The
BODHRÁN
MAKERS

To Elaine with love

Bodhrán (bow'rön): the first syllable is pronounced as in the *bough* of a tree, the second syllable as in *drawn* without the *d*. The bodhrán is a shallow, single-headed drum of goatskin which resembles a tambourine but is larger; it is played with a small stick called a cipín, or else with the hand.

The
BODHRÁN
MAKERS

JOHN B. KEANE

FOUR WALLS EIGHT WINDOWS
NEW YORK

© 1992 John B. Keane

Published in the United States by:
FOUR WALLS EIGHT WINDOWS

First printing October 1992.

First published in Ireland by Brandon Book Publishers Ltd.,
Dingle, Co. Kerry.

Library of Congress Cataloging-in-Publication Data:

Keane, John B., 1928—
    The bodhrán makers/John B. Keane
    p.   cm.
    ISBN: 0-941423-80-8
    I. Title.
    PR6061.E2B34   1992
    823'.914—dc20   91-33771
                      CIP

Printed in the United States

Preface

Thomas Cuss turned carefully off the main road and drove slowly through the open countryside of Dirrabeg. He parked the Mercedes next to a five-bar iron gate. The gate opened onto a spacious roadside field of sixty-one acres. The field in itself was marginally larger than the entire home farm from which he had just driven.

'We'll count separately,' he told his seven year old grandson, 'and see if our figures correspond.'

Tommy Cuss stood on the uppermost bar of the gate, a hand on his grandfather's shoulder, eager eyes working in conjunction with silently moving lips as his gaze moved swiftly from bullock to bullock.

'Sixty-seven,' he shouted triumphantly, awaiting his grandfather's tally which always took longer than his. Tom Cuss smiled and continued with his count.

'You have a good head,' Thomas Cuss conceded at the conclusion; 'sixty-seven is right. Let's go on now and count the others in the next field but let us give more time to it because now we'll be taking stock of yearlings and two year olds. They might not stand still as obligingly as these sober chaps here.'

The grass in the seventy-two acre, second field was fleecier and of a richer green than that of the first. The cattle had only begun their grazing the day before. At the rear of both fields were eight-feet-high turfbanks no longer in use. These ran parallel with the roadway and enclosed the acreage, vast by local standards, in a long green rectangle.

Grasslands, turfbanks and a blackthorn ring-fort astride a small uncultivated hillock accounted for the total domain of Dirrabeg.

'There were people and houses all along here one time weren't there granda?' Tommy Cuss turned to his grandfather hoping he would dwell awhile for the umpteenth time on the poverty-stricken but colourful lifestyles of the smallholders who had resided in Dirrabeg when Thomas Cuss had been a young man.

There was no sign now of human habitation, no paths or by-roads nor trace of the high whitethorn hedges and deep dykes which once divided the tiny fields. The remains of Dirrabeg National School, roofless and crumbling, were the last visible testimony to a vanished community.

Thomas Cuss did not indulge his grandson at once. He remembered only too well the humble abodes and the colourful characters. It had taken him twenty-five years and countless thousands of borrowed pounds as well as sleepless nights and constant anxiety to raze the dwellings and outhouses before reclaiming the soggy cutaway which had once supported the scraggy cows of the Dirrabeg smallholders.

Thomas Cuss had no qualms of conscience after the exodus of the early fifties. He had paid a fair price for the cutaway and there had not been a solitary smallholder who had not wished him well. The one thing to which he would never accustom himself was the mortifying silence imposed by the broad tract which he had reclaimed.

One

'CAN I COME to town with you?'
Donal Hallapy applied the finishing touches to the clamped sods which towered perilously above the confines of the assrail before answering. Between the shafts the Spanish mare arched her rump uneasily.

'There's too much snow,' he replied, not unkindly, 'and anyway there won't be any shopping.'

'Not even the pub?' his eleven year old daughter asked, prompted by her mother who stood behind her, hidden by the dark interior of the kitchen.

'Not even the pub,' he answered patiently. Trust his beloved spouse to come up with one like that, using the innocent child to throw out her barbs.

'Go on now,' he addressed himself to the mare, 'you've carried heavier in your time.' The animal started slowly, carefully, picking her steps along the snow-covered, dirt passage which led from the house to the by-road. She paused uncertainly at the junction where there was a steep incline, awaiting his guidance.

'Look,' Hallapy told the eleven year old, 'I could be late. I have business to settle but I'll bring you something and for God's sake tell your mother not to wait up for me.'

'She has no such intention,' young Katie Hallapy echoed the wifely sentiments coyly. At the top of the incline he took

9

the reins in his hands and flecked them gently. The mare strained at the ancient harness, her rear hooves failing to find purchase. He draped the reins over the hames and seized the back shafts in his powerful hands.

'Hup girl,' he shouted, lifting and pushing with all his strength. She responded gamely. Between them they managed to power the ponderous cargo, intact, onto the by-road. The clamp had swayed, even shuddered, but not a sod had moved. He smiled grimly remembering his father.

'You'll remember me, you son of a thatcher,' that worthy had once told him as they sat drinking at a wrendance. 'Whenever you build a clamp on an assrail or start a winter reek you'll remember what I taught you.'

Others might not agree but his friends would boast that when Donal Hallapy clamped turf it stayed clamped. The narrow bog road which led from the house to the main road was covered with freshly-fallen snow as were the many turf reeks. As yet it had made little impact on the heather-covered boglands: There was the faintest impression of white, no more. It would need several inches to envelop the heather. The surrounding hills were white and so would the roadside fields be white as he proceeded to town.

The town: it was a bad time of evening to make the four-mile journey. Darkness was beckoning and the main road would be slippery, not that he worried for the safety of the turf-load. The mare could take care of herself but there would be cars and lorries to contend with and it wasn't the widest road in the world. Still there was no frost, at least not yet. With such a leavy load the mare, for all her experience, would not be able to cope, not with frost. He tightened the sugán rope which bound his heavy black coat and turned down the tops of his wellingtons.

His thoughts turned to his brother-in-law. Damnatory phrases turned over in his mind: a useless, good-for-nothing, rotting drunkard; a dirty, foul-mouthed corner boy; a craven,

10

cowardly wife-beater. His sister would deny this last but Donal knew she was often at the receiving end of a drunken punch.

He found none of the many descriptions of his sister's husband to be even remotely adequate. He wouldn't be trudging to town now if the wretch had seen to his winter firing. Donal's sources in town had revealed that there wasn't a sod of turf in the corrugated iron shed at the rear of the house. The children were being sent to bed the minute darkness fell and made to stay there until morning. At school the older ones would find heat at least and they would be out of their mother's way while she scrubbed and polished for the better-off townsfolk. It was that or starvation.

'God knows she don't deserve it,' he spoke to the mare, 'and God knows before she met him she was never cold and she was never hungry. By Christ we always had spuds and cabbage and milk and we were never without a flitch hanging from the ceiling. No money, maybe, but full bellies and a warm hearth. I'll kill the bastard. Some night I'll kill him!'

The mare's ears twitched. They were on the main road now and she was finding the level surface to her liking; it was almost free of snow thanks to the traffic. What compounded his brother-in-law's all too numerous transgressions was the fact that he too was responsible for Donal Hallapy's not being on speaking terms with his wife.

The day before he had encountered a neighbour of his sister's on the by-road near the house. The man was a council worker, Moss Keerby, an honest-to-God fellow who had hired out a cob and rail for the day to bring home some of his turf. Moss had produced a packet of Woodbines and the pair had retired to the lee of a tall reek for a chat.

'What's new in town?' Donal posed the question after they had pulled and inhaled the first drag.

'Good few home from England. More expected before Christmas.' Moss Keerby dragged on his cigarette, awaiting further questions. None came. He spat loopingly into the roadside

11

grass. This act was followed by a long silence, Donal waiting for news of a more personal nature, unwilling to press for it. He had hoped that Moss Keerby would go on.

'Dammit man, how's Kitty?'

'Kitty's fine and so are the children but there isn't a sod of turf in the shed. There's no sign of your man either. I haven't seen him since Thursday.'

Donal digested this unexpected piece of news for some time. Then he proferred his verdict.

'Thursday was dole day. I daresay he drank the money as usual and went to bed.'

'I don't think he's in bed. I think he's gone.'

'What do you mean gone!'

'I don't know,' Moss Keerby continued cautiously. 'Maybe off somewhere on a booze. Maybe one of his trebles came up and he's laying it out somewhere.'

Donal shook his head. Trebles, he well knew, came up occasionally but never his brother-in-law's. He was too greedy.

'Tell Kitty I'll be in as soon as I can with an assrail, tonight if possible.'

'I'll do that,' Moss Keerby assured him. After they had parted Donal turned into the milking of his four cows. The yield was slight, just sufficient for the household needs. All four would be calving in the spring. As he drew upon the ungenerous paps his thoughts turned once more to his brother-in-law and he remembered one of his last conversations with his father as the old man lay dying in the crowded main ward of Trallock General Hospital. The older man had seized the younger by the coat sleeves with a surprisingly strong grip.

'Whatever you do, Donal, you must never beat him up. Kitty will turn agin' you and the children will turn agin' you. You hear me now. No matter how sorely you're tempted you're not to strike him.'

'All right, all right. He'll suffer no harm from me.'

'You promise now.'

'I promise Dad.'

In the kitchen of the tiny thatched house he transferred the milk from the tin bucket to a muslin-covered enamel one which his wife Nellie had placed on the table.

'Not much,' she observed, 'not near enough to make a gob or two of butter.'

'I'll bring butter from town,' he said. He didn't have to turn round to observe the change of expression on her face. Her lips would be pursed silently in disapproval wondering what new emergency precipitated another of his all-too-frequent trips to Trallock.

'I have to take a load of turf to Kitty,' he explained without turning round.

'Again!' The word was full of rebuke.

'Again,' he said. 'She hasn't a sod and your man seems to have gone off on some kind of shaughraun.'

'Willie is it?'

'Yes dammit. Willie. He disappeared on dole day. God knows where the wretch is by now. Willie Smiley.' He repeated the name contemptuously. 'What a monicker for that big, blubbery, misbegotten bastard!' His clenched fist smote the table in rage and frustration.

'And no doubt you'll take her a fine clamped rail?'

'Well, I might as well do the thing right as I'm doing it at all. She'd do as much for us.'

'I don't begrudge her. You know that.' Nellie Hallapy moved to the far side of the table and faced her husband: 'But for heaven's sake, Donal, that's six rails since September. The boys want new boots. Katie wants a pair of shoes. I haven't had a new stitch of clothes on my back these three years. Those rails of turf would fetch the money we need. Christmas is only ten days away and I haven't a copper.'

'Don't worry woman.' He raised a consoling hand but she turned away.

'There's more rails,' he comforted.

13

'There isn't all that much left. I've seen the reek and 'twill no more than do us till summer.'

'Ah there's a handful still in the bog. I always keep a trump for the last play.'

'I have no butter.' She refused to be comforted: 'And I have no margarine and I have no dripping while Vincent De Paul is off to town with the makings of good money.'

'We'll fry bread with bacon lard and we'll throw down a few eggs while we're at it. We never died a winter yet woman.'

Silently she set about preparing the supper, unwilling to be party to his banter.

She hadn't bid him goodbye before he left. She had, however, spoken through their daughter which meant that all lines of communication were not severed. There had been times when she had withdrawn absolutely into herself. Most of their fallings-out had to do with his kindness to Kitty; the rest were generally over money. Sometimes there would be enough but mostly it was the rarest of commodities in the Hallapy household. She liked to dress well but there was never enough money for new clothes, at least not for her.

'It's as if you were rearing two families,' she once fumed when she surprised him as he filled a bag from the potato pit in the haggard at the rear of the house. He had to concede that she was nagging with good reason. The pit was nearly run out at the time. Worse still he had selected the best of its dwindling contents, not for his own household but for another. He acknowledged this perverse streak in his nature for what it was – love of his father's family, the first family to which he had belonged. However, he knew he had been less than fair to his own in this particular instance and he had been somewhat less liberal since then.

Beside him the mare plodded slowly but surely townwards. Whenever traffic approached from front or rear he signalled his presence with a small cycle lamp. He was relieved to enter the well-lighted suburbs of the town. On either side there were well-built, fashionable bungalows and ornate two-storey residences, all with well-groomed gardens and lawns to the fore with intricately designed wrought-iron gates opening onto neat doorways. Houses and surrounds had the signs of professional care. The area was known as Hillview Row and in truth there was a fine view of The Stacks Mountains to be had from every select abode.

'This is where the money is boy,' he addressed the words to himself. 'There's Phil Summer's, the accountant's, seven bedrooms they say, and here now is Doctor O'Dell's, five bedrooms only but antiques to burn or so Nellie his wife told him. Rare antiques and every imaginable labour-saving device. There's Micky Munley's, the bookies.' No one of his acquaintance had ever set foot inside the house but if rumours were anything to go by the place was a veritable palace. 'A good scholar Mickey! Almost as good as myself that couldn't even finish my national schooling!'

He turned the mare to the left before reaching the main thoroughfare, Healy Street, which hosted the town's chief business houses until it ended in the town square. He looked at his watch: twenty minutes to seven. The journey had taken an hour and fifty minutes, well outside the mare's average.

The street in which he now found himself, Carter's Row, was the town's secondary thoroughfare, an amalgam of small businesses and trades, housed mostly in modest two and three-storey residences.

All the shops were closed except one. This was Faithful Ferg's, the soubriquet bestowed on the ramshackle green-grocery, crockery, newsagent, bacon and provisions store of Fergus Whelan, who closed only when the bell of St Mary's Catholic Church in the town square called forth the midnight hour. Neither did he close on Sundays, although he did make one small concession to the Sabbath by seeing to it that only the side door was used.

When taken to task by Trallock's venerable parish priest,

15

Canon Tett, about his Sabbatical activities he had explained with a tear in his eye and a shake in his voice that his conscience bound him to serve the needs of any man, woman or child who might require a loaf of bread or a quarter stone of spuds on a Sunday. The canon had lowered his priestly head and over the rims of his bi-focals surveyed the unlikely paragon dubiously. Ferg's gaze had remained steadfast and when he had thrust a five pound note into Canon Tett's hand with the injunction that he might pray for the holy souls, not merely of Ferg's immediate kin but for the souls of all the faithful departed, the subject of Sunday closing had been suspended there and then.

'Whoa girl!' The mare drew gratefully to a halt, her neck craned forward, her hooves spread wide the better to distribute the dead weight over her tired body. Donal fumbled in his fob pocket and found what he wanted underneath his watch. There were two half crowns and three florins, a total of eleven shillings. His features puckered as he went through some elementary mental arithmetic before entering the shop.

'How's Donal? You're out a bad night, boy.'

Donal knew from the smug intonation, especially contrived for the benefit of the several shawled female customers who stood waiting to be served, that Faithful Ferg knew exactly what had brought him to town.

'I'll take two pounds of sausages, Ferg.'

'Two pounds of sausages. That will be two and fourpence.' Ferg advertised the sum loudly and wrote the amount into a large jotter under his hand on the counter. This was to intimate that the customer was free to back off if the price was not right or if the requisite amount of cash was not forthcoming.

Ferg never filled an order unless the money was first laid down on the counter and it had to be the exact amount to the nearest halfpenny. All requests for credit were greeted with stentorian guffaws during which he would hold on to his side as though he were about to burst. Sometimes he would rest a hand on the shoulder of the customer nearest to him in order to sustain the outburst.

'I'll take two large pan loaves and a quarter pound of butter.'

'Two large pan loaves, two shillings, quarter o' butter ninepence. That it?'

'That's it for that order. What's due you?'

'Five shillings and one penny.' Ferg raised his head from the jotter, placed both hands palms downwards on the counter and stared solemnly at the space between his hands. A huge smile lighted his thin features when the money appeared on the spot where he had been staring. He scooped up the coins, placed them in the till and handed Donal one shilling and eleven pence in change. From beneath the counter he selected a used cardboard box. Bread, butter and sausages fitted snugly as though to a pre-arranged measurement.

'Now,' Donal rattled his remaining monies in the fist of his right hand, 'a second order and you'll secure this one with twine as I'll be taking it home. Let there be a half pound of butter.'

'Half pound of butter, one and a tanner.'

'Threepence worth of gallon sweets and one small barmbrack.'

Faithful Ferg pursed his lips at this latter, unexpected inclusion but made no comment save to announce that the amount of the item in question was 'one shilling and three pence.'

'Ten Woodbines. I'll carry those in my pocket.'

'Ten Woodbines, one and twopence,' came the mechanical voice from behind the counter. 'All told that comes to four shillings and tuppence.' At once he assumed his usual posture, not budging until the money was paid over. He dispensed the order quickly and held his pencil over the jotter awaiting further instructions.

'That it?' he asked.

'Just one more thing.' Donal produced a small, handstitched, canvas satchel from inside his shirt.

'Put sevenpence worth of oats into that will you.'

Another merchant might have smiled or even laughed at the meagre amount but not Faithful Ferg. Sevenpence worth of good quality oats was a rare treat for a donkey. He lifted his long, spare frame across the counter with a well-calculated vault. He thrust the wooden-handled tin scoop deep into the oats but the amount he withdrew belied the depth of the thrust. He tossed it on the scales-scoop, withdrew another smaller scoopful and sprinkled part of it over that already on the scales-scoop until the sevenpenny worth balanced with the weights he had laid out beforehand. He selected several grains, placing them on his palm where he examined them closely before transferring them to his mouth.

'Best food for man or beast is your oats Donal my boy!' Donal hardly heeded him. His thoughts were taken up with his remaining finances. He had altogether expended nine shillings and tenpence. By all the powers that be that should mean that there was exactly one shilling and tuppence left in his fob. In his trousers pocket there were five coppers which left him with one and sevenpence which was the price of a pint of stout. First things first, however.

'Go on, girl.' The mare needed no further spur than the oats bag which he shook tantalisingly close to her now-twitching ears as she moved off to take another left-hand turn of her own accord into a narrow laneway of small, single-storied houses, many of them thatched with straw, more roofed with sheets of corrugated iron while a privileged few were covered with slates.

The mare halted without bidding at a small, thatched dwelling at the end of the laneway. The whitewashed front was composed of two tiny windows at either side of a narrow door without lock or knocker. Here lived Kitty Smiley née Hallapy, only surviving sister of Donal and wife of the runaway Willie Smiley. There had been two other sisters and a brother but all three had succumbed to the ravages of tuberculosis in their late teens.

Donal gently kicked on the door with his wellingtoned right foot. In his hands were the cardboard boxes and oats bag. The door opened immediately to reveal a small, neatly kept kitchen whose chief feature was a Stanley Number 8 range which gleamed from constant polishing. A bare electric bulb hung from the ceiling. The door was opened by the eldest of the seven Smiley children, Tom, a likeable, easy-going lad in his thirteenth year. There were two other boys in the family and four girls. The girls had arrived after the boys, year-in year-out, unfailingly. The youngest was three-year old Josie and after that there had been one miscarriage. At the table sat the two younger boys and the oldest girl Sophie. There were some schoolbooks in evidence. The children looked pinched and pale but Donal guessed it wasn't from study. He placed the boxes in a corner, retaining the oats bag.

They had leaped about him as soon as he entered. To them he spelt affluence, the gift-laden, wealthy uncle from the prosperous countryside beyond the cramped world of their laneway. None, if they were asked, would be able to recall a time when he had arrived empty-handed.

'Where's the rest? Where's your ma?'

'Out working,' Tom answered. 'The girls are in bed.'

'Have you had your supper?' He had not failed to notice that each pair of eyes was directed every so often towards the cardboard boxes.

'No supper yet,' Tom informed him. 'We're waiting for ma.'

Donal went to the doorway. 'Go on, girl,' he called to the mare. Immediately she turned at the side of the house and followed a path to the turf shed. Donal returned to the kitchen.

'You proceed with your studies,' he cautioned. 'I'll heel the rail into the shed. I won't be long. We'll eat when I come back. Meanwhile one of you could by laying the table and cleaning the frying pan.' There were joyous whoops as he left by the back door to heel the rail. He was followed by Tom. He undid the bellyband and withdrew the pins from the top

19

of the back rail. Lifting the front shafts he heeled the load into the shed while Tom leapt gingerly into the base of the cart and kicked the remaining sods into the shed.

'Tell me,' Donal said as he tied to oats bag over the mare's head, 'was it a treble?' His nephew nodded.

'And was it much?'

'It was but I don't know exactly how much.'

'Did he give anything to your mother?'

'No.'

'To any of you?'

'No.'

'Any idea where he's gone?'

'They say England.'

'Who says?'

'They all say.'

'Do you miss him?'

'No.'

'The others?'

'No. They were too much afraid of him. How could you miss someone who beats you for nothing and beats your mother for nothing?'

'You're the boss man now Tom.'

They sat on the heap of sods, listening to the mare munch her hard-earned grain. Outside the cosy confines of the shed the snowflakes, increasing now in density, drifted noiselessly past. From the house came the excited outcries of the children. The back door opened. Mary and her two brothers came barefoot to the shed and departed, silently, with armfuls of turf.

It did not take Donal long to become aware of another sound. First it was no more than a gentle sobbing. Then there came a succession of semi-strangled, almost inhuman cries. Donal found it difficult to accept that anything so piteous could emanate from one so young but then he thought: thirteen years of anguish seething under a moryah carefree surface! If the boy didn't weep and weep his fill he would scarcely have been

20

human. That kind of woe is better out than in, he thought. He would give him his time, sit with him till the final gasp of wretchedness had been wrung out of his system.

The mare had finished. Now she was nosing the corners of the satchel for the last remaining grains. There was silence in the shed. Donal decided to sit and wait. The mare threw the satchel from her head and snorted. She was ready for the road. She would wait awhile yet.

'Come on away in Uncle Donal.' Donal was pleased the suggestion had come from his nephew. In the kitchen all was in readiness. Cups and saucers covered the bare boards of the table; there were neither plates nor side plates. A bright fire burned in the Stanley and the frying pan sat atop the main ring.

While the sausages hissed and spat in the heated pan Donal and Tom cut slices of bread and buttered them from the quarter-pound pack. So intent were all with the business in hand that nobody noticed the back door ajar and the silent figure standing there. It was Kitty Smiley. Without a word she loosened her headscarf and then, suddenly, pressed it to her eyes as the tears came. Instantly they were all around her but before they had time to express concern or show care she was herself again. She pointed to the range.

'Turn the sausages somebody, don't they burn.'

Donal hastened to the pan and shook it energetically so that the browned undersides of its contents were plainly visible after the upheaval. Just then the remainder of the family came racing in from an adjoining bedroom wearing only their long night-shirts. They were the younger sisters, Kathleen and Maura and the three year old baby of the family, Josie.

'I declare to God,' Donal exclaimed, 'that's hearing for you. They knew the sausages were being turned!'

The family ate ravenously. Donal joined in but Kitty would eat nothing.

'Mrs O'Dell insisted I have my dinner,' she explained. 'I'll always be fed where I work. It's these I'm worried about.'

Donal took note of her drawn face. He was always pleased to see that she retained her good looks: that was some consolation.

The house consisted of two bedrooms and kitchen. In the parental bedroom there was one bed and a cot where Josie still slept for want of better. The other three girls slept in one large bed in the second bedroom while the boys slept on two mattresses on the kitchen floor. These were stored in the girls' bedroom until nightfall. Donal and Kitty repaired to this room.

'I won't cry,' she promised as she sat on the edge of the bed making room so that Donal could be seated also. 'All the crying is done and I know in my heart he's going to be gone for a while. I'm resigned to it now.'

'So his treble came up,' Donal opened.

'He always said it would.' She shook her head at the irony of it.

It transpired that he had collected his winnings from Mickey Munley's Trallock office in Healy Street before going next door to a licensed premises known as Journey's End. Kitty was surprisingly well informed on the subject of her husband's last movements in his native town. Information about a missing husband is rarely tendered to the victim. However, Kitty had many friends and after the first few days all the pieces had fallen into place; all, that is, save the extent of his coup.

In the Journey's End he treated himself to a glass of Jameson and a bottle of stout. It was at Journey's End that he counted his money. From there he moved further down Healy Street until he came to Farrelly's Drapery where he purchased a pinstriped, black, three-piece suit, a white shirt and a tweed hat, grey in colour. Not only was Kitty Smiley well informed on her husband's purchases but all of Trallock was as well. The whole business was something of a nine-day wonder.

Willie Smiley's next move was downwards into the town square where he purchased a pair of suede shoes for the unprecedented sum of four pounds seventeen shillings and sixpence.

22

This was to occasion snide remarks in later years whenever a man with a dubious background appeared wearing expensive footwear.

'Another Willie Smiley,' wags would say or, 'Shades of Willie Smiley,' as though the man who appeared in the shoes had no right to them.

Willie's splurging was finally contained with the purchase of one white handkerchief. Some felt it odd that he had not invested in an overcoat with the weather turning colder every day but then, as others pointed out, he was not a man for overcoats, never having been seen to wear one.

The last person to see him in Trallock was Canon Tett's housekeeper, Nora Devane. On her way back to the presbytery, after the morning shopping, she observed him leaving the Trallock Arms and making his way covertly with his hand on his hat to where the Dublin-bound bus stood waiting. He entered the vehicle just as it was about to depart on the first stage of its long journey to the metropolis.

Nora Devane, although burdened at the time with two bulging bags of groceries, hurried to the window near which Willie Smiley had taken up his seat. There was no doubt but that it was he. He looked down at her through the glass and with a fleeting smile he lifted his hat before leaning back in his seat and pulling the newly-acquired headgear down over his eyes.

'What makes you think he'll stay away?' Donal produced the Woodbines pack and proferred it before putting one in his own mouth. She declined.

'He always said that if he ever brought off a big win that was the last Trallock town would ever see of him.' Her tone was one of total acceptance, as if the inevitable had happened.

'Wait till the money runs out. He'll be back with his tail between his legs because he won't do any better.'

'I'm not saying he won't come back some day,' she spoke with quiet authority, 'but it won't be today or tomorrow or next year or the year after. He'll have to be on his last legs

before he thinks of coming back here.'
Donal found himself believing her. Women were intuitive about such things. His only regret was that he hadn't administered at least one decent hiding to the scoundrel.
'Yourself and the children will come out to Dirrabeg Christmas Day.'
'What about Nellie?'
'Let me worry about Nellie. Just remember Dirrabeg, Christmas Day. Hire a car around midday. I'll get you home.'

Two

AS DONAL LED the mare into the laneway in front of the Smiley home he noticed that the falling snow had turned into a watery sleet which was just as well, he thought, for it would melt whatever snow might have since accumulated on the roads and by-roads.

He climbed into the rail and directed the mare towards the junction of Carter Street and Healy Street. From here he drove down Healy Street and into the town square. The streets were unusually quiet but this, more than likely, was because few townspeople would be abroad during the run-up to Christmas. The pubs would be all but deserted save for the presence of those who might be on holiday from England for the Yuletide period. They would remain quiet until Christmas Eve when the only problem would be clearing the packed premises of drunken patrons before midnight mass in St Mary's.

Donal drove around the square twice, making the sign of the cross each time he went by the church. Eventually he saw what he wanted to see, a solitary Civic Guard standing near the main entrance to the church. Donal identified him as Tom Tyler, an elderly lackadaisical custodian of the law who always displayed a marked aversion towards raiding public houses even when ordered to do so by his superiors. Whenever he was obliged to inspect a licensed premises after hours he always managed to overlook fleeing customers and to take no account of partly-filled glasses or smoke-filled snugs.

Donal flicked the reins and the mare trotted gingerly under a stone archway which led to the rear of a public house known as the Bus Bar. He hitched the mare to one of a number of wooden posts provided for such a purpose and rapped with his knuckles four times on the wicket of a large corrugated-iron gate. A minute went by and the better part of another before he heard footsteps approaching from the inside.

'Who's out?'

Donal recognised the voice of Minnie Halpin, wife of the pub's proprietor.

'Donal Hallapy,' he replied at once and then, 'Donal of Dirrabeg.'

The wicket opened and he stepped into a cobblestoned courtyard with decrepit outhouses and stables on either side. Minnie Halpin led the way to the back door of the pub turning her head once to enquire after Nellie and the children. Donal assured her of their wellbeing and then went on to ask her if she might require an assrail of high quality black turf for Christmas.

'I don't know Donal,' she seemed reluctant, 'one of the sheds over there is full of turf.'

'But not like mine,' Donal boasted. 'Every sod in my clamp will be as black as the ace of spades and that clamp itself will be a good three feet above the rail and all for a pound. You won't do better.'

'Bring it along,' Minnie Halpin spoke resignedly before turning to her left into the kitchen, allowing Donal to continue along a narrow corridor to the bar. This was a glittering palace of blinding brightness, its shelves stocked with hundreds of bottles, each glistening with its own individual radiance while scores of gold-labelled Baby Powers dangled attractively from specially designed brackets. Every shelf and every cranny behind the polished pine counter was filled with bottles large and tiny, new and ancient, plain and ornamental. Underneath

26

the counter but concealed from view of the patrons, two wooden half-tierces of stout were on tap, one highly conditioned, the other almost flat, each so primed as to compliment the other and to ensure that the creamy white collar remained atop the black stout until the last drop was swallowed.

Behind the counter stood the proprietor of the Bus Bar, portly, moustachioed Fred Halpin, an acknowledged expert in the handling and conditioning of stout. Even Guinness's representative, a taciturn fellow, not above dipping his thermometer into suspect pints and half pints, was prepared to concede that Fred Halpin's dispensing was as near to perfect as dispensing could be.

'What will it be, Donal a mhic?' The voice was deep, albeit hardly above a whisper lest it carry into the square outside and nestle in the wrong ears.

'A pint if you please, Fred.'

'A pint it shall be, a mhic.' Fred Halpin selected a pint glass, examined it carefully for residue and other imperfection and bent to his task. First a squirt from the high barrel and then a brimming flow from the low barrel. Allowed to mingle on the counter before the customer's eyes. Slowly the suffusion of the brown and the white became distinguishable from each other. The creamy head began to form, turning whiter all the time as the brown beneath turned to ebony. There were old men in Dirrabeg and in the other townlands surrounding the town of Trallock who would declare that there was no man born of woman able to fill a pint of stout like Fred Halpin. Not even a stain of moisture was to be seen on the counter when Donal lifted his glass, having first counted out his one and sevenpence.

'Anyone out?' Fred Halpin's sensitive thumb and forefinger touched up the waxed ends of his moustache.

'Only Guard Tyler,' Donal assured him.

'We're in safe hands.' The remark came from a grey-haired, red-faced man, neatly dressed, seated at a table near the blacked-out front window. There were several other patrons

27

present but these seemed too intent in their own exchanges to worry about the forces of law and order ranged against them in the world outside. Donal, pint in hand, joined the man at the table.

'Well Donal, how's the world using you?'

'Not too bad, Monty, and yourself?'

'That's a question of total irrelevance, Donal, but I'll answer it and tell you that I was often worse. You see, somebody told me this very evening that I didn't look in the least like my brother Ferg or Faithful Ferg as he is so inappropriately called by the poor of the parish. I was so touched, Donal, that I came straight here to Fred's in order to celebrate, so finish that like a good fellow and have another.'

'Thanks all the same, Monty, but I'll have to head for home after this.'

'I should have known, Donal,' Monty laid a hand on his arm, 'that you would accept a drink from no man unless you were in a position to buy one back. Dammit man, make an exception this once.'

'Some other time,' Donal told him. Donal liked Monty Whelan. So did most people. He wasn't without enemies and Donal knew this well. Monty had a caustic tongue which he sometimes exercised without discretion. He was a teacher by profession and although in his mid-forties was still without a school of his own. He taught as an assistant in Dirrabeg National School, four miles to the north of Trallock. Donal's children were among his pupils. His principal was an austere spinster named Ciss Fenley, Miss Fenley to most. The school manager was Canon Tett, parish priest of Trallock.

'You wouldn't know anyone lookin' for an assrail of turf, well clamped, black as coal, heavy as lead?'

'Heavy as lead. I like that. It's an exaggeration but I like it. I could use a rail of it if the price is right.'

'A pound,' Donal tendered.

'It's a deal,' Monty Whelan extended a hand. Donal shook

28

it. 'And while you're at it you might dump in two rails to Daisy Fleece. I'll fix up with you after delivery. Just keep your mind to yourself.'

Donal had heard stories about Daisy Fleece, mostly from his friend Moss Keerby. Apparently she could be an obliging sort of a damsel when the fancy took her or so it was rumoured.

'And who the hell should blame her,' Moss Keerby had said at the time, 'with a husband in Coventry and him sleeping with another.'

'And who's to blame Monty Whelan,' Donal thought and him a widower with ten years and childless at that.

'That's three rails altogether.' Donal rose and finished the pint. He stood silently for a while before leaving, his puckered, unshaven face indicating that he was in the process of framing a question, a question he was reluctant to ask but one for which he would have to find an answer sooner or later.

Monty Whelan sat stock still, knowing that Donal would speak in his own time. A strange man, Donal Hallapy, strange, that is, if you did not know him well.

'I know him better than most,' Monty thought, 'and yet I hardly know him at all except for a few unusual aspects of his past, known to few, and the fact that he works hard. Then there's the inescapable fact that he has a beautiful wife, beautiful in a tragic way and neglected. But by whom? By herself certainly as her deteriorating teeth would prove and her dark hair, riotous but uncared-for.' At forty Donal Hallapy was something of an enigma. Townspeople, while admitting that he was a Trojan worker, felt that he was backward, even a little repulsive. Monty Whelan knew that this was an estimation which was both skimpy and unfair. Donal had been in the Irish army during the Emergency years of the early Forties. He married not long after. He had spent a few years in England leaving his wife and two children behind with her parents. Then he had returned when his father was taken ill. When the old man died he inherited the eleven acres of cutaway which maintained four milch cows and a donkey. Together with five acres of good quality turbary there was almost enough for a man of Donal's rude strength and agricultural skills to barely support a modest family.

Donal never spoke about his time in the army or of the period he had spent in England. 'No doubt,' Monty Whelan thought, 'these would be early chapters in his life which he would like to see re-written or deleted.' He had similar chapters in his own, middle and late as well as early.

Suddenly Donal was seated again. He permitted his fingers to beat a nervous tattoo on the table.

'About this treble,' he opened.

'You mean the Smiley treble?' Monty submitted encouragingly.

'God sake man, what other treble is there? Do you know or don't you?'

'I have the simple facts of the case, as the man said, if you want them. It was a cheeky treble, audacious in fact. It could only happen in the National Hunt season and it could only happen to Willie Smiley. He picked these three horses. I wouldn't have picked them; neither would anybody who has the least interest in horse racing. The first won at ten to one. This was no great surprise. The horse, Charming Monarch, had been in the frame twice. It was on the cards he'd win a race some day and he did. I'll lay odds he'll never win again. The second horse came in at fourteen to one. Apparently the going was like putty and he was as much a work horse as he was a race horse. The third horse came in at twenty to one after five of the eight-horse field came down at the second last. Two of the remaining three horses were interfered with and Willie Smiley's final selection came home in a common hack.'

'How much did he get?'

'Patience Donal, patience like a good man. I met Mickey Munley, the bookie, last night as he was taking his constitutional around the square outside and he informed me that Willie

Smiley's bet was a half-crown treble on the three aforementioned nags. Mickey Munley imposes no limits on singles,
doubles and trebles where the wager does not exceed a half-
crown. Consequently the odds in Willie Smiley's investment
amounted to three thousand, six hundred and fifteen to one
which comes to four hundred and fifty two pounds, give or take
a few shillings with no tax deducted since the investor had the
foresight to pay his tax in advance.'

'Four hundred and fifty-two pounds!' Donal Hallapy shook
his head in bewilderment. 'I wouldn't earn it in years, not if I
was to put out my bundún, but imagine, not a solitary penny
did the miserly bastard hand over to his wife and family.'

'Good riddance maybe.' Monty rose and taking his empty
glass moved to the counter.

'Do you think you might stomach another drink now?'

'No!' Donal was adamant, 'but I'm thankful to you all the
same Monty. They're expecting me at home; 'twill be midnight
against the time I get there.'

Minnie Halpin escorted Donal over the cobbled yard to the
wicket. Opening it noiselessly she peered out into the night.
She looked up and down several times lest a hostile Civic Guard
surprise her before she could give the all-clear to Donal. The
mare's ears twitched as he climbed into the rail. A flick of the
reins and he was forced to restrain her lest she gallop blindly
into the square. She was anxious to be home, that was clear,
home to her mud-built stable with its abundance of hay and
shelter from the cold of the night.

The watery sleet had now transformed itself into persistent
rain. He sat in the body of the rail as soon as he was clear of
the town, trusting to the mare's instinct to bear him home
safely. In this respect she had never failed him and was unlikely
to do so now. There had been one particular night during
Trallock's summer carnival. He had spent the day drinking
with some friends after disposing of a rail of turf. Somebody
had assisted him into the rail after the pubs had closed and he

31

remembered no more until morning when he woke up to find himself still intact in the rail outside his own door with his head between his knees.

The mare proceeded at a steady trot while he went back over the events of the night. A motor car passed, its horn blaring in protest at the unlighted conveyance.

'At this exact point in my life,' he told himself, 'I haven't a penny to my name but I have my health and I've orders for four extra rails of turf and if I haven't the turf to fill those orders itself there's others that have. And what else have I? Haven't I a lovely wife and children and haven't I butter for them and barm brack and sweets.'

He stretched his hand to the corner of the rail where he had concealed the box which contained the luxury items with a covering of turf mould. There was no trace of the box or its contents: wet turf mould in plenty but nothing more. Murderous thoughts galloped through his mind. He stood erect in the rail, heedlessly facing the driving rain, fuming at the monstrous injustice of the theft, and theft it was. There was no way the box could have fallen through the laths of the rail. Some sly urchin had noticed his movements earlier in the night and taken advantage of his brief visit to Fred and Minnie Halpin's Bus Bar. Urchin my foot, he thought. It was no urchin. An urchin would have neither the patience nor the guile. He was very nearly flung from the rail as the mare took the turn on to the by-road on one wheel.

'Steady, you bitch!' he screamed. 'Easy, easy girl,' he called secondly in more mollified tones. He upbraided himself instantly for his harshness. He had confused the mare, who was accustomed to more conciliatory tones even when she made mistakes which was rare enough. He could sense her uneasiness between the shafts. Despairingly he knelt in the rail and felt all around in case he might have unwittingly passed over the missing box. He covered every corner inch by inch, but to no avail. What would he tell Nellie, long-suffering although not

32

silent? Katie would be asleep and would not awaken unless he called her. He should have known better. To leave an un-attended box of groceries, however small, in a backway in Trallock in the middle to winter was surely the act of a thoroughgoing amadán. The punishment certainly fitted the crime in this case.

His mind flashed back to Faithful Ferg's. There had been four shawled women in the vicinity of the counter where he had paid for the two boxes of groceries. It could have been any one of the four. All knew him and his likely destinations. Child's play for any one of them to avail of the square's numer-ous shadows before emerging and slipping under the archway to the back of the Bus Bar. No one would know her beneath the shawl. It would not have been her first time as many a drunken countryman would testify to his cost when he returned to his cart to find his meat gone, his groceries, even the eight stone sack of flour which provided his daily bread. No such magnitudinous calamity had ever befallen him: this was his first contribution to the hungering inmates of Trallock's desol-ate laneways; it would certainly be his last.

His late mother had worn a shawl regularly as had most of her contemporaries. Only the wives of the more prosperous farmers, business and professional people and, of course, the few remaining local Protestants, wore coats in public. Most of Trallock's older women still wore black shawls. Donal's neighbours, farmer's wives excepted, all wore shawls. As Monty Whelan was fond of saying 'they cover a multitude.' No matter how dowdy, worn or tattered the garments underneath they were safely concealed by the shawl as were secret pregnacies and other ill-gotten goods. For those who could not affords the luxury of a coat for mass-going the shawl was a heaven-sent blessing. Its owner could hide her identity and her poverty at the same time.

Shawls were the bane of Faithful Ferg's life. In his early days after taking over from his father they very nearly contributed

33

to his ruin. The more rapacious and desperate of his female customers carried pouches, secret pockets, even sacks attached to the dress or apron beneath. Pilfering was made easy since Ferg could hardly undertake to search every suspect, not that he was likely to be permitted to do so in the first place. Finally he had a card printed which he hung from the most conspicuous shelf in the shop. 'Shawls off before leaving premises,' it read. Shawled women, his brother Monty would argue, were no less honest or dishonest than any other. It was just that Ferg attracted the wrong types. 'Ferg brings out the worst in people,' Monty would explain upon hearing of some act of larceny perpetrated against his brother.

Thoughtfully Donal untackled the mare. He decided that his best course would be to tell the truth, at least as far as the disappearance of the barm brack and other items were concerned. Under no circumstances would he tell her about the groceries he had purchased for his sister. She would be sure to misconstrue although, in fairness, it should be obvious to anybody that his sister had triumphed over his wife again, had scored infinitely better as a result of his journey to town. He had not intended things to turn out that way. It was a cruel quirk of fate that they did, perhaps inevitable that they did. Nellie Hallapy had never worn a shawl, rightly or wrongly she identified shawls with melancholy and poverty.

'Did you bring the butter?' It was the first question she asked as soon as he entered the bedroom.

'I did and I didn't,' he said and proceeded to outline for her the disastrous developments of the latter part of the night. She allowed him to finish before posing the next question.

'What am I going to put on the children's bread and they goin' to school?' she asked.

'There's jam left isn't there?'

'There isn't,' she answered without a trace of emotion.

'I recall seeing jam before I left,' he argued.

'We ate it before coming to bed. Anyway all that was left

was a few spoons, barely enough to cover the bread.'

'Well now, they can do without butter for one day. It won't kill them.'

'No, only half kill 'em!' she responded bitterly turning her face to the wall.

'I have orders for four more rails,' he countered cheerfully. 'With the usual six that will come to ten pounds. We can draw five on the creamery. That's your Christmas taken care of. I'll look after the drop o' drink.'

'Fifteen pounds,' she sat up on the bed as he kicked his wet trousers into a corner. She left the bed without a word, located matches and lighted the minature oil lamp which stood on a small table by the bed. She lifted the wet trousers and entered the kitchen where she hung them from a wooden peg extending from one of the side walls of the hearth. He had slipped into the warm bed during her absence wearing only a shirt, a collarless, well-worn flannel, one of several from a bargain lot Nellie Hallapy had purchased at the market place in Trallock from the hustings during the height of a forgotten summer when shop-soiled flannel shirts and woollen undergarments were to be had for half-nothing. That had also been the summer of the new coat. She had not been in a position to buy one since. She could have had coats but none were of the quality of that summer's coat.

Returning to the bedroom she closed the door carefully behind her. She folded her hands and surveyed him quizzically.

'With fifteen pounds,' he said as though reading her thoughts, 'you can buy yourself that new coat and shoes for the children and still have enough to buy a dacent Christmas. You'll get a twenty pound cock turkey or bigger for two pounds. You can buy all the butter you want and all the jam you want and all the cakes you want and all the tay and sugar you want. You can buy wine and lemonade and biscuits. I'll look after the heavy liquor. You can buy chocolate and sweets and presents for the young wans.'

'I have my shopping list made out this long time thank you,' she chimed in curtly but it was clear that she was not unaffected by the prospect of money to spend at long last.

'There should be enough,' she conceded, 'for a coat all right and for the children's shoes.' Mentally she amended her Christmas list and might have been deliriously happy for a moment but then the realist in her surfaced.

'The very most the reek can spare,' she said accusingly, 'is five to six rails. We can't do without the rest.'

'I told you there's a good handful left in the bog,' he said.

'There's no turf of ours in the bog,' she countered.

'All right,' he said patiently. 'There's no turf of ours in the bog but there's turf other than ours in the bog.'

'I won't be party to stealing turf.'

'You don't have to be. You remember the turkeys that disappeared on us?'

'I'll never forget them,' Nellie Hallapy sighed, recalling the loss. 'I never reared a poult since and never will again.'

'Well,' Donal spoke matter-of-factly, 'you'll be paid for those turkeys presently because the turf I'll be taking to Trallock belongs to the man that stole them.'

'And do I know the man?' Nellie asked.

'Indeed you do. He's the Dancer Deely.'

'He's the curly-haired, sallow man with the cottage between Dirrabeg and town?'

'The same curly-haired man with twenty fine donkey stoolins of black turf standing in the bog not far from our own.'

'And how did you find out he was the man?'

'He had turkeys for sale yet his wife didn't rear any. No one else but ourselves had turkeys stolen. It took me a while to figure it.'

'He ruined our Christmas,' Nellie spoke vengefully.

'We won't ruin his,' Donal told her, 'but we're entitled to compensation.'

'You should steal every sod he has.'

'Wouldn't work woman. We'll take the value of the turkeys and let bygones be bygones.'

'Is there any danger of being caught?'

'No danger whatever,' Donal informed her, 'if the job is done properly and we keep our mouths shut.'

'Will he suspect?'

'Let him,' Donal replied. 'It should keep his mind occupied across the winter.'

'There's no danger then?'

'No. His turf banks and ours are identical. Both yield six sods, blackening to the bottom sod from the third with the top three sods dark brown or light brown. We both use the same make of sleán and all in these parts cut the same size in sods. There's no way you could know a sod of his from a sod of ours. I'll manage on my own although I could do with a look-out.'

'Well now, Donal Hallapy,' there was cheer in Nellie's voice. 'If you'll be wanting help with the lifting of that turf you needn't go farther than the room we're in.'

'That's good news indeed.' Donal reached for the Woodbine packet which he had placed near the oil lamp. Holding the end of the cigarette over the globe he drew briskly. The cigarette lit immediately.

'I'll need you along,' he told her. 'If there's no moon we'll do the job tomorrow night. If there's a moon we'll wait. Now come on into bed.'

He topped the burning red ash from the cigarette into a calloused palm. He smothered the ash between both hands, crushing it swiftly. He placed the cigarette butt next to the oil lamp and gently placed his arms around her.

'It's an awkward time,' she whispered.

'Why don't we use one of those things we got from England? They're under the mattress.'

'No. I won't. I can't.' She sounded adamant.

'But why not?'

He lifted her nightdress and drew her closer. 'Because if I

37

let you use one of those things I won't get absolution from
Canon Tett.'

'He'll have to give you absolution.'

'Will he now! Do you know that last Easter he would only
give me absolution on condition I never permitted the use of
one of those things again. He made me promise. "Don't come
back to this confession box again," he said, "if you violate
God's most sacred law."'

'And what am I supposed to do?'

'Withdraw in time,' she said bluntly.

'But according to Canon Tett that's a sin too. I heard him
say so one Sunday. Waste, he called it.'

Suddenly he kissed her lips and drew her beneath him.

'Whatever you do don't put me in the family way again. I'll
be going to confession to Father Butt, the senior curate. He'll
take no account of wasted seed when I tell him I've had mis-
carriages but they're all against the other things, curates and
canon alike.'

'They can be a mischievous clan at times.' Donal muttered
the sentiment half to himself.

'Who're a mischievous clan?' Nellie asked.

'Who but the clan of the round collar that puts a damper
on every damned thing that's any use. Now stop the chatter
and apply yourself to the job for which God designed you.'

Later as they lay silently together he reached across and
found the cigarette butt. He lit it from the lamp which he then
extinguished.

'Tell me about Willie Smiley,' Nellie said.

Donal began by relating his meeting with Monty Whelan
and ended with an account of his visit to his sister. He included
Tom Smiley's grief and Kitty's premonition that her husband
would not be quick to return.

'I never seen wolves in the flesh till a few hours back,' Donal
recalled. 'It was when Kitty's young wans tore down into the
kitchen when they smelt a few sausages frying. Like wolves

38

they were with the hunger.'

'I think,' Nellie Hallapy spoke after she had considered all she had been told. 'I think we should have Kitty and the children out here for Christmas Day. The least we owe them is their Christmas dinner.'

'Now, now!' Donal registered his disapproval with a sly smile in the darkness, 'you have enough to do without catering for a second family.'

'They can hire a car to come out and you can take them home that night in the rail,' Nellie was adamant.

'Whatever you say missus,' Donal acquiesced. Still smiling he was quickly asleep.

Three

THE ONLY FURNITURE in the dining-room of Trallock presbytery was a venerable suite which consisted of one mahogany table and six chairs. Two large pictures hung from the distempered walls, one a hastily completed portrait of a former canon and the other an enlargement of a professionally-taken photograph of the Trallock Gaelic football team of nineteen forty-six, which was the first and last time a Trallock team had won the district football league.

Ancient, immovable window drapes kept daylight permanently at bay. The only concession to brightness was a single sixty-watt bulb whose luminance was sombrely muted by a small circular shade, dark brown in colour. If the room was austere it was no more so than its sole occupant on that particular Christmas morning.

At seventy-eight Canon Peter Pius Tett sat, blue-eyed and clear-skinned, at the head of his table, belying his age by a dozen years or more, awaiting the arrival of his housekeeper and senior curate. The latter was the first to enter: meekly he took his place at the bottom of the table.

'Good morning, Father.' Canon Tett was the first to speak. It was one of a number of unspoken rules of the presbytery that the first word of the day belonged to the Canon. New curates were so informed immediately after their arrival and those who forgot the edict were greeted with a stony silence until they exited and entered again and awaited their turn in the order of conversation. They never forgot thereafter.

'Good morning, Canon,' Father Butt returned and then, 'it's a hard day outside, Canon.'

'The thing then,' Canon Tett threw out without a smile, 'is to be hard enough for it.'

Father Butt was a pasty-faced, rather self-effacing man in his early fifties. Physically he contrasted greatly with his superior. The Canon stood six foot three in his stockinged feet, was spare as a whippet, his peach-red face glowing with rude health, his whole being still exuding nervous energy, irreversible in his outlook, impervious to contradiction however justified and quite capable of traversing several miles of rough countryside before his breakfast.

Father Butt was a mere five foot four, flabby although not obese with dark hollows beneath his eyes which gave him an almost saintly look but for a lower lip, puce and full and drooping which detracted in the final analysis from his appearance of sanctity.

In his early years he had flirted briefly with golf and badminton but abandoned both after failing abysmally to make the least leeway in either. The people of Trallock would tell you that he was not a man of the world. It was their way of justifying his timidity. They liked and respected him. They might have liked him even more had they known that he lived in constant fear of Canon Tett, a fact not unknown to the Canon who relished keeping his curates on their toes.

'The collection seems to be somewhat up,' Father Butt tendered the news in the hope that it might humour the older man. Canon Tett pretended he hadn't heard. He always held that it was no concern of the curates how the finances of the parish progressed and in this instance, which was the occasion of the Christmas offerings, he refused to be drawn.

His housekeeper Nora Devane looked after the various sums collected, after each mass, in the sacristy. To each of the teachers in charge of a particular collection she would hand over a receipt for the amount. It was the function of the National teachers of the parish to look after all collections having to do with the parish. Names of the contributors with their addresses and the amounts offered had to be accurately taken down and would be read from the pulpit during each mass on a specially-chosen Sunday around the middle of January. The slightest error might well be the cause of the most acute embarrassment. The reading of the names often accounted for a period of time longer than the mass itself.

'You'll be going home today as usual?'

'Yes, Canon. Whenever it's convenient, although I sort of made a half promise to my sister that I would arrive before three. She promised to hold over the dinner until that time.'

'Let me see now.' The Canon looked into a space directly over Father Butt's head. 'Miss Devane and myself will be dining at the Convent as usual. I understand dinner is to begin at one-thirty. Now unless you want us to choke ourselves there is no way we could finish before two-thirty which means we won't be back here until twenty minutes to three.'

'That will do fine, Canon.' Father Butt might have told him that his sister lived over forty miles away to the south of the diocese but he recalled that the Canon was well aware of this already and might have taken it into account if he so wished.

'You'll be back tonight Father!'

'Of course, Canon.'

'What time, Father?'

'Before ten, Canon.'

The Canon nodded his ancient head in agreement and pointed at the door which had been tapped upon from the outside.

'That sounds like the breakfast Father. Open the door like a good man and let in Miss Devane.'

Father Butt arose dutifully and stood aside as Nora Devane, burdened with a large silver-plated tray, pattered noisily over

42

the wooden boards to the head of the table. Known unflatter-
ingly throughout the parish as the Dexter Devane, the tiny
housekeeper was the Canon's chief link with the world outside
the Presbytery. He had never once felt the need to call her
accuracy into question. Her knowledge of the parish and
parishioners was deep and comprehensive. Her sources were
numerous and while all were not as reliable as she would like
there evolved in time a system whereby she had no trouble
sifting the grain from the chaff. With an audible sigh she laid
the tray on the table, whipped off the linen cloth which covered
its contents and made straight for the door where she turned
and stood before delivering her curtain line. Both priests sat
erect awaiting the announcement for the day.

'Whelan never showed up,' Nora Devane spoke accusingly.
The Canon frowned. Monty Whelan, whose responsibility it
was with his principal Ciss Fenley to supervise the eleven
o'clock mass offering, could not be relied upon anymore. There
had been other irksome violations of the parochial code but
none as flagrant as this. Legally there was little the Canon
could do but as manager of all the National Schools in the
parish there was much he could do. Time enough for that,
however. Already he had transferred this thorn in his side from
Trallock town school to the remoter Dirrabeg school, remote
in a parochial sense. He had reckoned at the time that the
humiliation would force Whelan to re-consider his general
attitude to authority. He knew now that he had been mistaken.

'Did you say something Father Butt?'

'Nothing really Canon except would you mind passing my
egg and some of the toast if you please. I have the last mass
you know.'

The Canon surveyed him for a moment with mixed feelings,
not knowing how he should respond to the request. He allowed
a few seconds to pass before removing his own breakfast from
the tray and several more before he pushed it down the table
to his curate. Father Butt's breakfast consisted of a separate pot

of tea, jug of milk, bowl of sugar and one boiled egg. There were also two slices of buttered toast. All bread, toasted or untoasted, whether for Canon or curates was buttered beforehand.

On the surface the Canon's breakfast looked no different from that of his curate. However, instead of a boiled egg served in the conventional eggstand the Canon's eggs had been emptied into a cup and peppered and salted to his taste. There was good reason for this. If, as Nora Devane had pointed out one afternoon during a briefing on presbyterial economics, it was seen that himself was in receipt of a brace of eggs the curates might well deem themselves worthy of the same. The Canon had readily acquiesced to this and to other money-saving suggestions all carefully directed at the curates.

As he munched his toast Father Butt thought of his sister's home and the welcoming arm of his nephews and nieces. His brother-in-law, although bumbling and amiable, poor fellow, was somewhat intimidated by the clergy and as soon as the dinner was finished he would betake himself into the wild outdoors to count his sheep and cattle. The children would be too preoccupied with their Christmas gifts to pay any heed to their uncle's soul-baring over a two-hour period. All the time his sister would listen, the most sympathetic of looks on her worried face. Now and then she would take his hand and utter gentle phrases of consolation.

'A penny for your thoughts, Father.' Father Butt spluttered guiltily over a mouthful of egg.

'Nothing worthwhile, Canon,' he replied after he had recovered from the initial shock.

'Now Father,' Canon Tett poured himself a second cup of tea, 'I will be along during your mass to say a few words regarding the spirit of Christmas and a few other pertinent matters to do with the parish, that is, of course, if you have no objections?'

'Oh no, Canon. None whatsoever.' He managed to conceal his bitter disappointment as he rose and excused himself pre-

44

paratory to leaving the dining-room. His Christmas sermon, dealing with the power and purity of family life, had taken him several long nights to assemble and now there was to be nothing. He fervently prayed for the courage to release his pent-up grievances. Instead, by way of explanation for not finishing his breakfast all he said was: 'I have a few chores before mass. Please excuse me.'

On leaving the dining-room he pulled on his hat and overcoat and went out through the back door into a laneway at the rear. Hurriedly he by-passed the rear entrances of several houses before finally knocking at one. He waited for the best part of a minute but there was no answer. He knocked louder and looked about him fearfully lest the Canon or his housekeeper emerge suddenly from the backdoor of the Presbytery. There was still no response. He dared not knock any louder. His final assault on the door was one of sheer desperation. After what seemed like hours rather than minutes the door opened. Monty Whelan, hair tousled, wearing only pyjamas and unlaced shoes stood framed in the doorway, a look of utter mystification on his face.

'What's the matter Father?' he asked.

'Good God Monty don't you know what time it is?'

'It's half ten,' Monty confirmed after inspecting his wrist watch.

'It's half eleven man and you've missed the Christmas collection.'

'Oh Christ, it would take me. What am I to do?'

'In heaven's name man get dressed and present yourself at the sacristy at quarter to twelve. You can say you thought you were supervising the last mass collections instead of the earlier. Anything is better than not showing up at all.'

'What's the point? He won't believe me anyway.'

'In God's name will you do what I tell you? You're out on a limb, man. He has a dossier on you.' Here Father Butt looked away. 'He also knows about Daisy Fleece.'

45

'What are you talking about?' The tone was one of outrage but when Phil Butt's frank eyes confronted him again Monty Whelan bent his head.

'I'll be up right away,' he said, 'and thanks, Phil, thanks a million.'

At the Presbytery Father Butt was met by the Canon just as he closed the rear door behind him.

'You're all out of breath Father. You would want to keep yourself in condition. Look at me now. I'm one-and-a-half times your age and I'd be prepared to wager I'd outwalk and outrun you over any distance you care to name.'

'I'm sure 'twould be no trouble to you Canon. I'm afraid I was never an outdoor man.'

The two priests stood silently for a while, appraising each other, the older at the foot of the stairs, the younger with his back to the door he had just closed.

'You don't read a great deal either do you Father?'

'I'm no bookworm that's for sure Canon.'

'And have you any hobby at all Father?' the Canon asked with feigned innocence, knowing that his senior curate was currently obsessed with billiards, a game which he played at every opportunity. One of his priestly duties was a nightly visit to the parochial hall. Here were span new billiard and snooker tables, recently purchased out of a legacy donated to the hall's upkeep.

'You used to be a classical scholar used you not Father?'

'Used to be is right Canon.' The Canon, as Father Butt well knew, was a product of the Irish College of Salamanca in Spain. He looked askance at any sort of academic qualification. He held no degrees himself although he had read philosophy and theology up to the time of his ordination in nineteen hundred and four. Father Butt overheard him to opine that academics made poor curates and even worse parish priests.

'Let them teach like they're supposed to do and leave the running of parishes to fellows like me who're cut out for the job.'

If the Canon had gone to the trouble of examining Father Butt's Curriculum Vitae with any degree of thoroughness he would have discovered that his curate's academic qualifications were as modest as they could be by Maynooth terms. He had taken a pass B.A. in Irish and Latin with considerable difficulty and made it clear to all that he had no intention of chasing any further academic distinction. He was ordained in nineteen twenty-seven, assigned to his first parochial duties shortly afterwards and although he plunged into his work he failed to make any impression on his first parish priest.

His second, several years later, turned out to be an easygoing man with an outlook liberal for the time and it was on this unlikely model that he based his subsequent attitude to the Church. He was now in his ninth year, first as junior and then as senior curate in the parish of Trallock – urban population two thousand and eleven and parochial four thousand two hundred and ten.

The junior curate had been granted special leave on Christmas Eve to be with his father who had succumbed to a stroke some days before Christmas. It was unlikely that he would be back before Saint Stephen's night which meant that Father Butt would be obliged to forego his usual midwinter break of one night and a day and a half in his sister's home.

'Well, if there's nothing else Canon I'll be on my way.'

'Nothing for now Father.' Father Butt stood transfixed at the doorway. Nothing for now! What could he mean by that? What had he in mind? Was there something up his sleeve which he was holding back to serve as some form of post-Christmas castigation?

At the top of the stairs Canon Tett chuckled.

Nora Devane sat with folded arms surveying the sheafs of ten shilling and single pound notes. Extracting one arm from the other she slowly joined her palms together prior to entering the amounts gathered before and after the three masses up until noon. Eight o'clock had been disappointing but ten and eleven had shown significant upturns on the previous year. The Canon would be pleased. Most of the professional and business people had already contributed by cash or cheque in privately delivered envelopes. The Canon would divulge the contents of these in time but it was more than likely that the improvement would be reflected there also.

Laboriously she entered the figures underneath those of the year before. Normally this should have been the duty of the senior curate but the Canon had insisted that the less a curate knew the better for the curate in question and the better for the parish. All monies contributed by way of Christmas dues were the sole property of the Parish Priest. At the end of the holiday season when the businesses of the town re-opened Nora would discreetly deposit the money in the Canon's private account in the National Bank. She was never obliged to queue at the deposit counter like so many others. One of the clerks would immediately vacate his desk and silently intimate to Nora that he would be delighted to relieve her of the metal deposit box at an unfrequented area of the counter. Neither did she have to await the receipt. Later in the day this would be returned, safely locked into the deposit box, by the bank messenger.

Trallock was a thriving parish, probably the best-off in the diocese. Before funerals mass offerings would flow in, sometimes in their hundreds, depending on the importance of the deceased. Father Butt scored heavily here and Nora was not unaware of the fact. She went as far as she could, encouraged by the Canon, to divert mass offerings intended for the curates to the Canon and very often she succeeded. The only other sources of income available to the curates were nominal stipends of ten pounds per annum and an annual contribution from the parishioners to cover the cost of petrol and car mainte- nance. This was still known as Oats Money, a legacy from the earlier part of the century when priests travelled by horseback or in horse-drawn gigs and traps. It hardly sufficed to cover the transport costs of the curates who were frequently obliged to fall back on members of their families when a new car was required or major repairs made too-heavy inroads into their slender resources. There was also the fact that the first half-crown out of every pound subscribed went traditionally to the Parish Priest. Thereafter half of the monies went the same road while the remainder was divided equally among the two curates.

Board and lodgings were provided, as the Canon never tired of putting it, free, gratis and for nothing but when the fare did not measure up to the curates' expectations there was no redress. There were times at the height of a particularly unsavoury meal when the Canon would notice the pushed-aside, unfinished plates. He would seize such opportunities to launch, for the hundredth time, into one of his favourite stories.

'Did I ever tell you Fathers about Archdeacon Dooley of Drumleer?' Father Butt was often tempted to respond by saying that they had the story by heart but all he would do was exchange martyred looks with his junior.

'He was an awful man so he was,' the Canon would proceed between mouthfuls of the obviously relished mutton which the curates had found unchewable. 'There was this curate, an impertinent scoundrel if ever there was one.' This would be accompanied by a sustained guffaw articulated to add to the discomfiture of his listeners. 'Oh, a thoroughgoing buck who wouldn't eat what was put in front of him and you wouldn't mind but he was getting the same as the Archdeacon which was boiled mutton, the best of it.'

'"I'm entitled to a decent bit of steak now and then," he starts off to the Archdeacon, "and I'm entitled to a cup of tea and a slice or two of cheese if I can't stomach my dinner."'

Again there would be a sustained guffaw from Canon Tett. '"I'll tell you what you're entitled to," Archdeacon Dooley told him, "and that is no more and no less than what every other curate in this world is entitled to which is a Christian burial when you die and no more and no less."' After a final bout of

49

derisory laughter the Canon would bolt the mutton remaining on his plate and then with extended, talon-like hands would remove the rejected portions from the plates of the curates and transfer them to his own from where he would wolf them down with noisy relish.

Nora Devane, without taking her eyes from the money, felt among the many keys hanging from the huge ring attached to a link on a leather belt which she constantly wore. As she bore the money to the steel safe in the parochial office she considered the sacred condition of trust which the Canon had reposed in her. She wore a suitably solemn expression as she bent to unlock the safe. As the key turned she became all the more aware of her responsibility and consequently when she beheld, for the first time, the dossier on Monty Whelan she instantly felt it was her bounden duty to investigate.

The Canon would have hardly entrusted her with the keys of the safe unless he wished her to be privy to its contents. He would, she knew full well, never say it in so many words so that her conscience was clear when she opened the slender file having first consigned the money to its rightful corner on the floor of the safe.

Nora Devane turned the several pages silently, absorbing the contents of each. Her face registered no surprise as she read. She was already familiar with most of the Whelan heresies so religiously detailed by the Canon. However, the revelations on the final sheet drew from her an involuntary gasp and a series of subsequent exclamations which served to illustrate her total shock and surprise. 'Fleece Daisy', the relevant paragraph read. It consisted of an account of the recent comings and goings of Daisy Fleece to the house of Monty Whelan. Times and dates of each arrival and departure were meticulously included. His regular nightly and occasional daily visits to the Bus Bar and to several other of Trallock's better-known hostelries were also faithfully recorded.

Most damnatory of all, however, was the final inclusion

50

which outlined a visit to Dirrabeg National School by the aforementioned Daisy Fleece no more than seconds after it had been vacated by its pupils and principal teacher Ciss Fenley on the afternoon which heralded the beginning of the Christmas holidays.

Nora Devane shook her head in wonder and admiration at the extraordinary detail to be found in the report. For the life of her she could not identify the Canon's source or sources. She would apply her mind to this vexatious question later in the day in the privacy of her room. Disappointment tinged with envy lingered long after she had closed the safe: disappointment that the Canon had not asked her to confirm, as he always did in like circumstances, the Monty Whelan exposé and envy at the professional manner in which the Canon's informant had gone about his or her work. The saddest thing of all for Nora was the knowledge that she could never even aspire to the accuracy and authority which contributed to the authenticity of the Monty Whelan file.

Father Butt had but barely commenced his brutally edited Christmas homily when Canon Tett sidled noiselessly in from the sacristy and stood with bent head and joined hands, the picture of true humility at the opposite side of the altar from where his senior curate was holding forth in front of the wooden lectern which had replaced a rather vulgar pulpit, which had been sold to a secondhand dealer. Father Butt winced visibly when the Canon uttered the faintest and politest of coughs. He alone of the vast congregation knew that the seemingly innocuous utterance was an ultimatum to cut his sermon short and make way for his Parish Priest.

Utterly intimidated he mumbled his way through the final sentences when he should really have been clearing his throat preparatory to making inroads into the body of his intended address. Rather than add fuel to the Canon's irritation, and Father Butt knew from his moment of entry that the Canon was in a belligerent mood, the senior curate withdrew from the limelight and seated himself obsequiously behind the lectern.

The Canon, as was his wont, thrust his hands temporarily into his trousers pockets and closed his eyes. A number of scuffling exits told him that these were the victims of seasonal coughs removing themselves to the transepts where their outbursts would be less audible from the altar. Women with young children also betook themselves to obscured areas near the exits where their charges might be speedily removed should they begin to cry. The Canon was in one of his moods. This was apparent to the more seasoned members of the congregation from the moment he closed his eyes. They would remain closed until there was total silence. The rustle of adjusting posteriors and other positional changes of the many bodies seated throughout the church all amounted to a minor furore. Those who had been slumped were now sitting upright. Those whose eyes had been half-closed from want of sleep or from the excesses of the Christmas celebrations were now alert and committed, their faces aglow with anticipation.

The Canon had never failed them in the past when he had adopted his closed-eyes pose and there was no reason to believe he would fail them now. In fact a long time had elapsed since he had enunciated anything of a controversial nature in public.

The reason for his anger was comfortably ensconced in his usual place in the Bus Bar. Seated at either side of Monty Whelan were Minnie and Fred Halpin. All three had glasses in their hands. Monty was the first of a select few specially invited for Christmas drinks before the Christmas dinner which was served in every household in the area between the hours of one and two in the afternoon. Monty made no mention to the Halpins of his brush with Canon Tett. He simply told them that he wasn't feeling well and would be going home after the one drink. He had gone straight to the sacristy after Father Butt's visit, not bothering to shave or dress properly. He had merely changed his pyjama trousers for his everyday trousers and donned an old raincoat which he hoped would conceal any irregularities in his apparel. His shoelaces were still untied. His reception from the two teachers, one of whose positions he might seem to be attempting to usurp, was frigid to say the least.

'This isn't your mass Monty,' Tom Tierney, principal of Trallock Town Boys' School, informed him coldly, 'and which is more Monty,' he continued in an even icier tone, 'you know it.'

'As God is my judge, Tom,' Monty tried to brazen it out unsuccessfully, 'I got mixed up. Out all night you know.'

'Go back to bed Monty.' This came from the other teacher, a young man by the name of Jonathan Murray, a sometime drinking companion of Monty's.

'I'll go the minute the Canon comes,' Monty promised, 'just to let him see that I got my masses wrong.'

'For God's sake man,' it was Tom Tierney again. 'Ciss Fenley your own principal made out the lists. You were notified by letter and she told you personally. Now cop on man and get the blazes out of here before the Canon appears.'

'I'll wait. I have no bloody choice but to wait. I'm in his bad books often enough as it is. My job could be in jeopardy.'

'Well let me tell you, Whelan,' Tom Tierney was at his most righteous, 'you're putting our jobs in jeopardy as well.'

'Dammit man, will you not be so bloody sanctimonious. I've made a mistake. Can't you see? Didn't you ever make one Tierney?'

'Take it easy Monty.' The mild admonition came from Jonathan Murray: 'look at your laces, man. You didn't even bother to tie them.'

The young teacher knelt in front of the older and arranged a neat bow on either shoe. He was still on his knees when Canon Tett entered the sacristy.

'Get up!' he shouted. Immediately the younger man shot to his feet. 'And you,' the Canon pointed scornfully at Monty Whelan, 'how dare you appear here after missing the mass for

53

which you were appointed.'

'It was a mistake Canon,' Monty tried not to sound flustered.
'Will you look at the cut of him?' the Canon asked of the
others – Tom Tierney grim-faced and vindicated, Jonathan
Murray with head averted. The Canon took in the unshaven
face, the partly exposed collar of the pyjama jacket, the bleary
eyes and the other signs of recent debaucheries which had
ravaged Monty's face, now drained of colour.

'How dare you!' the Canon thundered. 'How dare you defile
this holy sacristy with your nightclothes and your foul breath.
How dare you contaminate the precincts of my church on
Christmas morning.'

For once in his life Monty Whelan found himself speechless.
In all the previous exchanges between himself and the Canon
the latter had always come off second best. His cudgelling
denunciations had been no match for Monty's biting sarcasm.
Now Monty was practically defenceless. His head throbbed.
His hands shook. He searched vainly for something to say but
no word came. The Canon pointed to the outer door of the
sacristy.

'Go!' he bellowed, 'go back to whatever brothel it was you
came from. I'll deal with you when you return to your sober
senses.'

Without another word the Canon had turned triumphantly
and entered the still more sacred terrain behind the altar.

'I'm going to tell you all something now,' he opened after
the silence which his closed eyes had induced made itself felt
in every corner of the church, 'and what I'm going to tell you
is this,' he continued after a long pause. 'If it were any other
day we had bar Christmas I would blind you with the tales of
lechery and debauch from people in high places but this is the
day Christ was born so I'll temper my words in deference to
the infant Jesus and ask you all to pray with me that the sinners
of this parish might see the light ere this day runs its course,

ere this day takes its toll and maybe dispatches one or more of these diabolical wretches to everlasting fire, sizzling fire, roaring fire that sears every part, inner and outer, of the human body. Our Father who art in heaven.' The response was instant and tumultous.

The second part of the Canon's address was less apocalyptic. He spoke of peace in the world and reminded his listeners that Christmas dues were still being accepted in the sacristy and that he could not call to mind words of condemnation strong enough to describe those who neglected to pay these same dues.

'Now there is another matter and it is something that has been playing on my mind for a long time.' Again he closed his eyes and waited. The silence he sought imposed itself naturally. 'Tomorrow,' the Canon continued, 'is the feast of the martyr Saint Stephen and so we call the day after him. We who are true to our faith and our fathers' faith know tomorrow as Saint Stephen's Day. We know it by no other name but alas in this parish there are people who, through ignorance or sheer perversity, will not call the day our great Christian martyr died by its proper title. They will persist in dishonouring the memory of one of the great saints of the Catholic Church by calling the day otherwise and what do these benighted wretches call it? They call it Wren's Day.

'They would have us honour a wren before a saint. Would you believe it, dearly beloved brethren, a wren before a saint? Tomorrow morning and indeed late this very night the countryside and the town will be treated to the spectacle of mobs of self-styled wrenboys with their wretched drums, their so-called bodhráns, and every mob on the make for money, intimidating men, women and children alike, not caring who they terrorise with their wretched mummeries and their distortions of native music, with their blackened faces and their tawdry costumes, and what will they do with the money they collect?' Here the Canon paused and with extended palms solicited an answer to his question.

'Will they hand it over to charity? Will they give part of it to charity? Will they give a solitary halfpenny to charity? They will not. They will spend every last copper on drink and they will stay up all night drinking and part of the following day drinking until they are sated and what do they call these drunken orgies? They call them wrendances. Dances indeed! What do you call something where you find men, women and children out of their minds with drink? You call them orgies, my dearly beloved brethren. Dare they come to the presbytery when they land in Trallock with their deafening bodhráns and their broken down concertinas and their home-made fiddles! I tell you that if they knock upon my door 'tis not money they'll get but the kettle filled with boiling water so that they won't come back again. Do not support these wretches. Do not go to their so-called dances. Support your own parochial hall on Saint Stephen's night where you have fine orchestras and wholesome dancing and where the profits made go to the upkeep of your church.' Wishing his wrapt audience a happy and holy Christmas the Canon swept from the altar and exited into the sacristy.

Father Butt sat in a trance not fully able to believe his ears. He had expected an attack on wrenboys and wrendances for some time but he had been completely unprepared for the tirade which had just assailed his ears.

The congregation was no different. It sat numbed and perplexed. Wrenboys had been part of Saint Stephen's Day since time immemorial. Indeed there were many in the church who had attended wrendances on numerous occasions. Most of the young children in the town of Trallock would blacken their faces and turn their clothes inside out and go on the Wren on Saint Stephen's Day. They would call to houses in their respective neighbourhoods where they would be treated to lemonade and cake and presented with a few coppers after they had sung the Wren song in any one of its many variations:

The wren, the wren, the king of all birds
On Saint Stephen's Day he was caught in the furze;
Up with the kettle and down with the pan
And give us a copper to bury the wren.

It was not Canon Tett's first onslaught on the ancient custom
of the wrenboys. Three years before he had accused the several
bands of wrenboys in the parish of cruelty to the smallest of all
the birds. However, it was quickly pointed out to him that a
live wren had not been used for well over a generation nor was
the wren any longer hunted and killed on Christmas Day.
Instead a cloth effigy of the bird was used.

Father Butt suspected that the Canon's hostility to wrenboys
arose from two factors. Firstly there was a long-standing tradition in the presbytery of Trallock that all established bands of
wrenboys which fulfilled the traditional requirements were to
be presented with a pound by the parish priest and a half-crown
by each of the curates. The previous year the Canon had given
nothing. The curates, for their parts, had observed the tradition
and handed over their contributions. The Canon's other
reason, or so Father Butt surmised, was that attendances at the
parochial hall were slightly reduced whenever a wrendance was
held in the parish. It had not taken the senior curate all that
long after his arrival to realise that anything likely to reduce
the parochial income was complete anathema to the Canon
no matter how worthy or ancient that custom might be.

After mass groups of people gathered outside the church and
in other parts of the town square. Faithful Ferg's rasp-like voice
was to be heard clearly from a large group congregated in the
archway entrance to the Bus Bar.

'Serve 'em right,' he was saying, 'nothing but a crowd of
bums looking for porter money.'

Not many agreed with him although there was little vocal
support for wrenboy customs on that particular Christmas
morning. Kitty Smiley stood impassively with her brood in the

57

centre of the square. What she had heard troubled her. She had been attending wrendances all her life, there was nothing else to look forward to from one end of the year to the other. People looked askance at unaccompanied married women in the parochial hall whereas at the Dirrabeg wrendance, celebrated at different venues each year, she was received like visiting royalty and was assured of as many dances as she wished with no strings attached.

Willie Smiley had never attended the Dirrabeg wrendance. There were too many people from that part of the world who were convinced that he might have done better by Kitty. Her eldest boy Tom had earlier disappeared through the archway and was by now in the Bus Bar purchasing a bottle of whiskey for his uncle Donal and intimating to Martin Semple the hackney driver that the family was ready to be driven to Dirrabeg.

Monty Whelan had a clear view of Kitty and the six children from his front window. He knew the children well and had taught most of them. There was Teddy and Bill and the girls, Sophie, Kathleen and Maura and the youngest not yet schoolgoing would be the baby of the family, Josie. But where was Tom? Ah yes, there he was now with Martin Semple in tow. No doubt they would all be going to Dirrabeg. Monty finished the whiskey in his glass and looked at himself in the mirror. He recoiled at what he saw. He decided to have one more drink before shaving. Then he would wend his drunken way to the abode of his brother Faithful Ferg in Carter's Row where he would join the family for Christmas dinner.

Ferg's wife Maimie had first extended the invitation the Christmas after his wife had died and when he had not shown up she had kept knocking at his door until he was obliged to open it out of sheer exhaustion. Maimie Whelan was a good-natured, easy-going creature, the opposite of her husband in her dealings with customers.

'If we allowed your mother into the shop,' Ferg once

58

explained to his only son Fergus junior, 'we'd be in the County Home inside of a year.'

Soon the square was deserted. Monty Whelan withdrew from the window and replenished his glass. A shave was what he needed. A shave and a little Brylcreem to keep his hair down and then as the song said: 'Who knows what mystery the night may bring?' He sang the words as he went in search of his razor.

Four

NO SOONER HAD the wrenboys assembled at the cross of Dirrabeg than the argument began. Not all were dressed in the traditional garb which consisted of plaited straw hats, straw leggings and coats made from white calico. Several wore their everyday clothes. A spokesman for this group was a man from Upper Dirrabeg, a countryside consisting of several foothills belonging to the Stacks Mountains which extended for twelve miles to the south-west. His name was Darby Kallihan and from the beginning it was clear that he was opposed to travelling the countryside on this occasion.

'The clergy is agin' us,' he warned, 'and we won't have luck nor grace if we go on the Wren.'

Murmurs of approval came from those who were without uniforms. Heartened by this Darby Kallihan issued further warnings: 'People is in dread of the clan of the round collar,' he cautioned, 'and we'll be sure to find many a door closed in our faces if we go on the Wren today.'

'It seems to me, Kallihan, that you never had any intention of going on the Wren. You came without instrument or uniform. Therefore you are not a wrenboy and have no business here.'

The words were spoken by a neighbour of Donal Hallapy's, an elderly man decked out to the fullest in traditional garb with blackened face and an outsized bodhrán held over his chest.

60

His name was Bluenose. Most of those present had either forgotten or were unaware of his proper name but it was clear his
opinions were respected.

'I go along with that,' Donal Hallapy, who was also dressed
in wrenboy garb, supported the old man. Others approved with
nods and handclaps.

'You're entitled to your opinions,' Darby Kallihan pressed
his case, 'but it's flyin' in the face of God to oppose the priests.
This is a Catholic countryside and the priest's word is the last
word.'

'Bullshit!' Bluenose countered. 'I've been going on the Wren,
man and boy, for nigh on sixty years and my father and his
father before him went on the Wren, man and boy like me. It
would be an insult to their memory if I was to renege on the
Wren and let me tell you another thing my fine friend from
Dirrabeg Upper where the crows ate the man, it is not the
priests who are against us it is the Canon, oul' Tett, that
wouldn't give you his spit and a few other cantankerous oul'
clerics here and there who are against every damned scheme
they didn't hatch themselves.'

'That's no way to talk about the Canon or any of the clergy,'
Darby Kallihan contradicted. It was the stentorian delivery
that put Donal Hallapy on his guard. He knew there and then
that every word spoken at the crossroads would be borne back
to the Canon through the medium of his housekeeper. She has
connections here, Donal told himself and maybe a relation or
two to boot. Nobody would know this better than Kallihan
who would be well aware that the Dexter had a sister in a
townland contiguous to Upper Dirrabeg. Time to intervene,
Donal thought. He raised a hand for silence.

'We could be here all day my friends,' he opened, 'and
nothing would be resolved in the end. It's clear that we have
two sides from what has been said. Let us now have a vote on
the matter one way or the other and when the vote is cast let
there be no tales out of school.'

61

'Or we might all be turned into goats,' Bluenose added mischievously.

'Right then, gentlemen.' Two voices spoke of one accord. They were those of the Costigan twins, two middle-aged stepdancers who were impatient for the road, 'let us have a show of hands and have done. All agin' raise their right hands.'

There followed a pause during which no word was spoken or gesture made. Then slowly Darby Kallihan raised his right hand. Several others followed suit until a total of nine was counted.

'Now,' said the Costigan twins, 'let us see who is for going on the Wren.' Instantly a score of hands shot upwards, and the demonstration brought a prolonged cheer in its wake. A count revealed that there were twenty-two wrenboys in favour.

'That settles it,' Bluenose struck his bodhrán repeatedly with the twin-knobbed, home-hewn drumstick known as the cipín which he carried in his right hand. The other bodhrán players joined in while the Costigan twins turned somersaults on the roadway.

'Ye won't have luck nor grace,' came the parting shot from Darby Kallihan as he led his supporters towards Upper Dirrabeg. Their going would leave an almost irreplaceable gap in the ranks of the Dirrabeg Wrenboys. The absentees were musicians in the main, expert concertina and melodeon players with enviable reputations throughout the length and breadth-of the parish. The real tragedy was that there had never been any form of rift before.

'Line up boys!' the order came from a stern-faced, middle-aged man on the outskirts of the party. Of all the wrenboys he alone had an unblackened face. Instead of the customary straw headgear he wore an unusually tall hat bedecked with sprigs of red-knobbed holly except for the base which was bound with tendrils of ivy. On his hands were white gloves, immaculately clean. He wore an ancient swallowtail coat which in its heyday had been black as ebony but now bore a definite tinge of ven-

62

erable green on its fringes which seemed set to impose itself all over.

On his large feet he wore hobnailed boots, one laced with red ribbon and the other with green. In his right hand he bore a stout, freshly-cut hazel staff, six feet in length and straight as a broomstick. The staff was also bedecked with ribbons, multicoloured and flowing to a length of eighteen inches. He was a tall, well-made man with close-cropped hair standing over six feet six inches in height and there was about him an aloofness and calm dignity which set him apart from all the others.

He was the Captain of the Wren, a commission which had been entrusted to him some twenty years before when the old Captain had taken ill. He was conferred with the rank for a probationary period before the appointment was made permanent. His word was law. It was he who decided the routes that should be followed and it was he who decided where and when the Wrenband might partake of refreshments. Drunkenness was punished by dismissal, the culprit being sent home as soon as it became apparent that he could not carry his drink. It was the Captain who took charge of the proceeds of the collection at the end of the day and it was he who decided at what licensed premises the drink for the wrendance would be purchased. Solely with him rested the right to veto undesirables or to eject troublemakers from the house where the wrendance would be held. His name was Rubawrd Ring and his appearance alone was an assurance that he was well able to fulfil all the obligations which his role demanded.

There were three females with the group. Their dress was similar to that of the men. Two, Noranne and Trassie Ring, were the unmarried daughters of the Captain. Noranne was an accomplished bodhrán player, Trassie a concertina player. The third female was Donal Hallapy's daughter Katie, a singer of traditional songs, mostly through the medium of Irish in which she had been most assiduously schooled by her teacher Monty

Whelan. She was possessed of a pure and gentle voice ideally suited to the *sean-nós* style which her rare and sensitive repertoire demanded.

As soon as the wrenboys had formed into a line along the margin of the roadway their Captain drew himself up to his full height and ordered his charges to draw themselves to attention. This they did smartly and in unison while the man in command inspected the rigid line which now confronted him. He moved slowly examining the features and the garb of every single wrenboy. When one lurched forward under his stony appraisal he came in for immediate censure.

'You have drink taken, you scoundrel.'

'Only a few and them was for a chill I picked up over the Christmas,' came the defence.

'Come out here on the roadway and let's see you walk. Right now! By the left, quick march.'

Rubawrd Ring barked out the orders without mercy as the accused party put his best foot forward. The first steps were even and fairly well paced but when the order was given to halt and about face the drunken wrenboy staggered all over the roadway, finally falling in an ungainly heap at the Captain's feet.

He arose with some difficulty and was directed in the general direction of his home and told to rejoin the group later in the day when he had slept it off. Resignedly he staggered homewards taking the two sides of the road, never once looking behind. The Captain continued his inspection. Occasionally he would pause when his highly trained sense of smell divined the fumes of freshly-consumed whiskey. He passed on quickly, however, well aware that the imbibers, like himself, had merely fortified themselves in moderation for the rigours of the morning march. It would be well past midday before a public house would be encountered. It would be true to say that there wasn't a man in the company who hadn't addressed himself to some sort of bottle before leaving home that morning.

At the end of the line Rubawrd Ring handed his hazel staff to the wrenboy nearest him, placed his hand on his hips and surveyed the cloud-filled sky. He turned full circle slowly, his eyes focussed on distant formations as well as the slow-moving, mixed masses overhead. The great, rolling, silent ramparts were not as informative as he would have wished. He turned his uplifted face into the prevailing wind, still continuing mild since the dawn of Christmas. His nose twitched as he sniffed its wintry contents. It blew gently and directly from the south-west where the clouds had recently assumed a darker hue than those over his head. It was a wind devoid of seasonal stings but in it were unmistakeable overtures of change. His nose twitched again. Still held aloft, it sought information from every source.

'There will be rain,' he spoke with quiet authority, 'but it will remain dry till well into the day and it would not surprise me at all if it held off until dark.'

'You could be right there,' Bluenose spoke, pointing a hand in the south-westerly direction. 'It will come from that quarter and when it comes it will drench the countryside.'

'Right then, this is what we'll do,' Rubawrd retrieved his staff and directed it towards the south-west. 'We'll gather ourselves directly and march into the wind so that when the rain comes it will pester our backs rather than our fronts. We should have all of Lower and Upper Dirrabeg collected before the light weakens. We'll go on then in a circle and see what's to be had from the other townlands of the parish. That should bring us well into the night and into Trallock town where the public houses will be gathering crowds and growing lively. We will collect the town beginning from Hillview Row and proceeding on through all the lanes and streets until we end up in the town square. There we will end the day's march at the Bus Bar. The money will be counted and the wrendance order made out. Any questions?'

'Will we be calling to the Presbytery?' The query came from one of the young men of the group.

65

'We will not be calling to the Presbytery,' Rubawrd Ring responded drily. 'It is not the practise of the Dirrabeg Wren to call where it is not wanted. Now gather yourselves and by the left, quick march!'

As the command was given the bodhráns sounded, led by Bluenose, Donal Hallapy and Noranne Ring. Soon the instrumentalists struck up a marching tune and the party of wrenboys found itself briskly marching through Lower Dirrabeg towards the foothills of the Stacks Mountains. The march, 'O'Donnell Abú', was a spirited one which would sustain them for many a mile. There would be others, lively and brisk, to see them through to the end of the day.

In all there were twenty-one wrenboys, roughly two-thirds of the usual number but sufficient to pass muster as an authentic wrenband. The group was at its weakest in the concertina sector although Trassie Ring, Rubawrd's other daughter, would suffice admirably. She would not be called upon as might the concertina players of Dirrabeg Upper to provide a solo performance. She had neither the skill nor the experience for this but there was no real problem since her playing would be partially drowned out by the band's three skilled accordionists and two button melodeon players.

There were three exponents of the tin whistle. Three others had departed with the Upper Dirrabeg dissidents but their absence would occasion no great deterioration since those who remained were held in high esteem in every townland of the parish. There were two step-dancers and in this respect the Dirrabeg Wren yielded to none for the Costigan twins were renowned for their bewildering footwork and variety of interpretations of even the most commonplace traditional dances. Their jigs and hornpipes were inherited from their late father, a dancing master without equal. Then came the tippers or bones players, their instruments pairs of polished rib bones extracted from the carcases of bullocks or cows. There was but a solitary fiddle player, one Mossie Gilooley, the others having thrown in their lots with the breakaway group. He tended to break rank while marching but playing a fiddle while on the march was no easy task in the first place. Neither was he addicted to keeping in concert with the other musicians but there were nuances and native skirls to his music possessed by no other. There had been three singers but the renegades, as Bluenose was to christen them later in the day, accounted for two of these. There was no worry, however, on this score since the remaining singer, young Katie Hallapy was quite capable of charming the birds off the bushes. Finally, there came the cashiers, two easygoing, inoffensive farmers' boys with little imagination and rocklike honesty.

Their job would be to gather and safekeep all the day's contributions, great and small. They had proved reliable in the past and since good cashiers were hard to find the Dirrabeg group considered itself fortunate to have them. Their task was simple enough when the band called on isolated homes but when a group or huddle of houses was reached at a crossroads or valley the group would perform on the roadway for the benefit of all while the cashiers called to the houses or collected from those who left their dwellings and circled round the band on the roadway.

Katie Hallapy marched by her father's side as they approached their first port of call. This was the dwelling house of a strong farmer where, year-in year-out, they were warmly welcomed. Soon the stone-flagged kitchen was filled with the wild music of the wrenboys, enriched by the muted drumming of the bodhráns. A dance was called for by the farmer's wife. This was in keeping with custom and the first strains of an ancient hornpipe had the entire household, young and old, tapping their feet and when the dance was ended a song was called for by the head of the house, Thomas Cuss, a gnarly, ham-fisted son of the soil with a surprising appreciation of wrenboy convention. In fact the entire occupancy of the house looked the most unlikely repositories of any form of cultural patronage. When the performance ended the older cashier was presented with the sum of five shillings. All were agreed the amount was a more than generous donation.

An offer of drink was turned down since it was no more than token in the first place in view of the large number of wrenboys but protocol demanded that the offer be made and rejected. The second house was a labourer's cottage but the welcome they received was no less than the first and at the end of the proceedings a florin was handed over. And so they proceeded at a lively pace, primed and fortified by their own music, omitting no house, no matter how humble, along their itinerary until they came to their first crossroads. Here several hillside families awaited them rather than impose upon them the necessity for a time-consuming trek to houses several hundred yards in from the roadway. They had come in donkey, mule and jennet carts as well as pony- and horse-traps and, of course, by bicycle and Shanks's mare. Here the band provided their first performance of length and the Costigan brothers excelled themselves on the hard surface of the roadway accompanied this time by bones and melodeons only.

Katie Hallapy's gentle voice brought peace and composure to the rustic gathering and when she finished her lamentation, through Irish, for a long lost exile her listeners demanded more. She sang again, a more joyful refrain on this occasion and would have been retained for the afternoon had not Rubawrd smitten upon the roadway several times with his hazel staff indicating that the next item on the programme was about to be implemented. As the entertainment proceeded the cashiers moved silently among the audience. The jingle of coins was constant and generous and when every source had been tapped they re-joined the band for the finale which consisted of a set dance in which all the wrenboys and most of those on the sidelines took part.

It was a thoroughly enjoyable occasion and when the wrenboys assembled at the command of the Captain for an all-out assault on the first hill of the journey they were greeted with prolonged applause. Several of the younger bystanders accompanied them to the brow where they waved and cheered until the marching column was lost from their sight. The cashiers were two pounds the richer after the encounter.

After four hours of constant travel, during which time they covered thirty-four houses and four well-attended crossroads, they found themselves at the first public house of the day. It was an ancient, thatched structure, depending solely on a rural clientele but it was a friendly establishment and no sooner had they been sighted than the landlord and his wife appeared in the doorway to greet them with a personal welcome. The time was one o'clock; they had been marching since nine that morning but as yet no one had complained of fatigue. Before any member of the group was given leave to enter all were first obliged to gather round the Captain whose instructions would be rigidly adhered to as soon as they were made known.

'Boys,' he addressed them, 'we surely have the best part of fourteen pounds gathered since we left the cross of Dirrabeg this morning early but if we are to have a dacent wrendance we'll need to gather another twenty at the very least. Every member of the Wren will now sojourn at this public house. We will submit an order for a sufficiency of meat sandwiches and each member will qualify for two pints of stout and a half glass of whiskey to be paid for out of funds. Any man found exceeding this quota will answer to me. We still have wide ground to cover and we don't need drunken men to hold us back and maybe even disgrace us in the eyes of respectable country people. In the pub we will first perform and collect and afterwards' – here he pointed his staff at the cashiers – 'the pair of you will see to the wants of all. Gather yourselves now, one and all, by the left, quick march!'

To the accompaniment of a rousing march they entered the pub where the patrons made them welcome with whistles and handclaps. Their performance was greeted with roars of delight.

69

Indeed they excelled themselves, inspired by the prospect of the liquor and edibles in the offing. Afterwards they took seats in various parts of the premises. They ate and drank with great relish and gusto, the Ring sisters as well as any. Donal saw to Katie's needs and the landlady made much of her, handing her a mug of giblet soup along with her sandwiches.

'That was for the man of the house,' Katie's benefactor explained, 'but I'm thinking you'll want it more before the day is out.'

Before they left an argument broke out between a local wit and Bluenose. The wit maintained for the benefit of his listeners that Bluenose needed no make-up such as blackening or raddle stick since he already had a wrenboy's face what with his generous mouth and nose of striking blue. Blows might have been exchanged had not Rubawrd Ring intervened. He ushered Bluenose out of doors and with one mighty hand lifted the old man's tormentor over his head for all to see. He held him aloft effortlessly until the remainder of his contingent of wrenboys had departed the confines of the pub and arranged themselves in marching formation outside. He then lowered him slowly and placed him gently upon a chair abjuring him to forego further comment until the wrenboys of Dirrabeg were out of earshot.

'What you say may be true,' Rubawrd conceded grudgingly, 'but it wasn't a kindly way to treat an old man.'

For a mile or so after leaving the public house there was an unevenness and sluggishness about the formation and movement of the band but this was quickly dispelled when they arrived at a cluster of thatched houses where a sizeable crowd awaited them. As the cashiers went to work the Costigan brothers came to life and before the entertainment was ended the effects of the drink they had taken had disappeared altogether. As they neared the end of the hill country they had all but completed the circle which would lead them into the suburbs of Trallock. When darkness fell the lights of the town were plainly visible as they descended in double file to the last, most lucrative stage of their journey.

Heavy rain began to fall. It had been preceded by a cloying mist but with the advent of a fresh breeze its force and density increased. The wrenboys were driven before it like leaves before an autumn gale. Fortunately, as Rubawrd had forecast, it beat upon their backs rather than their faces. The worst of the day's journey was behind them. The streets of the town would provide partial shelter from the rain.

Five

FATHER BERTIE STANLEY, junior curate of the parish of Trallock, arrived unannounced at the parochial house just as darkness fell on the afternoon of Saint Stephen's Day. He found Canon Tett in the dining-room seated close to the miserable remnants of a turf fire on one of the six creaking chairs which failed to take the bare monastic look from the musty room.

Stanley senior, after very nearly succumbing to a severe heart attack prior to Christmas, had made a surprisingly speedy recovery and would be set to leave hospital before the new year.

'How's your father?' the Canon asked brusquely.

'He's fine, Canon, thank you,' Bertie Stanley answered.

'Good,' said the Canon, 'maybe now we can expect a period free from illness so that you might catch up with your parochial obligations.'

'Please God, Canon,' Bertie assented, 'but there's talk abroad that newly ordained priests will be sent to England for a period.'

'Let's hope it stays at talk,' said Canon Tett icily, intimating that he wished the conversation to come to an end.

'Apparently, Canon, you don't seem to have heard of the Emigrant Chaplaincy Scheme.' Perseverance was one of Bertie Stanley's most noticeable characteristics. 'Of course you would have no way of knowing,' Bertie spoke forgivingly, 'but the fact of the matter is that the Irish bishops, with our own noticeably to the fore, have initiated this scheme and now, apparently, they are ready to make their findings known.'

'And, of course, they've confided in you before anybody else,' the Canon spoke witheringly.

'Not exactly, Canon,' replied an undeterred Bertie, 'but you might say that I have my ear to the ground, or another way of putting it might be to say that I have a friend in court. Actually, I met the bishop's secretary on Christmas Eve. He called to pay his respects and to convey the bishop's sorrow at my father's illness. He informed me that the scheme was as good as through and that I should be prepared for notification any day now together with all the other newly-ordained priests of this and all the other Irish dioceses.'

The Canon was about to interpose an opinion but Bertie provided him with no opening.

'In fact,' he continued, 'it's high time this scheme was put into operation. What it means is that Irish emigrants, especially the young and the forgotten, will have priests calling on them on a regular basis, to their lodgings or rooms or whatever and even to the tunnels, oil refineries, motorways and housing estates under construction at the moment. The idea is to bring them back to the faith and particularly to mass even if that means mass on sites or in lodgings.'

'You say newly-ordained curates, Father?' the Canon's tone was sceptical.

'Newly-ordained, Canon,' came the eager response.

'Well all I can say,' said Canon Tett, 'is God help those unfortunate emigrants if they are to be left to the mercy of newly-ordained priests. I'd sooner send out my parish clerk than a newly-ordained curate.'

'Oh, there will be a stiff course, Canon. We'll be put through our paces before we arrive at the front line.'

'And what's to stop me from vetoing your trip, Father?'

'Oh, it won't have anything to do with you, Canon. This is the brainchild of the Irish bishops and I don't see anybody torpedoing them.'

The Canon grunted unintelligibly before posing his next question. 'I suppose Father Butt took off the minute you set foot inside the door?'

'That he did, Canon, but you must remember it's his day off and that he was only standing in for me until my return.'

'Well now, Father, am I to take it that you'll be going out no more?'

'Not quite, Canon. I have a few chores to do and a few calls to make.'

'Well you can postpone them because I have no notion of going out on any sick calls this wet night. You'd hardly expect me now at my age to be gallivanting through bogs and hills in the middle of the night.'

'Well I won't be an hour all told Canon.'

'You haven't been listening Father.' There was petulance in the Canon's voice. 'I said you will not be going out again tonight unless it's a sick call. That is an order and if it's not obeyed to the letter I will ring the bishop this very instant. I'm tired both of your impudent manner and your continued prattling. God what a pair I'm saddled with! Now sit down and be quiet or go to your room.'

Bertie Stanley decided to opt for the privacy of his room. There was no point in arguing with a stone wall. He had come well prepared for any likely confrontations with the Canon. Only that very summer over a drink in the seaside resort of Ballybunion one of his professors, Monsignor Gallagan, had confided to him that he was forever grateful to the Almighty God for not having been sent as a curate to Canon Tett in Trallock.

'Tett, my boy,' he had said, 'is the devil incarnate with a round collar. He is all the things a priest should not be and the bother is that the dioceses of Ireland are full of Tetts. Money to burn and absolute power is Tett's idea of the priesthood and you know where they get this power? From Rome?

74

Not likely, my boy. They get it from a people who have never flowered, an abject race of pseudo-moralists who let their priests do their thinking for them. The people of this country are refugees from reality. We are text book neo-colonialists. We swapped our so-called independence for the tyranny of priest rule. Look around you, Bertie. Watch the way people stare at me because I have a black suit and round collar. Watch how their behaviour changes. Their joy is suddenly diluted. It's a good job we're drinking in a hotel. If we drank in a public house we would scandalise them. Come to think of it, if we drank in a public house we'd probably be excommunicated. Can you imagine how oul' Tett would react if it came to his ears that a priest was seen drinking in a pub in his parish? You know what the people of Ballybunion say, "Ballybunion," they say, "where parish priests pretend to be sober and bank clerks pretend to be drunk."'

After Nora Devane had removed the supper tray from the presbytery dining-room the Canon stoked the dying fire and added three small sods to the few glowing coals that remained. Neither of his curates had shared his supper table. Father Butt, he knew, had numerous friends, friends of dubious quality in the Canon's estimation, who would be only too happy to dine and wine him and he knew for some time that Father Stanley sometimes took snacks in his room. The Canon found this absence of absolute dependance on the presbytery disturbing. An insipid tongue of flame struggled from the fireplace casting weak shadows on the walls. The Canon sighed contentedly knowing he would not have to vacate his chair for more than an hour when he would be visiting friends in the square. The invitation had come that morning.

'It pleases me mightily,' he told Nora Devane; 'the Crollys are the town's oldest and most respected family, apart from being the biggest employers and real pillars of the church.'

The Canon crossed one long leg across the other, glad that there would be no intrusion into his thoughts. He drifted into a contemplative mood, wondering why the Crollys had invited him in the first place. He felt singularly honoured since it was well known that the Crollys never entertained. The thriving business was made up of hardware, drapery and furniture. There was a five-ton Bedford truck, a Comber delivery van and a company car, a well-kept Ford V-8 which was used solely by the business's representative on the road. Orders which he solicited from the village and country shops throughout the six days of the week were delivered unfailingly the following week. Crollys' transport was never late. The Canon put his mind to work endeavouring to find out what favour they might require of him. Whatever it was he would do all in his power to oblige. He had never found the Crollys stingy in the matter of mass offerings and other contributions and he would never forget the hundred pounds which he found one morning in an envelope which had been thrust under the front door of the presbytery. It had arrived on the eve of his first and last trip to the Holy City. A gift card was enclosed and it read: 'Have a nice holiday. The Crollys.' How could anyone forget such a magnificent subvention? 'And of course,' as the man said, 'there is plenty more where that came from.'

'I have come a long way,' the Canon spoke half to himself, half to the spiritless flame which could not quite make up its mind whether to live or die. 'For the simple son of a simple hill farmer I have come a very long way indeed and I will go a lot farther,' he assured the flame. He would never declare, publicly or privately, however, that the Roman collar had been his only means of escape from a life of drudgery as a clerk in some hardware or grocery store, the alternative to the emigrant ship which transported most of his neighbours' children to countries such as America, Australia and England. Another alternative had been to marry into a nearby hill farm after several years' hard work overseas amassing the requisite fortune, but what was this but slavery under another guise. No, his passport to freedom and dignity had to be the priesthood and so he found himself, a young seminarian in Salamanca in far-away Spain, hopeful of one day donning the round collar and ultimately being appointed to his own parish but never dreaming that he would end up as the parish priest of Trallock.

Before the Trallock appointment he had been in charge of two other parishes, first in the doubtful capacity of acting parish priest and secondly as the legitimate and sole pastor of one of the poorest parishes in the diocese, but here he had made his mark by building a new church and presbytery in record time without recourse to diocesan resources. He had mounted a series of raffles, football tournaments, dances, boxing tournaments and concerts and crowned his achievement by undertaking whirlwind tours of England and America where he extracted the maximum subscription from anybody and everybody of parochial descent in addition to milking contributions from every Irish association in both countries.

The bishop could do nothing but marvel at his boundless energy. In the course of time he was offered a bigger parish but he refused on the grounds that he deserved better, pointing to past achievements. He was a firm believer in the maxim that a dumb priest never got a parish. Then one bleak November day he was summoned to the palace and informed by a newly-elected bishop that a parish was vacant.

'My Lord, with all due respects,' the then Father Tett had interjected, 'would you mind telling me the name of the parish?'

'I am not obliged to,' said the bishop, 'not just yet.'

'Then I'm not obliged to take it,' said Father Tett curtly, 'because I don't believe in buying pigs in pokes.'

This comment had terminated the interview. The bishop, a former lecturer in theology, appointed a younger man to the vacancy. The younger man was somewhat addicted to intoxicating liquor and turned out to be a bitter disappointment to the bishop, Doctor Collane. He made several other serious errors before it dawned on him that there was more to running a parish than a pleasant disposition and high academic qualifications. When the elderly parish priest of Trallock died in nineteen forty Doctor Collane summoned Father Tett to the palace. The bishop, who had never once been disappointed by the commitment of Father Tett in response to demands for financial projects at home and abroad, decided not to beat about the bush this time. The parish of Trallock was up to its ears in debt and, quite simply, there was nobody in the diocese apart from the man before him capable of restoring its fortunes without undue delay.

'As you well know, Father,' the bishop opened cautiously, 'the parish of Trallock is vacant due to the death of our dear departed friend Canon Moriarty, never a man of the world you might say and consequently we are saddled with substantial debts in that part of the world. Nevertheless, there are many well-qualified aspirants to this prosperous canonric and I need hardly tell you that my ears are sore from unsolicited recommendations. I feel, however, that it is a parish that needs a firm hand, for the moment at any rate. It needs a man who can put the books back in the black in record time. Are you interested?'

'I'll take it, my Lord,' Father Peter Pius Tett shot back.

'You know what you're taking on, Canon?'

Father Tett could not resist a chuckle at this first use of his new title.

'I know what I'm taking on, my Lord.'

'And you think you can come up trumps?'

'If I saw the books my Lord I could tell you how long it would take me.'

'They're here,' said the bishop. 'I'll give you a quick rundown.'

The new canon listened intently as the bishop revealed the parlous condition of parochial finances. At the conclusion Bishop Collane asked him if he could provide a long-term forecast.

'I'll need five years,' said the Canon; 'with luck less but let us say five years.'

78

'That's most reassuring, Canon.' The bishop rose and took the Canon's arm as he led him out of doors to his car. 'I think I've made a wise choice, Canon, and I think you have been wise to accept.'

It had taken him less than the five years he had allowed himself to clear the parish debt. Now there was a healthy balance in the bank across the square and on top of that many other parishes in the diocese had benefitted from his business acumen. The bishop had begun to form the habit of calling him in whenever one of the poor parishes had exhausted itself.

'There are lazy priests as well as lazy people,' he once told the bishop, 'but whereas you'll always find someone to feed a lazy priest you'll find few to feed lazy people. That is why lazy priests don't have to beg.'

As he sat recalling past glories he suddenly pricked his ears and listened. He inclined his head towards the window the better to confirm his suspicions that it was some form of drum-beat which had intruded into his reminiscing. There it was again, unmistakeable this time. He rose from his chair and left the dining-room. Opening the front door of the presbytery he was forced to retreat by the driving rain. He took an umbrella from the hallstand and opened it. Covering his head and shoulders he went out into the teeming rain as far as the seven foot high wall which enclosed the presbytery grounds. He might have gone out into the square but this would mean exposing himself and that was the last thing he wanted. He dare not give it to say to his parishioners that he exhibited the least interest in the wrenboys' band which had just entered the square.

'Ah, there they are now, leaving one pub and, no doubt, facing for another.' Even the persistent rain failed to drown the sound of the music and drums. Canon Tett decided to remain where he was 'just to see if the scoundrels would have the gall to approach the presbytery. They have more sense,' he spoke the thought aloud, 'but on the other hand they could well be possessed of drunken courage. Drunk or sober I'll clear them from my door.'

As the rain beat its own tattoo on the umbrella the menacing sound of the bodhráns drew nearer until the band reached the presbytery. It seemed for a moment to the Canon that the sound of the drumbeats grew more subdued and that the volume of the music decreased. Also he felt that the pace of the group slowed down as it passed by. The Canon felt cheated. That morning after breakfast he had carefully rehearsed his lines and now the performance had been called off. The music drifted into the centre of the square. But what was this emerging from the presbytery with an umbrella over its head? It could only be his young curate, Father Stanley. Where was the fellow bound? Nobody had called requesting the services of a priest and the phone had not rung. He would have heard if it had.

'Where do you think you're going?' The Canon's question stopped Father Stanley in his tracks. The curate raised the umbrella and peered through the curtain of rain. He was astonished to see the Canon standing by the wall, umbrella now lowered for confrontation.

'Answer my question. Where do you think you're going?' He relished the apparent shock written all over his curate's face and the inability to answer by one who had always been master of the trite response up until this moment.

'Come on man. Answer my question,' the Canon shouted.

When Bertie answered his words came slowly and with absolute clarity. 'I'm going out,' he said, 'just for a moment to pay my respects to the wrenboys and to give them the half-crown which is their due.'

'You will turn on your heel, you impertinent buck and you will go back into that presbytery or I'll have you before the bishop for deserting your post.'

The Canon was delighted to note that his curate was taken aback. He pressed home his advantage. 'Go on. In with you.'

'I am not a prisoner,' Bertie Stanley returned. 'I am not

deserting my post. All I'm doing is going into the square for a second to give the wrenboys this half-crown.' He made a move towards the door but the Canon forestalled him.

'If you go out that door,' the Canon mustered all his authority and drew himself up to his full height as he closed his umbrella, 'it will be locked behind you and that will be the end of your prospects of ministering to the lost souls of England.'

The Canon raised the umbrella as though he would use it in the event of the curate trying to force his way past. Bertie lowered his head and closed his own umbrella; silently and dejectedly he re-entered the presbytery.

Outside in the square the rain had suddenly stopped. The Dirrabeg Wren marched in dignified fashion past the presbytery, eyes fixed in front, drumming and music restrained as ordered by Rubawrd Ring the Captain.

'Halt!' At the command the band, without ceasing to play, came to a standstill.

'Dancers forth!' Rubawrd called whereat the Costigans came to the fore and stood stock still, right legs firmly anchored to the ground, left legs poised for dancing. The brothers excelled themselves but the expected audience failed to appear. A small number of women and children, the former wearing shawls which totally concealed their identities, stood watching, among them the Smiley family, all dripping wet yet with eyes alight and innocent faces absorbed by the spectacle.

The cashiers made their way amongst the onlookers but the response was meagre. In other parts of the square, notably its corners, small, unidentifiable groups stood huddled, more out of curiosity than support for no sooner had the cashiers approached them than they vanished into doorways and under archways. It was clear too that there were faces at every window but none dared come out into the square after the Canon's condemnation on Christmas morning.

In Trallock's thirteen public houses the wrenboys were roundly abused by the more self-righteous of the town's drun-

81

kards. Other drinkers availed of the Canon's castigation in order to refuse subscriptions, explaining that while they might not be strong and perfect Christians they were nevertheless Catholic enough to take note of their Canon's strictures. He was, after all, the spiritual leader of the parish. Most of these would have found some other escape route anyway. They always had in previous years but on this occasion they delighted in offering the new pretext, many of them intimating that large sums would have been forthcoming but for Canon Tett's embargo. This sorely annoyed the Dirrabeg wrenboys who were not so easily duped. They saw in the refusals nothing more than the age old bias of town against country. Donal Hallapy, in particular, thought this treatment by his urban neighbours despicable. He personally knew most if those who declined to subscribe. Over the years he had supplied them with assrails of turf. They could never be trusted to honour an agreement and he was often obliged to sell at a low price rather than return home with a full rail. He was, in fact, still owed money by a few.

Most of the houses along Hill View Row had not opened their doors. Neither had they opened windows which would be the wont of the house-holders when there was rain falling. Then they would drop coins from upper storey windows while the wrenboys provided entertainment down below. This time the response had been minimal. Apart from Doctor Joe O'Dell and Mickey Munley the bookmaker, the all-round reception was dismal. In Carter's Row and in the tiny laneway where Kitty Smiley lived the response was much better but subscriptions in these areas had always been confined to coppers rather than silver. Healy Street had been a disappointment with only a few of the business people responding. Kitty Smiley had informed them that only three other groups had called that day so that there could be no doubting that most wrenboys had taken the Canon's words to heart.

At the bottom of Healy Street before they entered the square one passer-by had called them a gang of beggars. Bluenose had

to be restrained but the others took it in good part and proceeded with their march as if he had said nothing. The square
had been the biggest disappointment. Two of the three public
houses in that part of town closed their doors. The business
people had simply ignored the wrenboys. There were a few
exceptions. Father Butt had called Donal Hallapy aside and
thrust five shillings into his hand, explaining that one of the
half crowns was a subscription from the junior curate Father
Stanley. The incident happened in Monty Whelan's spacious
sitting-room. Monty Whelan and Father Butt had been standing at the sitting-room window which overlooked the square
when the wrenboys appeared.

'There's nothing like the sound of the bodhrán to rise the
blood in a man,' Monty had said. Father Butt, a glass of whiskey
in his hand and a cigar in his mouth, acquiesced. They watched
as the wrenboys tried house after house, knocking futilely on
closed doors. A few householders flung silver coins downwards
from upstairs windows but the majority withdrew from other
windows through which they had been watching as soon as the
cashiers approached.

In Monty Whelan's sitting-room two bottles of whiskey went
the rounds. The wrenboys did not stand on ceremony. Drinking
glasses were rejected and the gurgling bottles, their contents
steadily diminishing, went from mouth to mouth. Monty,
aware of the band's financial setback in the town pressed a five
pound note into one of the cashier's hands.

'Never let it be known,' he said proudly, 'that the wrenboys
of Dirrabeg were not nobly received in the town of Trallock.'

'A five pound note!' the news was echoed in awesome
whispers around the room.

After Katie Hallapy had sung one of Monty's favourite Irish
ballads the band trouped out into the square and marched to
the Bus Bar which would be their final call of the night. After
they had gone Monty and Father Butt resumed their positions
by the window. The square was deserted save for a solitary

83

shawled figure who moved slowly and deliberately towards the archway which led to the rear of the Bus Bar.

'I'm blessed to God if that isn't the Dexter,' Monty declared.

'Where?' There was a note of alarm in Father Butt's query.

'In the shawl,' Monty pointed a finger at the tiny figure. 'It's the walk. I'd know it anywhere. It always reminds me of a waterhen.'

'I wonder if she saw me come in here?' Father Butt asked anxiously.

'Naw,' Monty assured him. 'She's been trailing the wrenboys since they came to town. At the first beat of a bodhrán she got down to business like a greyhound from the traps. Compose yourself. You're the farthest person from her thoughts this night.'

They watched, scarcely breathing, as the tiny housekeeper made a final round of the square before returning to the presbytery. Father Butt marvelled that she could navigate the dark pavements and cobbled archway entrances with such skill especially since her face seemed to be completely covered by her shawl. Monty Whelan knew better. There would be just enough room to see out but none to see in. But for her distinctive gait she would have been impossible to identify. Satisfying herself that the square retained nothing worthy of her attention she entered the presbytery.

'What's this?' Father Butt's voice trembled. He sounded quite agitated.

'What's what?' Monty asked.

'Over there. In Crolly's doorway. It looks like Canon Tett.'

'It is Canon Tett,' Monty assured him. They watched as the Crollys shook hands with the Canon. The door closed behind him, the Canon looked up at the sky and opened his umbrella. Light rain had begun to fall. Though nothing compared to the intensity of the earlier downpour it added to the over-flowing gutters already contributing massive torrents of brown flood-water to the river Awnee which caressed the town in a wide semi-circle before joining the Atlantic several miles downriver. Canon Tett was well pleased with himself. The Crollys, J.P. and his wife Emily, had fallen all over him from the moment of his arrival at their dwelling place over the business premises. He was relieved of his overcoat and umbrella and made to sit in the most comfortable armchair in the cosy sitting-room. He was hardly seated when a glass of brandy was thrust into his hand. Although not a drinking man by any standards he accepted. There was a chill in his bones after his vigil in the rain and brandy was the very thing to banish it. They sat around a glowing coal fire chatting about everyday matters, refusing to raise the main issue until propriety had been fairly observed by reference to inconsequential trifles. They heard a band of wrenboys come and go. It was a small group if one was to judge from the sound. The Canon was delighted to note that the Crollys had made a point of ignoring the visitation. He found the brandy to his liking. He allowed them to add to his glass.

'Excellent brandy!' he observed after the first sip had found its mark.

'Delighted to hear it,' J.P. Crolly beamed and then produced a carefully rehearsed quip which flattered the Canon no end.

'It would take a Salamancan palate to acknowledge a good brandy,' he said. The Canon never mentioned the fact that the only wine he had ever tasted in Salamanca had been altar wine nor did he indulge in any alcoholic beverage whatsoever until he attained the ripe age of three score and ten and only then for medicinal purposes. If they wanted to make a connoisseur out of him he had no objection. The brandy was costing him nothing and taken in moderation would certainly do him no harm. After an hour or so of general parley tea and sandwiches were served by Emily Crolly. While they sat eating J.P. suddenly rose and cleared his throat.

'I hope you won't take it amiss Canon if I bring up a subject which is very dear to my heart.'

'Why would I take it amiss? Am I not in the house of a

friend. Please proceed, J.P.'

'Thank you Canon. The matter concerns my daughter Angela who, as you know, is a primary teacher in Dublin. Lately, my dear Canon, she has become most desirous of change and nothing would suit her better than a school near home. She is our only daughter as you know. The boys are happily married and doing nicely.'

'Better than nicely,' the Canon kept the sentiment to himself but it was well known to him that the four Crolly brothers would mind mice at a crossroads. The eldest was a successful dentist in Trallock, two more highly successful physicians in the city of Cork and Junior Crolly, the heir to the family business, was reputed to be even more astute than his father. The Canon was as familiar as any inhabitant of Trallock with the assessment of the Crollys by a local wag. Said he: 'The Crollys is it! Sure there's a fool in every family except the Crollys.'

'Poor Angela,' J.P. shook his head sadly. 'She longs to be near home. City life is not for her, Canon. She is a refined, gentle sort of girl, innocent of the world, Canon, so we were hoping that if there was any vacancy to arise in the future you might consider her.'

'I'll do more than consider her,' the Canon was emphatic. 'When a vacancy occurs she shall have it.'

'Of course we realise that it may be some time,' J.P. Crolly continued, 'and that there will be other claimants even more worthy.'

'Who could be more worthy?' the Canon asked, 'than the daughter of two of the best friends I ever had. And you may not have all that long to wait,' he confided. 'There are a number of impending vacancies due to age but those will be a year or two yet. However, I have certain changes in mind shortly and I think your daughter will benefit from one of these. Say no more for now. Bide your time and keep your own counsel.'

The Crollys exchanged puzzled looks. What had the Canon in mind and how would he fulfil a promise if there was no vacancy? Yet he was a man of his word and a man of his word must be taken seriously.

'I'll have to be going,' he said.

J.P. assisted him from the armchair, helped him with his coat and handed him an envelope with the express wish that he should utilize its contents to buy some token for himself. Later he was to discover with delight that the envelope contained a hundred pounds. As he left Crollys' he could not know that two pairs of eyes monitored his every movement. Neither could the owners of the two pairs of eyes know that the propietor of one figured prominently in the Canon's plans for the future.

Six

IT WAS UNANIMOUSLY agreed by the Dirrabeg wrenboys that the annual wrendance would be held on the second
Saturday night of January. At the conclusion of their Saint
Stephen's Day march they counted the proceeds of the day's
collection on the high counter of the Bus Bar. Silver and copper
coins were the dominant features of the money on display. The
count was conducted by Minnie Halpin. First the paper money
was withdrawn: this included Monty Whelan's fiver, two single
pounds and one ten shilling note, three separate contributions
these from a minority of the town's business community, and
finally two pounds, one each from Mickey Munley and Doctor
O'Dell. Coppers and silver amounted to twenty-five pounds
one shilling and one halfpenny making a grand total of roughly
thirty-six pounds.

The drink and sandwiches consumed earlier in the day
accounted for an extra five pounds. The collection was down
six pounds on the previous year. Nobody had any doubt as to
where the blame for this lay. But for Monty Whelan's generous
gift the day's outing would have been very near to a financial
disaster. As things stood it meant that instead of the customary
four firkins of stout there would now be only three. All were
agreed that this would seriously curtail the night's enjoyment
with every likelihood of a premature end when the stout was
exhausted. The solution came from Bluenose.

'If,' he argued, 'we was to buy no wine or whiskey we could manage another firkin.'

'The women won't like that,' Rubawrd Ring reminded him.

'Let the women drink porter the same as we all drink,' Bluenose replied. 'Once they gets accustomed to the taste you'll hear no complaints from that quarter.'

Eventually it was agreed that no whiskey would be purchased but that there should be some form of concession to the women by way of a few bottles of cheap wine. It was held that since most of them only tasted wine once a year they would not be able to distinguish between cheap cream sherries and established brands such as Bristol Cream and Winter's Tale.

It so happened that Fred Halpin had an abundant stock of a very cheap sherry known as Munster Cream but more frequently referred to as cooking sherry. It retailed at a half-crown a bottle and was much in demand by invalids who used it to leaven the taste of the raw eggs which they copiously swallowed in the belief that they reinforced the constitution and created no serious digestive problems. Fred Halpin generously pointed out that he would be prepared to offer a discount if a dozen or more bottles were purchased. It therefore transpired that for the modest sum of twenty-eight shillings twelve bottles of Munster Cream were acquired for the Dirrabeg wrendance. It would be consumed with relish to the very last drop.

No whiskey was purchased but Rubawrd Ring pointed out that there would be no embargo on privately purchased noggins or half pints provided they were concealed on the person and drunk out of the public view. Fred Halpin's bill came to twenty-six pounds. It also included a plentiful supply of cordials and minerals for the young folk and for older people who were teetotallers. Out of the ten pounds remaining a sum of six pounds was set aside for other commodities essential to the success of the wrendance. These would be purchased in the early afternoon on the actual day at Faithful Ferg's.

Niggardly as his subscription had been and miserly as was

89

his reputation no other business premises in Trallock was better equipped to supply the remaining needs of the wrendance. Several outsize barmbracks and a similar number of pigs' heads would be required as basic edibles as well as a batch of baker's bread consisting of thirteen tile loaves freshly baked, tea, sugar, butter and mixed fruit jam because it was the least expensive. The pigs' heads would be boiled in separate houses and brought to the house of the wrendance early in the evening. Neighbouring houses would be expected to provide extra cups and plates, knives, forks, spoons and fresh milk. Tea and sugar would complete the order at Faithful Ferg's.

In the bright warm kitchen at the rear of the pub Minnie Halpin prepared tea and cake for the females of the group and left them to fend for themselves while she went to her husband's assistance in the bar. The moment they had eaten the Ring girls, Noranne and Trassie, discarded their wet wren clothes and together with concertina and bodhrán placed them beneath the kitchen table before announcing that they intended doing a round of the town. They would have invited Katie Hallapy along to keep them company but she had already succumbed to the heat of the kitchen and was fast asleep in her chair, her head resting on her hands which in turn rested on the kitchen table.

In the bar the music was in full swing. Musicians from other bands had begun to arrive. The beat of the bodhrán was the dominant sound but fiddles, concertinas, melodeons and accordeons were in no way subdued by the many drummers beating out the age-old throbbing timbre of the bodhrán, thunderous when demanded, gentle and muted too as a solitary concertina player rendered a tune whose words told of heart-broken exiles in far-off lands. Finally only the bodhrán of Donal Hallapy was heard in accompaniment as the concertina player coaxed the delicate note, teased the long note, jerked the short and wrestled the powerful from the insignificant instrument.

A great cheer went up when the rendition spent itself

abruptly and deliberately.

'You're a mighty drummer,' the concertina player complimented Donal. 'You're the best in the parish of Trallock.'

'He's the best bodhrán player in the country,' Bluenose added.

'He may well be,' said the concertina player who knew better than to contradict the fiery ancient from Dirrabeg. The words were hadly out of Bluenose's mouth when the lights were suddenly doused and the voice of Fred Halpin was heard above all others.

'Silence,' he called. 'Silence all.' A prolonged hush followed and then Fred Halpin spoke in low tones to the silent assembly.

'It looks as if the Civic Guards are on the warpath folks so we'll keep it down until the danger passes.'

Thereafter all conversations were conducted in whispers. All business behind the bar was suspended. The most recurrent causes of outright raids on licensed premises were the giveaway tinklings of empty glasses and jinglings of coins. Civic Guards were ever on the alert for such sounds. An added hazard in the Bus Bar was the venerable cash register which was even louder and more strident then the ringing of a telephone. After several minutes of silence in complete darkness Minnie Halpin was dispatched to the rear of the premises with orders to open the wicket and make a careful survey of the scene outside.

It was agreed that if the Guards knocked upon the front door each customer would exit silently by the wicket at the back. Minnie returned breathlessly to report that the sergeant of the Civic Guards was in attendance in the backway. It was her considered opinion that a raid could be expected at any moment. Anxiously Fred Halpin drew aside the curtain of the front window and looked out into the square. His worst fears were realised. There was a Civic Guard stationed right outside his front door. From a moment his heart soared when he recognised the features of Tom Tyler. Tom could be trusted to keep his back turned while the customers were slipped out

91

silently before the back door was opened to the sergeant. Tom turned suddenly as if he knew he was under surveillance. He looked Fred straight in the eye and shook his head firmly, indicating by a barely perceptible uplifting of an eyebrow that there was another minion of the law in attendance not far away. Fred's eyes swept the square and sure enough they alighted after a while on the figure of a second Guard, poorly concealed by the shadows in a doorway not more than thirty yards from the Bus Bar.

The presence of the second Guard meant that a raid was inevitable. While he stood looking on, Tom Tyler was powerless. From the rear of the premises came the shrill sound of a whistle. It was this signal for which Tom Tyler had been waiting. He raised his hand and smote upon the door, uttering at the same time the all too familiar words: 'Civic Guards on public house duty'.

Fred Halpin delayed before opening the door. When he did Tom Tyler asked if intoxicating drink was being consumed on the premises, to which Fred replied that he was an upstanding citizen and that he would never countenance such a carry-on under his roof.

'In that case I'll be on my way,' Tom Tyler said. He was about to move away from the door when the second Guard emerged from the shadows. 'It looks as if I'll have to inspect the premises,' he said regretfully. 'It's the last thing I want to do, Fred, you know that.'

'I know that, Tom,' Fred spoke sympathetically, 'but what's it all about?'

'A complaint,' Tom Tyler returned.

'A complaint by whom?' Fred asked.

'Not allowed to say,' Tom spoke stiffly but his eyes were focussed on the presbytery further up the square.

'I might have known,' Fred clenched his fists in impotent rage and meekly stood aside to allow Tom Tyler access to the bar. Inside Minnie Halpin had turned on the lights. Upon entering Tom Tyler took off his cap and produced his notebook. 'Will you please admit the sergeant, Mrs Halpin,' he addressed himself to Minnie in the most respectful of tones. 'Now, my good man,' he spoke more officiously to Fred, 'how can you account for these people on your premises after official closing time?'

'I have no excuse to offer,' Fred answered lamely. When the sergeant entered he stood with hands folded and a broad smile on his sallow face.

'Looks like the biggest haul yet!' he scoffed. He was new to the district and by all accounts was only awaiting promotion and a transfer to a distant town.

'You'll be good enough to give your correct names and addresses to myself and Guard Tyler.' So saying, Sergeant Shee produced his notebook.

'And you'll be good enough to take off your cap.' The icy command came from Fred Halpin.

'I most certainly will not,' the sergeant barked back.

'You are in my home,' Fred Halpin spoke slowly, 'and while you are here you will remove your cap. I don't deny that we are here after hours and that we are breaking the law but you will not degrade my home by keeping your cap on in the presence of myself and my wife.'

Minnie Halpin darted forward suddenly and snatched the cap from the sergeant's head. She held it behind her back when he made an attempt to retrieve it. An angry murmur went up all around. It stopped the sergeant in his tracks.

'You can have it back when you're leaving,' Minnie conceded. One by one the names were taken; it was a tedious process. Several whose faces were still heavily blackened gave false names and addresses but the majority were known to Tom Tyler who had no option but to record their presence on the premises. Later they would be fined in the district court, two and sixpence for those who attended and five shillings for those who did not. The fine on the licensee was something heavier

93

and might vary from two to five pounds. He would also be expected to engage a solicitor. As their names were taken the offenders trooped out into the square where they huddled together under a street light and struck up a lively march. When the public house was cleared Sergeant Shee asked for his cap.

'I won't forget this incident,' he informed the Halpins, 'and you may be sure that I will bring it up in court and' – he raised a finger of admonition – 'I'll be keeping a special eye on these particular premises from now on and it might well happen that your license might be objected to at a future sitting.'

'If you come near these premises ever again,' Fred Halpin spoke slowly, 'I will report you to the chief superintendent who they say is a conscientious man. I will tell him that my premises have been raided three times already this year while other premises in the town can do as they please, as for instance Journey's End where you yourself do your drinking. You raid and convict those premises the same number of times as you've raided and convicted me and you'll be welcome here but until such time as you do, stay away from my door.'

'You heard what he said?' the sergeant, now trembling and pale-faced, turned to Tom Tyler.

'Every word,' Tom assured him.

'And you'll repeat what he said in court?'

'Of course I will,' Tom Tyler assured him, 'and when I do the judge will ask why in God's name those premises he mentioned are not being raided.'

The sergeant stood stock still for a moment, scarcely able to believe his ears.

'You'll hear more about this,' he informed Fred Halpin but his tone lacked conviction. He made his exit followed by Tom Tyler. Later in the barracks Tom would be roundly scolded by his superior and threatened with dismissal and although he might sport a chastened expression the reprimands would roll off him like water off a duck. He had ridden out the wrath of other sergeants and had survived without scars. In the square two score of bodhrán players and musicians gave of their best and while the sounds might have lacked sensitivity and perfection there was a rollicking abandon which was infectious. As Tom Tyler watched and listened from a discreet distance with his sergeant he found himself so caught up in the music that the sole of his right foot rapped the ground involuntarily. The sergeant's face registered disapproval.

'Let's move them along,' he said.

'What harm are they doing?' Tom Tyler asked.

'They are making a nuisance of themselves and they are preventing the residents of this neighbourhood from taking their sleep.'

Tom was about to point out that it was still early and that anyway the residents here were probably enjoying the music when the sergeant moved off briskly. 'Move along there,' he shouted, 'move along or I'll take your names for disorderly conduct.'

Some of the younger musicians handed their instruments to onlookers and confronted the sergeant. 'Since when was music made into disorderly conduct?' a hot-tempered young man to the forefront asked.

'Move along,' the sergeant's voice grew hysterical. He had been baulked once already that night. What Fred Halpin had said was true and it rankled all the more for that. The sergeant fumbled for his baton and as he did Tom Tyler suddenly arrived at his side.

'If you draw that there will be hell to pay,' he said. 'Now lads,' Tom raised his hands in a conciliatory gesture, 'start up the music and march away around the town.'

'Right boys!' Rubawrd Ring stepped forward, 'you heard what Guard Tyler said. Gather yourselves now and behave like wren-boys.'

Mumbling and muttering the young men retrieved their instruments. The older were already lined up for a final march

95

around the town. For generations it had been the practice of the various groups of wrenboys from the surrounding townlands to congregate in the square before parading en masse through the town and eventually dispersing after a complete circuit which saw them return to the square for the last time. Mudstained calico uniforms, wet and torn, were discarded by the majority of the wrenboys. The more fastidious would hold onto theirs until they were required again.

Throughout the week that followed the weather changed for the worse. Blinding hail and rainstorms swept across the countryside. During the infrequent lulls the smallholders of Dirrabeg replenished the fodder in stables and cowstalls from barns and hayricks. An intrepid few risked the journey to town for medicine or household supplies. Others availed of the all-too-short intervals to visit neighbours. Their stays were prolonged due sometimes to the sustained inclemency of the weather but more often than not because of the hospitality of the household being visited.

The Christmas purchases would not yet have been exhausted, especially the liquid element and since this was purchased, as a rule, by the man of the house, stocks often survived well into the New Year. There were many who would abstain from intoxicating liquor in their own abodes rather then be without adequate potation for visitors.

Donal Hallapy was not surprised when there was a knock upon his door at eight o'clock on the eve of the New Year.

'Come in,' he called expansively. Rubawrd Ring entered followed by Paddy Costigan, the more vocal of the Costigan twins.

'God bless all here!' both men intoned the time-honoured blessing together.

'There's no pair more welcome,' Donal came forward to greet them with extended hands. Without bidding the two Hallapy boys, Tom and Johnny, vacated their chairs by the fireside.

'Show me them wet caps and coats,' Nellie took the thoroughly wet headgear and garments and hung them to dry. Donal was delighted with his visitors. He was well supplied with liquor for the occasion, not having touched a drop of his own since Christmas night when his visitors had been Bluenose and his wife Delia. Present also had been Kitty Smiley and her brood. It had been a hilarious evening and night with Bluenose regaling all as he recalled his pugilistic exploits as a young man. The merrier he became the more boastful he became. Under the table at the time there happened to be two ancient pairs of boxing gloves which Donal had purchased at the Trallock hustings on Christmas Eve for his two sons.

'Come on,' Delia Bluenose taunted her husband, 'pull on a pair of these on you and I'll show you how to box.' She threw a pair of gloves at his feet and drew on the other pair before standing upright and shaping like a boxer.

'Sit down, you foolish oul' woman,' Bluenose advised her.

'Come on, you coward,' she called, fortified by the best part of a bottle of Sandeman's five star port.

'Go on, Bluenose,' the Hallapy boys entreated. Bluenose, a good-natured old man despite his sharp temper, decided to enter into the spirit of the thing and allowed young Johnny Hallapy to lace his gloves. Unsteadily he rose to his feet. Finding his balance on the kitchen floor he flicked the thumb of the right glove against his nose snorting several times like the old stager that he was. He danced around, shadow boxing for a while and then administered the most playful and tender of tips to the chin of his spouse. A fly would have done more harm. Again he threw out a gentle, open glove and then with a flurry of gloves and dancing feet he threw several clouts into the air, all the time loudly egged on by his audience.

'What do you think?' the question was addressed to Johnny Hallapy. Hardly were the words out of Bluenose's mouth than Delia swung with her left hand. She brought the wild swipe upwards from the floor and made contact with Bluenose's jaw.

97

It was a blow in a million.

His feet shot out from under him like a pair of automatic bolts. His rear plopped instantly on the floor where he sat stunned and speechless. Young Johnny Hallapy rushed into the arena and seized the old woman's hand. He held it as high as his height would allow, proclaiming her to be the heavyweight champion of Dirrabeg. For her part she stood amazed and fearful, wondering how Bluenose would react when he returned to full consciousness. She need not have worried for he took the incident in good part. The remainder of the night was taken up with singing and dancing and finally ghost stories of which Bluenose's wife had a colourful store.

Donal and Bluenose drank their fill and later all were agreed, especially the Hallapy children, that it was as good a Christmas night as ever they had experienced. Afterwards Donal had borrowed Bluenose's pony and cart in order to transport the Smileys back to Trallock. They sang the whole way to town.

On Donal's return, under a star-filled sky without trace of cloud, he had ample time to ponder his position at the year's end. It had not been a great year and, saving the bonus of the assrails of turf in defrayment for the stolen turkeys, there was nothing to enthuse about. He estimated that he had been far better off the same time the previous year. There had been two pigs fattening, one of which he had sold to pay the annual rates and the other of which he had killed and salted. There had been a weanling left from the four calves dropped the previous year. The weanling had been for unforeseen emergencies. This year there would be no weanling and of the four calves due in the spring two would be forfeited to pay the rates. He would carry the others as long as was feasible. Somewhere he would have to find the money to buy a pair of bonhams. Otherwise the household would be without meat across the Autumn and Winter. His turf reek and potato pit were at an all-time low. The future did not bear thinking about. Still there was the wrendance, always the most enjoyable night of the Dirrabeg year with no shortage of food and drink.

'No shortage of anything, eh Donal!' Bluenose had confided to him at the previous year's dance as they sat by the fire and watched the dancing girls whirl and leap, prance and pause, as they ogled the young men. Rubawrd Ring and Paddy Costigan gladly accepted the brimming glasses of whiskey which Donal thrust into their hands. Both declined the offer of water. Before drinking they raised their glasses and toasted the house and its inmates. They swallowed simultaneously until both glasses were emptied. Both gasped, took in huge lungfuls of air between their clenched teeth and shuddered as the whiskey found its mark.

Without a word Donal handed them two bottles of stout. Secondly toasting all and sundry they swallowed copiously until they judged the whiskey to be adequately diluted by the second, less potent draught. It had been apparent from their faces the moment they entered that they bore news of some import but to enquire what the nature of this news might be would have been bordering on the sacriligious. They must first be granted time to settle down and begin the proceedings with preliminary snippets. After a second glass of whiskey and several bottles of stout Rubawrd Ring cleared his throat and assumed an expression of the utmost dolefulness.

'There is bad news,' he said.

'Oh!' from Nellie Hallapy.

'No one dead, I hope,' from Donal.

'We might as well be dead,' Rubawrd Ring spoke dejectedly. There was an uneasy silence while Rubawrd and Paddy Costigan exchanged woeful looks.

'You tell him,' Rubawrd turned his face to the fire and abdicated responsibility for the cheerless revelation which was to come.

'Well,' Paddy Costigan began and he looked closely at the bottle of stout in his hand as though it were partly to blame, 'it looks like there will be no wrendance.'

'No wrendance,' his listeners repeated the tidings in awesome whispers and waited for more.

'It appears,' Paddy Costigan continued, 'that Mickey Lantry is not now prepared to give us his house for the occasion. He says that it would be flying in the face of God to do so.'

'The face of God meaning the dial of Canon Tett,' Rubawrd Ring spoke bitterly.

'He'll change his mind,' Donal said.

'He won't,' Rubawrd spat the words out, 'the wretch is adament. We've tried every tack with him but he's so terrified of the Canon that he won't even listen to us.'

'What are we to do?' the question came from Donal.

'There's little we can do unless we have a night in the Bus Bar and that wouldn't be the same thing at all. We could divide up the money but that wouldn't be any good either.'

'Is there any other house?' Nellie Hallapy asked.

'Plenty of houses,' Rubawrd assured her, 'but none with big enough kitchens or rooms where you could sit a crowd to supper.'

'For dancing the kitchen would have to be big,' Donal reflected, 'and there aren't that many big kitchens save farmers' kitchens and I know of no strong farmer that would give his kitchen even if Tett was to come and dance in it.'

'What we want is an old farmhouse kitchen with wide flags in front of the hearth where the stepdancers might do themselves justice, an old kitchen big enough for twenty dancing couples at the time.'

'There aren't many of those,' Donal poured a bottle of stout into a teacup as he spoke.

'There is one,' Rubawrd Ring informed him, 'but whether he'll give it or not is another matter.'

'Who would that be?' Donal asked.

'Bluenose.'

'But the house is falling down around their ears.'

'That may be,' Rubawrd conceded, 'but it has a big kitchen

and a fine room adjacent and dammit all man we only want it for one night.'

'They're too old. It wouldn't be fair to them and besides they may not want to give it. Then there's the family to consider.'

Discouraging as were Donal's remarks, Rubawrd pressed his case.

'The family is in England,' he said, 'and if I know them there isn't one would refuse us. The couple might be old but they don't think they're old and that's mighty important. Anyway it isn't up to them alone, it's also up to you.'

'Up to me! How could it be up to me?'

'Now, now, now Donal we all know that Bluenose regards you as his closest friend. There is nothing he'd refuse you.'

Donal frowned. 'I hate asking them,' he said. 'I feel I'd be taking advantage of them.'

'It's that or no wrendance,' Paddy Costigan put in.

'It's a mighty burden on an old couple,' Donal pointed out; 'there's a night and a morning in it.'

Nellie Hallapy turned to her husband. 'All the women in the townland will help out. Katie and myself will clean up after.'

'Where is Katie?' Rubawrd Ring asked.

'In bed since the wren,' Nellie explained.

'A touch of a cold,' Donal added.

'Nothing serious, I hope,' Rubawrd asked.

'Nothing serious,' Donal assured him.

Katie Hallapy's illness had been born out of humiliation. When in Trallock for the Christmas shopping she sensed that the costume she wore was an object of ridicule: the skirt no longer reached to her knees but because of the economic circumstances of the household she had decided to keep her mind to herself. She had also resolved that she would feign illness rather than attend the wrendance.

The subject of the wrendance location was temporarily set aside as Nellie Hallapy laid the table, assisted by her sons. The trio at the fire spoke of the devastating effects of Canon Tett's

101

Christmas Day sermon. Other priests in other places frequently referred to wrendances as porter balls or round the clock booze-ups and mostly there was no malice in their imputations. Canon Tett's voice, however, was undoubtedly the most powerful in the parish of Trallock.

'The wren will never be the same again.' The gloomy prophesy came from Paddy Costigan.

'The wren will die,' Rubawrd Ring countered, 'only if we let it die. Priests have spoken out against wrendances before.'

'Yes, but not like this. The wren is beginning to become a bad word in Trallock.'

'That won't last,' Rubawrd assured him. 'What matters now is to find a house.'

'All right,' Donal spoke resignedly. 'I'll put it to them first thing in the morning. You can take it there will be a wrendance. Now let's finish this bottle of whiskey.'

Seven

AT FORTY-FIVE Monty Whelan was one of Trallock's more controversial figures. The very mention of his name almost always gave rise to argument. Noted for his outspokenness, he was admired by the more liberal members of the community and regarded with the deepest suspicion by the more conservative. There were some who envied him and there were some who hated him for one reason or another. A poll would have revealed that a slight majority of the townspeople held him in no great esteem. On the other hand it would show that his stock was very high amongst a strong minority and also in the outlying areas of the parish, particularly Dirrabeg where he was assistant in the two-teacher school. He might have been principal but then he might also have been principal of the main school in Trallock town.

When his wife had died after ten years of marriage he had turned to drink. People thought him fortunate not to have been dismissed after allowance had been made for his loss. This ran into a period of almost two years after which time the patience of his principal teacher had grown thin although the latter had repeatedly covered for him and continued to do so despite internal and external pressures.

Monty was an excellent teacher. Despite his many absences and irreverence for punctuality the fourth grade class which he harangued and nurtured in turn always transferred itself to the

103

next grade with full mastery of the curriculum which included arithmetic, geography, history, reading and spelling in Irish and English. He also managed to include a little natural history which had been dropped from the curriculum by the Department of Education so that more time might be made available for the teaching of Irish. His mastery of the native tongue was never disputed nor was his ability to engender a love of the language in his pupils. What they learned from Monty Whelan they never forgot. In after years in public houses and elsewhere they would tolerate no criticism of him.

Corporal punishment had always been anathema to him. With his vast knowledge of the town where his family had traded for several generations he knew how and when to make allowance for those under his care who were under pressure at home. He called every boy by his christian name and no matter how excessive his alcoholic intake the night before his charges never suffered as a result. His enemies came from the settled, self-styled respectable people of the town. Chiefly the enmity might be attributed to his free and easy lifestyle and obvious opulence. His wife had left him everything and this was reckoned by shrewd observers to be a sum that, for all his apparent profligacy, he would never manage to spend in the solitary lifetime at his disposal.

Generous to a fault, he was known to be a soft touch although he knew where to draw the line when he felt he was being put upon to excess. The house in the square had been the venue for many wild parties in the early years after his wife's death and as is the way in every closeknit community exaggerated accounts of the awful orgies which took place there spread like wildfire, initiated by people who had not been invited and who would have no way of knowing what had taken place.

As the years went by and the pain of his wife's demise subsided somewhat the parties diminished in number and in size but he was not yet above inviting a number of friends and casual acquaintances for a drink or two when Fred Halpin called time in the Bus Bar. It was at one such get-together that he came to know Daisy Fleece.

The Trallock Gaelic football team had earlier won a junior league game against a neighbouring parish and Monty, who was one of the team's three selectors, took advantage of the occasion to indulge in a mild celebration. When Fred Halpin delivered his usual mild ultimatum Monty had invited all those present for a drink in his nearby house. Daisy Fleece had been present at the time with her sister who happened to be home from England on an annual visit to her mother, an invalid who had adamantly refused to make the journey to England where most of her offspring now resided. Daisy had volunteered to stay with the old woman on condition that the other members of the family contributed to her upkeep and the upkeep of the modest family home on the outskirts of the town.

Daisy had married at sixteen the second son of a farmer from the Upper Dirrabeg hill country. It had been a shortlived affair by parochial standards. She had given birth to three daughters, the first a few weeks after the marriage and the third two years later. The day after the christening of the third child her husband, Walter Fleece, vanished from the scene. He had never returned. Rumour had it that he re-married in Coventry where he was a successful sub-contractor. The daughters, now in their twenties, were successfully married to Englishmen, all of whom were reportedly model husbands. The girls had never returned to Trallock and had repeatedly written letters entreating their mother to join them in England. She had always refused although she was present at their weddings and had holidayed with all three on a regular basis, hiring a local woman to look after her mother during her absence. The girls bore a deep and abiding hatred for the town of Trallock, a hatred that they would never lose. They explained to their husbands who often expressed the desire to visit the town that they had been degraded there and made to feel inferior by a number of children fortunate enough to have fathers who stayed put and whilst

105

most people were kind and sympathetic the slur was always there.

Monty Whelan had earlier noticed Daisy Fleece and her sister in the Bus Bar. He had always been attracted to Daisy and if he had been asked to nominate the handsomest woman in the town of Trallock he would have opted for either Kitty Smiley or Daisy Fleece. At forty Daisy was nearer his age. Since his wife had died his name had never been linked with that of any woman. There had been overtures galore, mostly instigated by his well meaning sister-in-law Maisie, but he could never manage to muster sufficient interest. Anyway, his late wife had been a beautiful looking woman and Maisie's candidates, while presentable and shapely, could not even remotely measure up to the cherished memory of the only woman he had ever loved.

As he sat in the Bus Bar in the middle of a group of friends his eyes wandered from time to time to the place where Daisy and her sister were seated. On his way to the toilet he stopped and enquired after the health of the mother. He remembered her as a most redoubtable virago who took her ire out on teachers who endeavoured to chastise her sons. On being assured that the old woman was well he proceeded to the gents where he pondered further on the charms of Daisy Fleece. Later he had invited the sisters to his house. Daisy politely refused, explaining that her mother would be expecting her, but her sister declared that she needed a break from the mother. Between them they persuaded Daisy to dally for a short while.

The party had been a success and afterwards Monty had insisted on walking the sisters home.

'Only for the hour that's in it and only for Maggie here,' Daisy declared, 'I wouldn't allow myself to walk with you, Monty Whelan.'

'For God's sake why not?' Monty had asked, taken aback.

'Because you have too much to lose by being seen with me.'

At the house Maggie invited him indoors for a cup of tea. The local woman who had been sitting up with the old woman could not conceal her astonishment upon beholding the visitor.

'See what I mean,' Daisy explained. 'Tomorrow, Monty, you'll be the talk of this neighbourhood and it's nothing good they'll be saying.'

On the pretext of suddenly acquiring a headache Maggie retired to bed. Monty and Daisy sat on in the kitchen.

'Suppose someone were to see you leaving here,' she pouted, 'what would they think?'

'The worst,' Monty replied. They sat for an hour reminiscing about their youth. There was no mention of absent husband or deceased wife. When Daisy suggested that it was time for him to go he asked if he might see her again.

'Why?' she asked dispassionately.

'Because you are the most beautiful-looking woman in the town and on that account I feel I have the right to ask. I'm a single man, remember.'

'You may be single,' Daisy reminded him soberly, 'but I'm not. I'm still a married woman. What would people say?'

'It wouldn't worry me one way or the other what people might say,' Monty answered.

'Well, it would worry me, not but I'm sure that people have me down for a loose type already but it would worry me for what it might do to you.'

'To me?'

'Don't be naive, Monty. If we were seen together it would scandalise the parish. You seem to forget you're a teacher. Respectable people would not want an adulterer teaching their children.'

'An adulterer! What are you talking about. We have no obligation to anybody, either one of us.'

'Listen, Monty,' Daisy placed her hands over his on the kitchen table. 'I think far too much of you to be seen in public with you. It could cost you your job. Let me finish. You're not the first man, not even the first professional man in Trallock to want to have a relationship with me. Ever since he left me

107

nearly twenty years ago there's never been a time when I haven't attracted would-be lovers. Some were pillars of the church; others the opposite. Some were wealthy, some from the top families in town. They've begged me to accommodate them, even to meet them for a chat as it were but there was always one snag. Our relationship would have to be secret. No one must know. If you heard the proposals! Meet me on such a stretch of roadway at ten o'clock at night or I'll slip in your back door some night, just leave it unlocked. Then there were the offers of a weekend in some city. They promised to book me into the best hotels, wine and dine me and even finance my wardrobe, but nobody must know. You're somewhat like them, Monty, but not altogether. At least you are prepared to be seen with me in public. I respect you for that but I can't allow it although if it's any consolation to you I like you a lot.'

She removed her hands and folded them. 'I think it's time you went home.'

'I suppose it is at that.' Monty tried to conceal his disappointment. 'If you change your mind you know where to find me.'

Daisy had laughed at this. 'The bloody weird part of it now,' she said, 'is that I'll have to leave you out by the back door as if we were adulterers.'

Monty took her hands in his as they rose. 'Well,' he preened with mock boastfulness, 'I have one up on all the others. At least I have the distinction of being let out your back door.'

Later when he emerged into the street he felt distinctly elated. He might not have succeeded in establishing a relationship and he probably never would but at least she had singled him out for honourable mention. She could have been contemptuous and she would have had every right to be, but no. She had been sympathetic, had not, in fact, been in the least dismissive which gave him hope. He dared not read too much into her good-natured response, however. He could not imagine her being disdainful towards anybody. He wondered who her suitors were. Respectable, church going, how dare they! He found himself laughing at his newly-discovered self-righteousness. Basically his own secret aspirations could not be all that different from those of her other admirers except for the fact that he was no longer married. That particular segment of his life was carefully stored away. The grief had passed but the void remained and would always remain to some degree. Sometimes he felt that if they had been blessed with a family things might not have been so depressing. At least he would have someone of his own to turn to.

Hard to conceive that Daisy Fleece was the first woman in his life since his wife's death: not the first woman, rather the first woman he had genuinely desired for more than basic reasons in that long interim. There had been others who had evinced interest, lonely widows, hopeful spinsters seeking security and one he dared not contemplate. He wondered if she had fully recovered.

Not since that first and only terrifying revelation had she ever by word or deed as much as remotely intimated the slightest interest. It had happened shortly after his enforced transfer from Trallock Boys' School to the more remote mixed school of Dirrabeg. It had taken him some time to get used to the demotion and demotion it was no matter what his friends might say although rusticated might be the more appropriate word. The transition had almost proved too much for him. But for his principal Ciss Fenley he would have succumbed altogether to the bottle. She had stood by him all through those first months, overlooked his transgressions, taken his classes when he failed to show up and after a while took to driving him to and from the school in her Morris Minor until eventually the teacher in him began to surface and he was able to fend for himself.

There came a time when he became totally involved with his classes. His charges had a vast repertory of native ballads, many in the Irish language, also a wide variety of local folk tales and a command of speech enriched and coloured by words

109

and phrases from the Irish which their grandparents had spoken and of which a substantial residue had been retained by their parents although until Monty's arrival this remnant too was in danger of disappearing. He arrested the decline and through dint of cossetting and commitment managed to preserve the inheritance which his pupils had been in danger of losing.

'It was God that sent you,' Rubawrd Ring once told him after he had accidentally overheard some of the older schoolchildren conversing in Irish in the schoolyard.

'The soil was rich,' he returned, 'and the seed was there.'

In time he came to love the children of Dirrabeg. They had a freshness and innocence rarely found in the town. It came to be the most rewarding time of his entire career as a teacher. He saw himself as a preservative and repository rolled into one. All would have been perfect except for the one pitiful incident which still brought a blush to his cheeks whenever it confronted him. They had been returning from school in the Morris Minor when he had remarked innocently that it was high time he brought his own car into use. Almost a full year had passed since he had taken up the Dirrabeg appointment. A fine rapport had developed between them. Little did he know that she cherished a far different interpretation of their relationship.

'There's no need for you to do that,' she had said generously, 'you know I don't mind driving you.' Then after a pause: 'I'd drive you anywhere, Monty. I think you should know that by now.'

At first he could not believe his ears. She was the last person in the world to whom he would have given a romantic thought. He pretended he had not heard the ominous words but she was only beginning.

'We have grown very close have we not, dear,' she said, taking his silence for shyness. Words began to pour out in a torrent. He sat dumbfounded, unable and unwilling to contribute a word of his own. He closed his eyes and prayed silently that the whole, terrifying business was all a dream. He felt her

hand on his squeezing as the spate of words still poured forth.
'Aren't you going to say anything?' she asked after what had
seemed like hours. He searched in vain for some form of
response.
'I understand,' she said and squeezed his hand all the more.
He never longed for any sight just then as he longed for the
suburbs of Trallock. She drove at a snail's pace, availing of
every second before depositing him at his door. Even then she
still held his hand. She turned and looked at him. For all her
ardour she could not but recognise the pained expression on
his face. She slowly released her grip on his hand. He searched
and searched for something to say, anything to relieve the
oppressive atmosphere in the car.
'Oh Christ!' he prayed silently and more fervently than ever
before in his life, 'give me something to say.' Nothing came.
She was babbling again, this time less coherently, phrases like:
'What a fool I've made of myself,' and, 'why did you let me go
on! Why didn't you stop me, do the kind thing and tell me to
shut up!' She went on until she had exhausted herself. Then
came a period of sobbing. Outside in the square life went on.
People passed to and fro, totally unaware of the drama close-by.
She was speaking again, this time in a more precise tone.
'Do you feel anything for me?' she asked, 'anything at all?'
'Of course I do,' he grasped the lifeline and held on, unwilling
to be drawn ashore by any hands other than his own.
'Of course I feel for you,' he told her. It was his turn to
babble now. It was the only course open to him. 'I regard you
as a dear friend and I always will. You've been a tremendous
help to me in the school. I honestly feel that I could not have
carried on without your help. Look, Ciss, let us pretend that
this never happened. Nobody will ever hear anything from me.
Let us return to where we were.'
'Do you feel anything for me?' she asked, vainly endeavouring
to salvage some small scrap of consolation, something on which
she might build.

111

'I do. I do,' he said, 'but you must know that I cherish the memory of my wife more than anything else in this world and that there can never be anybody to take her place.'

'I'm not asking to take her place, Monty. I can't imagine what gave you that impression. What I had in mind was that we might visit each other's houses now and then, go out for a meal maybe or if you'd fancy a drink we could go to the hotel.'

Monty winced visibly. It did not escape her. Neither did it divert her. She was a year older than he. Never before had she been presented with what she believed to be such a golden opportunity. Add to this the fact that she came from stock who persevered to the ultimate when it came to making the most of the slightest chance in the matrimonial stakes.

'We're both alone in the world Monty. My parents are dead and your wife is dead.'

'Of course, I have my brother and his family,' he was quick to correct. He never dreamed he would find himself falling back on his brother Fergus. The role of hypocrite was one to which he was not used. Still, he would adopt any role if he was sure he would emerge from this unwanted situation cleanly; he sensed that even minimal concession would eventually lead to total surrender. This was no artless colleen he was dealing with. He had come to realize this since she had begun her play, the sum total of which was that there must be some kind of firm understanding between them. Try as he would he could devise no firm line of dismissal, no curtain line which would end the matter conclusively. Lamprey-like she refused to surrender her grip. It began to dawn on him that a decisive move was required if he was not to surrender the absolute freedom he had enjoyed for so many years. He could never see her in the role of subject missus sitting happily by his side while he supped whiskey and stout in the Bus Bar. As far as he knew she did not drink.

'If I get out of this unscathed,' he silently promised his creator, 'I will make every effort to mend my ways and I promise

112

never again to be remiss in the matter of daily prayer and observance of the sacraments.'

There was no immediate heavenly response to his desperate plea. He resolved to clinch the matter. He sat upright in his seat and partly opened the car door. Steeling himself he addressed her with what he believed to be a mixture of calm logic and irrefutable fact.

'I am no use to you my dear Ciss or to any woman. I'm an inveterate drunkard and I am firmly ensconced in the single way of life. It is not my intention now or at any time to have any relationship whatsoever with any female whatsoever and that is absolutely my final word in the matter.'

So saying he erupted from the car, banging the door as forcefully as he could, daring not to look behind lest some yet unrevealed womanly wile forestall him. He made straight for the Bus Bar where he ordered a glass of whiskey from Minnie Halpin.

'What's the matter with you?' she asked.

'Why?' he asked calmly.

'You're shaking. Your hands are shaking, even your knees. It's as if you were after seeing a ghost.'

He pondered her observations and was obliged to concede that she had struck the nail on the head.

'Not quite a ghost,' he announced half to himself, half to the wall, 'more of an ogre really.'

He decided to stay at home from school for the remainder of the week. He would indulge in a few more whiskeys and retire to his bed having first sent word to Doctor O'Dell that he required his services whenever convenient. He would need a certificate.

Later, after a routine examination, Joe O'Dell withdrew his portly figure from his patient's bedside to the centre of the room where the maximum amount of light was available for the reading of the thermometer he had just withdrawn from Monty's mouth. Joe shook his head.

'There's nothing the matter with you that's visible to the naked eye or within the limited ken of a general practitioner,' Joe O'Dell returned the thermometer to its case, 'except that you are probably drunk, certainly half drunk. Is there something you're not telling me?' He poured himself a stiff dollop from a half-filled whiskey bottle which stood on the table beside the bed. 'I'll give you a cert all right on the grounds that you'll almost certainly be sick in the morning if you drink any more whiskey. Why don't you tell me what's troubling you? You know me, Monty, that's as far as it will go.'

Joe O'Dell listened between sips as Monty unfolded his tale. His good-natured face registered no sign of either joy or sorrow until the end was reached when he poured himself a second whiskey.

'So you think a few days away from the school will allow things to blow over?'

Monty nodded eagerly. He looked hopefully at his physician, silently praying that he would approve.

'I don't agree at all,' came the measured response. 'If you don't present yourself at school tomorrow there is nothing surer than that Ciss Fenley will come here to find out what's wrong.'

'The door will be locked.'

'Locked doors are poor proof against a determined woman my friend. Your only hope is to go to school. Otherwise you could very well find her here in this room before the day is over.'

'All right, all right. I'll be there.'

'Good.' Joe O'Dell poured himself a final whiskey and sat on a chair near the bed.

'There's another thing you would want to remember. Calculate your every move and be on your best behaviour for a while to come. Don't forget that hell hath no fury like a woman scorned.'

'What do you mean exactly?'

'I mean she's your superior. I mean she's been rebuffed and that can hurt when you're an ultra-respectable, middle-aged woman who has gone blindly overboard. She's never gone all out before which means she's never been rejected before. She's wounded. Therefore she's dangerous and will be dangerous until the wound heals if heal it ever will.'

Monty's face expressed genuine alarm at this fresh disclosure.

'Isn't it possible,' he said, 'that you might be reading more into this than is already in it?'

Joe O'Dell sipped thoughtfully from his glass before venturing a reply.

'It is possible,' he said, 'but the opposite is also possible and, having said that, I'll say no more, except that to be forewarned is to be forearmed.'

At school the following day Monty could discern no distinct change in Ciss Fenley's attitude. At lunchtime she stayed on while he returned to Trallock where he partook of a pint of stout and a ham sandwich in the Bus Bar before returning to Dirrabeg. When school closed in the afternoon they exchanged a few words about the weather, making no reference whatsoever to the bewrayment of the day before. She seemed as charming as ever as she stood silently, smiling and agreeable, awaiting any further comments he might choose to make about the likely dispositions of wind and rain.

'Well, that's the way,' he had breezily concluded, perhaps too breezily, before suddenly hotfooting it to his car and to departure.

He thanked his stars on his way home that she had taken it so well. He had expected her to be cool to say the least or perhaps distant. He felt greatly relieved, delighted too that he had taken Joe O'Dell's advice and opted for school instead of bed. The Doc was a wily old coot. One had to hand it to him.

If Monty had only known that Ciss Fenley regarded the incident of the previous day as no more than a bad opening round in a full distance contest he would have gone straight to the Bus Bar after arriving in Trallock and there partaken of a stiff whiskey. Instead he went directly to his study and wrote

115

a letter to Daisy Fleece. Whether it was because of the nerve-racking encounter with Ciss Fenley or genuine infatuation with this new object of worship he could not be sure but he poured out his heart in the missive and posted it at once lest by any chance he change his mind. He knew instinctively, even if he dared not hope for a reply, that the letter was in safe hands and that there was no fear its contents would ever be divulged to anybody.

When after a week he had received no response he wrote again and told her that she might expect an epistle every other day for the remainder of her life unless she consented to meet him. As time passed and his many letters remained unanswered he took to walking past her home in the hope that he might meet her. Whether by chance or intent she was not to be seen. On a number of occasions he was tempted to knock at her door but always he had second thoughts, realising that an act of such rashness would destroy any slender chance he might have of furthering their relationship.

Then one late night, several weeks after he had penned the first letter, there was a knock at his front door. He had left the Bus Bar an hour earlier. In fact he had been the last to leave so that it was highly unlikely to be one of his cronies from that centre. It could be Father Butt but he would be more likely to knock at the back door. It could be Jonathan Murray, the young assistant teacher at Trallock Boys' School. It was just the sort of hour he was fond of picking to seek advice about teaching methods. Tom Tierney, his straight-laced principal would not approve, hence the late hour, or more likely it would be a denizen of his beloved Dirrabeg, stranded in Trallock because of a stolen bicycle or bereft of the means to hire a taxi home, probably Bluenose or Rubawrd Ring or even Donal Hallapy. On the other hand it could be Tom Tyler, the genial guardian of the peace. He had knocked in the past when the night without was too foul even for the law and Monty's sitting room light shone warm and promising behind partly drawn curtains. They had often demolished a bottle of whiskey together as Tom reminisced about his native Mayo, the scene of a poverty-stricken but carefree boyhood. It would hardly be Tom. The night was too mild. Nothing sort of sheer desperation induced by unbearable weather would ever force him to intrude and even then the knock would be diffident and low key. Monty inserted a marker between the pages of the book he had been reading and rose wondering.

He opened the door to behold a shawled woman, her head slightly averted. He noticed the wellingtons on her feet and thinking his caller was a tinker woman his hand shot involuntarily to his trousers pocket where he located a half crown.

'It's not your money I'm after, sir,' came the voice.

'God, don't say it's you, Daisy. I don't believe it. It's too good to be true.'

'It's me all right but don't you dare raise your hopes. I'm only here to tick you off, Monty Whelan.'

'You're here and that's what matters,' he whooped. He ushered her into the sitting room before she could protest. Inside he stood at a respectful distance. The shawl fell to her shoulders.

'I declare to God,' he crowed with genuine delight, 'but you are the prettiest sight I have seen this many a long day. He threw back his head and sang a couplet from one of his favourite songs:

'As if from out the sky above an angel chanced to fall
'Twas my little Irish colleen in her oul' plaid shawl.

'Sit down. Sit down,' he said expansively, 'and by all means castigate me but don't go away. Just don't go away and leave me.'

Across the square a mystified Ciss Fenley sat by her window. She had seen the shawled woman knock at the door. She had seen her enter; nay, she had seen her being made to enter. Could the poor man be reduced to currying favours from itinerant women after midnight or was the shawl a guise? She would wait and see. Ciss Fenley had longed for many things in her life but now she longed with all her heart for a pair of binoculars. Still, all was not lost. She would wait and failing to identify she would follow in the shadows and find out what she wanted to know.

The tall, irregular edifices of the square, shopfronts obtruding, private residences discreetly withdrawn, provided a sufficiency of night-time shadows and varied angularities of concealment to suit her purpose. The bother was that these recesses were sometimes occupied, mostly by courting couples but also by solitary members of the Civic Guards. Still others sought shelter there when unexpectedly waylaid by heavy rain showers which meant that she might well be seen and, being seen, leave herself open to question. The answer, of course, was a black shawl. There was one of her mother's in the house, in an old wardrobe in the attic. She would retrieve it and bide her time.

Eight

THERE WAS THE usual disquiet and discontent among the younger members of Dirrabeg Wren during the bleak days leading up to the wrendance. For the first time too the same despondent feelings began to spread among the older people, especially those with young families. The womenfolk were well used to grousing from the younger generation. After every Christmas and summer when the exiles had left for England a number of disillusioned boys and girls would follow in their wakes.

This was understandable. The Dirrabeg exiles were resident for the most part in the English midlands where there was no scarcity of employment. In addition wages were good, astronomical by Dirrabeg standards. Many had purchased their own homes, houses with dining rooms and sitting rooms as well as bathrooms with hot and cold water, undreamed of luxuries in Dirrabeg.

In fact save for the few houses of the larger farmers there were no indoor toilets or bathrooms and in many no electric light. The light had arrived elsewhere but there had been too many obstacles in Dirrabeg. Many of the older cottiers and small farmers refused to join the group scheme which would provide electricity at relatively moderate rates. Engineers from the electricity board had failed to resolve the impasse. The oldsters stoutly maintained that it wasn't worth their while, that their offspring were settled in England with every intention of staying there permanently and that they had no notion of allowing themselves to be saddled with monthly bills on top of the initial outlay. The engineers argued that the electricity was cheaper than in any other part of Europe, that paraffin, candles and home produced peat were costing infinitely more. They had figures to bolster their arguments but the old people did not want to hear. Different, they maintained, if there was any hope of their children coming home but there seemed to be no likelihood whatsoever of that, now that they had established themselves in the new country.

Between Saint Stephen's Day and the night of the wrendance the score or so young men and women who had returned home to Dirrabeg for Christmas had drifted back across the Irish Sea leaving resentful boys and girl behind. The exiles had been a generous bunch with a recklessness that appealed to the deprived youth of Dirrabeg. In the public houses in Trallock they had spent prodigiously, never reckoning the cost and displaying wage dockets which carried details of unbelievably high weekly earnings.

Older people on being told of the amounts were sceptical but not so the younger folk. They had seen the money. They had been witnesses to the abandon with which it was spent and they had been included in every spree by young friends, neighbours and relatives whose accents bore strong traces, after less than a year of exile, of the areas where they worked overseas.

The exiles were impeccably dressed. Some had even rented cars for the duration of their short Christmas holidays. There were many in Dirrabeg in their thirties and forties with families to support who failed to see any future in the land of their birth. Many had brothers and sisters already well established in England and indeed there were many of those who remained behind in Dirrabeg who were heavily dependent for survival upon subventions from their exiled kinsfolk. Two-thirds of the population of the townland had emigrated over the previous dozen or so years.

As they lay in bed one wet and windy night Donal Hallapy spoke of his fears and worries to his wife. She listened as he listed his shortcomings when faced with the future. In the end she consoled him with the age-old saying which had comforted many like him in the generations past.

'We never died a winter yet,' she said but although she would never admit it to him she was even more apprehensive than he. Her major worry was their daughter Katie. She would be twelve in the oncoming April. They had both vowed that she must not enter service in Trallock. As a girl Nellie had endured three years of servitude in a number of different homes in Trallock where often her main concern after the completion of her chores had been the preservation of her virginity.

When she complained to her mother on the first frightening occasion the whole business had been pooh-poohed. She was told that she was old enough to look out for herself. In fact she recalled what her mother had said when she complained about the lord and master of the house where she had first worked as an all-round drudge.

''Tis the nature of the bashte, child,' her mother had said without any trace of emotion, 'he's only an oul' fool runnin' around after his own tail. He'll tire of it when he sees you're not the free and easy sort.'

She had not fully comprehended her mother at the time although she got the gist, more or less, of what she was endeavouring to convey. What was quite clear to her was that the money she earned was desperately needed to feed her brothers and sisters at home. They were all now in England and although she had been sorely tempted to write to them for help on many an occasion she had always managed to hold out.

Her daughter would never go through what she had been forced to go through. Her mind was firmly made up in that respect. She recalled a dismal evening during which she had

121

found herself alone in her place of work with one of the sons of the house. On that occasion she had very nearly been raped. She had complained to her mistress and was dismissed from her post the following day after consultation with the man of the house and a fabrication from the son that she had led him on. Katie would go to the secondary school in Trallock. Already Nellie had spoken to the Reverend Mother of the Presentation Convent where the school was housed.

Mother Columba was a formidable-looking woman, of impressive girth with the most forbidding of faces but nevertheless a woman who was always accessible to women like Nellie Hallapy. She was also possessed of a sense of humour and a rather resigned outlook on life. Her predecessor had been an extremely pious female with little interest in the outside world. Columba was the opposite and she was the bane of Canon Tett's life. She was well informed on the prevailing scandals and everyday goings-on in Trallock and surrounding townlands. On one occasion the Canon had approached her on behalf of Nora Devane.

What Nora required was an intelligent girl who could answer the phone and receive callers to the presbytery. Additional duties included light housework on a six day per week basis. The Canon intimated that he would require the girl immediately. He had made no mention of payment and it was the first question Columba put to him. He mentioned a paltry sum which the Reverend Mother scorned.

'What you really want, Canon,' she had informed him without putting a tooth in it, 'is somebody who will work for nothing. I don't educate my girls for slavery.'

Canon Tett was shocked beyond words. It had been his first formal encounter with her. He mumbled some incoherent threats and made a vague reference to the bishop.

'Fine,' said Mother Columba rising from her chair. 'You get in touch with the bishop and let him decide upon wages. I recall he spoke very trenchantly about cheap labour in a pastoral

122

a few years back.'

Tett had left the convent in a rage but there was little he could do except to make certain he would be well prepared for future encounters with the Reverend Mother. When Nellie Hallapy made her approach concerning Katie she explained that no financial contribution whatsoever would be forthcoming for the first year and indeed it was likely that some years would pass before she could even begin to settle her account. Neither would she be able to provide text books although she felt that a school uniform might be just about within her scope. Columba had asked several questions, chiefly about Katie's attitude to religion and study. She was already acquainted with her National School record. There had been a letter from Ciss Fenley, solicited by Donal Hallapy, and in it was a restrained but laudible account of Katie.

There was, however, no mention of her pre-occupation with ballads and singing or of her fluency in spoken Irish. These omissions were taken care of one evening when Monty Whelan paid a visit to the convent. He had known Columba for many years. They had a high regard for each other. As always they conversed in Irish.

Columba selected a tiny key from a bunch which she carried attached to the shining black belt which encircled her waist. She opened a locker in the sitting room and withdrew a bottle of Paddy Flaherty whiskey together with one glass. She filled it to the brim despite Monty's feeble protestations. Over a period of an hour or so they spoke about teaching in general and then addressed themselves to the real purpose of the visit.

'It would be a terrible shame,' Monty had opened, 'if this girl was allowed to go into service. She has an extraordinary flair for the native ballad and already she's well able to converse in Irish.'

'What of her character?' Columba had asked.

'No worry on that score,' Monty had assured her. 'I will personally vouch for her and if there's any problem about school books or any other expenses I will also see that all obligations are discharged.'

'Now, now!' Columba had assured him, 'there won't be any need for that, later maybe but not for the first few years. There are intermediate and leaving certificate scholarships you know, my dear Monty, and if the girl is as good as you say she is there should be no problem about finances. There is also the fact that I am empowered to make sure that no worthwhile girl in the locality is deprived of a secondary education.'

'You have a great heart, Columba,' Monty had said as she proceeded to re-fill his glass.

'I have as big a heart,' Columba had responded, 'as I'm allowed to have.'

When Nellie Hallapy's visit with Columba had ended both were in a happy frame of mind, Nellie because Katie would be assured of at least a few years' secondary education and the Reverend Mother because she sensed that Katie Hallapy would bring something to the school which had been far too subdued up to this, a traditional country influence, natural and unspoiled. It was settled that Katie would commence studies at the Presentation Convent at the end of the following September. Nellie had made no mention of a bicycle. She decided that she would cross that bridge when she came to it.

On that score she need not have worried. Monty Whelan had decided shortly after his meeting with Columba that a new bicycle would be a fitting present for his star pupil when she left Dirrabeg National School for good in July of the following year. He would so inform her father when next they met. He fully realised that without a bicycle Katie's hopes of a secondary education would be dashed. He also decided that he would monitor her progress and tender discreet financial assistance whenever it was required. He had no doubt about her ability to acquit herself well. She was retentive and intelligent and would be sure to master French easily, the only new language which she would be required to learn.

124

Before the closing of Dirrabeg School for the Christmas Monty had noticed a hardening of attitude on the part of his principal. Bearing in mind the advice he had received from Joe O'Dell he trod warily. Disheartening enough to be in the bad books of his parish priest and school manager without having to watch his every movement and every word while his principal hovered in the vicinity. At the back of his mind there were times when he sensed that a conspiracy of some sort was being discreetly contrived which would eventually do him no good. He had nothing tangible to go on but there was a furtiveness and hostility about Ciss Fenley's behaviour in recent days that left him uneasy.

Then there had been the afternoon when Daisy had stopped at the school. According to her it had beeen purely unpremeditated. In fine days, after bedding down her mother for her post-luncheon snooze, Daisy was in the habit of cycling into the countryside. On many an occasion she had cycled past Dirrabeg School but that had been before Monty had signalled his interest. On the last day of the term she found herself inadvertently pedalling towards the school. She had encountered some of its cheering home-going scolars as she approached and was about to dismount preparatory to returning the way she had come when Monty appeared on the roadway in front of the school.

Ciss Fenley had already departed. Daisy decided to maintain her course but when Monty extended both hands outwards from his sides she was obliged to brake hard or run into him. She chose the former. When she dismounted she hastily explained that it was purely by chance that she found herself where she was.

'I believe you,' Monty had told her. 'A woman who has spent so much time avoiding me over the past weeks would be highly unlikely to confront me on my own ground.'

Overhead in the darkening sky a large flock of lapwing dipped and wheeled in unison, their weeping cries a fit requiem for the fading light.

'What are they?' Daisy had asked. 'God knows I've seen them often enough but it never occurred to me till now to ask what kind of birds they were.'

'They're lapwing or crested plover,' Monty explained. 'If you were to ask one of the schoolchildren they would most likely tell you that the birds were pilibín which is the Irish name for the species.'

'Are they native?' Daisy asked, anxious to keep the conversation on an impersonal basis.

'No, they are not native. They come from Scandinavia more or less. When winter is over they'll return and we'll not see them again till next winter.'

'Do you have an interest in birds?' Daisy asked him.

'No. You are about the only bird who really interests me.'

'That's a nice thing for a school teacher to say to a lady passing the road.' Daisy pretended to be perturbed.

'There are any number of nice things I would like to say to you, Daisy Fleece, but the most important one is what would you like me to buy you for Christmas?'

'Now that's another thing,' Daisy said crossly.

'What's another thing?' he asked innocently.

'Those two assrails of turf which you had Donal Hallapy bring me.'

'Did Donal say I sent them?'

'He didn't have to. It couldn't have been anybody else. "An admirer," he said. Of all the cheek! Donal will be sure to tell Nellie and Nellie. . .'

He forestalled her before she could continue. 'And Nellie will tell nobody and we both know that because she is a woman who minds her own business.'

'But you shouldn't have sent them.'

'I wanted to send them. The thought of you trembling with the cold over Christmas was more than I could take. Now what would you like me to buy you for Christmas?'

126

'Don't you dare buy me anything. God, you'd swear you were my boyfriend or something.'

'I wouldn't mind being your boyfriend,' Monty told her. The sincerity in his voice was unmistakeable, 'although being your something sounds more interesting.'

'As I've told you already Monty, I am a married woman. A married woman cannot and must not have a boyfriend. I can't even be friends with you. All it would take to ruin both of us is to be seen together more than once. Then the tongues would wag and we might as well be dead. You seem to forget that it would be completely irresponsible for you and I to have any sort of relationship.'

The injunction was hardly out of her mouth when the skies overhead opened and the drops came teeming down.

'Quick,' Monty shouted, seizing her arm with one hand and the bicycle with the other. Before she had time to object he had the school door opened and in a moment the bicycle and its rider were safely inside. Outside the rain pattered against the windows of the classroom where they found themselves. It was one of the school's three compartments apart from a crude toilet which stood several yards to the rear of the building. The third and smallest of the indoor sections was a cloakroom cum storeroom. At one end there was a neatly clamped heap of good quality turf. This had been supplied free of charge by the parents of the pupils. There was a fuel allowance but as Monty had once pointed out to a reluctant contributor the allowance would hardly buy enough turf to fill the bowl of a goodsized tobacco pipe.

In earlier times each of the pupils brought a solitary sod of turf every few days but the practice had been supplanted by a system whereby each parent would be obliged to replenish stocks with the occasional assrail or pony rail. Fires were kept going in the two classrooms on a constant basis across the spring and winter and at other times when the temperature dropped below par. There was still a glow in the grate of the room where

127

Monty taught.

'Is this were you teach?'

'This is where I try to teach,' he replied. 'Here, have a seat.' He indicated a small bench near the fire. 'The young lady who normally sits there,' Monty informed her, 'is very nearly as pretty as you.'

'Do I know her?' Daisy asked.

'You know her father, Rubawrd Ring. The lady in question is his youngest daughter Moira. Like yourself she has me in the palm of her hand.'

He sat atop a nearby bench. They both looked into the dying embers, neither saying a word while the rain still fell outside. It was a cosy room, cluttered with bric-a-brac of an educative nature. There was a shelf of books in Irish and English, mostly pictorial and orientated towards children. There was an ancient globe of the world which Monty had resurrected in an equally ancient auction room while on a visit to Cork City. On the walls there was a variety of maps and charts.

'I've never seen a schoolroom like this,' Daisy announced after she had looked around.

'Feel free to call anytime,' Monty said. Daisy changed the subject by asking him what sort of relationship he had with Ciss Fenley.

'As good as can be expected,' he responded cheerfully, 'when you consider that she's the boss.'

'Everybody says you're the better teacher. In fact they say you're the best teacher around.'

'Tell that to Canon Tett,' he laughed, 'or better still tell it to Nora Devane and she'll tell the Canon for you.'

'I would imagine,' Daisy proceeded mischievously, 'that with a man and a woman working together day in day out that some sort of close relationship would be inevitable after a while, especially where both are unattached.'

'You would, would you?' He left his seat and knelt in front of the bench where she sat. 'Let us not talk about my affair

128

with Ciss Fenley. Let us instead talk of more relevant matters such as my relationship with Daisy Fleece.'

'Tell me about Ciss Fenley first.'

'You really want me to reveal all?' The tone of his reply puzzled her.

'I'm only joking,' she suddenly put in.

'And I'm deadly serious,' he said as he took up a position near the window. The rain had stopped and the outlines of the hills had become barely visible in spite of the strengthening darkness.

'Ciss Fenley means absolutely nothing to me,' he said after a while, 'but alas and alack I seem to mean something to her.' Monty went on to unfold the whole story of the uneasy relationship which existed between his principal and himself. By the time he had finished dusk had fallen. Daisy made no comment for several moments. She sat absolutely still.

'I shouldn't have asked,' she said eventually.

'Of course you should have asked,' he said. 'You're the only person who knows apart from Doctor Joe O'Dell and I had to tell him on professional grounds.'

'In one way I'm glad you told me,' she confided, 'because it turns our relationship, little as it is, into something extremely dangerous. You must see now that under no circumstances can we ever meet again.'

'I'm not having that,' he shouted the words across the room at her. 'What I feel for you is genuine and I'm not ashamed of it. Now stand up and listen to me.'

Too surprised to do otherwise she stood upright. He took both her hands in his before speaking. When he did speak his voice was tender yet filled with a new power and confidence.

'I'm in love with you, Daisy. I haven't loved a woman since my wife died. It's taken me a long, long time to get over her loss and now when at last I have found somebody worthy of replacing her I am told it's all over.' He placed his hands firmly on her shoulders. 'It's not all over Daisy. It's just beginning.

129

You,' he allowed the word to hang in the air for a minute, 'are my girlfriend as of now and don't you dare contradict me.' Gently he drew her into his embrace. She offered no resistance. 'Every time I see you, Daisy Fleece,' he whispered, 'I want to put my arms around you.' They kissed in the darkness. It was the fulsome, sustained searching kiss of a couple who had been lonely overlong. She made no attempt to extricate herself from the embrace. There was no second kiss. Both knew that to prolong the experience would be provocative and improper under the circumstances.

'When can I see you again?' he asked.

'I don't know,' she replied.

'Please let it be some time soon. It can be so bloody lonely.'

'I know. I know,' she answered eagerly. 'I know enough about loneliness to fill volumes but you must let me think. Give me a little time.'

'Of course, but how long is a little time?'

'It's so dangerous for both of us,' she cautioned, 'for you in particular.'

'Let me worry about me,' he said.

They stood silently by the window, the glow in the hearth all but gone, the sky overhead alight with stars recently released from the cover of the heavy rolling rain clouds.

'Give me a few days and I'll be in touch,' Daisy assured him, 'and don't worry if you don't hear from me for a while. I promise I'll be in touch. I need you Monty. Before this I would be totally ashamed to make such an admission to any man but in your case it's true. I'll tell you what I'll do. I'll try to get to your place on the night before Christmas Eve. If I don't make it don't fret because I'll make up for it some other night.'

'Will you come dressed as before, in shawl and wellingtons?'

'Yes. That will be best. At least nobody will know me.'

'Will you come to the front door like the last time?'

'Oh dear no! It will have to be back door this time.'

'I'll leave it partly ajar,' Monty said.

130

'If I'm not there by eleven I won't be coming. It will mean that my mother will be having one of her nights. She has one from time to time. She just won't fall asleep. Chances are that everything will be alright and if so I'll be at your back gate in shawl and wellingtons at eleven of the clock.'

'I can hardly wait,' he told her as they embraced finally.

They agreed that it would be best if she did not drive back to Trallock with him. Dark as it was somebody would be sure to notice. He watched her cycle homeward over the narrow roadway, returning along the route by which she had come. He stood for a long while in tune with his surroundings, delighted that at last she had agreed to meet him. As he stood surveying the changing sky he thought he heard a noise coming from the rear of the school. He looked but could see nothing. It had been a scurrying sound, more than likely some wild creature on the prowl or one fleeing for its life. The area around the school was vibrant with wildlife.

Daisy Fleece had been as good as her word. She came dressed in the ancient shawl and wellingtons and although the square was all but deserted she managed to present an unobtrusive image, staying close to the houses, her head bent, her eyes concerned with nothing save the ground under her feet. She could have been any one of a hundred shawled women in the parish. Normally addicted to long, sweeping steps which would make her identifiable under any guise she now resorted to a short, fast gait common to stubbier women. It would, she felt, make her all the more difficult to recognise. She encountered only one person in the Square and that was Tom Tyler. She bade him a mumbled goodnight as they passed. He returned the salute without pausing to inspect his hailer as he normally would.

At the time Tom was quite incapable of executing any such manouevre. While he managed to present an outward facade of sobriety a long sojourn at the Bus Bar as a pre-Christmas guest of Fred and Minnie Halpin had taken its toll. He wisely

131

decided that as soon as he finished his rounds his safest course would be to make for his home in Carter's Row where he would slump into his favourite chair in front of the fire which his wife would have waiting for him. While there was no other presence in the square after Tom's departure there were two pairs of eyes trained on the area. The first were those of Nora Devane who had a partial view from an upstairs window at the rear of the presbytery. The others belonged to Ciss Fenley who had been sitting at her front window since visiting the church three hours earlier.

It was not the first time that night that her vigil had been interrupted by a shawled figure. The difference was that she had been able to identify all the others. Since that first occasion Ciss Fenley had been convinced that Monty Whelan's visitor was a tinker woman. Now she wasn't so sure. Firstly it was widely known that tinker women never prostituted themselves. Secondly Ciss was now ready to believe that Monty's caller was a local woman and a woman of some importance at that. It was the affected walk which directed her towards this new train of thought. When the expected knock at Monty Whelan's front door did not materialise she was deeply disappointed but when the shawled woman paused near the archway which led to the rear of the Bus Bar and several other houses including Monty's she was immediately alerted. When the figure disappeared under the archway Ciss Fenley hurried upstairs and located the shawl which she kept in readiness. She had no doubt whatsoever that the shawled woman was headed for Monty Whelan's back door. From her presbytery eyrie Nora Devane kept an eagle eye on the proceedings in the square. Not having as much to go on as Ciss Fenley she was mystified. To Nora it was generally no great feat of detection to identify any and all shawl-wearers in the parish. Having ascertained that the shawled woman was not a local shawl-wearer she deduced that the shawl was a disguise and that its occupant was affecting the short steps which seemed to Nora not to be

132

completely in tune with the body's disposition.

What then was the creature's purpose? Nora concluded that the woman was probably on her way to the rear of the Bus Bar with a view to purchasing liquor to which she was secretly addicted or that she was a damsel of easy virtue bringing so-called solace to some lonely male residing at that side of the square.

Only one lonely male came to mind and that was Monty Whelan. Nora went at once to the wardrobe and found her own shawl which she always kept in readiness.

Monty received Daisy Fleece with open arms. When she explained that her mother was restless and for that reason she could not stay long he simply took her in his arms and held her there while he kissed her face and hair and throat. She made no effort to resist him. When finally he released her he led her into the sitting room and to an armchair by the fire. He sat on another nearby, holding her hand in his. He poured out his loneliness to her. She listened, nodding patiently and sympathetically. She accepted his offer of a drink but insisted that it be no stronger than sherry. In all they spent an hour in each other's company.

'I've already stayed too long,' she explained as she arose from the armchair. 'Next time I should be able to stay longer.'

'When will the next time be?' Monty asked anxiously.

'I'll let you know,' she promised.

'Pray it won't be long,' Monty said.

'As soon as ever I can,' Daisy assured him.

'A kiss before you go,' he begged. She smiled and for the first time placed her arms around his neck. They kissed for a long while until eventually she withdrew herself from his arms.

'I really have to go,' she said. 'My mother needs as much attention as a newborn babe.'

She wrapped the shawl carefully around her until only her eyes were visible. As he closed the back gate behind her he felt the years fall away from him. Here was a girl in a million, he thought, and she cared for him, really cared for him, but how would they resolve their seemingly impossible problem? The last thing he wanted was to drag her into a shoddy relationship with marriage always out of the question. Anyway he wasn't so sure that she would agree to such a union although he felt in his bones that inevitably their relationship must become closer. The problems looked insurmountable although the important thing was that she was willing to come and visit him and that she was willing to stay in his arms while he kissed her. This was what really mattered for the present.

When Daisy appeared in the archway she looked carefully to left and right and stood for a few moments while her eyes searched the square. There was nobody about. Ciss Fenley watched from behind the curtains while Nora Devane, from a less favourable viewpoint, concentrated all her energies into her inadequate vision, inadequate for the task in hand. The moment Daisy emerged from beneath the archway Ciss Fenley silently closed her front door behind her and allowed her quarry a longish start before setting off in pursuit. She had decided in advance that it would be a sound idea if she were also to change her gait under the circumstances. She followed discreetly at a distance. Departing the square Daisy grew less cautious about her manner of walking and very nearly lapsed into her normal manner. As she neared home she sensed that she was being followed. She looked round and caught a glimpse of a shawled figure in the distance. She quickly turned left into a grassy, rarely-used by-way which would take her to the back door of her home. As soon as she found the grass under her feet she ran for all she was worth and was safely indoors before the shawled figure appeared at the entrance to the by-way. Here Ciss Fenley contented herself with long looks up and down before turning for home.

Never before in her life had Nora Devane found herself so confused. Upon entering the square she was just in time to see the first shawled figure making her departure. Hot on her heels

134

although some sixty to seventy yards behind was the second shawled figure. Nora had no doubt but that one was following the other but why? For all her experience in shawl detection she could identify neither of the women. She followed the pursuer until she re-emerged from the entrance availed of by the pursued.

Nora quickly re-traced her steps lest she herself be identified. She entered the presbytery by the side-door. She ran all the way upstairs to her room but after keenly searching all the visible parts of the square through the open window cound find not a living thing. Ciss Fenley had outsmarted her for no sooner had she entered the presbytery side-door than Ciss bolted for home, arriving there just as Nora Devane was about to enter her bedroom.

Daisy Fleece stood with her back to the door, heart throbbing, breasts heaving, barely able to catch her breath. The shawled party had been on her trail. Why else would she have turned back at the entrance to the by-way? Daisy's modest house was the second of a row of twelve on the outskirts of town, two hundred yards or so from the square.

Her tracker, whoever she was, was now in possession of solid information. Any intelligent woman should be able to deduce that she had run the remaining yards to her home which automatically excluded several older women who lived in the row. With the additional fact that Daisy was a taller than usual type of woman, discovering her identity should be no problem. Daisy was absolutely correct in her assessment of the situation. Ciss Fenley now knew, beyond doubt, who Monty Whelan's shawled visitor was. She knew the moment she saw the deserted by-way.

'The dirty rotten wretch,' she mouthed the phrase fiercely. She was not referring to Daisy Fleece whom she regarded as a mere pawn. The object of her frenzy was Monty Whelan. She would repeat the phrase and many others of a similar nature before sleep overtook her in the late hours of the morning.

Nine

ON THE FIFTH of January Father Bertie Stanley rubbed his palms together gleefully as he awaited the arrival of his breakfast. It was not the prospect of the fare which Nora Devane would presently transport into the characterless dining-room which prompted his manifestations of delight. Rather was it an epistle he had received by the morning's post from the bishops's secretary. The tidings contained in the letter were not unexpected but he had anticipated them later rather than sooner.

He was to present himself before his lordship Doctor Collane a bare five days hence on January tenth where he would receive formal instructions concerning his transfer to England as part of the Emigrant Chaplaincy Scheme. He looked forward to a time when he might peruse a daily newspaper with his breakfast. Only religious newspapers were allowed in the presbytery and while these were commendable in themselves the young curate felt that a man of his calling would need to be more comprehensively informed if he was properly to fulfil his ministry.

'Come in,' he called as soon as he heard the housekeeper's toe sounding on the partly opened door.

'Where's the other fella?' she asked as soon as she entered.

'Are you referring to Father Butt?' Bertie Stanley asked, the reprimand in his voice unmistakeable.

'And pray who else would I be referring to?' Nora Devane

136

asked as she lay the well-worn, silver-plated tray on the table.
'He'll be along in a minute,' Bertie told her.
'Well now, what could be keeping him and he knowing the
time it is.' She heaved a long sigh of pretended sufference as
she placed a boiled egg in front of the younger curate. Next
came the toast rack with its four buttered slices, the tiny milk
jug and the bare requirements in sugar, pepper and salt.
'Where can he be?' Nora Devane asked of nobody in particular.
'Oh now, now,' Bertie Stanley spoke distantly, 'we must not
concern ourselves about such matters. We should be looking
after our own business and leave others to their own affairs.'
'All I'm saying,' Nora Devane returned, 'is that his egg will
be cold and it won't be fit for eating.'
'Don't concern yourself like a good woman. Just run along
and let me dispose of these morsels in peace.'
Nora was surprised by the curate's attitude. She would have
given him a piece of her mind there and then but on second
thoughts she decided that there were other and better ways of
putting him in his place. Cold soup is a great eye-opener, she
told herself with a grin, or better still a rub of a peeled onion
across the butter. No need to worry that the Canon might be
contaminated. He had taken to eating in the kitchen lately,
not that he would be likely to notice anyway since he ate
whatever she put in front of him. The curates were far more
sensitive, especially Father Butt who was likely to be put off
by the least thing.
The senior curate arrived as Nora was leaving. Silently he
took his place after an exchange of nods with his junior. Earlier
Bertie had told him about his imminent transfer. Father Butt
had been genuinely pleased and had congratulated him profusely but he was also apprehensive. Father Stanley would have
to be replaced and heaven only knew who his successor might
be or what fads and eccentricities he was likely to bring with
him.

137

'I wish to high heaven I was in your shoes!' Father Butt expressed the sentiment fervently as he uncapped his egg. 'Look at the freedom you'll have. You'll be surrounded by National Hunt meetings and then there's the cinema and the theatre. I don't begrudge you Bertie, you know that, but I really would give anything to be in your place.'

'Your turn can't be far away now.' Bertie Stanley dabbed his mouth with his handkerchief and sat back in his chair. 'It has to be the next time. You're the most senior.'

'Dammit to hell man,' the senior curate thumped the table with uncharacteristic anger. 'I was the senior man the last time and what good did it do me?'

'That was different and you know it. The man who pipped you had service in the foreign missions. That put him up in the placings.'

'I doubt it.'

'Tell me one thing and no more,' Bertie Stanley folded his arms and cleared his throat, 'have you spoken to his Lordship?'

'No. I have not. There are times when he doesn't like being spoken to by curates and I'm terrified lest I pick one of those times. You could speak to him. You're his whiteheaded boy with your master's degree and your incredible capacity for work.'

'You really want me to speak to him?'

'Of course I do,' Father Butt replied on the verge of tears. 'I'll crack up if I have to endure another year in this awful dive, this accursed purgatory of a place.'

'I'll speak to him,' Bertie Stanley promised.

'You won't tell him I put you up to it?'

'Of course I won't,' the young priest promised. 'The minute I find an opening I'll make a case for you.'

'God bless you, Father,' Father Butt heaved a mighty sigh of relief. At least the bishop would soon be aware of the fact that he existed. Both priests were about to rise from the table when Canon Tett appeared.

'What's the hurry boys? What's the hurry?' he asked with

138

clearly affected good nature.

'No hurry at all Canon,' the younger of his two curates cheerfully informed him.

'In that case, stay where you are a while and we'll have a
bit of a pow-wow.'

Father Butt was well used to such ploys. The Canon wanted
to find out something, his normal sources having failed him.
His hail-fellow-well-met attitude would last only as long as it
took him to discover what he wanted to know. They were soon
to find out.

'Boys,' he said expansively, 'there may be a way in which
you can come to my aid. I wouldn't ask you but it's for the
good of the parish.'

'We'll help you any way we can, Canon,' Bertie Stanley
assured him.

'That's the spirit, Father,' the Canon lifted Father Butt's
unfinished egg and scooped out the contents with his index
finger. He ate it with relish.

'What I want to know is this boys. How many porter balls
are being held in the parish this year and where they are being
held?'

Both curates were quick to inform him that they had no idea.

'Neither have I,' he admitted. 'Normally I would be fully
acquainted about such goings-on but this year for some reason
unknown to me there is a tacit silence in regard of wrendances.
So what we'll do is this. You both keep your ears to the ground
and if that doesn't yield results ask around, particularly country
gorsoons ye might see in town with rails of turf. I want to know
the exact nights and the houses where they'll be taking place.
Now that shouldn't be too much trouble.'

Father Butt suppressed a smile. He knew exactly what was
amiss. Nora Devane had no spies in Dirrabeg proper. The wrenboys of Upper Dirrabeg were no longer members of Dirrabeg
Wren having opted out of the collection on Saint Stephen's
Day. Normally Nora would be acquainted with the dates and

139

locations of each and every wrendance in the parish and indeed for miles around by her agents in Upper Dirrabeg. Since these renegades as they were called in Dirrabeg proper no longer had access to the councils of their Dirrabeg counterparts Nora Devane was left in the dark.

'So you'll do that little favour for me boys,' the Canon beamed as he rose from his chair. Father Butt made no answer. He exited swiftly and silently and was gone from the presbytery before the Canon could corner him and extract a definite promise.

'I'd love to be able to help, Canon,' Bertie Stanley assumed an apologetic tone, 'but unfortunately I won't be around. I was waiting for an opportunity to tell you.'

'Tell me what, you silly fellow? What in God's name are you on about.'

'Don't you remember, Canon? We spoke about it before Christmas.'

'Spoke about what?' The Canon's irritation was beginning to get the better of him.

'The Emigrant Chaplaincy Scheme, Canon.'

'Oh, that nonsense,' the Canon was at his most dismissive.

'Nonsense or not, Canon,' Bertie Stanley came back, 'today is my last day as a curate in Trallock. I had a notification from the bishop this morning. I am to report to the palace on the tenth to be briefed about my impending trip to England.'

'Well, I've heard nothing from the bishop and until I do you'll carry on with your duties here.' The Canon was adamant. It was a situation which Bertie enjoyed beyond words.

'I'll tell you what I'll do, Canon,' he became suddenly expansive. 'I'll postpone my departure until after lunch to give you a chance to get in touch with the bishop. Meanwhile you had better have a gander at this.'

Bertie produced the official letter from his breast pocket and handed it to the Canon. The Canon fumbled through his pockets in search of his reading glasses. As he read he sniffed and snorted in mounting disgust. He returned the letter without a word.

'I'm sure the bishop will be in touch with you Canon. Meanwhile I have any number of jobs to do before I depart for good. I hope we'll meet again sometime.' He raised a hand in farewell and breezed out of the dining room. Canon Tett was at first amazed at the impertinence of the younger curate and then livid when he remembered all the ways he might have dressed the scoundrel down. The day wasn't over yet. First he decided to check his post. His worst fears were realised for at the top of his correspondence which was neatly stacked on the hallstand awaiting his inspection was a letter from the bishop.

Hastily he opened it and read it through. What the young pipsqueak had said was the truth. He had always credited Bishop Collane with more sense. There was to be a temporary replacement until a permanent appointment could be made, more than likely in mid-Spring when it was anticipated that a number of important diocesan appointments and changes would be made. One elderly priest in the south of the diocese was in the process of retiring . A successor would have to be named and this in itself would lead to numerous changes of curacy.

The Canon went out of doors and had a look at the morning sky. He located his heavy overcoat and hat and took with him an umbrella. His first call was to P. J. Crolly's. He was greeted by a clerk who asked in what way he could be of help.

'You might give me a receipt for that like a good man,' the Canon informed him handing him a bill he had received together with the corresponding payment in cash. The clerk made haste to the office where P. J. Crolly himself ruled the roost.

'I'll take charge of that, Tom,' he told the clerk. The amount was for three pounds, seven shillings and some odd pence. He marked the bill paid and joined Canon Tett at one of the shop's many counters.

'Ah, Canon Peter,' P.J.'s greeting could not have been more

141

effusive. 'Your receipt.' He handed the Canon the slip of paper together with the money he had earlier tendered to the clerk.

'Such a paltry amount, Canon. You shouldn't have bothered.'

The Canon pocketed the money and enquired after P.J.'s wife. On being assured that she was in excellent health he enquired after the daughter.

'Angela's poorly enough Canon, thank you,' P.J. told him with despondent face. 'She's been in bed the past few days with one thing and another.'

'Tell her from me, P.J., that she is constantly in my thoughts. She should be hearing from me very soon.'

'Oh, that's good news, Canon Peter. The poor thing is lost entirely in the city.'

'She won't be lost for long I promise you. There is something you can do for me P.J.'

'Anything, Canon. Name it and if it's in the power of man to do, it will be done.'

'Find out for me will you if there's to be a porter ball by the Dirrabeg wrenboys and the when and the where of it like a good man.'

'No trouble, Canon. I have a Dirrabeg lad works as a delivery boy. I'll give you a ring at lunchtime.'

Nelly Hallapy passed the Canon later in the morning as he journeyed into the countryside on one of his much-vaunted constitutionals. She preoccupied herself with the guiding of the mare, flicking the reins and gidapping unnecessarily until Canon Tett had safely gone by. The Canon hardly noticed her. In her coat pocket Nellie had three single pounds and a ten shilling note. The money was for the purchase of a new coat, her first in more years than she cared to remember. She would proceed by appointment to Kitty Smiley's, her sister-in-law's where the mare and cart would be looked after by the Smiley children until her purchases were completed.

Kitty had taken the morning off in order to assist with the

choice of coat. Nellie dared not trust to her own judgment in such a monumental undertaking. She had waited so long that she dared not risk all without a second opinion and she would be glad of Kitty Smiley's company.

No sooner had she entered the suburbs of Hillview Row than she was greeted by several of the Smiley children who had been informed of her coming and had come part of the way to greet her. As they scrambled aboard the now railless cart she noted the bare feet of the three boys, Tom, Teddy and Bill and the well-worn dresses of the older girls, Sophie and Kathleen. Not one of the five wore an overcoat and yet they glowed with health and an infectious happiness.

'No matter what,' she had often heard her husband say, 'you'll always find the Smileys cheerful.'

All five stood rather than sat in the body of the cart. Tom asked if he might be entrusted with the reins and Nellie surrendered them willingly. She was sure the boys had shoes. She had seen them on Christmas Day when they had eaten the Christmas dinner as she had never seen children eat. The shoes, she guessed, would be kept for special occasions. She wondered about the two younger girls and asked if they were all right. She was assured of their health and happiness by the laughing cartload, all five completely overwhelmed by the novelty of their transport.

As they passed the elegant home of Phil Summers, the accountant, Nellie winced. She always did whenever she remembered her brief sojourn there. Randy Phil, as he was called, had given her many a run for her money, short as was her stay under his roof. His son had been no better while the pious mistress of the house had no hesitation in laying all the blame at Nellie's door. She had never worked at Doctor O'Dell's but girls to whom she had spoken had nothing but praise for the Doc.

She winced again as though she were being physically stung by some unknown pest. Here was the abode of Junior Crolly.

143

She had been fortunate to escape serious molestation when she worked, briefly, in the Crolly home in the square of Trallock. It was the hypocrisy of such people that really revolted Nellie. She could understand need and loneliness but the surface righteousness sickened her.

As she passed bookmaker Mickey Munley's she smiled. Locally regarded as a ladies' man he was anything but as Nellie could verify. She had married from Mickey Munley's. It was Mickey, in fact, who had volunteered to drive her to Trallock parish church despite the protestations of his wife. Mickey had often intimated to Nellie that he wouldn't mind accommodating her himself if Donal Hallapy was unable to rise to the occasion. Often too he had told her how pretty she looked but at the back of it all he was harmless, a lonely man with a wife who made no attempt to understand him.

Nellie regarded Estelle Munley as the most conceited woman she had ever met. Estelle would never have enough. Most women envied her the generous and carefree husband who was always at pains to make little of her shortcomings. The trouble with Estelle, if one was to believe her neighbours and limited circle of friends, was that she suffered constantly from acute illusions of grandeur and, according to wiser matrons of Trallock, this was the deadliest disease of all for it brought nothing but disillusionment and sorrow in its wake.

During her period with Mickey Munley Estelle had treated Nellie like the dirt under her feet but Nellie could never bring herself to dislike the woman. She was aware that for all her possessions she would never know contentment and while she did not feel sorry for her she could never take her seriously enough to like her or dislike her.

Kitty Smiley stood in the doorway of the small thatched cottage with her two youngest daughters, Maura and Josie. As the sisters-in-law headed for Crolly's Kitty Smiley asked in a whisper if the date and venue for the wrendance had been decided.

'At Bluenose's next Saturday night,' Nellie whispered back, 'but keep it quiet. We don't want the wrath of the clergy on top of us, at least not until it's over and done with.'

'My lips are sealed,' Kitty Smiley promised. 'It's the one night of the year I could not do without, seeing all the old friends and neighbours and listening to that lovely wholesome music, our own songs and our own dances.'

Kitty Smiley had been always hard put to comprehend the attitude of the townspeople, her departed husband included, to the traditional songs and dances of Dirrabeg. The country singers were frequently mimicked in the town's public houses and distorted imitations of the reels and jigs which had been the pride and joy of country people for generations were the source of great amusement to townie onlookers. Kitty would not have minded so much but those who mocked the most were those who were themselves no more than a generation removed from the traditions they endeavoured to degrade.

It was the same with the Dirrabeg accent which was heavily influenced by the Irish which had been spoken widely within living memory. Many phrases and exclamations were still in everyday use as well as several hundred topical words for which there were no accurate translations in English. With its guttural and nasal inflections, legacies from the spoken Irish, the Dirrabeg accent was easy to ridicule.

There was even a local comedian whose party piece was Hamlet's soliloquy spoken in a Dirrabeg accent. On one occasion Donal Hallapy, Bluenose and Rubawrd Ring were present in an unfamiliar public house in Trallock when the comedian delivered the immortal lines. Bluenose had to be restrained when it became apparent that the spoken language of his beloved Dirrabeg was being traduced. It took his two friends all their time to subdue him and indeed had it not been for the intervention of Monty Whelan who happened to be in the pub on the occasion there might have been an all-out row. Monty explained to Bluenose that if Shakespeare himself had

145

been listening he would have felt highly gratified at this most complimentary and unique interpretation of his immortal monodrama.

Crolly's New Year Sale had been well advertised. Nellie's only interest was in the female drapery section where a large and varied selection of women's coats had been drastically reduced if one could believe the advertisement in the local paper. It was already crowded when Nellie Hallapy and Kitty Smiley arrived there.

'Over here,' Kitty led the way to a corner where several racks of coats were arranged to catch the eye. Green, grey and black were the fashionable colours but these were interspersed with red and blue and even an occasional white.

'I wouldn't have the courage to wear red or white,' Nellie confided to her sister-in-law.

'Neither would I,' Kitty Smiley agreed. Nellie tried coat after coat. The prices were pretty uniform at three pounds with, here and there, an odd-looking garment which had been slashed to the minimum price of one pound. Both Kitty and Nellie recognised these particular garments as Crolly Specials. They were in the habit of surfacing at Crolly sales year after year and could only be described as genuine hand-me-downs.

Eventually Nellie's choice was narrowed to two: one a fawn-coloured, three-quarter length, smartly-cut mantle and the other a grey, full-length serviceable tweed of comfortable yet modern design. Both were priced at three pounds which was well within Nellie's range. While she held one and then the other at arm's length she could not help but notice that she was being observed by the now-ageing youngest son of her former employer. His face was wreathed in smiles and they were unreservedly directed towards her. Again she winced when she remembered how he had tried to take advantage of her and how he had very nearly succeeded through dint of brute force alone.

Slowly, deliberately she returned both coats to the rack and turned towards the exit.

'I don't think I'll bother,' she confided to Kitty.

'You need a coat,' her sister-in-law reminded her.

'Isn't there a teenage shop after starting up somewhere in the vicinity?' Nellie remarked as though she had not heard.

'It's a small place in Carter's Row,' Kitty confirmed. 'Actually it's on our way.'

The two women left Crolly's. Junior Crolly stood with his right hand absently placed on the hip of a female dummy, a pained, puzzled look on his pale, indoor face.

The teenage shop had been opened shortly before Christmas by a girl who used to be a counterhand at Crolly's. Nellie knew her by sight. She wondered briefly if Junior had ever tried to force his attentions on her. Knowing Junior she would not put it past him. She felt instant sympathy for the girl who came forward to greet them as they entered the shop.

'I'm looking for something for a girl of twelve, thin, about your own size,' Nellie told her.

'Have you anything particular in mind?' the girl asked.

'How about a costume?' Kitty Smiley suggested.

'She already has a costume since her confirmation although she's completely outgrown it. I don't think she would like another costume.'

'How about a smart coat?' the girl asked at the same time absently extending a practised hand and extracting a coat, light blue in colour, from a nearby rack. Kitty and Nellie examined it while the girl held it at every conceivable angle.

'It's lovely,' Nellie conceded.

'It's lovely all right,' Kitty agreed, 'but I bet the price is lovely too.'

'Not really,' the girl contradicted. 'It's only three pounds, four shillings and elevenpence and if you want any alterations made after you take it home there won't be any extra charge.'

'I'll take it,' Nellie said withdrawing her purse from her coat pocket.

147

'You'll throw something off,' Kitty Smiley suggested.

'All right,' the girl assented. 'Three pounds and a half crown then.'

When the coat was wrapped Nellie handed over the money and awaited her change.

'Will she be needing a hat?' the girl asked.

'Thankfully no,' said Nellie. 'She has quite a good hat since her confirmation. Her head is still the same size although I don't know what this new coat will do to it.'

When they left the shop Nellie looked about her and saw what she wanted.

'Faithful Ferg's,' she said. 'Let's treat ourselves to a cake, Kitty.'

Inside Ferg stood with his hands spread across the counter, palms downward.

'Kitty! Nellie!' he saluted them in turn.

Later on her way home Nellie was unable to resist the urge to take a quick peek at her new purchase. It never occurred to her that she had made a sacrifice. Rather did she look upon it as a treat for herself as well as her daughter. The important thing was that Katie's delight would far outweigh whatever minor pangs of disappointment she herself might feel.

She had had a long, intimate chat with her sister-in-law over the tea and cake. There had been no word from Willie Smiley since his departure.

'I really don't blame him all that much,' Kitty had told her. 'I mean, I can understand his feelings. I wouldn't want him back though. I don't think I ever want to see him again and as for the children, they don't seem to care. They're good kids, really good kids. I have that much to be thankful for and I have admirers by the dozen.'

Here she laughed and slapped her palms against her thighs. 'I have them married and single and every one of them thinking that I'm likely to be fair game with Willie gone. Oh, there's many would take his place gladly, but, of course, in a private capacity only as the man said.'

They had laughed loud and long as the list of would-be lovers was revealed.

'I'd never have thought of it of most of them,' Nellie Hallapy confessed. 'I mean many of those bucks are old enough to be your father!'

'Oh dear me,' Kitty laughed, 'age has nothing to do with it.'

'I mean, most of them are so religious.' Nellie's incredulity made her sister-in-law laugh all the more.

'I know. I know,' she said between bouts of laughter, 'they have paths worn to the altar rails. So have their wives in fact and maybe that's part of their troubles.'

'Who's to say?' Nellie Hallapy said.

'My father used always say,' Kitty spoke thoughtfully, 'that too much religion was nearly as bad as no religion at all.'

They parted promising to meet at the wrendance.

'Will you bring the children?' Nellie asked.

'And spoil my chances!' Kitty flung back. Then seriously she said: 'No. It would be too late for them but I have a friend who wants to come if it's all right.'

'Do I know her?' Nellie asked.

'Indeed you do,' Kitty told her. 'It's Daisy Fleece. If she can get somebody to look after her mother for the night she'd love to come.'

'I'm sure she'll be more than welcome,' Nellie Hallapy assured her. 'Daisy could do with a night out more than most.'

Ten

SINCE HER PERUSAL of the Monty Whelan dossier on Christmas Day Nora Devane was able to decide that one of the shawled figures she had perceived in the square a few nights before was none other than Daisy Fleece. Neither was there any doubt in her mind but that the chief contributor to the Whelan dossier was the other shawled party. But who was the other shawled party? A resident in the town square most certainly but which resident? No one that she knew from that ultra-respectable part of town wore a shawl.

As she sat by her bedroom window watching the comings and goings of the townsfolk and endeavouring to determine the business that had them out of doors so late at night her face grew first puzzled and- then positively squinchy as she searched her memory for recent shawl wearers native to the area immediately within her ken. Figures came and went beneath her. Cars sped by as the night wore on and yet puzzlement and concentration remained on her face. She closed her eyes the better to concentrate on the solving of the mystery. Suddenly the look of bafflement was replaced by one of triumph.

'Blasht me!' she said aloud, 'why didn't I think of her before?'

The last shawled figure she recalled was Maggie Fenley and how alike to old Maggie was the second shawled figure she had seen a few nights before. For all her aping and shaping Ciss

150

Fenley had failed to dispose altogether of her departed mother's cantering gait. The shawl had accentuated rather than concealed her likeness to her late mother.

'So now where are we?' Again Nora Devane spoke aloud. She remembered how embarrassing it had been for the newly-qualified teacher whenever her mother appeared in public wearing the shawl. There had been reports of vicious verbal exchanges between mother and daughter concerning the same shawl. Eventually mother yielded to daughter and for the rest of her days Maggie Fenley had to content herself with a coat and hat. Privately she had confessed to Nora Devane that she felt ill at ease in her new outfit and would never really adapt to it. Nora Devane left her seat by the window well pleased with herself. The Canon might already know about Monty Whelan and Daisy Fleece thanks to the reports which he had been receiving up to this but he should be pleased to learn the identity of the hitherto anonymous donor of such reports.

The following morning he sat by the kitchen range opening the day's letters. Nora stood over the table having scooped the contents of two soft boiled eggs into a teacup. She added salt and pepper and a spoonful of butter before stirring the mixture with a spoon. Several slices of toast, already heavily buttered, lay neatly arranged on a small dish on the Triumph range, an elegant, immaculately polished kitchener, older in years than Nora Devane and indeed vying for seniority with the Canon himself. Nora had often seen him in better form.

'Come on over now, Canon, don't the eggs go cold.' She transferred the dish of toast to the table and set about arranging the curates' tray. The temporary replacement had come the day before, by name Father Alphonsus Donlea, a middle-aged, anaemic-looking man who had spent the greater part of his ministry in and out of sanatoriums, or so Nora Devane's usually impeccable sources maintained.

'Trust Collane to lob the likes of him over on top of us!' Nora muttered the words to herself. She lifted the tray and went as far as the kitchen door where she stopped and delivered the line which she was sure would titillate the Canon's interest.

'Did you hear anything about Whelan lately?'

'What Whelan?' the Canon asked in annoyance, irritated at being interrupted just as he was transporting a spoonful of egg to his already eggstained mouth.

'Yerra, what Whelan do you think, only our own Master Monty, the darling of the ladies.'

Nora exited at once. She tapped on the dining room door with the toe of her right foot before entering.

'Good morning, Fathers.' The salute was more of a command than a greeting. What it meant was that they should address themselves to the breakfast without undue delay and be off about the business of the parish. Both men had been blowing through their cupped hands for warmth as she entered.

'Don't say 'tis cold ye are!' She spoke the words in feigned surprise.

'There's a chill abroad,' Father Donlea ventured as he took stock of the scant fare.

'Fine healthy weather,' Nora Devane retorted with a laugh.

'Sit down, woman.' The command came from the Canon the moment she returned to the kitchen. She withdrew a chair from beneath the large oaken table and sat facing Canon Tett.

'Now what's that you were saying about Whelan?' He polished off the last spoonful of egg and folded his arms the better to savour the new revelation concerning this hateful scoundrel who was forever flouting his authority.

'Yerra nothing much, Canon,' Nora Devane replied off-handedly, 'except that he's sparking.'

'Sparking!' The Canon echoed the word in bewilderment.

'Sparking with Daisy Fleece. Don't you know the Fleece one that was left by her husband.'

'Indeed I do,' the Canon recalled, 'don't I visit the mother regularly so why wouldn't I know her?'

'Well that's the lady he's knocking around with lately but

152

sure I suppose you know that well enough so there's no need
for me to say more.'

Nora rose and proceeded with the collection of the breakfast
remains.

'In God's name will you sit down?' The Canon's curiosity
was now finely whetted. Nora resumed her seat and waited.

'I know a bit,' he conceded. 'There have been letters.'

'Oh!' Nora exclaimed feigning surprise.

'Anonymous letters,' the Canon explained.

'Anonymous my tail,' Nora Devane scoffed.

'You mean you know the author of these letters?'

'I didn't say I knew but I'm as sure as a body could be that
they were written by a lady not all that far away from where
we are now.'

'I would dearly love to know the name of that lady,' the
Canon leaned forward in anticipation.

'I'm sure you would,' Nora Devane responded tantalisingly.
'There is things we'd all like to know, Canon.'

'And pray what would you like to know now that you don't
know already?' the Canon asked.

'The first thing I'd like to know, Canon, is when the Dirrabeg
wrendance is on and where it's on.'

'And what would you want to know that for?' the Canon
asked.

'A friend wants to know, Darby Kallihan from Upper Dirrabeg. He feels he has a right to know.'

'That's easily answered.' The Canon allowed himself one of
his rare smiles. 'The Dirrabeg wrendance is on tomorrow night
week and as far as I can tell it will take place at one Michael
J. Herrity's.'

'Hereinafter affectionately known as Bluenose,' Nora
Devane put in quickly.

'Bluenose is what they call the fellow right enough,' Canon
Tett's smile was replaced by a grimace, 'and now will you be
good enough to tell me without further pussyfooting who wrote

me those letters?'

'Who but Ciss Fenley?' Nora replied with alacrity, 'and would you blame the poor creature, Canon, and she having to consort and collogue with that scoundrel five days of the week, under the one roof.'

'You're sure she's the person in question?' The Canon sounded doubtful.

'I'm as sure as a body can be, Canon.'

'Well you may be sure,' the Canon sounded convinced, 'that I don't blame the woman in the least for doing what she felt in conscience bound to do. The fact that she did not sign her name is neither here nor there. She has her character to think about and she has her position to think about.'

'And it was to yourself she wrote, Canon,' Nora Devane was quick to supply further justification for the attempted anonymity. 'She put her faith in the one man in the parish that can be trusted above all. She could have told her tale to others but she knew where her duty lay. The poor woman must have suffered her share not knowing where to turn. It was God directed her, Canon.'

'It was so. It was so,' Canon Tett agreed. 'As you say she suffered her share.'

'And then to ease the burden,' Nora Devane went on, ' she said to herself 'tis a load for broader shoulders than mine so she turned it over to yourself, for who's to say that she wouldn't be tainted and disgraced if her name was linked with this horrible affair.'

'Affair!' the Canon's exclamation exploded like a thunderbolt.

'Well now, Canon, 'tis not for me to say but Daisy Fleece is a married woman and Whelan as we all know is no angel.'

'No angel is right,' the Canon thundered in agreement, 'and what we have here is a very serious business indeed and I entreat you herewith as my servant and as a consequence a servant of the Lord to say no more of this to any man or woman until I

154

see what's to be done.'

Nora Devane displayed suitable reverence at the Canon's solemn enunciation and manner. She clasped her hands together and nodded her head solemnly.

'Go now,' said the Canon in a somewhat similar tone, 'and send word to your friend Kallihan about this infernal wren-dance.'

In the dining room the curates had completed their breakfast. Neither had made the slightest reference to the housekeeper or to the cold of the room. There had been an instant rapport between them. Father Butt had been in his final year in Maynooth when Father Donlea had been in his first and Father Donlea had not forgotten a kindness shown to him by the senior student. It had happened on the eve of the Christmas holidays. One of the younger student's suitcases had burst open unexpectedly revealing a huge bundle of unwashed shirts and underclothes as well as muddied football boots and stockings. It had been an embarrassing moment since the incident had occurred in a rather busy corridor in an establishment which was never without its fair quota of wags. The final year student had stopped and gone to the aid of the younger, helping him return the unsightly garments to the rent case and volunteering an unused travel bag of his own. The offer had been accepted and the bag returned at the beginning of the next term.

Father Donlea had for years been a martyr to tuberculosis and had very nearly succumbed to its ravages on several occasions. Although fully recovered it had taken its toll and it was clear to Father Butt that the new curate was not a robust individual, cheerful and willing beyond doubt but he would have to be careful lest he overtax himself. Father Butt resolved that he would, therefore, act as a buffer between Canon Tett and the newcomer.

Further south in the warm if stodgy dining room of the bishop's palace Doctor Collane and Father Bertie Stanley faced each other across the massive dining room table. The breakfast consisted of freshly-made wheaten bread and grilled kippers. There was, by comparison with the last ecclesiastical dining room Father Bertie had known, an abundance of fresh butter and a toast rack of gigantic dimensions. The breakfast had been Bishop Collane's idea. Earlier they had discussed the predicament of Father Butt. The bishop had not been nearly as sympathetic as Bertie had hoped he might be. Any immediate prospect of the senior curate acquiring his own parish was not on the cards nor was there any prospect in the foreseeable future.

'But,' the bishop had reminded his protege, 'things have a habit of changing suddenly and when they do your friend will come into contention.'

When asked why Father Butt was not to be considered for the most recently vacated parish in the diocese the bishop had informed Father Stanley that it was none of his business and that he was just beginning to try his patience. However, seeing how taken aback the younger man had been at this rebuff the bishop relented somewhat and explained that the parish in question was possessed of a sizeable Gaeltacht area and that the eventual incumbent would need to be possessed of a sound knowledge of Irish, both oral and written. This automatically excluded Father Butt, whose knowledge of Irish was no more than rudimentary.

'Let these matters in my hands,' the bishop had said finally, 'and be assured that nobody will be victimised.'

Afterwards the talk ranged over Father Stanley's new assignment. Already there was a curate from the diocese ministering to emigrants in the London area. He occupied a flat in Cricklewood and was loosely attached to a number of parishes. His duties consisted of supervising lay workers who would greet new arrivals from Ireland at Euston and Paddington Stations, endeavour to direct them to fruitful and useful occupations and make sure that they kept in touch with the local Irish centre. Then there were weekly visits to the building sites of such esteemed employers of the Irish labour force as Laing, Murphy and McAlpine. If necessary mass might be celebrated on the sites in question provided the foremen had no objection. The whole object of the exercise was to make sure that emigrants kept in touch with the sacraments. It meant visiting venues as far apart as ballrooms like the Galtymore and the Gaelic playing fields in New Eltham. No Irish centre was to be overlooked nor any public house or dancehall where the Irish emigrants foregathered.

'The London area is pretty well catered for,' Bishop Collane told Bertie Stanley. 'The problem is the English midlands where the number of freshly-arrived Irish workers runs into tens of thousands, migrant workers in particular, and there are thousands of them being deprived of the sacraments through no fault of their own. Some have given up the faith altogether and the number attending mass is small indeed. Many of these unfortunates are shift workers who are either too tired or too lazy to make out local Catholic churches. Anyway, right now there aren't enough Catholic churches to contain all the Irish emigrants. You'll do what you can Father, improvise where necessary. A Nissen hut could make a fine temporary church or any kind of hut for that matter. Bring them the mass and you'll be doing fine. If we fail them they'll drift and they are drifting already. The pub is the new home for innocent gorsoons not all that long loosed from their mothers' apron strings, foolish green saplings who couldn't put a single penny on top of another before they left home. We are losing them, Father, and the tragedy is that some are lost forever, so get over there where you're needed and devote yourself to the welfare of your fellow Irish. You'll be on your own, left to your own devices, faced with every kind of problem and every kind of temptation but you have the grace of God and with that on your side you won't fail.'

Father Stanley had listened gracefully. There had been questions he would have liked to interpose such as the matter of

157

initial funding for the venture but it had begun to dawn on him that the bishop meant it when he said that he would be left to his own devices, meaning he would have to make do with the limited finances in his possession. These consisted of a hundred pounds from his parents, money they could ill afford. There had been a hasty whip-round amongst the teachers in the parish of Trallock as soon as they heard of his appointment. This came to fifty pounds.

Together with a few other gifts his total financial possessions amounted to two hundred and fifty pounds. Out of this would come his travelling expenses and the price of some sort of second-hand car. He would have to depend heavily on the generosity of the Irish emigrants if he was not to starve. Reports, however, indicated that these emigrants, even those who had drifted down the road to perdition, were notoriously generous.

'You'll have a roving commission,' the bishop cut in on his thoughts. 'You will concentrate naturally on emigrants from our own diocese. You will be attached in the loosest possible meaning of the word to the Diocese of Nottingham which as you probably already know consists of the counties of Derby and Leicester and you will also be available to the Diocese of Northampton contingent upon exceptional circumstances. Our people seem to have been attracted chiefly to these dioceses for one reason or another. It could be that council houses are more freely available and then, of course, you have the common emigration pattern where one emigrant from one place follows another from the same place blindly. It could also be that the type of work available or the work conditions indigenous to these areas might be the explanation.'

'Who is to be my immediate superior, my Lord?' Father Bertie interjected at what he thought was an appropriate moment.

The annoyance showed clearly on Bishop Collane's face. His flow had been interrupted but the expected reprimand did not come.

'As I have pointed out to you already you have a roving

158

commission so I dare say that the parish priest of wherever you find yourself at a given time would answer the description of your authority but don't be restricted by local protocol. Observe the proprieties by all means but your superiors whoever they may happen to be are as aware as I am that these are exceptional times with the huge inflow of Catholics, the greatest since the Famine. It is a statistical fact that an average of fifty thousand men, women and children have begun to leave Ireland each year and of these the vast majority are destined for Great Britain. It's a haemorrhage which would exhaust most countries although with our high birth and unemployment rates it could be a godsend. One dare not contemplate the alternatives. Anyhow, Father, you'll be breaking new ground. If there is a major problem contact me right away. I don't foresee any real problems, however. Write regularly and when you arrive home in the summer come and see me. I'll be anxious to hear your report and maybe we might find time to talk about your future.'

The bishop rose and stood at his end of the table awaiting the young curate's departing handshake. As he stood silently a smile flashed across his face.

'Did I ever tell you, Father, what my bishop said to me the first time I went abroad? Don't forget to say your prayers, he said. Imagine that! Don't forget to say your prayers; not another word and I no more than a boy heading for distant Nigeria.'

At the table top the bishop extended his right hand. Father Bertie grasped it. The bishop placed a hand on his shoulder, smiled for a moment, imparted his blessing, turned and disappeared into his study without another word. Father Bertie had expected a subvention, some form of funding to tide him over until he was established but it was the one business which had never cropped up. Disappointed but still eager he left the presbytery.

To the north of the diocese in the townland of Dirrabeg the Hallapy family sat together at breakfast. It was a happy occasion. After a long but enjoyable wrangle it had been agreed that Katie and the two boys, Tom and Johnny, would be allowed to attend the wrendance on the following night. Certain conditions were attached. All would have to leave on the stroke of twelve. As soon as the breakfast was over the two boys would tackle the mare to the rail of bogdeal, consisting of eight half-sacks, each filled to the top, which Donal had chopped into chips and manageable blocks from partly-buried bog oak, centuries old. The chips were without peer when it came to starting a morning fire across the winter and the larger faggots mighty boosters to dull or fading fires. The blaze of a bogdeal-aided fire was luminous and cheerful. In the course of its burning sooner or later all the hues of the rainbow were sure to appear in the leaping flames and not merely the standard colours but all their known variations often for no more than a bare instant. Then at other times, if the kitchen was dark, the scene would be lighted by a sustained unearthly hyacinth often followed in turn by a swirl of ruby or an eerie flickering of lavender which purpled every face around the hearth. Add to this the crackling and the spitting and the fuming as the flames took hold and the scene was set for spooky tales of pooka and banshee or hair-raising recollections of ancestral ghosts.

All that was needed to prolong the mood was the addition of a sliver of this venerable bogwood. The going rate for a bag of bogdeal was a shilling. When the bags were disposed of the boys would tender the entire sum together with a carefully drawn-up list of groceries to Faithful Ferg. Included would be a small treat for themselves. The remainder would consist of absolute household necessities such as tea, sugar and butter. On this particular morning there was no butter for breakfast in the Hallapy household. In its stead was a glistening lump of freshly-heated, salted bacon lard against which the bread slices might be pressed or rubbed. The bread was home-made, a mixture of maize meal and white flour, hard as a board when stale but delectable when freshly baked as it was now. Nellie had boiled three eggs in a tiny saucepan which had been placed atop a small bed of coals at one side of the hearth. When the eggs were boiled the coals were returned to the fire proper. The eggs had been allowed more time than usual since two would have to be divided between herself and the three children. Halving a soft boiled egg was a daunting task whereas a hardboiled egg was easily and fairly bisected. A full egg was allowed to Donal Hallapy for as soon as breakfast was over he would betake himself to one of the lowest and wettest of his tiny fields to spend the day scouring the dykes therein. He would return before dark to fodder and bed the cows.

Spotlessly clean and shining on the window sill were three dozen of hen eggs. Later in the day these would be carefully washed a second time before transportation to town by an itinerant egg-buyer. They would fetch enough to pay for a long-overdue hair-do. Nellie quite properly felt that nobody would question this luxury on the eve of the wrendance. Katie would spend the day assisting Bluenose's wife in the preparations for the dance. Later that night there would be a secret meeting of the elders of the Dirrabeg Wren for the purpose of screening buy-ins.

A buy-in was a man who although not a wrenboy might be well disposed to the Dirrabeg group and therefore most anxious to attend their annual festivities. Buy-ins were mostly farmers who had neither the time nor the inclination to spend a day collecting for the Wren. Other buy-ins might be those who, because of some mental or physical infirmity, would hardly be able to endure the hardship of a long day traversing the countryside. Then there were a few approved townies such as Monty Whelan, The Halpins Fred and Minnie and Moss Keerby. Gagers was the local name given to the men who would approve or disapprove of would-be buy-ins. An applicant would declare his intention of attending the wrendance some days before.

161

The amount he would be obliged to pay was determined by his appetite for intoxicating liquor although a set sum of seven and sixpence was the recognised charge. There was no admission fee for lone females. They would merely be partaking of the Munster Cream Sherry which was not regarded by the gagers as legitimate liquor under the circumstances. Even for quality sherries there was nothing but contempt and if a man was seen drinking sherry he became suspect ever after. Different with whiskey. No mature wrenboy would consider going to a wrendance unless he was possessed of a half pint of Paddy, Powers or Jameson which would serve as a booster over the course of the celebrations.

'Only for the regular dose of the hot stuff,' Bluenose was fond of saying, 'there is no way I would stay the course.'

The committee of gagers consisted of Bluenose, Donal Hallapy, Rubawrd Ring and Paddy Costigan. They sat for an hour or more considering the applications. Excluded out of hand would be those who were given to profane or abusive language and all townies with a few honourable exceptions. The standard charge of seven and sixpence would be imposed on Fred and Minnie Halpin, Monty Whelan and Moss Keerby. The male trio were better than average drinkers and would normally be subjected to double the usual fee but it was well known that they would be already fortified with freshly-consumed whiskey upon arrival and that they would also be possessed of at least a half pint apiece to supplement the stout which they did not regard as sufficient in itself to sustain them over such a long period.

Other applicants were rejected out of hand. Certain of these offered to pay well in excess of the normal amount but for a variety of reasons they were turned down, one because he was argumentative in drink, another because he was offensive towards women and a third because he had intimated that he was not prepared to pay a penny more than seven and sixpence although the committee knew full well that he would drink

162

twice that amount without putting any great strain on himself.
There was considerable argument concerning the application
of the final buy-in. The man's name was Patsy Oriel, a gentle,
smiling, inoffensive fellow in his late thirties. He hailed from
a townland at the other end of the parish. It was also known
of him that he was a notorious womaniser.

'I wouldn't mind,' Paddy Costigan announced, 'but the
scoundrel has a wife and nine children by his marriage and
heaven only knows how many by-blows scattered all over the
countryside. I propose he be turned down.'

'On what grounds?' Bluenose asked.

'On the grounds stated,' Paddy Costigan responded indig-
nantly.

'And I say,' Bluenose countered, 'that it will be a black day
for Dirrabeg if we penalise a man because he has an industrious
penis.'

Bluenose looked about him for support. Donal Hallapy was
non-committal, not knowing what to say. He had no strong
feelings one way or another. Rubawrd Ring looked his most
solemn. He stared into his empty whiskey glass and reserved
his decision until after Blueneose had poured the remains of
the second bottle of whiskey into their four glasses.

'I believe as you do,' Rubawrd addressed himself to Bluenose,
'for although it may not be proper it is natural and who is to
say that we here tonight have not turned our minds towards
other men's women from time to time. I say let him in.'

'And I say against,' Paddy Costigan insisted, 'because it's
shameful and sinful.'

'Agreed,' Bluenose backed him up, 'it is without doubt
shameful and sinful but it's no crime and until it is made a
crime I have no objection to the presence of Patsy Oriel in my
house.'

To resolve the impasse Rubawrd suggested that there be a
show of hands. There were three in support of Patsy Oriel's
application, Bluenose, Rubawrd Ring and Donal Hallapy.

Paddy Costigan voted against.

'Then it's carried,' Bluenose put the jowl of the whiskey bottle in his mouth and swallowed the few remaining drops in order to conceal his satisfaction.

'I can't for the life of me see why you should be worried,' Rubawrd Ring turned to Paddy Costigan. 'I mean you have no wife and neither has your brother a wife. Different now if it was one of us who objected. We would have good reason, being possessed of fine presentable women and, therefore, having more to lose whereas you and Timmie have nothing whatever to lose.'

Paddy Costigan made no answer. Donal Hallapy guessed that it was resentment rather than righteousness that was responsible for his objections in the first place. The Costigan twins, now in their early forties and relatively well off with seven cows and a pony had fared poorly when it came to women. Both would marry instantly if they could find suitable partners. Alas, all the eligible girls in the district had emigrated over the years. The Costigan parents had passed away but a few short years before and it was the general feeling in Dirrabeg that the twin brothers had allowed time to slip while their father and mother were alive. They were identical twins and this was no help either. The few remaining spinsters in Dirrabeg might have considered one or other of the brothers seriously but they looked so much alike that none could tell one from the other most of the time even though the spinsters were well enough acquainted with the pair.

There were other Costigan brothers but these had emigrated to the English midlands shortly after the war and were now settled with wives and families. The twins had often given serious thought to pulling up stakes and heading for England where their marriage prospects would be greatly improved but always at the last minute they would have a change of heart. Once they went so far as to put the farm up for sale but when the deal was about to be closed they suddenly changed their minds.

'All buy-ins will pay at the door,' Bluenose turned to Rubawrd Ring. 'You'll collect, Rubawrd.'

'No trouble there,' Rubawrd assured him.

'The money will give us a bit of leeway.' Bluenose awaited other comment.

'What will it come to?' Donal Hallapy asked.

Rubawrd Ring busied himself with some hasty mental arithmetic.

'It will come to exactly three pounds,' he informed them.

'That much?' Bluenose whistled.

'Eight times seven and sixpence is three pounds,' Rubawrd estimated.

'Three pounds would buy a few bottles of whiskey,' Paddy Costigan deduced.

'Exactly what I was thinking,' Rubawrd agreed.

'No,' Bluenose cut in. 'One bottle of whiskey is plenty. We'll drink the rest when we go for the stuff. Fred Halpin will give us credit till the buy-ins fork up.'

It was decided that Bluenose and Donal Hallapy would set out for Trallock before dusk on the following day. They would take Bluenose's pony and cart. They would arrive in Trallock just as darkness was descending. They would bring pony and cart into Halpin's cobblestone yard and repair to the pub proper where they would be met by Rubawrd Ring and Paddy Costigan. There they would drink the buy-in monies and afterwards load up the cart with stout, wine, minerals etcetera before stopping at Faithful Ferg's to collect the edibles. Donal would accompany Bluenose in the cart while Rubawrd Ring and Paddy Costigan would follow behind on their bicycles. There were all too many townies only too willing to waylay an old man with a carload of drink and choice food. It would not have been the first time a wren cart had been looted on a lonely road. The guardians of Dirrabeg would give their lives rather than allow it to happen on this occasion.

Eleven

THE MORNING OF the second Saturday of the New Year broke cloudily and mistily. The hills of Upper Dirrabeg were shrouded in fog but in Dirrabeg proper the cloying mist had lifted long before the noon of the day. The majority of the inhabitants of Dirrabeg remained in bed until well after noon. Normally they would be out and about after first light but on this occasion they would need all their energies before another day dawned.

Many would return to their beds after tending to the few chores which necessitated their rising in the first place. There was little to be done. The cows were heavily in calf with little or no milk to give. All stock had been supplied with a sufficiency of fodder the evening before, enough to satisfy their needs until the following evening.

Most cows were not due to calve until February or March. Their owners prayed fervently that the blessed creatures would behave normally and bide their time until the wrendance ended but it was accepted that cows could be most inconsiderate in this respect and had a habit of calving at times which could not be more inconvenient to their owners. Yet one never heard a derogatory word about the milch cow. She was, after all, the chief source of income, placid and easygoing in temperament, rarely capricious or excitable and prepared to eat cabbage, potato or mangold, turnip, straw or hay, bran, meal, pollard,

166

oats, wheat or barley, and indeed any form of non-poisonous greenery or any denomination whatsoever of grain.

Donal Hallapy's four cows would all calve late in February. They were his main stock apart from the donkey and one yearling heifer which would be sold at the cattle fair in Trallock in mid-March in order to pay the rates. Donal would have preferred if he didn't have to dispose of the yearling. The Hallapy acres were capable of maintaining five milch cows and as many as three yearlings. The cows would need extra care and nourishment until the time they calved, particularly the week preceeding birth and for a few days afterwards.

Donal Hallapy's economic plight had kept him awake nights. He should be carrying five cows but barring a miracle he would be obliged to wait until he could afford to retain one of his heifer calves. Of the four calves which would be born in the weeks ahead two would have to be sold after a few weeks. Only two flitches of bacon hung from the ceiling and the calves would go towards the purchase of a pair of bonhams, one to be fattened for the Hallapy household and the other to be sold. He would hold on to the two other calves for as long as he could but it was certain that he would be unable to keep even one across the winter of the following year.

There were many items he needed desperately. There were for instance a supply of paraffin, a new sleán and two three-prong pikes to cope with the turf-cutting in late April or mid-May. At least two sacks of yellow meal would be required if the pigs were to be fattened properly. The donkey mare was in dire need of new britching. The roof needed thatching. The straw and scolbs he could supply himself and although he was a tolerable enough thatcher a professional would have to be commissioned if the roof were not to collapse altogether.

The boys would want new boots before the year was out and he himself required new wellingtons. Katie's clothing requirements, with secondary school in the offing, simply did not bear thinking about while his wife's need of new clothing confronted

167

him morning, noon and night.

There were numerous other necessities which just did not bear contemplating. Never before in his life had he been faced with such seemingly insurmountable odds. The best he could hope for by the end of the year was to be able to keep his head above water and this provided the calvings went right, that the pigs survived without succumbing to swine fever which had been rife the previous year. Should it be a wet year his output of turf would be down which meant that there would be less rails for likely customers in the town of Trallock. Shortly after noon on the second Saturday Donal released the cows from their pens in the stall and guided them to fresh water in a stream a few hundred yards north of the house. It was a tiny roadside rill but it was consistent throughout all seasons. Its source was a spring nearer the house which was the sole water supply of the Hallapy household.

The water was crystal clear with a slightly sulphuric taste but this was regarded as beneficial rather than otherwise. The cows would amble at a snail's pace picking at vetches and decaying grass clumps as they meandered towards the gap in the whitethorn hedge which allowed access to the stream.

While they were watering Donal cleaned out the stall, supplemented the dwindling hay and spread freshly-cut rushes all over the floor. His cows were well looked after although not as well as he would have liked. For the next few weeks he would add potatoes and freshly-pulped turnips to their diet and during the final week before calving he would cover the turnip and potato mix with a sprinkling of yellow meal. There were only three stones of this precious supplement left but it would help the cows over the most difficult period. After the births was also a demanding time for the exhausted creatures. For this special or emergency period he had a small supply of bran put aside. As soon as a calving was complete he would prepare a substantial bran mash which the cow would swill, slavering and dribbling with noisy relish. Donal often wondered which the cow liked best, the freshly-made, steaming bran mash or the newly-arrived calf.

Between coming and going the cows would spend roughly an hour on the road. They needed neither guidance nor stimulation. Their instincts warned them that it would be more profitable indoors than outdoors with daylight declining and the unmistakeable sting of frost in the air. Already the roadside bushes were greying with the rime of hoarfrost and soon the surface of the roads would be glinting and slippery.

That morning as soon as he returned from the cow stall Bluenose had predicted that it would freeze before the day was much older.

'What a lonesome tale you have for us,' his wife had countered.

'Mark my words,' Bluenose had warned as he sat down to the plate of oatenmeal porridge which made up his breakfast, 'but you'll be turning into me in the middle of the night.'

'Not this night I won't you poor oul' dotard. This night I'll be waltzing with Patsy Oriel the ladies' man and others of his like.'

'I always knew you had a lightning streak in you, you Jezebel,' Bluenose quipped as he thrust a calloused hand under her dress when she came near the table.

'Bullocks' notions is what you have you poor oul' thing,' she cracked as she moved out of his reach.

'Go up to the room at once and strip and you'll see what notions I have,' Bluenose bawled out the words between bouts of laughter.

'Oh, you dreadful monster that should be on its knees repenting. You're bound for Beelzebub's furnaces sure and certain. I'll have to consecrate the house after you. Eat your porridge now like a good boy and mind you moderate your language when Katie Hallapy comes, don't we be the talk of the parish.'

'And pray where are you bound for?' Bluenose asked.

'Out to know would I gather a brace of blue duck eggs for

169

your dinner before you go to town, you worthless ruffian that won't wash nor shave.'

The pair would go on happily all day exchanging insults but, nevertheless, seeing discreetly to each other's needs, each aware that age was beginning to take its toll and that they needed, now more than ever, to be fully aware of each others comings and goings.

'Mind you be back quick,' he shouted, 'or you'll feel my belt on your rawny oul' behind.'

At the door she turned and spoke seriously: 'What time are you going to town?'

'Around the two mark,' he answered, 'and barring calamity we should be back here with the light.'

'It's not the first time I heard that story,' she taunted.

'Well, this time you can believe it because we have no choice but be back.'

'There's one thing sure and certain,' she called haughtily before leaving the kitchen, 'and that is when I marry again I'll marry a nice, curly-haired boy.'

She was gone before he could reply. His eyes focused on the door after her departure. From a crook thereon hung a freshly-made bodhrán.

'You gave me a deal of trouble, you did,' Bluenose addressed the instrument before rising to apply the finishing touches to his latest and what, he had vowed while making it, would most certainly be his last bodhrán.

His hands were no longer steady and even when aided by powerful spectacles his sight was poor. Still, all things allowed, it was probably the best bodhrán he had ever made and he had made a few. It was to be a gift for Donal Hallapy. He had hoped that it would be completed for Saint Stephen's Day but of late the days and nights were inclined to come around faster than ever before. The important thing was that the finished product would hold its own with any other. All that now remained was to sandpaper the surface for the final time.

It was acknowledged by all those who understood the complexities of the business that Bluenose was the best of all bodhrán makers. There were some who would argue that he was too fastidious. Others would say that his instruments were too refined but there were none who would not say that they were special, that they had a unique timbre and a rolling resonance found in few bodhráns.

Certainly he had never before taken such care. He had waited for over two years to locate a suitable animal and in this repect he was lucky for he had begun to despair of ever acquiring a hide to suit his purpose. He had seen the three-year old nanny goat at the October cattle fair the previous year in Trallock. He had approached its owner with a heavy step and a long face and explained how his wife had for some time been the victim of a deadly rash which neither apothecary nor doctor could cure.

'A man told me,' Bluenose went on, 'that the milk from a white nanny goat would drive away all forms of itch so if you don't want to see my poor wife in her grave before her time you'll knock down this goat at a low price.'

The owner, a pock-faced itinerant by the name of Carty, knew Bluenose well and knew why he wanted the nanny goat.

'I'm sorry about your poor wife,' he said, 'for I have a wife of my own that I would sorely miss even though the river isn't her master for non-stop chatter, so what I'll do is this my lovely man. I'll knock a crown off the asking price and we'll say no more.'

'And me thinking,' Bluenose retorted, 'that a crown would be the whole price.'

At this Carty laughed loud and long.

'This is as fine a specimen of she-goat as ever nibbled on ivy,' he boasted. 'Her mother was sired by a snow-white puck from the island of Inisheer and if that isn't pure breeding I don't know what is, and which is more,' Carty warmed to his task, 'there isn't a blemish on her from top to tail and all the

171

kids she has thrown is one. But be that as it may all I'll relieve you of is a solitary pound note for I may tell you I wouldn't close an eye tonight with thinking of your poor woman and she knocked up with the itch.'

While Carty rambled on about the goat's forebears Bluenose went on his knees and ran his hands through the nanny's white coat. His fingers probed the hide in its entirety.

'If it's sceartáns you're looking for,' Carty told him, 'you'll find none for she's clean as a whistle in that regard.'

Sceartán was the Irish name given to ticks and these were the bane of all bodhrán makers. A feeding tick always left a fresh perforation on the hide. Through this puncture the tiny parasite would gorge itself with the animal's blood. Once the tick was removed the skin healed fully in the course of a week or two but if the tick was not removed before the goat was slaughtered the pinhole showed up when the hide was stretched in the process of tanning. Such hides made poor bodhráns and were lacking both in tone and volume. Satisfying himself that the creature was free of all forms of insect, Bluenose rose to his feet and after intimating that the price was too high bade goodbye to Carty. He had hardly put ten paces between himself and the itinerant than he heard his name being called.

'Ah, Bluenose, don't go like that,' Carty shouted after him.

Displaying some reluctance Bluenose returned and informed Carty that he should have his head examined to be looking for such an outrageous price for a common she-goat. After considerable haggling the nanny exchanged hands for fifteen shillings.

Bluenose did not slaughter the goat at once. He fed her with bran and new milk and richly-clovered hay until her condition could not be further improved upon. Three weeks before Christmas he led her to the haybarn where he tied her four legs together. Then he lifted her slightly by the right ear and inserted the knife. He very nearly made a thorough muddle of the business, so much so that he was obliged to extract the knife from

172

the bleating, struggling creature and transfix it a second time until its bloodstained tip appeared under the left ear. After the second insertion the nanny goat died instantly.

He skinned her immediately and removed head, legs and tail before trimming the hide neatly with a heavy scissors. He brought it then to the kitchen where he laid it on the centre of the table. It would remain there for twenty-four hours despite his wife's protestations. The following day he covered the hairy side of the hide with a liberal sprinkling of lime and rolled it over neatly but not too tightly.

'Tis a wonder I'm not in the mental home years ago,' his wife scolded, 'with all the blood and butchery that goes on around here.'

'If you don't be quiet,' he countered, 'I'll give you a sprinkling of lime, although I'd say your oul' hide is too tough to suffer any damage.'

With the hide under his arm he journeyed along the roadway until he came to a part of the stream where the chuckling waters flowed swiftly. Here between two stones he laid the limed hide, covering it finally with several layers of lattice wire to protect it from eels and rats.

Other bodhrán makers would bury the fresh hide in a heap of stable manure on the grounds that the heat generated therein would hasten the decomposition of the hair. This was alright if one was in an almighty hurry and if a body did not care about the dull brown and green colour which the tanned skin would carry later. Bluenose favoured the water treatment because afterwards the hide disported its natural fawn shade as a result.

Without his knowing it his wife would regularly, secretly, visit that part of the stream where the hide was submerged. There was always the danger of a freshet after the stream had been enriched by heavy rains or melted snow and hail. Delia Bluenose would make certain that the lattice wire remained in place. More than once in the recent past the wires and hide had drifted apart and the eels had terebrated the skin in several

173

places, rendering it worthless for bodhrán making.

After nine days Bluenose removed it from the stream. Together with Delia he examined the now hairless hide on the kitchen table.

'It's a lovely hide,' his wife announced after she had run her fingers all over the still wet coating.

'The goat was right,' said Bluenose, 'and that is what really matters. There was never such a nanny as this. She was born to be made into a bodhrán.'

He lifted the hide lovingly and brushed it against his face the better to savour its texture. He sniffed and fondled it before weighing it in the palms of his gnarled, horny hands.

'This will be the sweetest drum that was ever sounded. There will be no outdoor work for this drum. This is a drum for the hall and the hearth. This is a drum fit for a king.'

He walked around the kitchen still feeling the texture, delighted that at long last Donal Hallapy would have a bodhrán to match his talents. Donal had possessed excellent drums before but they had been either too strong or too light, too thick or too thin.

'Aren't you the vain old pensioner,' his wife teased, 'going around like a child with a féirín and you having a foot in the grave. Your vanity will be your undoing you randy oul' devil you.'

'Cackle away you oul' crone but you may be sure that this bodhrán will be sounding long after we're shoving up the daisies.'

He handed her the hide and went out of doors. She would spend the best part of the night patiently scraping away tiny tufts of hair, scruff and other impurities. Bluenose's hands were no longer steady enough for such delicate work. He would never admit this nor would she bring it up but she would refer to his superior judgement as she worked, asking him every so often if such an area needed more scraping or if her progress met with his approval.

174

'Yes. Yes,' he would reply with seeming impatience but he was pleased nevertheless that she sought his opinion and even more pleased that she never made any reference to his infirmities.

Under no circumstances was a finely-edged implement to be employed in the scraping of the skin. The slightest slip of the fingers or other miscalculation and the hide would be worthless. Bluenose's wife used a well-worn, ancient, triangular section from a mowing machine. While it was slightly blunted from usage it was still sharp enough to remove tufts and other defacements and there was no likelihood that it would nick or penetrate. At the end of the night the hide was without flaw. Bluenose expressed satisfaction at his wife's handiwork.

'You have it destroyed entirely,' he told her, 'but it will have to do.'

The following morning he tacked the hide to the bottom half-door of the ancient thatched stable to the lee of the dwelling-house. The top half of the door would remain open so that the western breezes would have unhindered access and allow the hide to dry out properly.

Every other day Bluenose would stretch the hide a little more tautly until at the end of eight days he decided that it had been stretched to its limit. He then submerged it in a barrel of rainwater. Here it was allowed to soak for twenty-four hours before being attached to a specially prepared rim which was shaped from a narrow strip of plywood four and a half feet long and four inches wide. Bluenose set a small skillet full of water to boil while he prepared an even smaller glue-pot, the bottom of which he would immerse in the water as soon as it came to the boil.

When the glue was ready, with Delia's aid, he applied the sticky substance to both ends of the plywood strip and then stuck them together so that a perfect circular rim was formed. Then he applied two small cramps which would hold the plywood ends together until the glue had dried.

175

The following day he stretched the cured goatskin over the rim, cutting away the raggedy skirts until the hide extended uniformly for an inch over the rim. Then stretching it as tautly as he felt necessary Bluenose hammered it gently on to the rim with five dozen upholstery tacks. Later when he was out of doors Delia Bluenose would remove those tacks which did not conform to the even line which glistened around the rim. Gently she would hammer them into line until the task was completed. The making of the bodhrán had been carried through by Christmas but Bluenose judged that it was far from ready for use. He therefore decided that he would not present it to Donal until the night of the wrendance. Beyond doubt it was the best bodhrán he had ever fashioned. It had a sonorous and most melodious tone and it carried farther than any instrument of its kind that he had ever heard. It shivered and trembled when struck, its booming reverberations circulating around the kitchen long afterwards and diminishing delightfully until they were no more.

'That's where heaven is,' Bluenose explained to Delia. 'Where the sound ends and the silence begins.'

The finished article was, however, still quite a long way off. The sandpapering of the surface was a task which the pair of them took on in turn. It required a gentle and consummate skill in case the skin was scratched or rasped. It was, Bluenose felt, a bodhrán which would respond better to the knuckle of the human hand than to the twin-headed drumstick known as the cipín. Even when tapped with the fingers it released an extraordinary volume of sound, each beat possessing uncommon musicality.

'I declare to God,' Bluenose exclaimed after he had played it one night for a long period, 'the fairies wouldn't make one better. I tell you oul' woman that this is a magic drum and it wouldn't surprise me but you could call up the corpses from their graves with it on May Eve or All Souls' Night.'

'Well, you may be sure that if you go before me, you oul'

hoorie, I won't drum you from the clay.'

'Long enough I've had to suffer your cackle day in day out,' Bluenose replied, 'and what harm but I could have blondes chasing me all around Trallock dare I but spend a few nights there.'

'Well now,' said Delia, 'my way is clear for that lovely curly-haired boy I does be always dreaming about. I'll marry him for sure the day they lay the scraws on you.'

That night he had held her close as the cold penetrated the unheated bedroom.

'I've slept with the best of them,' she whispered before she fell asleep, 'and you're still the hottest thing around.'

As Bluenose sandpapered the bodhrán for the last time he contemplated the long night and morning ahead. Please God all would go well and the wrendance would be a resounding success. It would not be his fault if it wasn't. He still had certain misgivings about the granting of his house, not that he feared the priests or what the priests might say but the prospect of an accident of some kind arising from the occasion would be interpreted by ignorant people as a sign from the heavens, an indication that he had incurred God's wrath by allowing the wrendance to take place under his roof.

As he gently applied the sandpaper to the finished surface an idea came to him.

'I declare to God,' he said aloud, 'but it's a pure inspiration.'

It was half an hour yet before he would tackle the pony to the open cart for the journey to Trallock to collect the drink and provisions. Time enough to spare, he thought, for the execution of his plan. In the room off the kithen which would be the didling area for the night he heard Katie Hallapy's unstinted laughter as his wife related some outrageous tale. Katie knew nothing about the bodhrán. In fact she had not noticed it and certainly his wife would not tell her after all the trouble they had taken to surprise Donal. Bluenose decided to take his wife into his confidence. He went to the room door after he had placed the bodhrán outside the front door of the house.

'Come down here you lazy hussy that has that lovely little girl distracted.'

'What's up with the oul' codger now?' she addressed young Katie before joining him in the kitchen. He whispered his secret into her ear but did not wait for her reaction. He would have been pleased to see the delighted smile which the imparting of his whispers had imposed on her ancient face.

On an extensive knoll at the highest point of Bluenose's rushy farm there was an ancient fairy fort, a ring of centuries-old blackthorn which enclosed a small level sward clipped closer than a golfing green by its plentiful population of rabbits. By the simple expedient of setting fire to the thorn and scrub Bluenose might have increased his limited acreage of arable land but this would have been unthinkable for any interference with a fairy fort was regarded as a form of desecration so vile that it did not even merit contemplation.

It was to this hallowed spot that Bluenose betook himself before his trip to Trallock. The bare blackthorn trees were frosted white and grey, their intricate branches filigreed by nature's elaborate tracery. When Bluenose entered the sacred circle a pair of chattering blackbirds broke noisily from their cover and disappeared into the midst of some nearby bushes leaving in their wakes an enchanted silence. Bluenose stood with his feet wide apart, his head held high, his outgoing breaths plumes of white in the icy afternoon air.

Firstly he allowed his powerful fingers to ripple the bodhrán's surface. Then he smote upon the drum with the clenched knuckle of his right hand. At once it vibrated into life, its outgoing beat unimpeded by wind or rain so that its varying tones now rippling, now plangent, now resounding were carried for miles across the still countryside. He paused for a moment and moistened his lips before breaking into a mild puss music, for no other purpose than to provide a consistent and rhythmic

178

tempo which would be a true test of the instrument's range. Diddling was the local name applied to this type of puss music which of itself was regarded as a highly developed form of intonation. Bluenose chose a reel called the Rolling in the Rye-grass as the ideal vehicle for his rendition. As he diddled the drum spoke without impediment, its clear tones racy, uninhibited and vigorous. At the end Bluenose felt a great satisfaction mingled with a physical ease he had never before experienced. He was also aware of a new mental tranquility which words could not adequately describe. In short, he felt like a superior being.

When he returned to the house he hid the bodhrán in the hayshed and hurried to the haggard where the mare was waiting. There was a time when he would be obliged to spend hours in pursuit of her before she finally yielded and submitted her rippling body to harness. Now she waited patiently when he approached and meekly followed when he stroked her flowing mane. As he tackled her to the cart his wife and Katie Hallapy appeared in the doorway of the dwelling house. Katie called out excitedly and asked if he had heard the bodhrán sounding from the direction of the fairy fort. Bluenose shook his head.

'Never mind him,' his wife said. 'The poor old dear is deaf.'

'My hearing is as good as it was when I was a gorsoon,' Bluenose responded, 'but I heard no bodhrán.'

'We heard it plainly,' Katie Hallapy assured him.

'And you say it came from the direction of the old fairy fort?' Bluenose asked, screwing up his ancient face until every wrinkle was at its most pronounced.

'It was from the fairy fort alright,' Katie Hallapy spoke fervently, 'as plain as the day and it like no bodhrán that was ever heard before.'

'Then you may be sure it was the good people,' Bluenose said, 'for they are possessed of magic bodhráns and all those that hear their sound will never be without an ear for music.

179

The only body that should not give ear to them is an oul' woman, especially one that gabs all day for as sure as there's meat on the skin of a wren the next time she goes near the sea she'll be carried off by the tide.'

'And what about young girls?' Katie Hallapy asked anxiously.

'Young girls,' Bluenose was at his most convincing, 'especially them that's pretty, will trip through life without strain or sorrow and that's as sure as I'm standing here idle with your father waiting below for me. Get up with you now,' he called to the mare as he lifted himself stiffly into a sitting position next to the shaft.

'Don't you dare leave the yard, you rotten heathen, till I cast the holy water on you.'

So saying, Delia Bluenose hurried indoors and re-appeared moments afterwards with a black porter bottle partly filled with the sacred water which had been blessed and sanctified by Canon Peter Pius Tett in a hundred-gallon barrel on the Easter Saturday of the year before outside the entrance to the transept of Saint Mary's Church in the town of Trallock.

'Here child,' Bluenose's wife handed the bottle to Katie, 'sprinkle the wretch well with it. Maybe your innocence and virtue might knock the harm from him and separate the ungodly scoundrel from his brother Satan.'

Bluenose pretended to be stung by the blessed liquid which Katie Hallapy showered over his head and shoulders but he made the sign of the cross on himself nevertheless before sending a flicker along the reins which set the pony on its journey to Trallock.

After his departure Delia Bluenose and Katie decided to take a stroll through the surrounding countryside. Their steps led them to the fairy fort where they both crossed themselves before entering the sacred ring.

'There is no fear of us,' Delia assured her young companion, 'for once you make the sign of the cross and cross a running stream the fairies won't bother with you and we have done

180

both so there's no fear at all of us.'

Delia smiled to herself when her eyes alighted on the flattened rabbit droppings. Only herself and Bluenose knew the identity of the fairy bodhrán player who had imprinted his signature with such uncharacteristic humility.

'I came here with my grandmother in the summer of eighteen eighty,' Delia Bluenose recalled, 'and in those days there was a cabin and a potato garden wherever you'd turn even though we were after two famines and many of our people had vanished into the ground or across the seas. I was no more than eight or nine and God help me I recall that the people were pure paupers entirely with nothing left to them only their songs and bit of dancing. Down there beyond the whins,' she pointed downwards, 'was Din Dinny Jerry's and over there,' she pointed to another tiny knoll a few hundred yards away, 'was poor Patsy Fiachal, so-called because he had one mighty fang of a tooth and no more. Over beyond the sally grove was Liam Shawn's. What a flaming stepdancer he was! You'll see his steps tonight when the Costigans dance for us. Over there,' she pointed again to a small copse of black alder and thorn, 'was where Shamus and Brid Ní Nuallain lived and now if you look my loveen you'll not see a trace of any habitation. There was no one to take over when the old people passed on. The bogland claimed back what was its own and there wasn't a gorsoon left to chastise the crows that nested in the rotting chimneys. All gone and no trace of a potato drill or an oats garden. The Lord have mercy on all of them and may He grant them silver beds in heaven for they were a shining and a proud people that never demeaned themselves.'

She uttered the last sentence in Irish to Katie Hallapy's delight.

'Have you more Irish?' Katie asked.

'Hardly any I'm sorry to say,' Delia replied sadly, reverting to English again. 'It was swept from us by time and by the shoneen and the foreigner but my grandmother had great Irish

181

though her English was very rough and she could make little or no fist of it. My own poor mother died young and carried nearly all the Irish with her to her grave. Maybe if she had lived I'd have my plenty of Irish now.'

'But you have some,' Katie pointed out, 'and I have some and very soon I'll have a lot more.'

'For sure you will,' Delia encouraged, 'for 'tis you have the soft voice for it and the love for it.'

Before they descended to the farmhouse Delia pointed out the crumbling ruins of other mud-built cabins where once there had been life and laughter but illness too in the shape of tuberculosis which had always taken its toll of Dirrabeg people.

'Those people who left,' Delia shook her head in regret, 'will never return. My own will never return. They have houses now in Northampton and Leicester fit for a king with bathrooms and hot and cold water and gadgets I never heard of. They'll come for the odd holiday and they won't forget us for the Christmas but when Bluenose and myself kicks it that's the last Dirrabeg will see of them. May the grace of God follow them wherever they go and may good fortune and good health shine on them and that the begrudgers might be drinking bogwater when they'll be drinking tay.'

Twelve

RUBAWRD RING WAS shaving when the beat of the distant bodhrán assailed his ears. Because he was obliged to contend with a sturdy five-day-old stubble he had taken himself out of doors where, although dusk was imminent, the light was nevertheless better than indoors. Even with the aid of the paraffin lamp there had been insufficient light in the small dark kitchen with its tiny solitary window. The last thing he needed was a cut or scar on this day of all days with the wrendance only a few hours away and Paddy Costigan due to call at any moment to accompany him to Trallock where they would meet, as arranged, with Donal Hallapy and Bluenose.

Rubawrd Ring's shaving accoutrements were somewhat primitive. For a basin he simply upturned the cover of the twenty-gallon milk tank and placed it, upperside down, on top of the tank. While he stropped his razor his daughter Noranne filled the cover with hot water. His youngest daughter, Moira, watched fascinated from the kitchen door. His other daughter, Trassie, and his wife were still in Trallock where they had journeyed that morning by foot to keep an appointment with a hairdresser. Rubawrd would need the bicycle for his impending trip to town. First he immersed his two powerful hands in the hot water and allowed them to remain submerged until he was obliged to withdraw them because of the stinging heat. Immediately he applied them to his face, repeating the exercise

183

over and over until he adjudged the bristle to be sufficiently softened for the application of soap.

Noranne held this in readiness until she would be asked to tender it, after which Rubawrd would submerge it in the upturned cover while she returned to the kitchen for extra hot water. As she poured Rubawrd rubbed his hands together preparatory to recovering the soap and creating a rich lather between his heated palms. As he creamed his face with the freshly made lather Noranne stood by attentive as a ward sister awaiting the nods and becks of the surgeon.

'Razor,' he called and in a flash it was thrust, handle first, into his hand.

'Mirror,' he cried and it was raised to a level with his face and held as firmly as if it were attached to a fixture. Spreading his legs wide apart and flexing the muscles of his mighty shoulders he cast a cold appraising eye over his chin, cheeks and throat.

'Teeth,' he called and Noranne, with her free hand, thrust a set of upper dentures into his open mouth. All his upper teeth had been extracted some years previously but he rarely used the false replacements save when chewing bacon or shaving as he was now.

With a sure stroke he ran the razor down the side of the face to the very corner of the lip. He repeated the movement a second time when Noranne withdrew a cloth from her apron. This he used to clean the lather from the razor before addressing himself to the other side of his face. This completed, he made a determined assault above the upper lip before elevating his narrow jaw so that he might be provided with a clearer view of the throat. As he shaved this delicate area he held the skin which covered his Adam's apple firmly between the fingers of his free hand. A tiny tuft of hair would remain here sacred to the memory of all those hairs which had been so skillfully and carefully shorn. It was a sign of manliness not to interfere with this tiny area nor was it considered right or proper either to pluck hairs from the nasal apertures or the ears. This was one of the numerous distinguishing features between the males of Trallock town and those of Dirrabeg. Townies removed all hairs indiscriminately during shaving. The men of Dirrabeg, although often under considerable pressure from their women-folk and from the few remaining teenage males, adhered to the old ways.

'If it was good enough for my father,' Rubawrd had once informed his wife and daughters with a finality which brooked no further questioning, 'then it's good enough for me.'

Five of his eight children were in England; all were married and although none had come home to celebrate Christmas they had sent modest subventions. The Ring parents were well aware that without these seasonal tokens and other assistance throughout the year the remaining daughters, young Moira excepted, would have no choice but to depart Dirrabeg and find employment across the Irish Sea.

Rubawrd Ring was a three-cow farmer who, like Donal Hal-lapy and most of the other smallholders in Dirrabeg, lived from hand to mouth. Rubawrd was possessed of some excellent turfbanks which provided adequate and good quality fuel. Unlike Donal, who sold his produce by the assrail in nearby Trallock, Rubawrd disposed of his by the rick or by lorryload drawn from two roadside ricks, valuable surpluses after his own needs were catered for. Between the income from the cows, a modest weekly sum from duck eggs and hen eggs and an occa-sional day's hire from the bigger farmers whose extensive hold-ings greened the vista between Dirrabeg and Trallock, Rubawrd managed to survive. There was a certain amount of regular employment available when road work was undertaken by the county council but priority was given to cottiers who had no land and no visible means of support or to those with strong political affiliations.

Like Donal Hallapy and the remaining small farmers of the countryside surrounding Trallock Rubawrd spent many a sleep-

185

less night wondering from what mysterious source the next shilling would come. Sometimes he was fortunate enough to find himself with a spare half crown or two, sufficient to purchase a space at Fred Halpin's Bus Bar on occasional Sunday nights. Most of the time his pockets were empty.

'I envy you one thing above all others,' Bluenose once told him as they journeyed home from Trallock after a Sunday night session in the Bus Bar.

'It can't be my children,' Rubawrd replied, 'and it can't be my wife because you already have a family and wife without equal and it can't be my stock and it can't be my house and it can't be my land because the last two are wet as often as they are dry.'

'I envy you your cabbage,' Bluenose told him. 'You have the best cabbage in Dirrabeg.'

'Cutaway cabbage is the best cabbage,' Rubawrd answered modestly.

'Aye,' was Bluenose's rejoinder, 'but there's others has cutaway and their cabbage is very ordinary.'

What Bluenose said was true. Rubawrd Ring had cabbage without peer. Sometimes he would dispose of a bag or two to the greengrocers in Trallock but the market was unreliable and the one time he planted extensively he found himself feeding most of the crop to the cows. Rubawrd had almost completed his shaving when the bodhrán sounded from the direction of the fairy fort.

'What in Christ's name is that?' he called out almost knicking himself with the razor.

'Sounds like a bodhrán,' Noranne said.

'Yes, but what is a bodhrán doing up in the old fort in the middle of the day and such a bodhrán. It's like no drum I ever heard.'

'Could it be the fairies, da?' Noranne laughed as she posed the question.

'Don't ever laugh where the fairies are concerned. We'll

never know for sure whether they're there or not but who in God's name is drumming this time of the day?'

The same question occurred to the Costigan twins and to Donal Hallapy and his family. All listened while the drumbeats sounded, all exchanging wondering glances. Donal smiled to himself as he identified the melody from the pattern of beats.

'It is lorgadáns, dad, or what?' young Johnny Hallapy asked.

'Who's to say?' Donal tried to sound mysterious.

'What is it, Donal?' Nellie Hallapy moved closer to her husband. Donal winked at her behind the backs of his two sons.

'I'll tell you this and I'll tell you no more,' he intoned solemnly, 'any mortal man that says his prayers regular before he pulls the quilt over his head need never worry about them that's belting that bodhrán.'

The Hallapy brothers exchanged determined looks, both resolving never again to let a night pass without petitioning their maker.

Donal Hallapy was aware that Bluenose had invested in a white nanny sometime during the fall of the previous year but as far as he knew it was Bluenose's intention to breed from his new acquisition and as soon as the kid was suckled to slaughter the mother with a view to using the hide for bodhrán making. Now he knew why Bluenose had purchased the nanny. For a long time he had been aware of Bluenose's dream of manufacturing the perfect bodhrán. Judging from the distant sounds the new instrument was certainly out of the ordinary. He would suspend judgement, however, until he was granted permission to play it.

In the Bus Bar Monty Whelan and Fred Halpin sat on high stools outside the counter. Fred's only son Jerome, home from university where he was studying medicine, had taken over the running of the premises for the evening and night. His father and Monty had started drinking a half hour earlier, merely to whet their appetites, as they had explained to Minnie, in preparation for the celebrations that would be taking place later in Dirrabeg. None who would be attending the wrendance had divulged the night or the location to outsiders. Canon Tett had been misinformed and but for the astonishing perception of his housekeeper would have remained in the dark until the dance was over. P. J. Crolly had rung him as promised and had told him in good faith that the wrendance would be held in Bluenose's farmhouse on the Saturday of the following week. So he had been informed by a member of his staff, one Mattie Gilooley, a son of Mossie Gilooley, the Dirrabeg wrenband's outstanding fiddler who had taken his son aside earlier and told him that if anybody asked him he was to say that the dance was taking place at the later date and if there was to be retribution afterwards from P. J. Crolly the fiddler's son would explain that he had been deliberately misguided by his parents who wished nobody to know when and where the dance was being held.

'And if he sacks me?' the fiddler's son had asked.

'If he sacks you,' said the fiddler, 'all it means is that you will be joining your brothers and sisters across the water sooner than any of you thought. You don't ask Mister Crolly about the dates and places of his shindigs, therefore he has no right to go asking you about ours. So like a good man tell him what you were told to tell him and keep a straight face.'

From the moment Canon Tett had informed her about the wrendance Nora Devane had been somewhat sceptical. For one thing it was too late into January for the holding of a wrendance and for another the Dirrabeg porter-swillers would have neither the patience nor the discipline to wait that long to drink their ill-gotten gains. She became convinced as the days went by that whoever it was who imparted the information to the Canon had been a victim of the duplicity of certain Dirrabeg agents.

On the morning of the second Saturday in January she set out as usual from the presbytery on her weekly mission of provisions replenishment. Among numerous other forenoon visitors to the town she had encountered Nellie Hallapy in the vicinity of Faithful Ferg's in Carter's Row. She presumed at the time that Nellie was on her way to visit with her sister-in-law Kitty Smiley and thought no more of the matter. Later, however, she observed from the interior of a butcher's shop, Kit Ring and her daughter Trassie as they passed by, intent on some business or other. They bore no grocery bags so that their business in Trallock must be of some extraordinary nature.

'What in God's name,' Nora Devane asked herself, 'are they up to?'

The matter slipped from her mind as she haggled with the butcher over prices. It was not until Nora was about to enter the square from Healy Street that the third and most vital clue presented itself. Normally she would not have noticed the fiddler's wife Gertie Gilooley so self-effacing and effectively shawled was she during her trips to town but on this occasion there was a complete transformation, for instead of wearing the black shawl which was her usual garb she was now decked out in a coat and headscarf and was perched atop her husband's rickety bicycle, the uppers of her wellingtons barely managing to make contact with the pedals. It wasn't the transformation from coat to shawl that excited Nora Devane's interest and made her turn around to follow the parting figure after she had cycled by. Rather was it the change in Gertie Gilooley's demeanour for no sooner did she cast eyes on Nora Devane than she abandoned the saddle and stood on the pedals the better to accelerate and disappear from the gannet eyes of the housekeeper.

'Four from Dirrabeg and all in the one morning,' she whispered the words to herself as she stood stock still watching the retreating figure of Gertie Gilooley.

'Blasht me for an ape!' Nora Devane blurted out the exclamation as it dawned on her where Gertie must surely be coming from. Where else in the world but a hairdresser's with that tightly-bound headscarf and that flushed face fresh from the

189

electric dryer. Nora hastened homewards and made straight for the kitchen where she guessed the Canon would be heating himself near the Triumph range.

'Canon,' Nora asked excitedly, 'when is that you said the Dirrabeg wrendance would be taking place?'

'Saturday week wasn't it? Why?'

'Because, Canon, it is my belief that the wrendance is on tonight.'

'And pray who told you that?' the Canon asked, certain that his own intelligence service would prove to be superior.

'No one told me, Canon, but I have eyes.'

'Come to the point.' Canon Tett raised a bony hand impatiently.

'I will to be sure, Canon. I will to be sure. Will you tell me, Canon, why is four females from Dirrabeg and maybe more having their hair done this morning?'

'I don't know, woman,' the Canon spoke wearily, 'but I would entreat you, if you know the answer, will you for pity's sake tell me?'

'To be sure, Canon. To be sure. Why else would they be getting the hair done unless for a wrendance?'

'Is there any way we could make sure?' the Canon was on his feet now.

'That's the easiest ever, Canon. All that needs to be done is for myself to have a look into the hairdressing shops with a view to making an appointment. I can see the customers and make sure they don't see me.'

'Along with you then,' Canon Tett ordered, 'and don't be all day like a good woman.'

In the Bus Bar Fred Halpin and Monty Whelan had retired to the kitchen to join the Dirrabeg foursome who had silently arrived there unknown to anybody. After the second whiskey Fred Halpin was inclined to be expansive in his speech. It was his son Jerome who respectfully suggested that the kitchen would be a less public place if they wished nobody to know

190

their business.

Said he: 'If anybody walks in and sees my father outside the counter at this hour of the day they won't be long putting two and two together.'

'Wisely spoken,' Monty Whelan had concurred. They were warmly received by the Dirrabeg men and invited to participate in a round of drinks about to be ordered. Rubawrd explained the predicament of the buy-in monies and Fred Halpin gladly agreed to provide credit until he would be fully reimbursed that night when the contributions would have been paid over.

After four whiskies Bluenose suggested to Fred that it was high time the pony cart was loaded.

'The women will be wondering what's keeping us,' he explained.

'One for the road,' Monty Whelan called.

'Not for me thank you,' Bluenose stood to attention awaiting Fred Halpin.

'You boys have the drink,' Bluenose suggested, 'while me and Fred are loading, but let that be the last for we have a call at Faithful Ferg's and a long and icy road before us.'

There were solid murmurs of assent at this sage observation. Later the pony cart, covered with canvas to conceal its cargo from curious eyes, was seen to exit from the archway next to the Bus Bar. The sole occupant was its carter, Bluenose Herrity. He would be joined according to plan at the junction of Healy Street and Carter's Row by Donal Hallapy who would lead the pony by the head thereafter, because of the slippery conditions underfoot, until they reached their destination. After a given headstart of two hundred yards they would be followed from the suburbs onwards by Rubawrd Ring and Paddy Costigan. None of the four considered the precaution really necessary but had heartily acquiesced when Rubawrd made the suggestion.

'Better be sure than sorry,' he had announced solemnly when the arrangements for transportation were being finalised.

191

As they proceeded into the freezing countryside the steam rose in a wraithlike mist from the labouring pony. But for Donal's steady guidance and Bluenose's continuous flow of assurances the creature must surely have floundered. Between them they provided her with the necessary confidence until she found a slow but even rhythm which made her burden less onerous. All the time Donal kept pace, his presence a guarantee that the required restraint would be forthcoming should her hooves be deceived by a particularly skiddy patch of roadway. Overhead every star in the heavens was clearly visible, each as though striving to outglimmer each other. A full moon shone radiantly, silvering the roadway and the frozen pools in the adjoining fields. All around from human habitations, near and far, thin white columns of smoke ascended the silent, windless night. As he led the pacified pony over this slippery roadway Donal Hallapy felt elated. The whiskies he had consumed together with the utter beauty of the star-filled night helped him to forget the all too numerous problems which had plagued him since the new year dawned. Then there was the prospect of a glorious night's music and dancing with no scarcity of drinks or edibles, with the friends of one's bosom in the vicinity and the fair prospect of ravishing his certain-to-be-inebriated spouse at some celestial stage between the night and the morrow. Who cared for past misfortunes or for the uncertainties of the future?

It was a night of immense promise with a magical moon that rode bright and handsome in the high heavens. To be out of doors in the countryside on such a night was a tonic in itself but to be sharing the responsibility for the transportation of such a pleasure-inducing cargo gave him a feeling of superiority the likes of which he had never experienced. He felt like shouting his freshly-generated euphoria to the moon and stars, unable to conceive of any other bodies worthy of receiving such exhilirating personal tidings. The mood remained until they reached the turning which would lead them into the moonlit land of Dirrabeg. Slowly, carefully, exerting the utmost caution and aided by the gentle endearments of Bluenose, the pony felt its way from tar road to bohareen. The secondary road through the boglands was rough and uneven but there was no danger of the pony faltering or slipping. The sturdy creature snorted as soon as she found herself on familiar ground. Soon she would be home in the cosiness and comfort of her tiny stable, safe from cold and hunger, in that happy, hay-filled place. A mile or so in the distance the lights of the Dirrabeg homes guided them onwards, Bluenose's at the highest and most distant point, Martin Gilooley's the nearest, Hallapy's, Costigan's, Ring's and the others in between, ever-decreasing over the years.

At first Donal Hallapy could not explain the pony's unwarranted action. She reared and plunged, almost discharging her cargo there and then. It tested his utmost reserves of strength to keep her from bolting. He leaned with all his weight on her withers, his feet off the ground. Bluenose was thrown instantly on to the margin of matted grass and briars so that his fall was broken. He lay stunned for a while before managing to scramble to his feet. When the pony reared a second time both men held on to the reins and winkers at either side of her head and with the utmost difficulty succeeded in partly mollifying her. When she bucked and snorted Donal held her vice-like by the forelock with his right hand, his left still holding the reins.

From the alder clumps and sally groves at both sides of the roadway clods of turf were now being pelted in their direction. Entrusting the reins to Bluenose Donal Hallapy emitted a mighty roar, alerting Rubawrd Ring and Paddy Costigan who trailed them by some two hundred yards. After a second cry of alarm Donal leaped the roadside stream and headed in the direction from where the clods had come. He might have more profitably remained at his post for no sooner had he vaulted the stream than a number of men, their faces blackened, converged on Bluenose from both sides. At once Bluenose guessed

193

their intent which was either to destroy or appropriate the cargo. Knowing that Rubawrd would be along at any moment he wisely decided to cling for better or for worse to the reins and winkers and to ignore the blows which might descend as soon as the attackers realised that he had no intention of relinquishing his hold.

He was first struck on the head and secondly on the back of the neck. Neither blow had the slightest effect on him. The third blow was carefully timed and professionally delivered. Stars and flashes appeared before his eyes but he held on grimly. He was to receive no more blows that night for just as he was about to be beaten to the ground Donal Hallapy appeared, dragging a semi-conscious clod-thrower behind him. With a cry of fury he launched himself amid Bluenose's assailants. As his fist made contact with the jaw of the man who had all but felled Bluenose Rubawrd Ring and Peter Costigan arrived on their bicycles and without bothering to dismount drove straight into the raiders, as Bluenose held on firmly to the pony's head. A fierce fist fight ensued.

Although outnumbered by more than two to one the more determined Dirrabeg men managed to hold their own. The tide of battle ebbed and flowed, the Dirrabeg trio fighting like Spartans. They battled in a tiny phalanx which had the features of a triangle. This way, one or more always faced the enemy and there was a guarantee of protection from behind. In addition, if a man went down, the others would be near at hand to provide him with cover against the knee and the boot until such time as his footing and senses were restored to him. The trio complemented each other in several ways. Rubawrd Ring was the most orthodox of fighters, relying almost completely on a straight left which was rarely off target and then, unexpectedly, he would deliver a right cross, a most damaging blow when it landed. Donal Hallapy was a dour fighter with a preference for in-fighting. Given the opportunity he could stun a man with a glancing blow from either hand or fell a man when he found a suitable opening. Paddy Costigan was by far the nimblest of the three. Not a great warrant to deliver a blow, he was impossible to nail with any significant sort of wallop. Consequently he drew a great deal of fire. All three defended themselves with open palms, clenching their fists into powerful weapons only when golden opportunities came their way.

The triangle had seen action together in the past, the first time being some fifteen years previously when Dirrabeg had its own junior or second division Gaelic football team in the Trallock and district league and championship. A fight had erupted towards close of play in the semi-final of the championship. The conflagration was caused by the awarding of a penalty to the Trallock side who were two points behind at the time. The Dirrabeg players insisted that the referee, himself a townie, capitulated because of pressure from the Trallock supporters who outnumbered the Dirrabeg supporters five to one. Nevertheless, because of their fiercer commitment and premeditated strategy they won the fight hands down but exited ingloriously from the championship.

'If you wanted to field a Dirrabeg fifteen tomorrow,' Rubawrd Ring frequently commented, 'you'd have to scour the building sites and factories of England for players.'

The fight had now reached a stage where victory must go one way or the other. The fury had long since departed from the exchanges and the gasping, the puffing, the blowing and the grunting were now the dominating sounds. The exchanges were as earnest as ever but fatigue was taking its toll. All the time Bluenose had been loudly exhorting his fast-tiring comrades to greater endeavours but now he was silent as his gallant companions still refused to yield.

He watched anxiously until he could stand it no longer.

'To hell with the pony,' he thought, 'and to hell with the cargo. These are the friends of my heart.' He patted the animal smartly on the rump. 'Go on girl,' he urged gently, yet firmly. 'Go on away home now.'

195

The pony moved off at a brisk walk just as Bluenose entered the fray. To those who might not have been acquainted with his past pugilistic accomplishments he must surely have seemed like the easiest meat ever. His age and awkward gait suggested that his movements would be far from fluent and that should he by some off-chance land a blow there was little likelihood that it would do any damage.

Bluenose's approach to fistfighting was the very essence of deceit. Instead of advancing into the thick of the uneven contest as had his friends, he stood on the verge of the proceedings and quietly but astutely landed several telling blows before one of his victims realised that the pony had disappeared and that its owner was now to be reckoned with. The man who turned on Bluenose was a well-made, strapping fellow in his prime. He smiled grimly behind his black make-up. He would quickly dispose of this elderly dodderer who had dared to strike him from behind. The truth was that Bluenose never struck from behind for the sake of getting in a cheap or cowardly wallop. His aim was to attract one or more of his friends' assailants so that they, against the decreased odds, might render a better account of themselves.

He succeeded in provoking the ablest and youngest man on the enemy side. If it had been an older man Bluenose would have been deprived of the element of surprise for he would have known or heard of the Dirrabeg veteran's penchant for unorthodox tactics. When confronted with a foe Bluenose had a habit of twirling his open palms aimlessly in short, varying arcs about each other until his quarry was convinced that he was dealing with a half-wit and so might move in and proceed with the business of demolition. Bluenose's opponent did exactly this and paid the price in no uncertain fashion. The moment he made his move Bluenose unleashed two powerful backhands made doubly damaging by the looseness of finger and knuckle. At his time of life there was only one remaining blow of any consequence left in Bluenose's armoury. If it failed

196

he would be at the mercy of his opponent. This was a left hook but it would require every ounce of strength remaining to him and it would have to be delivered with such momentum and abandon that its dispenser was sure to lose his balance if the blow went harmlessly wide of its mark.

Bluenose swung from the hip as the younger man wiped the blood from a cut over his eye. The old man grimaced with delight when he felt the burning pain run up the wrist of his left hand. The younger man's feet shot involuntarily out from under him and in a thrice he was sitting on his posterior, not fully comprehending what had happened to him. When he tried to rise he fell again. It was the turning of the tide for, upon beholding their fallen hero, the attackers lost the intitiative whereas the warriors of Dirrabeg, on becoming aware of the extraordinary achievement of their ancient chieftain, redoubled their efforts. Palms still twirling aimlessly, Bluenose sought a second victim but there was none.

The ambushers, apart from the young man on the ground, fled helter skelter in several directions, their cries rising like the plaints of affrighted curlews in the rare and frosty air.

'Three cheers for Bluenose!' Paddy Costigan lifted the deadly left hand in the air while the cheers rang forth. Almost at once they were joined by some of the womenfolk who were already in attendance at Bluenose's, preparing the house for the dance. They had heard the fray and seen the pony and some carried weapons. Bluenose's wife bore an old iron tongs so heavy that it needed both hands to hold it aloft, Kit Ring a four-pronged pike which she had found embedded in a manure heap and Nellie Hallapy an ancient holly cudgel which was part of Bluenose's arsenal lest some night he be attacked in his home by robbers. Other females arrived to convey the joyful tidings that the pony and cargo had arrived intact in Bluenose's yard.

Meanwhile the young man who had fallen foul of Bluenose's left hook had struggled to his feet but was still in a state of grogginess. Nevertheless he squared off and adopted a fighting

197

stance.

'Come on,' he shouted, 'all together or one by one.'

Kit Ring would have impaled him there and then on the prongs of her pike but her husband intervened. The four Dirrabeg men were astounded but at the same time greatly impressed by the spirit and courage of the still groggy young man.

'Here now!' Rubawrd Ring uplifted a restraining hand, 'it was never the way of the Dirrabeggers to fight a man who is outnumbered.'

'And weren't the Dirrabeg men outnumbered,' his wife cut across, 'for all this wretch cared.'

'Now. Now!' Bluenose calmed her, 'he fought fair and he fought game and even now he could run like the others and outdistance us but he prefers to hold his ground like a fighting man.'

'Put it there, young fellow.' Bluenose extended the same devastating left hand which had so recently rendered the young man hors de combat.

The young man regarded the proferred hand with unconcealed suspicion. He withdrew a step not daring to take his eyes from such an instrument of destruction.

'Go on,' Rubawrd Ring egged, 'take his hand.'

'Take it,' Paddy Costigan and Donal Hallapy called in turn.

Still cautious, the young man advanced a step and tentatively extended his right hand. Bluenose took it in his and peace was made.

'You will come with us,' Rubawrd Ring informed the young man, 'and your cuts will be tended. Then, if you wish, you will be welcome to stay the night.'

There were some murmurs of protestation from Kit Ring and Gertie Gilooley. Bluenose turned on them with a stare frostier than its natural counterpart.

'The Captain of the wren has spoken,' he said crossly. 'This young man will now be regarded as a friend.'

198

'Hear! Hear!' the spontaneous assent came automatically from Noranne Ring. Immediately she had spoken she covered her mouth with her hands. She was the first to recognise the strapping youth from Upper Dirrabeg. She had seen him frequently at dances in Trallock and he was a lad much admired by the young ladies of both town and country. She knew him to be the youngest son of a widow. His brothers and sisters had emigrated to England as soon as they entered their middle teens. His name was Conor Quille and he was later to confess that all members of the attacking force were the wrenday renegades from Upper Dirrabeg who had planned the ambush shortly after Christmas as a retaliatory measure against the wrenboys of Dirrabeg proper. Conor Quille had been enlisted the night before and was given an assurance by Darby Kallihan that it was to be a fair fight with equal numbers on both sides. Before he had time to reprimand the renegades who had deluded him he realised that it was indeed a fair fight, such was the courage and strength of the outnumbered Dirrabeg men. He professed shame and remorse at having participated in such a cowardly attack. He had no idea as to the identity of the person who had informed the renegades. When the black polish was wiped from his face and his cuts and bruises ministered to the women of Dirrabeg were of the unanimous opinion that such a handsome and innocent youth would not have hand, act or part in anything underhand.

Thirteen

DAISY FLEECE AND Kitty Smiley arrived at Bluenose's house at nine o'clock. It had taken them less than an hour and ten minutes to cover the four miles between Trallock and Dirrabeg. No sooner had they set foot inside the door of the wrendance than they were swept off their feet, Bluenose taking strong hold of Kitty Smiley and Donal Hallapy presenting himself for acceptance to Daisy Fleece. The dance was a polka in which several couples were already taking part. The new arrivals were not even allowed time to divest themselves of their heavy coats or to change into the well-worn dancing slippers they brought with them in their coat pockets.

The wrendance had not yet come fully to life but the advent of the newcomers attracted more couples to the floor. Rubawrd Ring finished the contents of the mug which, to this time, had been held closely to his breast. It had contained a noggin of undiluted whiskey which he had been sampling in measured sips between cups of freshly-drawn, highly-conditioned porter. The breast pocket of his shortcoat contained a second noggin. He had promised himself that its contents would not be savoured until well after midnight when he might be in need of its boosting properties at the halfway stage of the joyous proceedings.

He placed the mug carefully at his feet and invited his wife Kit to take the floor where Gertie Gilooley was held, vice-like, by the beaming Patsy Oriel. From time to time he would convey the most intimate tidings of his infatuation to her freshly perfumed ears. Gertie Gilooley did not know whether to laugh or cry. She was well aware of Patsy Oriel's reputation. There was no female present who had not been warned at one time or another of his amoral tendencies, of his uncanny capacity for timing the instincts and emotions of unwary females and for luring them to secluded bowers and other romantic places where it was said he had the capacity to stimulate hitherto impervious females to inconceivable summits of rapture.

It was believed that he could divine at a single glance any weak chinks in the armour of even the most redoubtable matrons. Gertie Gilooley found him entertaining and stimulating but found herself in no danger of being lured out of doors. When he received a resounding slap on the back from Paddy Costigan with the injunction that he should straighten himself up and dance like a man Patsy Oriel took not the least offence. He drew himself to his full height and with a straight face held Gertie Gilooley at a respectful distance while he reverted to the orthodox steps of the polka.

The musicians had arranged themselves centreways on the stairs which climbed from a corner of the kitchen to a loft no longer in use. It had served as a bedroom and later as a storeroom for seed potatoes. When Bluenose's sons and daughters returned from England with their young families for the summer holidays it was brought back into temporary usage; otherwise it lay idle.

Three musicians occupied the stairs: Mossie Gilooley on the fiddle, Trassie Ring on the concertina and Delia Bluenose on the bodhrán. They would be relieved after an hour's playing by other musicians who themselves would be relieved after roughly the same period. Mossie Gilooley divided his attention between his instrument and a mug of porter which rested between his feet. There was a glazed look in his eyes partly due to the porter and whiskey he had drunk but compounded by the passion and energy which the agitated movements of his whole body transmitted to the fiddle.

Noranne Ring sat by the fire. Later her turn would come to play on the bodhrán. Conor Quille knelt by her side, his mouth stained with traces of recently-consumed porter, his young eyes filled with admiration for this laughing girl whose complete captive he now was and forever would remain or so he swore to himself between cupfuls of porter.

When the polka ended the musicians were loudly applauded after which the young Hallapy brothers, Tom and Johnny, made the rounds with two small buckets of porter, freshly-drawn for the occasion by Timmie Costigan who was an acknowledged expert in the tapping and handling of barrels having been thoroughly instructed on numerous other occasions by none other than Fred Halpin himself. Neither Fred nor Minnie had yet arrived. It was known to all, however, that the Halpins together with Moss Keerby and Monty Whelan had arranged to be driven to Dirrabeg by Martin Semple the hackney driver, neither Fred nor Monty being willing to trust their own vehicles to the hazards of the icy roads. Given the fact that both would almost certainly arrive at a state of somewhat incapacitating intoxication before the night was over, it was reckoned by the folk of Dirrabeg that hiring Martin Semple was a very sensible thing to do under the circumstances. It was also an accepted fact that Martin Semple was an inspired driver while under the influence. He had never been involved in a crash or accident although his passengers could tell of miraculous escapes over the years.

In the room off the kitchen the large mahogany table was covered with newspapers for the occasion. Neither Delia Bluenose nor others in Dirrabeg who were possessed of table-cloths had been willing to volunteer them for an occasion such as a wrendance with porter being spilled and sloshed at every hand's turn. The great advantage about newspapers was that they were great absorbers of drink and could be replaced after each sitting. There would be several sittings since no more than eight at a time could be hosted at the table. On an ancient walnut sideboard the edibles were on display. Here too most of the Munster Cream Sherry awaited distribution. Already three bottles had been consumed. The remaining nine bottles would meet a similar fate before the wrendance came to an end.

The older women, unknown to their menfolk, would have secretly subscribed before Christmas to a bottle or two of high quality sherry and port. These would be stored in a makeshift cloakroom off the dining area. No man dare venture into this holy of holies. Neither were some of the Dirrabeg matrons above concealing a glass or noggin of brandy on their persons, to be taken in moderate doses during visits to the cloakroom where the secreted sherry and port might also be tippled in comfort and privacy. Meanwhile the Munster Cream Sherry was distributed without any effort at concealment in the more public confines of the kitchen where it was imbibed graciously in the most ladylike fashion.

Each guest would partake of two substantial refections, the first between the hours of midnight and two o'clock in the morning and the other between the hours of six and eight o'clock in the morning. All food for the occasion had been purchased at Faithful Ferg's. Mean he might be but the quality of his provisions could always withstand close inspection. By ten o'clock all the guests were present, the contingent from Trallock being the very last to arrive. They were warmly welcomed by Rubawrd Ring in his capacity as Captain of the Wren, then by Bluenose and Delia. Acting on instructions from Rubawrd Ring seats were immediately vacated near the fire.

Quite by accident Monty Whelan found himself seated on a sugawn chair next to Daisy Fleece. Before he had time to exchange greetings a mug of porter was thrust into his hand by Katie Hallapy. Minnie Halpin was tendered a brimming glass of five star port by Kit Ring. Fred Halpin produced a bottle of whiskey from his overcoat pocket and presented it to Bluenose who promptly uncorked it and poured a glass for the bearer of the gift and for Moss Keerby.

'I must say you look very well, very well indeed.'

The words were conveyed in low key by Monty Whelan to Daisy Fleece.

'Thank you, sir,' she whispered in return.

More people present than they would ever have thought possible were aware that some sort of relationship existed between them. Kitty Smiley knew but had divulged her secret to nobody. Daisy Fleece had confided in her on their way to the wrendance that a close friendship was fast developing between them, that after initially endeavouring to discourage it she was now prepared to let it run its course, resigned to the fact that the relationship would have to be an underground one.

Kit and Rubawrd Ring knew. They would never divulge the secret to anybody. The news, surprisingly, had come from their youngest daughter Moira, who with a playmate of her own age had remained in the vicinity of the school after it had closed for the Christmas holidays. They had peeped through the classroom window sometime after Daisy and Monty had entered. They had remained concealed until the couple left the school. Then they had hidden behind the low wall at the rear of the school and had remained perfectly still when Monty investigated the scurrying sounds which had attracted his attention after Daisy had left.

When Moira Ring arrived home just as dark was falling her distracted mother chided her for her tardiness and demanded an explanation. Innocently Moira had revealed how she had seen the Master put his arms around Daisy Fleece who was well known to both herself and her companion, a seven year old from a small farm straddling the boundaries of Lower and Upper Dirrabeg.

Later that night when the rest of the family was abed Kit Ring had informed Rubawrd of what Moira had seen. After digesting the news Rubawrd assumed the gravest of countenances.

'This is a very serious matter,' he told his wife. 'Do Noranne and Trassie know?'

'They know nothing,' he was assured.

'And they must know nothing,' he cautioned, 'for well meaning and all as they may be they haven't the guile or the craft to contain such a dangerous piece of information.'

Without another word he entered the tiny bedroom where his youngest daughter slept in one large bed between her two sisters. Gently, noiselessly he lifted her into his arms without disturbing either of the bed's sleeping occupants and bore her into the kitchen where her surprised eyes focussed first on one parent, then on the other.

Rubawrd seated her on his lap while Kit raked the ashes for coals in an effort to nurture the dying fire into life. As soon as Moira was fully awake Rubawrd smoothed her hair backwards from her face and tilted her chin upwards, kissing her on the forehead. Rubawrd smiled down at her before speaking. The smile was returned with interest.

'What you saw today in the school?' he opened. Moira nodded her head, a serious look replacing the smile. 'You must never, never again say to anybody because if you do something bad will happen to Master Whelan.'

Moira nodded comprehendingly, impressed by the solemnity of her father's tone.

'Will you promise me that on your heart, my little jewel?' Rubawrd asked gently.

Again his daughter nodded. Rubawrd knew that Moira would never deliberately break her promise. With a farewell kiss he returned her to bed.

'But what of the other?' he asked anxiously.

'One of the Drillies,' his wife informed him.

'There are worse than the Drillies,' Rubawrd conceded.

'She's not as bright as Moira and she may have forgotten by the time she reached home. She's a dull child,' Kit Ring summed up.

'In the wrong hands such information could be very damaging,' Rubawrd shook his head before posing a final question. 'Mickie Drillie is nothing but an old slowcoach and a man of few words. He won't be likely to carry the tale farther in the event of his finding out but what of the wife? Is she a blabbermouth or is she close?'

'No looser or no closer than most,' Kit Ring replied.

'Go on away to bed let you,' he advised her. 'I'll stay here awhile and tease the thing out. Maybe nothing will come of it.'

'Daisy was on the road this evening right enough,' Kit recalled, 'but the dark was coming down and even if there were others on the road they'd be hard put to place who she was. Anyway, Daisy Fleece is a decent woman.'

Her husband smiled to himself. 'There's no one decent in the eyes of the story-carrier,' he said sadly. ''Tis the decent ones that have the most to lose.'

Nellie Hallapy was aware that some form of understanding existed between Monty and Daisy. She deduced this from what Donal had told her concerning the two rails of turf which Monty had ordered to be delivered to the house in the suburbs. Young Katie Hallapy knew shortly after Monty had taken up the seat beside Daisy, not that Monty had chosen the chair for himself. Delia Bluenose it was who proffered the chair in the first instance. She had insisted that the school teacher take his place by the fire because, in her eyes, he was a person of rank.

Monty had accepted with alacrity. From the way he had spoken to Daisy, from the adoring glances he had bestowed upon her and from the gracious manner in which words and glances were accepted, Katie Hallapy knew instinctively, young as she was, that the pair were in love. She was pleased. Daisy Fleece was reserved and modest, friendly too and still very pretty. Katie Hallapy frequently worried about Monty. She thought about him a good deal, wondering if he would marry again, if he had a girlfriend, if he was still heartbroken after his wife who, by all accounts, was a gentle and beautiful woman.

206

Daisy Fleece should suit him nicely. In her innocence Katie Hallapy saw them as an ideal pair; no complications presented themselves to her guileless mind. A worry had been lifted from that mind. She saw her teacher as a vulnerable, kind and lonely soul who now, at least, would have somebody like himself to look after him.

'Round the house and mind the dresser!' The age-old call came from Rubawrd Ring. It was a dance in which man, woman and child were obliged to participate. Moss Keerby was first on the floor with Kitty Smiley. Again Gertie Gilooley found herself in the arms of Patsy Oriel. Her face was flushed from the heat of the fire and from two large measures of Munster Cream Sherry which had been laced by Bluenose with part of the whiskey which had been so generously donated by Fred Halpin.

Monty Whelan held the hand of Daisy Fleece as they awaited the thump on the bodhrán which would herald the music from fiddle, melodeon and concertina. Bluenose partnered Katie Hallapy, his wife her brother Johnny while Nellie Hallapy chose her son Tom.

Donal Hallapy sat on the stairs, cipín held high over bodhrán waiting until all in the house were partnered before smiting upon the goatskin. Noranne Ring looked up into the newly-blackened eyes of Conor Quille, awaiting the signal which would send them tripping around the kitchen, backwards and forth, forth and backwards, until they were overcome by breathlessness.

Then magically the knob of Donal Hallapy's cipín smote upon the drum. Ecstatic screams responded to the eagerly-awaited signal. Boots, shoes and slippers flailed the flagstone floor. Wild yells, rebellious and sustained, ascended the open fireplace and escaped through the smoking chimney into the night air. Affrighted snipe, screeching and crazed, darted all over the starry sky. Bluenose's dogs added to the tumult. Other hounds in distant places responded. In the stable the pony whinnied and snorted while the clamour from the excited fowl-

207

house enriched the unholy din out of doors.

Inside the musicians vied with the dancers in their efforts to surpass each other's contributions. Round and round the dancers tripped, sometimes brushing, sometimes embracing, sometimes colliding. On and on went the prancing until the sweat poured down from musicians and dancers alike and yet not a solitary participant, young or old, would cry halt. Suddenly the music ceased and a deafening handclap greeted the sublime efforts of the musicians. The dancers collapsed onto chairs and benches. Some sat on the floor and raised their legs aloft whooping and whistling to show their appreciation.

Others staggered into the cold refreshing night beyond the bounds of the kitchen. Here they drew mighty gulps of pure air, hands resting on overworked hips, panting and gasping as though the air in itself was not sufficient to restore them.

'I declare to God,' Fred Halpin confessed to his perspiring wife, 'I didn't think I had it in me.'

Out of doors too came the musicians. Donal Hallapy was followed by his wife Nellie.

'Come on away back to our own house,' he coaxed.

'I knew there was no good in your mind when you beckoned me,' she nudged him playfully.

'Come on,' he whispered, 'while we're young.'

'It's too cold,' she drew away from him.

'What cold, woman!' He placed a hand around her waist. 'You should see the banker of a fire I built before I left the house. It should now be just about glowing before collapsing altogether.'

'I'll say one thing for you, Donal Hallapy,' Nellie tittered, 'you were always able to build a decent fire when it suited you.'

'Come on,' he urged, 'we'll be back in half an hour.'

Nellie allowed herself to be half-borne, half-wheedled the few hundred yards to the Hallapy household.

'The fire needs checking anyway.' Donal tried to sound concerned.

'It's my head that needs the checking,' Nellie threw back, 'for giving in to you like I always do. I hope nothing happens.'

'We'll use one of the yokes from over the water,' he increased his pace.

'And what will I tell Canon Tett the next time I go to confession?'

'You don't have to go to the Canon. There's Father Butt and by all accounts there's a new curate after coming, a Father Dunlea.'

'Come on,' Nellie Hallapy whispered, a catch in her voice, 'we'll use nothing.'

'Let's go for a walk.' It was Monty Whelan who made the suggestion to Daisy Fleece as they found themselves together out of doors.

'Why not?' Daisy replied. They walked along the pathway which led upwards to the old fairy fort. After a while he took her hand in his.

'They'll be talking about us,' she cautioned.

'No they won't,' he said. 'Nobody's seen us. They are all too taken up with their own affairs.'

The cropped grassy sward within the circle of blackthorn shone like a burnished disc under the moon.

'It's very romantic,' Daisy Fleece drew closer to Monty. Their bodies touching, they walked into the circle. He lifted her face to his and kissed her lips. They kissed again.

'I never dreamed,' Monty whispered, 'that I would know such happiness again. I was on my way down and inevitably out until you came along and to think you were there all the time, going to waste under my nose. Whatever is to become of us, Daisy?'

'God is good,' she whispered, 'things will work themselves out in time, you'll see. You know where I am. When things get bad for you I'll come to you but we must be careful Monty for the present at least. We have each other. That's the important thing. And I love you; I really do. What a terrible place we live in. You're free and I've been abandoned but it's decreed that we must never unite, never, never, never come together. It's so cruel and heartless.'

He felt the warmth of her tears on his face.

'I promise you,' he held her by the shoulders and looked into her eyes, 'in fact I swear to you that we'll be married one day.'

'I can't see it.' She was sobbing now. 'I'm an outcast and I'd only be a worse outcast if I dragged you down with me.'

'You mustn't say that,' he entreated. 'You've brought me up, elevated me from the lowest level.'

They stood there silently, still in each other's arms.

'We'd better be getting back.' Daisy dried her tears with the handkerchief he had given her.

'When we reach the house I'll go in first by the back door. You follow later by the front.'

'Whatever you say, my love.' He took her hand as they descended the narrow, grass-covered bohareen.

Moss Keerby and Kitty Smiley leaned their backs against a roadside turf rick. Earlier after they had emerged from the dance Moss had asked her to walk with him. As they walked he poured out his heart.

'I would never have told you how I felt about you but for Willie leaving you. I've kept it inside all these years. I've always respected you, always tried to be on hand when things were bad. I told him once that if he ever beat you again I'd kill him. I used to hear your cries night after night. I would lie there, praying to Christ that he'd leave you alone.'

'When did you tell him you'd kill him?'

'It was the night Tom took your part, about a year ago. When he began to beat Tom I put on my clothes. My sister heard me. She told me it was none of my business. I met him the following day as he was coming out of Munley's betting office. I told him I heard everything the night before. I swore to him that I would most certainly kill him if he tried it again. I meant it, Kitty, and he knew I meant it.'

210

'You know he never touched me after that night. You must have really put the fear of God into him. I'm flattered, Moss. I really am. I knew we always had a special friendship you and I and I knew somehow that I could call you if ever he went too far. I'm honoured that such a fine man as yourself would consider an old throwaside like me.'

'Don't say that. Nobody I ever saw has your beauty. Don't ever speak about yourself like that again.'

'My dear Moss, what can I say to you? You must know that I could never have anything to do with another man. I have to consider the children. What would they think of me?'

'I love your children. I always have. One would have to love them! I've never seen such a good-humoured bunch.'

'And they love you. Do you know that? They really love you. You've been like a father to them.'

'You're not offended by what I said to you?' He stood facing her.

'How could I be offended? It's just that we are in an impossible situation. Anyway, I'm planning on going to England before the end of the year. I dread to think what might happen to the children here.'

'Will you try to find Willie?'

'No. I never want to see him again.'

'If you go to England I'll follow you.'

'Don't be foolish, Moss. You have your home and your job and your sister to support and what makes you think England would be any different? I'll still have my children to think about.'

Gertie Gilooley would always maintain to herself until the day she died that she had been transported to the hayshed of Bluenose Herrity by means other than natural and in truth she had no recollection of leaving the wrendance without her coat nor the vaguest recollection whatsoever of climbing the rickety wooden ladder which led to the top of a block of dry hay, still perfumed with the wild and fragrant scents of the bygone summer, warmer too and softer than any mattress. Most important of all, to suit the purpose for which she had been conveyed to this cosy spot, the ladder had been drawn up after him by her abductor. By what enchanted means he had managed to deposit her there she would never know. All Gertie Gilooley could recall was consuming two glasses of Munster Cream Sherry and being borne in the arms of Patsy Oriel round and round the kitchen to the strains of her husband's music. Others might recall the laughter on her lips, the abandon in her eyes but none would ever dream that she would end up in the hayshed, another notch on the tally stick of the arch-seducer, Patsy Oriel.

When she returned from that rapturous clime where some bewitching form of enticement had lured her she could not credit the fact that she was lying upon her back and that a strange man had just been astride her. She knew she should have screamed. It would have been the natural thing to do under the circumstances. Her instincts warned her, however, that it would have been inappropriate. She lay there momentarily stunned, her eyes seeking to penetrate the darkness in an effort to identify her companion.

'Are you alright there missus?' The hoarse enquiry came from somebody who was drawing on a pair of trousers and finding it difficult to do so on the shifting surface of the hay. Gertie Gilooley's position became suddenly clear to her when she recognised the figure of Patsy Oriel.

'Oh sweet, blessed mother, forgive me,' she intoned fervently after which she began to pray for all she was worth.

'If I was you, missus,' Patsy Oriel cut in on her heavenly entreaties, 'I would postpone the prayer and gather myself before your husband starts looking for you.'

The reminder did not alarm her in the least. Her husband was devoted to his fiddle and would be for the duration of the wrendance, an event which would not recur for another twelve months. If it was a fiddle now instead of herself that he had mislaid he would recruit wife and children and proceed with the search to the exclusion of all other business until the instrument was found.

It wasn't that he did not care for her. God knows she could never deny that he was a good and faithful husband even if she was obliged, on occasion, to acknowledge the superiority of the fiddle. It was the awful thought of being seen by one of the neighbours that worried Gertie Gilooley. She had the good sense to realise that there was little use in mooning over what had happened.

'You're a terrible scoundrel entirely,' she scolded.

Her paramour smiled in the darkness. He could sense from the tone of her voice that he was partly forgiven.

'God pity me, I stood no chance at all against you.'

'Ah now, missus,' Patsy Oriel was laughing, 'there was two of us in it.'

'Go along with you,' she countered. 'My name will be mud if I'm spotted climbing down from here.'

'I'll go first and make sure the way is clear. Don't put one of your dainty feet on the ladder till I give you the say-so.'

'Patsy?' her call was tentative. He paused, his foot on one of the uppermost rungs of the ladder. 'You won't ever say a word?'

'Words are not my trade.'

He threw the boast backwards with a laugh before descending. Several minutes elapsed before she heard his voice coming from the floor of the barn.

'Quickly now, missus, and mind your step whatever you do.'

He took her by the waist from behind before she reached the bottom rung, 'and make sure you clear the hay from you before you go into the kitchen.'

Nobody would ever know about their sojourn on the hay block. Gertie Gilooley was glad to come safely out of it. Her husband Mossie was first amazed and then extremely gratified by the affection and later the passion which was to be showered upon him during the nights after the wrendance.

'Will you be going to town one of the Saturdays?' she asked one night after a session which had been fulfilling and memorable for both of them.

'I can take you this Saturday,' Mossie Gilooley told her.

'Oh that would be lovely,' she said. 'I'll be able to go to the noonday confessions.'

'And pray,' her husband asked tenderly, as he held her gently, 'what would an angel like you want with confession that was only there just before Christmas?'

Gertie decided not to answer the question. Instead she returned her husband's caresses, heaved a deep, deep sigh and settled into sleep.

Around the wrendance fire Bluenose was reciting the saga of the bodhrán. He had heard it too, he explained to the crowd gathered around the hearth. The large fire of black turf and brown bogdeal threw the glow of its flames upwards and outwards.

'I heard the beating and I putting in the cows after they watering themselves.' His face took on a strange and distant look, his eyes peering at one watching face and then another. He looked up the chimney as though he expected the spirits of the fairy fort to be eavesdropping. He lowered the tone of his voice.

'As soon as I heard the drumming I straightened myself and made for the fort. As I climbed I saw a strange yellow light in the sky. It burned alongside the brightening moon awhile and then it sunk low till it was over my head. I followed it into the heart of the fort and there I saw three lorgadáns sitting on their haunches around a bodhrán.

'"Welcome, friend," one of 'em said but I made no answer nor did I look any of them in the eye. Look a lorgadán in the eye and he'll blind you. Speak to him and he'll strike you dumb but hold your tongue and the chance is you'll come clear.

'"You want this magic bodhrán?" one of 'em enquired and

214

then the three of them produced cipíns and started to play. I
never heard the like of the drumming. None of you would have
heard it because I myself was only barely able to hear and I
down on top of them. "You want it?" the same lorgadán
enquired again. I nodded my head. "It's yours," he said, "and
it will cost you nothing for you and yours have paid the price
this long time. You have never interfered with our fort and
you have never stopped our stock of grazing."

'Suddenly hundreds of rabbits stood on their hind legs in
front of me and I guessed them to be the stock he was talking
about. "Promise us now," said the three chanting together,
"free grazing for our stock for evermore, free access to water
and never bring a horse or machine to plough where we have
sown." I nodded three times and they seemed well pleased.

'"Come out herself!" they called and I declare to God didn't
a door in the ground open and this tall woman climbed out.
She wore no clothes but her hair was long and every tress was
brighter than the next. What did the creature do then but
hand me the bodhrán and the cipín and instruct me to play
and that would be the music that you heard today.'

'And where is the bodhrán now?' The question came from
Johnny Hallapy. Bluenose did not answer at once. His gaze
remained fixed on Johnny for a long time, the watchers
entranced as the flames flickered and the shooting sparks flew
upwards.

'There!' he shouted the word as Delia Bluenose appeared,
having a moment before emerged from her and Bluenose's bedroom. She bore the bodhrán aloft, her eyes closed. She mumbled an old Irish chant, half to herself, half to the watchers,
not once opening an eye, moving around and around until she
stopped in front of Donal Hallapy. Speaking in Irish she placed
the bodhrán in his hands.

'Let the bodhrán rest where it belongs,' she exclaimed in a
loud voice, much to Bluenose's satisfaction.

Donal refrained from smiling. What an almighty rogue was

215

Delia Bluenose and what a match for her husband. Donal accepted the bodhrán without a word. Privately he accepted it for what it was, a gift from his old friend.

'A story, Delia!' The call came from young and old alike. As the clamour rose she took her place near Johnny Hallapy and told the story of Bluenose, how he was not a real person at all and that was why the lorgadáns had entrusted him with the bodhrán.

'The fairies know their own,' she said. She went on to tell how Bluenose's mother gave birth one summer's morning to a bouncing baby boy with golden hair and bright blue eyes, how father and mother were overcome with joy and went forth, as soon as the mother was able, parading their prize before the neighbours and indeed further afield until the countryside grew tired of their carry-on. Then one day when the child was unattended the three lorgadáns stole down from the fairy fort and swept away the bonny blue-eyed, golden-haired baby and put a swarthy, ugly, cantankerous thing in its place.

'That ugly baby was Bluenose,' Delia informed all and sundry, 'and them three lorgadáns he met today are his lawful brothers. He grew up into a horrible, contrary creature until one day I saw him by chance at the horse fair in Trallock. I took pity on him and married him for better or worse and that's why we're here together this frosty evening and that the begrudgers might be drinking bogwater when we'll be drinking tay.'

A mighty round of applause greeted Delia Bluenose's tale. When the tumult had subsided she announced that it was time for the first supper.

'Those from the town will go up first,' she decreed, 'because it is them that has come the farthest.'

At a signal Nellie Hallapy and Gertie Gilooley lifted the large black iron kettle from its crook on the crane. Close to the fire in a bed of hot ash and cinders was a second kettle with steam issuing from its spout. Delia herself took charge of this smaller vessel and proceeded to rinse out the two large

216

teapots which had been in readiness from the outset in the corner of the hearth. Katie Hallapy first took one teapot and then the other and ran to the back door where the contents were disposed of. Gertie Gilooley and Noranne Ring skillfully arranged two glowing beds of coals to accomodate the freshly-rinsed teapots in which the tea would be drawn. Meanwhile the town party had been making their way to the dining room. Deliberately Daisy Fleece sat at the opposite side of the table from Monty Whelan. When the party was seated the tea was poured and the feasting began. Already the table was laid with full plates of boiled pig's cheek and streaky bacon. A sliced barm brack occupied a large plate in the centre while beside it stood two heaped plates of freshly-sliced pan-loaves. Two pots of jam, one marmalade and the other mixed fruit were also on display as were saucers of butter, brown sauce and mustard. All dined well, Fred Halpin declaring that it was the most wholesome and tastiest pig's cheek he had ever eaten. Monty Whelan concurred and the others were loud in their praise of the plentiful fare. There was much banter as the Dirrabeg women came and went with fresh pots of tea and saw to the needs of those whose plates required replenishing. Occasionally Monty Whelan and Daisy Fleece exchanged fleeting looks, cherishing the secrecy of their relationship and savouring the sweet memory of their stroll to the fairy fort.

All the time from the kitchen came the music of concertina, fiddle and bodhrán. There were yells and shouts of protest as partners parted and joined with others in the set dances. There were even louder expressions of delight when they found themselves together again. All around men and women who were not participating tapped the flagstone floor to the beat of the music, clapping their hands when the quicksilver feet of the more skilled dancers pattered bewilderingly intricate patterns of steps, the males of each partnership vying with each other, displaying seemingly random variations which would have been

217

carefully thought out and rehearsed for several weeks before. All the time freshly-drawn buckets of porter went the rounds. A second firkin had been tapped by Timmie Costigan and those who had consumed the contents of the first remarked how finely conditioned it had been and the great battle it had made considering the demands which had been imposed on it. The second firkin tasted even better than the first and much praise was showered upon the tapper and dispenser. Note too was taken of the fact that the supplier had been Fred Halpin. Experienced porter drinkers, and there were many present, displayed the most profound expressions of appreciation and announced that the Halpin-Costigan combination was one that could not fail.

The town party had returned to the kitchen and others from Dirrabeg replaced them at the table. In the kitchen there was no let-up in the music. Donal Hallapy, on his new and most prized bodhrán and Trassie Ring on the concertina replaced Bluenose, Noranne Ring and Mossie Gilooley who had been called to the second sitting. The occupants of the third, fourth and fifth tables ate handsomely but speedily rather than miss for too long the goings-on in the kitchen which had now arrived at a state of glorious abandon.

Old misfortunes had been forgotten, beguiled away by the drink and the cameraderie. A deep feeling of warmth circulated the kitchen. Imagined wrongs faded from memory. Men and women held hands as they spoke of times past and present and sought nothing but a bright and trouble-free future for each other. A deep tolerance was abroad, a spirit of understanding and compassion which superceded the pettiness of the poverty-stricken existences of most of those present. Inspired by a newly-found benevolence they saw deep into each other's beings discovering good and tender qualities in the melting pot of their celebrations.

When Minnie Halpin discovered that she was waltzing beyond the binding confines of the kitchen she was surprised

218

but not alarmed. Her partner, Patsy Oriel, was an accomplished waltzer, mindful only of his partner's problems and predicaments, faced as she was with the wild exuberance and physically overpowering presence of the younger pairs of prancers, steering her clear of every obstacle and gently but firmly restricting her to a safe and even course. Unobtrusively and unnoticed he managed to navigate Minnie Halpin, middle-aged, rocklike of sense and still prettily plump, away from the tumult of the kitchen and into the enchanted air of the frost-bedecked night.

Later as she sat alone, dazed and bemused in a sugawn chair in a corner of the hearth, she felt compelled to arrive at the conclusion that what had happened must have been a dream. It could not be otherwise. She set about convincing herself that the mixture of brandy and sherry was the cause of the hallucination she had just experienced but what a dream it had been and how real and how sensational and now that it was over how terrifying! Absently she lifted a wisp of hay from the sleeve of her blouse and, surveying it, slowly succumbed to a protracted spell of uncontrollable blushing. She hardly dared look around her as she remembered climbing the ladder. The rest she would never bring herself to recall. It was something which would never be permitted to surface, never, never, never!

After a long while she raised her head and looked around her. He was sitting on a turf sod under the stairs cleaning out the bowl of his pipe preparatory to filling it. She had heard his name frequently in the bar but had never paid any attention. Satisfied that he had properly scooped out all the ash and other motes from the bowl he withdrew a chunk of plug tobacco from his waistcoat pocket and with his penknife began carefully to pare thin flakes into the palm of his right hand. She watched fascinated, wondering how he had succeeded in isolating and having his way with her without her once being even remotely aware of his intent.

She wondered if she had been seen. No, he was too crafty

219

and experienced. His timing was impeccable in that respect. For a brief moment he lifted his eyes from his pipe as if he sensed she was watching him. Almost unseen he waved his tobacco-filled hand and nodded in such a respectful fashion that she instinctively returned his salute with a smile, instantly regretting it, fearful lest he get the impression that she was condoning what had happened.

Patsy Oriel sat contented, shredding the flakes of tobacco in his calloused palm. The night had been to his liking. Only his victims knew or would ever know what had transpired. Others might talk of him but for his part he would never boast of his exploits. He had too much regard, he told himself, for those who had temporarily entrusted themselves to his arms. Patsy Oriel, pipe held vice-like between knees, shredded and re-shredded the bowlful of tobacco he had cut from the plug. There is nothing exceptional about me, he thought, and nobody would ever know anything about me but for those early mistakes when I was at the threshold of my career. It was a career which would embrace over a hundred women.

Less than medium height, he never stood out in a crowd. His pale blue eyes gave no indication of the intrepid heart which was housed inside his less than average chest. He knew he was of little use at anything else. His neighbours regarded him as a suspect worker, willing but unable to concentrate or give of his best in the round of a day, a poor contributor in a team of three that went into the making of a sleán of turf.

He was a worse partner in the simple card games which were played in selected houses across the winter and as a result he frequently found himself unwanted. His wife was a large and obese woman who had lost all interest in her appearance after their ninth child. He had sired other children. Of this he was certain. Despite his smallness, his frailty of frame and lacklustre presence he had a way with women but only when he found them in his arms during a dance. He never questioned his power or tried to analyse it. Sufficient for him that it existed and that he was often able to capitalise on it. Tonight had been a better than average night. Both women had been in his sights for a considerable period of time. There he would be yearning after a certain female for years and suddenly came a night like the Dirrabeg wrendance and she would be in his arms with as little chance of escape as a feeble fly from a carefully-wrought web.

Filling the bowl of his pipe he heaved a great sigh of satisfaction before lighting and puffing until a red glow showed at the surface of the bowl and the smoke drew easily when he sucked it from the stem. He would dance no more that night. He would sit where he was and chew the honeyed cud of his experiences in the hayloft.

When Johnny Hallapy tendered a mug of porter Patsy Oriel accepted it gladly and felt in his waistcoat pockets until his fingers fastened upon a silver threepenny piece. Johnny accepted it thankfully and pocketed it but refused Patsy's offer to sit a spell on the grounds that he was under orders to ready himself for home with his brothers and sister. They had long outstayed their leave and already had received two extensions, one from Nellie and the other from Donal. Katie stood by the doorway, resplendent in her new coat, awaiting her brothers. She was the only person in the house who saw the motor car as it turned into the yard, its lights extinguished, its engine dead.

Fourteen

FATHER ALPHONSUS DONLEA had been asleep for two hours when he felt the pull on his shoulder. His first reaction was to shrug the demanding hand away and turn on his side. The hand would not go away, however. It kept pulling and dragging and nudging until he was obliged to respond to it.

'What is it?' he called out drowsily from his broken slumber. He could not, of course, see Canon Tett's towering frame looming over him. Although it was one o'clock in the morning the Canon was fully dressed. He had not gone to bed. He had waited by the range in the kitchen from eleven o'clock onwards which was the time Nora Devane had retired for the night.

The Canon had fortified himself every so often with sweetened cups of tea from the full teapot which Nora had left on the range. He had passed the time between the hours of eleven and one reading the *Messenger*, his favourite religious publication, a forty-eight page compilation of stories, poems, prayers and serials, all with a decidedly Catholic slant. It cost only two pence and because of its flimsy paper cover, red in colour, it was easily folded and pocketed. The Canon considered it ideal reading whenever he found time on his hands. When eventually he discarded it Nora Devane painstakingly withdrew the leaves and divided each into two equal parts. These she hung in a bleak outdoor w.c. which served as the

222

curates' toilet. It could be that she intended the bisected but still readable pages to serve as reminders of their priestly calling as well as fulfilling their primary toilet roles. Old newspapers cut into approximately the same size supplemented the *Messenger* contributions.

'God be with the youth of me,' Father Butt had once confided to Father Bertie Stanley, 'when the great outdoors was my toilet, a hundred square miles of mountain and moorland and no one to interfere with you save a frightened deer or a loping hare.'

Eventually Father Donlea managed to open his eyes fully and lift himself upright on the bed.

'What's the matter?' he asked as soon as he recognised his caller.

'There's nothing the matter, Father. Just get up and come with me.'

'Is it a sick call?' Father Donlea asked as the Canon turned away without answering. 'Has there been an accident?' he called out anxiously as he listened to the Canon's footsteps descending the stairs.

'Ours not to wonder why!' he spoke to himself as he hastily pulled on his trousers before instituting a search for his shoes. He found one under the bed and the other on the tiny dressing table honeycombed from the depredations of woodworm. He had but barely fastened his collar when he heard the booming voice of Canon Tett calling him from the foot of the stairs. Hastily he combed his thinning hair and dipped his hands in the ewer of stale water which dominated the dressing table with its attendant basin, chipped and cracked.

'What in God's name is holding you up, Father?' came the irritated voice of his parish priest.

'Coming, Canon,' he called from the doorway as he fumbled through his pockets to make sure his car keys were on his person. At the foot of the stairs the Canon was waiting. Awakened by the uproar Father Butt had appeared in his

223

pyjamas at the head of the stairs.

'What's happening?' he asked of the junior curate. Father Donlea shrugged his shoulders and hurried to join his lord and master.

'Is anything up, Canon?' The query came from Father Butt.

'Nothing that you need concern yourself about,' the Canon threw back matter-of-factly. 'Go back to bed like a good man or you'll miss your beauty sleep.'

Father Butt stood mystified at the head of the stairs. It could hardly have been a sick call. There was an extension from the doorbell attached to the wall directly over his bed and he would have been the first to hear. In fact it was his night for sick call duty and this puzzled him all the more. If it had been an accident the Canon would have instructed him to contact the Civic Guards and doctor or at least ordered him to be on the alert. There had been a time when he might have lain awake wondering and worrying about it but the years had inured him to the Canon's mysterious ways. He returned to his room and was asleep in minutes.

'Your car will do nicely Father!' Canon Tett informed his junior curate.

'Of course, Canon,' Father Donlea returned obediently, 'but is it any harm to ask where we might be going?'

'No harm at all, Father. Just bide your time and all will be revealed as the man said. Meanwhile get your car out and let us be on our way.'

'Yes but which way?' Father Donlea persisted with his questioning.

'In God's name will you get the car and don't be standing between me and my bounden duty!'

Father Donlea hurried to the curates' garage, a whitewashed decrepit building which had once been a stable. As they drove northwards through the square on the Canon's instructions Father Donlea could not help but wonder about their eventual destination. He knew it would be a waste of time putting further questions to his parish priest. When they came to the junction of Healy Street and Carter's Row Father Donlea eased his Morris Minor to a halt.

'I await your instructions, Canon,' he announced in what he hoped was a formal, yet respectful tone.

'Go on out the main road,' the Canon returned stiffly, 'and turn off for Dirrabeg. You know where Dirrabeg is, Father?'

'Oh yes, Canon. Father Butt took me on the grand tour the day before yesterday and I also made the rounds of the entire parish a few times on my own.'

'Very well if you did,' the Canon cut in. 'Just take it nice and handy now until you come to the crossroads and then douse your lights. Dirrabeg, you see, is a very curious place, full of curious people and we don't want anyone to know our business.'

During the short period since he had taken up residence in the presbytery, Father Donlea had experienced several occasions of perplexity, all motivated by Canon Tett's devious and inconsistent behaviour. Even without the advantage of a briefing from the senior curate Father Donlea's first impression of the Canon was that of a gruff and coarse old man who should be out on grass. He had known others like him, had in fact served under parish priests just as old and irascible. Yet, for all their senility and contrariness they had been basically good priests, shrewd administrators and, as he knew from personal experience, excellent confessors.

The trouble with them was that they had grown hardened against all forms of change and were suspicious of reform even when this was advocated by the bishops. They became dictatorial from isolation. There was no arguing with such men but he had to concede that there was much to be learned from them. What puzzled him most was their inexhaustibility and their eagerness, despite age, to remain in the firing line, ready for any form of confrontation. Father Donlea envied such priests their unshakeable convictions. For Canon Tett there was no doubt, no shady area, no wrestling with conscience.

225

For him it was right and wrong, right and left and black and white. Such men did not lie awake at night vainly endeavouring to distinguish between what was really bad and really good. They slept the sleep of the just. Their faith was unshakeable and their rules unbending no matter who suffered in the process. It wasn't that they had become blinded to what was happening around them. Canon Tett was aware of nearly everything that happened in his parish. He was not totally insensible to the need for intervention in certain delicate areas such as the all too numerous cases of extreme poverty and want. He was prepared to pay appropriate lip service but he would never harass his better-off parishioners into coming to the aid of the less well-off. To him token assistance was in itself sufficient. Industrious, good-living people could not be expected to give continually of their hard-won resources.

'Slow down, Father, and turn off your engine. The fall of ground will see us to our destination.'

'What is our destination, Canon?'

'Keep your eyes on the road like a good fellow and you'll know soon enough. Content yourself with the knowledge that we are about God's business this night. Be grateful that you have been chosen to act on behalf of the Father. Ask not why you are here but be glad you are here and be prepared to act on your Father's behalf.'

The Canon's recital became somewhat mumbled as the car moved slowly and noiselessly down the incline which would take them into the yard in front of Bluenose's abode. At first Father Donlea refused to believe his ears when he heard the faint strains of music. How, he asked himself, could there be sounds of revelry in such a remote place at such an unearthly hour? He lowered the car window and listened. Outside the night air sped past almost noiselessly, its icy breath fanning the car's interior.

'Close the window, Father, don't we get pneumonia.' The command came from the Canon who had ended his rambling

226

homily.

'Just a minute if you please,' Father Donlea returned, 'I'm almost certain I hear the sound of music.'

'Of course you do, Father, and so do I.'

'But how? Where?'

'From our destination,' the Canon retorted with a chuckle. Father Donlea did not close the window at once. The music was unmistakeably traditional, full of that strange mixture of life and antiquity. He found himself pursing his lips and silently breathing the music of the reel, and reel it was. He knew that much about traditional music. It seemed to him that a drum of some kind was the major feature of this rustic ensemble. He had no doubt identifying a fiddle, maybe two. There was also a melodeon or piano accordeon; he could not be sure which.

Father Donlea hailed from a quarter of the diocese where there never had been a wrenboy tradition. He had never seen, much less heard a bodhrán. After a second, curter injunction from the Canon he reluctantly closed the car window. Even with the window shut the music was still to be heard, its volume increasing as they neared their stopping place. As they alighted from the car in Bluenose's yard Father Donlea could only conclude that some sort of hooley or American wake was in progress or perhaps even the concluding stages of a wedding celebration. He began to revise his opinion of his parish priest. How thoughtful of him and how kind to invite his curate along! He wondered if the Canon made a habit of visiting late-night rural celebrations without the knowledge of his senior curate or housekeeper. The younger priest felt a warm glow for having being considered as a trustworthy companion on this secret and most welcome venture into the hinterland. So this was the Canon's Achilles Heel, a sojourn among the countryfolk who valued the traditional way of life. The visit, no doubt, was his way of endorsing their fidelity to ancient standards. Willingly he followed the Canon across the yard and into the kitchen. Following in the Canon's wake, he was amused and

227

surprised by the vigour and enthusiasm of the dancing couples. Countrified and uncultured they might be but there was a certain dignity in the way they disported themselves. Most of the men were drunk to be sure; he deduced this from their wild yells and glazed eyes. Some of the females were quite attractive, carrying themselves with poise and composure despite the extreme physical demands of the dance and he felt that without them the whole affair would have been a shambles.

As yet neither he nor Canon Tett had crossed the threshold and could not be seen by the kitchen's inmates. None, save a pretty little girl wearing a light blue coat, was as yet aware of their visit and she, or so it was apparent to Father Donlea, was so overcome by their presence that she seemed to have lost all power of speech and movement. After a while they were spotted by Johnny Hallapy who was in the act of transporting a bucket of porter from one corner of the kitchen to the other.

He advanced at once towards both newcomers and, dipping his cup into the sudsy contents of his container, brought forth a brimming cup which he presented to Canon Tett. It was only then that Father Donlea became aware that something was amiss and that the Canon's visit was more in the nature of a raid than a ratification.

The moment Johnny Hallapy tendered the cup the Canon smashed it from his hand. It fell with a crash, its contents spreading frothily over a floor already wet from the same carelessly-conveyed liquid. The smashing of the cup was the signal for which the Canon had been waiting. It suited his purpose ideally. He advanced into the kitchen, his right hand raised aloft, his eyes burning with the zeal of conviction. Behind him at the door a bizarre comedy, unseen by all save Patsy Oriel, was being enacted.

Undeterred by the Canon's rejection, Johnny Hallapy thrust his hand into the depths of the porter bucket and produced a second cup, this one cracked and without a handle. He handed it apprehensively to Father Donlea. By Johnny's childish reckoning it was only proper that the second priest should receive the same treatment as the first.

Father Donlea looked around and about desperately trying to ignore his would-be benefactor. The lad could have been no more than seven or eight, should have been abed hours ago, had no right to be posturing in a positively adult environment with a cup of stout at this unearthly hour of the morning. He looked downwards chastisingly and noted the perturbed look on Johnny Hallapy's sleepy-eyed face. The brimming cup was still extended in his direction. Father Donlea hesitated. There is something happening here, he told himself, which might well have a great bearing on mine and this young fellow's future. He accepted the cup and swallowed its contents without taking it from his mouth, wiped his lips and returned the cracked beaker to a grateful and mightily relieved Johnny Hallapy. It was a moment that Johnny would never forget.

Meanwhile, after a brief but paralysing silence imposed by Canon Tett's unheralded entry, the kitchen surrendered itself to bedlam. Shrieking women ran for their coats, crushing, bruising and knocking each other aside in the frantic scramble to escape the eagle eye of the Canon. Minnie Halpin slid silently from her chair by the hearth and would have toppled into the fire in a dead faint had not Monty Whelan observed her perilous position. With the aid of Daisy Fleece he succeeded in lifting her back onto the chair where she lay sprawled and helpless. Her husband Fred knelt by her side while all who could made good their escapes.

The men who had been involved in the dance had drawn their coats over their heads to hide their identities before escaping through the back door. The musicians, Trassie Ring, Mossie Gilooley and Donal Hallapy stayed put on the stairs, Donal still beating gently on the bodhrán which Bluenose had so lovingly made for him. As soon as the Canon's back was turned Mossie Gilooley and Trassie Ring tripped noiselessly down the stairs, Trassie to take up her position by her father's side near

229

the hearth and Mossie Gilooley to find his wife who had fled screaming into the night without cap or coat the moment she discerned the Roman collars.

When the Canon had raised his hand to claim attention the majority of the revellers had disappeared. The few who remained sat or stood silently, still overcome by the shock of his arrival. Bluenose and Delia stood together at the door of the dining room; Rubawrd Ring and his daughter Trassie stood nearby; Nellie Hallapy had joined Donal on the stairs. The town party sat by the hearth still ministering to the rapidly recovering Minnie Halpin. Seated on his turf sod beneath the stairs, Patsy Oriel also remained; he sat impassive and imperturbable, looking into the bowl of the pipe which he had just withdrawn from between his teeth.

Father Donlea stood with bowed head, hands clasped behind back, a despondent look on his tired face. He had grown suddenly weary. There was silence now save for the barely audible drumming of Donal Hallapy's bodhrán. The sound, if anything, served to stress the silence. The Canon spoke as if he were leaning against the altar of the parish church.

'How dare you abuse the Sabbath, you ungodly wretches?' was his opening admonishment. 'Here it is, two o'clock in the morning, with the first mass only five hours away and drunkenness rampant. How often have I told you that you may not hold these porter balls when they intrude on the Sabbath Day, the day especially set aside by God for worship? Have I not spoken from the altar of your parish church repeatedly on this subject or am I speaking to myself? Why have you deliberately flouted my decision on this question? There are other days in the week yet you deliberately choose the one day forbidden by your parish priest. What are you doing here?' The last part was addressed to Monty Whelan.

'It is none of your business where I go or what I do after I leave school,' Monty replied.

'Isn't it now, Mister Whelan? We shall see about that.

230

Remember that any behaviour on the part of my teachers likely to arouse concern or give scandal is my business and I will always make it my business because the school children of this parish must come before all else. I will say no more about this now but I expect you to come and see me after school on Monday. I shall have something to say to you then.'

'Say it now,' Monty Whelan demanded.

'Not now.' There was a menacing chill in the Canon's voice. 'This will keep till Monday and make sure you present yourself at the presbytery as soon as school finishes.'

As the Canon spoke his eyes took in the others in the kitchen. He noted the defiance on the faces but it did not deter him. His eyes rested finally on Daisy Fleece. The Canon surveyed her coldly and hostilely from head to toe before looking her in the face. She did not bend or deflect her head as he had anticipated. She returned his look without flinching until he was obliged to look elsewhere.

'If you have any sense now,' the Canon addressed himself to Bluenose and the others, 'you'll stop this tomfoolery and go to your beds. It's past two o'clock in the morning and you'll be entering the Church of God in a few short hours. Do not, under pain of excommunication, enter my church with the sign of drink on you. Go on along with you now and prepare yourselves for the Sabbath.'

Nobody moved. From the stairs the drumming of the bodhrán increased in volume. The Canon turned, anger flashing in his eyes, his face contorted.

'Stop that infernal sound,' he shouted. 'Stop it at once or I'll put God's curse upon you.'

Donal Hallapy placed the cipín behind his ear and placed the palm of his right hand on the surface of the bodhrán. Still the sound persisted, infinitely fainter now, almost inaudible.

'Put that thing from you!' the Canon commanded. There was no response from Donal Hallapy. His eyes were fastened on the hand which covered the surface of the bodhrán. There

231

was no movement from the hand but if one drew close and peered intently one might see that the fingers rippled almost imperceptibly on the goatskin. From a distance the rhythmic beat must seem to be generated by the instrument itself.

Father Donlea wondered at Donal's expertise. There was no movement from the hand that he could see and yet the muted, haunting, rippling tattoo persisted. Sometimes it seemed to come from a distance, yet all the time, vaguely sinister, it pervaded the kitchen, creating a strange tension. He noted too that the eyes of the man who held the bodhrán had closed. Yet he wasn't asleep. His body was too taut for that. A look of uncertainty had crept over Canon Tett's face. For once he was speechless. The uncertainty became transformed into puzzlement and from puzzlement once more to anger.

'Put that infernal contraption from your hand!' he called.

Donal reacted by snatching the cipín from behind his ear and belting the bodhrán with a ferocity and speed which alarmed Father Donlea. From where the curate stood the man with the bodhrán seemed to be possessed. The vibrant drumming filled the kitchen; it was almost deafening. The Canon placed both hands over his ears as Donal Hallapy with unbelievable dexterity wrenched the fury through the medium of the drumbeats from his being. Suddenly the drumming stopped. Donal opened his eyes and placed the cipín once more behind his ear.

The silence which followed was unnerving. The Canon removed his hands from his ears, the anger once more dominating his features.

'Throw that barbaric instrument away from you at once,' he called out to Donal.

'It is not a barbaric instrument,' Delia Bluenose flung back. 'It's a drum made by my man Bluenose and the likes of it was never made before.'

'It is barbaric,' he thundered, 'and as well as that it is the devil's drum.'

232

The devil's drum. The phrase was whispered by Delia Bluenose in awe and terror. It was here that Bluenose intervened for the first time: he stepped into the middle of the kitchen and faced the Canon.

'Listen to me, Father O'Priest,' he cried with his fists clenched. 'Listen wrendance-wrecker and joy-killer. Just as sure as your Christ and mine is the King of Kings so is the bodhrán the drum of drums!'

'Drum of devils,' Canon Tett shot back unchastened. 'Come on!' he turned on Father Dunlea, 'our business here is finished and scant help you were to me may I say.'

In the car there was silence until they reached the crossroads which would return them to Trallock.

'Where did your tongue disappear to?' Canon Tett spat out the words. 'You stood there like a danged dummy and let me do all the talking. What in God's name happened to you?'

'Nothing happened to me Canon. I was unprepared that's all. For the life of me I cannot see what right anybody has to upbraid those unfortunate people. All they were doing was drinking and dancing.'

'All they were doing!' The Canon spluttered. 'All they were doing,' he barked, 'was flouting God's law and you say I haven't the right to upbraid them. This is my parish, Father, and while I'm in charge I will speak out against debauchery of the kind we saw tonight. Now drive your car and don't let me hear another word out of you.'

Father Donlea drove silently, his eyes fixed on the road ahead. The whole business, in retrospect, seemed to him like a bad dream. Fragments of the scene flashed before his mind as they drew into the suburbs, the shocked faces of the people present, the terror of the fleeing women, the haunting sound of the bodhrán, the face of the youngster who had offered him the drink, the Canon's attack on the teacher and most vividly of all the old man's definition of the bodhrán. The Canon might have ended the dance but the bodhrán player had stymied

233

him and the old man's answer had rattled him. How will I ever justify my visit when I meet those people again, Father Donlea thought. I was party to a monstrous intrusion into the private activities of a whole community of people. I participated in their humiliation in the name of the Church and by my silence I betrayed them.

'May God forgive me,' he said aloud. 'May God in His mercy forgive me!'

Fifteen

NEWS OF THE Canon's raid reached Trallock at six
forty-five on Sunday morning. It was conveyed to his
his massgoing passengers by Martin Semple the taxi
driver who every Sabbath relayed several carloads of elderly
and isolated countryfolk to the various masses at Trallock parish
church. The early arrivals spread the colourful tidings among
the later arrivals until the seven o'clock bell rang by which
time the entire congregation was fully acquainted with the
harrowing proceedings of the early morning fiasco at Dirrabeg.

Martin Semple had arrived shortly after the priests had left.
Normally he would spend a few hours, at the behest of the
Captain, drinking and dancing until such time as his passengers
were ready for the road but on this occasion there was no
dancing and little drinking. The bottom seemed to have fallen
out of the celebrations by the time he had arrived. Over a mug
of porter Rubawrd Ring had given him a blow by blow account
of the sacerdotal offensive, accurately divulging every detail,
neither adding to or subtracting from what had taken place.

Martin Semple relished every word of what he was told,
realising that it would be of inestimable value to him in the
days ahead. His clientele, for the most part country people,
had insatiable appetites for news, particularly news of this kind.

Later Martin Semple would refine the story to its bare essen-
tials and then embellish the highlights in his own inimitable

style. If he strayed from the truth occasionally and brought his imagination into full play it was for the benefit of his passengers who expected to be entertained in such a fashion. Because there was a strong basis of truth in all his revelations his recensions and elaborations were also accepted without question. He was often quoted where doubt was cast upon the authenticity of a particular item of news.

'I have it from Martin Semple himself,' the bearer of the questionable piece would use the trump card to dispel any remaining doubts.

Father Butt, who celebrated the seven o'clock mass, was as yet unaware of the happenings of the early morning. That there was something out of the ordinary after occurring was clearly evident from the agitated undercurrents wafting altarwards from the body of the church. Even during the consecration he was made aware of the unrest which existed outside the altar. He would know soon enough. He never deliberately sought out news. Sooner or later he would be informed, if not by Nora Devane or the Canon for their own perverse reasons, then by the parish clerk, Shamie Deale, a withdrawn, rambling hulk of a fellow who liked Father Butt and felt that he should be filled in on the more noteworthy happenings outside the presbytery walls.

Faithful Ferg heard of the raid immediately after seven o'clock mass which was the time he opened for business on the Sabbath. He hugged himself with glee as the tale was unfolded, thumping the counter and changing regularly from one foot to the other which was his way of expressing his appreciation. The fainting of Minnie Halpin was, for him, the highlight of the night. Nothing could be more ludicrous in his eyes. No mention was made of his brother Monty although he guessed he must have been there. He was surprised to learn that Daisy Fleece had lent her presence to the occasion. Nice bit that, he thought. Pity she lived on the other side of town. So she had now taken to frequenting wrendances. He had always sus-

236

pected she was a bit of a flier. Of course, where there's smoke there's fire and there had been enough smoke in the Fleece one's case to prove the existence of a veritable bonfire. But how did one get at her? How did one make contact without being suspect? It was a matter to which he would have to give a deal of thought.

It was late in the morning before Nora Devane heard. She had been obliged to wait until after eleven o'clock mass for the details. She was well aware that the raid had taken place.

'How did ye get on last night Canon?' she had asked as the parish priest sat by the range preparatory to eating his chopped-up eggs.

'You'll hear soon enough,' was all the answer she managed to elicit. His mood was grumpier than usual. She had heard him nattering to himself in his room before he came downstairs. Perhaps it was the late night or could it be that he did not have matters all his own way in Dirrabeg?

'Did you hear anything?' he had asked her on two occasions.

'Such as, Canon?'

'Such as thumping or beating or the like.' She shook her head in perplexity. Could it be that he had started to dote a little?

Father Butt had proved to be even less rewarding but then it was possible that he knew less than she did. She pinned her hopes on Father Donlea. She found him alone in the dining room. In a few moments she was back with his breakfast. On this occasion there was a liberal supply of freshly-made toast, two boiled eggs and a large dish of butter.

'You must be jaded after the night,' she threw out the feeler as she placed the breakfast tray on the table.

'How did it go?' she asked.

'How did what go?' he returned.

'The wrendance last night?' she reminded him as she assumed a conspiratorial smile. He stood up instantly.

'I never again want to hear mention of last night,' he told

237

her crossly, 'and I'll thank you never to bring up the subject of wrendances again.'

He stalked from the dining room, snatched his hat from the hallstand and went out of doors.

'Your breakfast, Father!' she called after him. He acted as if he had not heard. He stood for a moment, sniffing the cold morning air as if he expected it to provide him with a sense of direction. The next instant he was gone. Nora Devane returned the breakfast tray to the kitchen. The contents would not go to waste. The two eggs and the ample toast, with a little re-heating, would provide breakfast for both curates the following morning. The Canon would drink the tea. Nora made contact with her own sources after eleven o'clock mass. If the account of the raid on Bluenose's brought her cheer it was dissipated by news of the total rout of the ambush party from Upper Dirrabeg.

Doctor Joe O'Dell heard of the raid from Fred Halpin when he called to the Bus Bar for a pre-luncheon pint after twelve o'clock mass.

'If it were my house,' he said angrily, 'I would be taking legal proceedings against him first thing tomorrow morning.'

'And could you do that?' Fred Halpin who was still groggy asked with some surprise.

'If,' said Joe O'Dell, 'a priest came into my house and disrupted a party I would sue him for invasion of privacy. If he threatened my guests I would throw him out on his ear and report him to his bishop.'

'Easy for you,' Fred Halpin pointed out. 'You are a doctor. Poor oul' Bluenose is only a four-cow farmer with a leg in the grave.'

P. J. Crolly and Emily heard it from their son Junior before they sat down to lunch in the Trallock Arms. Junior's wife, Aroon, sat in the foyer with her mother-in-law. Here she divulged the happenings at Dirrabeg to Emily Crolly. In the bar over pale sherries Junior filled in his father down to the minutest detail. By the time the affair had been conveyed to Junior Crolly, which was shortly after twelve o'clock mass, the story had been transformed out of all proportion.

According to Junior, bell, book and candle had been produced by Canon Tett before pronouncing the awful rite of excommunication. The debauchery which had been witnessed by both Canon and curate did not bear repeating. Emily Crolly managed to generate progressive expressions of shock and astonishment, incredulity and downright horror as her daughter-in-law unfolded gross indulgences of lust, lewdness and drunkenness embracing every age from eight to eighty. Emily Crolly expressed no surprise when Aroon revealed the identities of the visitors from Trallock.

'Oh, the poor Canon,' she dabbed her eyes with her yellow organdie handkerchief which matched in quality and colour the elaborate collar of the pink satin frock which had been partly revealed when she had opened her upper coat buttons lest the shock from her daughter-in-law's disclosure prove too much for her.

Emily Crolly, as she herself had so often pointed out to others, had an upbringing far more sheltered and genteel than anyone could possibly imagine and because of this she was liable to be weakened or even overcome by stories of an unpleasant nature. Nevertheless, she managed to survive the unhappy experience of having to subject herself to such a gross tale and even allowed herself to be beguiled later into accepting a second helping of the choice roast lamb in which the Trallock Arms specialised. The Crollys, father and son, were directors of the hotel and lunched there at every opportunity. It was rumoured that the other Crolly sons were also directors although it was believed that the manager, Tony Munley, only son of Estelle and Mickey Munley of Hillview Row, held a majority of the shares.

Tom Tierney, principal of Trallock Boys' School, heard the news from his wife Rita at three thirty in the afternoon.

239

'Whelan has been a scandal for many a day,' he told her. 'I don't know why the Canon puts up with him; why, he's even tolerated by the Gaelic football club, he's even allowed to be an officer of that club when everybody knows he's attended rugby games.'

Mother Columba did not hear of the Dirrabeg raid until late in the day. One of the older sisters had a chest ailment and seemed to be feverish and at five o'clock Columba rang for Joe O'Dell. After a lengthy examination of the ailing sister he wrote out a prescription and suggested that she be transported by ambulance to the Bon Secours in Cork without further delay. While they awaited the ambulance Joe related all he knew to the Reverend Mother.

'There's one thing about Columba,' he had once told his wife, 'you can tell her what you like and nobody will ever hear a word. She is the best listener in the parish.'

Columba listened as Joe O'Dell's tale unfolded itself. His was a true account, having been received first-hand from Fred Halpin.

'I can see Minnie Halpin clearly,' Columba smiled but she did not laugh, 'but as for Bluenose, there is nobody could win an argument with him. I tried a few times. He used to supply the convent with milk in the old days. It was good milk and Bluenose was honest enough. He'll never get over the shame of this.'

'The Canon had an infernal neck to go out there at all,' Joe O'Dell said.

'Of course, there is the question of arriving drunk to mass,' Columba said pensively.

'You know and I know,' Joe O'Dell told her, 'that he doesn't like competition, and that's how he views the wrenboys. Estelle Munley threw a party last night. It finished up at five in the morning. I know because I was there. How come Canon Tett didn't put in an appearance there?'

'There's no use in asking me,' Columba put in at once, 'I'm

240

not in the man's confidence.'

'He knows who to bully,' Joe O'Dell told her. 'Estelle Munley's Christmas dues would amount to more than the whole of the Dirrabeg contributions together. Our Canon, for all his alleged fearlessness, knows where to bark and where not to bark.'

Columba did not learn until the following day that Katie Hallapy and her brothers, Tom and Johnny, were present at Bluenose's at one thirty in the morning when the Canon and Father Donlea made their appearance. Word would eventually get about and it certainly wouldn't do Katie any good. There would be certain pious parents who might look askance at the idea of her enrolment. To them the wrendance was a debauch, a reflection on the parish and a cause for serious concern. Had not the Canon himself denounced such evil practices from the pulpit? Columba knew that the Canon would not condone the enrolment either. He might not say so in so many words but he would strongly disapprove. All too often he had hinted that service in a strict home was the best education for girls with dubious backgrounds.

'Or let 'em off to England altogether,' he once declared to Columba after she had accepted a girl from a troublesome family. Fortunately, as far as Columba was concerned, the Canon had no control over the secondary schools of the parish. He was, however, manager of the Convent Primary School just as he was of the primary schools in Trallock and Dirrabeg.

Columba was seriously worried for Katie Hallapy. There might be no open representations made but general disapproval would be made abundantly clear from the moment of Katie's enrolment. What of Katie herself? Would she be thick-skinned enough to endure the slights and the rebuffs of girls with so-called impeccable backgrounds or would she, like so many others, throw in the towel when the ever so carefully concealed taunting and cold-shouldering became unbearable? Some of it would be unintentional but some girls might be so manifestly

241

patronising that open hostility would be preferable. She might be lucky and find herself being championed by one or more of the more influential characters in her class but whether she was or not it would be up to her in the long run to establish herself. The first months would be crucial. If she survived the first term she would survive the second. There was the danger too of imagined slights. Columba had known girls who took umbrage at everything, at the way other girls looked at them or spoke to them. They saw something sinister in even the most well-meaning overtures.

Curse the wrendance! Katie's presence there at so late an hour might well prove to be an obstacle too many on a course where there were adequate hazards already.

Father Alphonsus Donlea returned to the presbytery in the middle of the afternoon. He had spent the intervening hours wandering through the countryside in a state of extreme distress. In the beginning, despite the fact that he had no overcoat and that the biting easterly wind was at its most penetrating, he felt no cold. When eventually he was overtaken by the first shower of sleet he found himself several miles from the presbytery. He turned for home and for the first time he began to appreciate the wintriness of the afternoon. As he proceeded towards Trallock he swung his hands violently to keep himself warm. He chided himself for having neglected to bring an overcoat. He contemplated the idea of seeking shelter in one of the numerous cottages and farmhouses on his way but because there was nobody visible near any of these abodes he decided against. He imagined the shock and embarrassment of a rustic householder at the sight of a coatless priest, wet to the skin. As he walked he grew weaker and there were times when he staggered like a drunken man. Always, however, he forged ahead, his heavy drenched garments chafing against his flesh. He was very nearly exhausted when a van drew up alongside.

'Are you going to town, Father?' the query came from Faithful Ferg who had spent the morning scouring the countryside for

242

cabbage, a commodity which was always in short supply during the mid-winter period.

'Throw that around you, Father,' Ferg handed his passenger an old potato sack. 'It will do until you get home and change.'

'That's very kind of you,' Father Donlea managed to reply between chattering teeth. 'I don't think we've met,' he said after he had taken stock of his benefactor.

'Oh God help us Father!' Ferg laughed submissively, 'where would we meet and me only a penny-ha'penny shopkeeper stuck on the side of a laneway. I seen you alright. I attended your mass and I heard your sermon. If people took what you said to heart, Father, it would be a better world. I often wonder how poor people like myself manage to shoulder our burdens at all with thieves and rogues at every side of us.'

Father Donlea could express only token acknowledgement of Ferg's disingenuous lamentation. He had never felt such cold in his life. It numbed his very senses.

'That was a mighty night's work yourself and the Canon did last night, Father.' Ferg was obliged to repeat the commendation. Father Donlea found it difficult to extract himself from his icy reverie. All feeling had gone from his feet.

'What did you say about last night?' He forced himself to concentrate. It would be churlish indeed if he did not tender his full attention to this Good Samaritan who had plucked him from the wilderness.

'The wrendance, Father,' Ferg reminded him.

'Oh that!' Father Donlea frowned, his mind temporarily taken away from the awful cold to which his aching body had almost surrendered.

'It took great courage, Father.' Ferg insisted on lavishing praise where he felt it was due. 'There's honest, hard-working people down on their knees this day that's more than beholden to yourself and Canon Tett. There are men and women who'll never forget the good and faithful priests who struck a blow against drunkenness and debauchery and God knows what else.

243

You'll go down in history Father.'

'I hope not.' Father Donlea's rebuttal was seen by Ferg as a gesture of self-effacement.

'You'll be remembered for it, Father, when a lot of other things are long forgot.'

'Oh no!' The tearful disassociation made Ferg all the more determined that Father Donlea should not be so dismissive of his achievements of the early morning.

'I'll tell you something, Father,' Ferg grew confidential as they drove into the square of Trallock, 'and it's as true as there's cabbages in those bags behind your back. Yourself and Canon Tett will go down as the men who purified Dirrabeg. By God you'll hear no bodhráns there tonight Father and you'll hear no bodhráns there for many a night to come. Sure, they hadn't a nanny goat left in the countryside between the lot of 'em. They'll come sober to mass from now on too and it's yourself and the Canon that must be thanked. There's many will talk and there's more will threaten but it takes the clergy to take the bull by the horns. You know, Father, I was often nearly stunk out of my pew by the smell of stale porter the morning after a wrendance. I saw a woman faint one morning after she was overcome by the fumes of stale drink. Is it true, Father, the Canon excommunicated them?'

Faithful Ferg did not wait for a reply. His thoughts turned, as they had been doing a lot lately, to Daisy Fleece. She had been in the shop the evening of the wrendance with Kitty Smiley. Two fine things they were to be sure and the shameful way they were going to waste. Half the bloody country must be lambasting that Fleece one and, of course, the Smiley one was not going to let herself go short. Whatever possessed Willie Smiley to leave a bird like that!

Father Donlea sat with his face in his hands, his head bent, his frame shuddering.

'Here we are Father and if you take my advice you'll swallow a good jorum of punch before you go to your bed.'

'Thank you, my good man. Thank you indeed.' The words were shattered and indistinct as they left his mouth. The praise to which he had been subjected had added to the aches which racked him all over. He had scarcely the strength to turn the door handle of the van. The key of the presbytery door fell from his hand as he tried to insert it. He was obliged to crawl on his knees before he found it in the wet grass next to the footpath. Safely indoors he heaved a pain-filled sigh of relief. In the distance he heard Nora Devane's voice. It came from far, far away, although as far as he could see she was standing at the kitchen door. She wanted to know if he had eaten. Rather than enter a debate on the matter he nodded his head silently and went upstairs slowly.

'You'd want to get out o' them duds quick, Father,' Nora Devane called after him.

In his room he stripped every stitch from his trembling body. Unable to stand he sat on the side of the bed and with the greatest difficulty managed to pull on his pyjamas. In the bed the cold would not go away. He drew the clothes over his head. His agitation was now so great that even the bed shook noisily. He began to tremble uncontrollably. It was in this condition that Father Butt found him an hour later. He rang at once for the doctor. Joe O'Dell was curt and noncommittal after concluding a hasty examination.

'Get that housekeeper to bring some warm blankets and fetch a pair of slippers for his feet.'

Father Butt hastened to carry out the doctor's orders.

'What's all the furore?' It was the Canon's voice. He had tiptoed noiselessly up the stairs after hearing Father Butt's ultimatum to Nora Devane.

'We have a sick man on our hands, Canon,' Joe O'Dell informed him. 'He needs oxygen. I'm taking him to hospital.'

'Where?' the Canon asked, his tone showing concern for once.

'I'm afraid Trallock General will have to do, Canon. I doubt

245

if he'd survive any kind of journey just now.'

'Oh the poor fellow!' The Canon peered closely at his curate. 'He was always delicate you know,' he informed Joe O'Dell. 'As far as I know he had T.B. for years.'

'Your curate has lobar pneumonia, Canon.' There was considerable apprehension in Joe O'Dell's voice.

Sixteen

CANON TETT LOOKED out the kitchen window at the driving snow. The flakes sped westwards as though pursued by some horrific enemy whose sole aim was to consume them. Some dawdled and postured in the vicinity of the window, their flight arrested by the shelter provided at the southern side of the presbytery. Some fell to the ground, others attached themselves to the window and melted but most rejoined the fleeing multitudes after a brief sojourn in the wind-suspended haven near the window.

Canon Tett was no lover of snow. He could admire its pearly patterns on the summits of the distant hills or watch it contentedly from a sheltered place but he hated its cold. Frost he could accept without question. He regarded frosty weather as healthy weather conducive to brisk walks and related exercises. He could tolerate rain. Nothing the matter with rain provided you had a good umbrella but snow was different, especially snow driven by an easterly wind as it was now. It brought with it the kind of cold that penetrated the imperceptible slits and chinks so common to ancient doors and windows. No barrier was proof against its infiltration and no matter how many pairs of socks or how redoubtable the boots he wore the cold would overrun his toes and remain firmly entrenched there even in bed when each foot was provided with a specially prepared hot water bottle by Nora Devane.

247

From its dawn the day had been otherwise depressing as well. Father Butt had been absent since eight o'clock and it was now twelve thirty in the day. The presbytery had been inundated with sick calls from early morning. At eight the Canon had received a call from Joe O'Dell: Father Donlea had been removed by ambulance to Cork city; there was no change in his condition.

He placed the blame for his curate's illness fairly and squarely on the Dirrabeg porter ball at which Father Donlea had arrived without either coat or hat, plain for all to see. The Canon had conveniently forgotten, although fully informed by his housekeeper, that Father Donlea had arrived at the presbytery on Sunday afternoon drenched to the skin and barely able to support himself.

'Of course he couldn't support himself,' the Canon agreed with her, 'how could he and he out at all hours last night, one of the coldest nights of the year without cap or coat in the course of his parochial duties. Those wretches in Dirrabeg are as much responsible for the poor man's condition as anything else. He was never a hardy fellow but he would persist in going. All he had to say was that he didn't want to go. I'm a reasonable man. There's no one will deny that. The reason I didn't take Father Butt was because I thought him better equipped for night calls. It wouldn't do to have a man with Donlea's health going out on night calls, especially this time of year.'

'I never seen you do anything but what was proper, Canon,' Nora Devane assured him.

Father Butt arrived back at the presbytery at one o'clock. His lunch consisted of boiled beef, parsnips and potatoes. There had been a tolerable soup beforehand but the beef was predominantly fat and the parsnips would have been more palatable if they had been dressed. For all that because he was ravenous with the hunger he made the most of it. At one of his calls he had snatched time for a cup of tea and was grateful for the fact that the woman of the house insisted on lacing it with

248

whiskey left after Christmas.

'Wasn't it terrible about Dirrabeg, Father,' she said in a shocked tone.

'Oh it was, it was,' he threw back rather than waste time contradicting her.

'And they say poor Father Donlea is knocked out after it, Father.'

'News travels fast,' he told himself as he finished the tea.

'And how is he now, Father?'

'He's not well at all missus,' he replied as he had been replying all morning.

'I'll pray for him, Father.'

'I'm sure you will missus. Prayer is about the best thing now.'

In the car he frowned as he remembered his conversation with Joe O'Dell. He had made a hasty call to the doctor's residence in Hillview Row before leaving Trallock.

'I've sent him to Cork, Father. I've just been on to the Canon, not that I needed his permission but I made the gesture out of courtesy. Father Donlea, as you know, has lobar pneumonia, not too bad in itself but his medical history is against him. I had him on oxygen and antibiotics but Cork will provide more intensive care and they'll have somebody specialising in this sort of thing. You believe in prayer, Father, and maybe there's something to it. I'd suggest to you that you pray as you never prayed before because the situation is dicey.'

'What's your personal opinion, Joe?' Father Butt asked anxiously.

'It's out of my hands. All I can say to you is that where there's life there's hope.'

Joe O'Dell placed a hand on the curate's shoulder. 'You mustn't blame yourself. It would have happened anyway, sooner or later.'

'I know. I know.' Father Butt's tone was contrite. 'But no matter what anybody says I must take part of the blame. I promised I'd look out for him and now this happens.'

Before Joe O'Dell could tender a word of consolation Father Butt was gone.

It was Nora Devane who brought word of the Dirrabeg defections as Canon Tett was later to describe them when he corresponded with the retreat master of the Orvertian Fathers in Belfast. As usual Nora Devane's sources were impeccable. What transpired was that a number of the male members of the Dirrabeg Wren had not presented themselves at any of the masses in Trallock Parish Church on the Sunday following the disrupted wrendance. To make matters worse it was widely known in Dirrabeg that they would not be attending mass until further notice.

'What of the women?' Canon Tett had asked.

'Oh, the women is all right, Canon,' Nora Devane assured him. 'Every solitary one of 'em was there and so were the children.' According to Nora Devane the Dirrabeg women resorted to the wearing of shawls rather than be recognised and humiliated by the respectable people of the parish.

The most noteworthy aspect of the Dirrabeg defection was the fact that it was not organised. In the Hallapy household Nellie was first out of bed. The time was half past eight. If they hurried they would be just in time for ten o'clock mass in Trallock. She called the children first, then Donal. Despite the fact that he was only four hours in bed he sat up instantly and ran his fingers through his greying hair.

By common agreement the wrendance had ended at four o'clock. There had been neither music nor dancing after Canon Tett's departure. Those who remained had seated themselves around the fire. There were important matters to be decided. There was, for instance, the question of the two untapped firkins of porter and the spare provisions from the second sitting which had been abandoned.

Fred Halpin agreed to take back the firkins. They could be surrendered at cash value or they might be drank in his pub, each wrenboy and buy-in to be allotted his fair share, to be drunk at his convenience. The latter proposal was found to be the more acceptable. Of the one hundred and twenty-eight pints of porter to be disposed of each man would receive five pints. Martin Semple volunteered to bring the firkins home in the boot of his taxi.

Of the three remaining barm bracks the Rings and the Hallapys were presented with one each. Each, it transpired, was also entitled to a half pound of butter. Before the party broke up Delia Bluenose retained one barm brack but distributed two heaped platefuls of pig's cheek amongst those who remained.

Patsy Oriel had slipped away quietly shortly after the Canon and Father Donlea had taken their leave. As he cycled over the white, moonlit road he took the pipe from his mouth and broke into song. The song he sang was a local one which told of the plight of a young man whose sweetheart was forbidden by her heartless parents to honour a tryst with him. In spite of this she stole from her bedroom when the moon rode high and in nothing but her nightdress ran across the dewy fields of buttercups and daisies to where her true love awaited her in a ripening meadow by a clear stream which flowed through her father's verdant acres.

The Hallapy children breakfasted well on the Sunday morning. The barm brack was a rare treat and for once there was an abundance of butter with nobody calling for moderation. Nellie sat on the side of the bed trying to prevail upon Donal to accompany herself and the children to mass.

'My mind is made up,' he told her before turning into the wall and drawing the clothes over his head.

'Aren't you getting up at all today young man?' Delia Bluenose dragged the bedclothes from over her sleeping husband. Bluenose sat up in the bed at once and rubbed his eyes.

'What's the matter with you now?' he called out peevishly feeling for the blanket which had fallen to the floor.

'Mass is what's up with me you horrid old pagan. Pull on your trousers now and let us be going. You have a pony to

251

tackle.'

'I'll pull on my trousers all right,' he informed her, 'but it won't be to go to mass, not while that oul' scoundrel is wearin' vestments.'

'Oh, come on!' Delia Bluenose begged, 'the mass is all we have to keep us clear of the devil.'

'Well, I'd prefer the devil to the likes of him that was here last night. I'll tackle the pony for you but don't expect me to go with you.'

Rubawrd was first up in the Ring household. He spread the ashes over the floor of the hearth and chose a number of small, glowing coals to re-start the fire. He broke the large turf sods into smaller pieces with his gnarled hands and laid them by the sides and on top of the coals. In minutes he had blown the smoking heap into bright flame. He hung the large iron kettle from the lower arm of the crane. Soon it would be boiling. From the doorway of the bedroom he addressed his wife.

'Make your own arrangements for mass,' he said. 'I won't be going.'

'Very well.' Kit Ring raised herself on the bed, her face filled with questioning.

'I'll take the double barrel,' he said solemnly, 'and I'll spend the day fowling. I'll see to the cows first.'

'What about your breakfast?'

'I couldn't bear the sight of food just now.'

'And is that why you're not going to mass?'

'No. The reason I feel the way I do is because I have a sick head from all the booze of last night and this morning. The reason I'm not going to mass is that my heart would not be in it, not after last night.'

Paddy and Timmie Costigan slept in adjoining rooms. They awakened at exactly the same time. Timmie called out to his brother to enquire which mass he might be attending.

'No mass for me today my brother,' he called back. 'You go if you wish but let me out of it.'

252

Timmie Costigan lay in his bed, undecided. If Paddy did not want to go to mass that was Paddy's business. Still, they had always acted in concert. After due consideration he revised his earlier ruling. If Paddy did not want to go to mass it was also his brother's business. He was his brother's keeper and how could he keep him unless he was in his company? He decided not to attend mass either.

Mossie Gilooley the fiddler advised his wife Gertie of his decision not to go to mass just as they were about to mount their bicycles.

'I cannot go,' he said. 'I wouldn't give those townie beggars the satisfaction of inspecting me.'

'And will you be going next Sunday?' she asked concernedly.

'They'll have to change Canons,' he replied, 'before the fiddler goes to mass again.'

'You'll be damned entirely,' Gertie Gilooley warned.

'That may be,' he answered resignedly, 'but for the present there's no devotions for the fiddler.'

Seven other members of the Dirrabeg wren absented themselves from the holy sacrament of the mass on the Sunday after the wrendance. This brought the number of defectors to thirteen.

It was Faithful Ferg who informed Nora Devane about the wholesale absenteeism from church. His suspicions were aroused when only the Dirrabeg females appeared to make their small purchases after ten o'clock mass. The Dirrabeg women would normally hang around the shop clutching their possessions until their menfolk arrived from the Bus Bar after a hasty pint or two; if the weather was fine they would stand in groups around the door.

On this morning there was no loitering, indoor or out. The women of Dirrabeg disappeared immediately their business was transacted. Their speedy departure was a loss to Ferg. Neither they nor their children ever stooped to shoplifting and Ferg found that he could relax while they were on the premises.

253

There was a time when the needier would ask him for credit, especially during the winter months. There were occasions when he had almost relented and he felt well and truly vindicated for not doing so. They were still his customers whereas if he had extended credit he would probably have lost them forever. Neither had any of them starved to death. They had turned up Sunday after Sunday as hale and hearty as ever. They never bought anything but the bare necessities except on isolated occasions when they might invest in a package of jelly or a pot of mixed fruit jam.

The snow was still drifting before a slackening east wind when Nora Devane announced that Master Whelan had arrived. The Canon stood with his back to the kitchen range. It was the only place where he found himself capable of keeping the cold completely at bay.

'What'll I tell him Canon?'

'Go about your business now like a good woman,' the Canon answered brusquely. 'I'll see to Master Whelan in my own good time.'

He looked at his watch. Whelan would have arrived from school at least a quarter of an hour ago. No doubt, the Canon thought to himself, he went to the Bus Bar to fortify himself before coming here. His likes always needed strong drink before facing up to unpleasantness. From where he stood the Canon could hear the stamping of the teacher's feet on the tiles of the draughty hallway. Then there came the clapping of gloved hands. In spite of the whiskey the fellow was still cold. Let him wait another bit. The Canon could not have been further out in his assessment of Monty Whelan's after-school movements. The Dirrabeg assistant had driven to Trallock by the most roundabout route which was through Upper Dirrabeg. He too had decided to keep his adversary waiting.

The Canon's thoughts had been taken up, before Monty Whelan's arrival, with devising suitable punishments for the schismatics of Dirrabeg. He saw them, in his mind's eye, as

254

Assyrians descending on the gentle fold of Christianity, his fold. He found himself reciting an almost forgotten stanza:

The Assyrian came down like a wolf on the fold
And his cohorts were gleaming in purple and gold.
The sheen of their spears was like stars on the sea
When the blue wave rolls nightly on deep Galilee.

Byron might be flawed as a man and as a Christian but by God he could write ringing poetry! Nora Devane looked up from the kitchen table in alarm when the Canon's voice rose to deliver two of the most appropriate lines in the poem as far as he was concerned:

But the Angel of Death spread his wings on the blast
And breathed in the face of the foe as he passed.

Oh, for the divine powers of that particular angel! Canon Tett never felt more in need of a numinous transfusion. Here he was about to face a most evil and formidable satellite of Satan himself whilst abroad in Dirrabeg and who knows where else in the countryside there was the makings of a second Sodom and Gomorrah with one of his curates lying at death's door whilst the other was too crafty and too weak-kneed to stand up and be counted.

'I might be alone,' Canon Tett addressed himself out loud to the ceiling, oblivious of the presence of Nora Devane, 'but God is by my side now and forevermore.'

'Follow me,' the Canon spoke brusquely as he led the way to his study, a tiny room on the second floor. Monty Whelan followed silently, his heart thumping so violently that he feared a seizure at any moment.

'Sit here,' the Canon indicated a rickety bamboo chair, one of two at either side of a table cluttered with religious tracts and pamphlets. Monty had never before set foot in this part of the presbytery. Taking the seat he took off his gloves and placed them in his overcoat pocket.

255

'Now!' the Canon opened, 'I will not beat about the bush, Mister Whelan. What I have to say is just as distressing for me as it will be for you. I have given the matter lengthy thought and I am now quite convinced that there is no other option open to me. On the day the school closed for the Christmas break was there a woman in your classroom?'

Monty did not answer at once. He decided to parry the question, thus forcing the Canon into posing a second question and maybe revealing the strength of his hand.

'My principal Ciss Fenley was in the classroom but only for a few moments Canon.'

'I'm sure Miss Fenley had good cause to be in your classroom, Mister Whelan, but I'm not talking about her. Now tell me was there any other woman in the classroom?'

'Yes,' Monty Whelan answered looking the Canon in the eye, 'and just like Miss Fenley she too had good cause to be there.'

'Who was she?' the Canon asked truculently.

'You already know who she is, Canon, so I don't see the point in this game of cat and mouse.'

'Suit yourself, Mister Whelan, but let me tell you that you were seen to have had your way with a married woman in the sacred precincts of Dirrabeg National School.'

'Have had my way!' Monty scoffed. 'If kissing and embracing a woman is having one's way then that is what I was doing and if a National School classroom may be described as a sacred precinct then what you say is true.'

'So you admit it!' The Canon leaped from his chair and slapped the table with his right hand. Tracts and pamphlets flew all over the room. A mottled cloud of dust ascended from beneath the disturbed foliage.

'I admit nothing,' Monty was also on his feet, 'except that I kissed a woman and embraced her in the empty classroom of Dirrabeg school after that school was closed. The woman was there by my invitation. I chanced to meet her on the roadway

256

and asked her in from the rain.'

'Who are you trying to fool?' the Canon shouted. 'You say you chanced to meet her as though you had not been meeting her before. Well, my fine fellow, I happen to have proof that you met Mrs Fleece, a married woman, several times in your home before that shameful day in Dirrabeg.'

'And what about it?' Monty Whelan shouted back. 'I'll meet whoever I damn well please, where I please and whenever I please without permission from you or from anybody else.'

'Oh no you won't you scoundrel. You won't meet any loose women in my school, not while I'm school manager you won't. You will not corrupt my schoolchildren in the sacred place which has been set aside for their education and for no other purpose but their education. Do you think I am going to tolerate fornication in that special place to which both the state and the Church has appointed me guardian. I am the custodian of every child that passes through the portals of the parochial schools.'

'I don't deny that,' Monty cut in savagely, 'but I'll have you in court and take what you have if you mention the word fornication in relation to me or to Daisy Fleece ever again.'

'What you will take out of here this evening will be very little indeed my fine fellow.' The Canon sat down smiling. Monty also sat. When the Canon spoke again his tone was softer. He thrust his hands into his trousers pockets and extended his long legs at either side of the table. He allowed several minutes to elapse before resuming the offensive.

'Now, Mister Whelan, here is what I propose. You will resign your position as assistant teacher at Dirrabeg National School. There is no great hurry. You can give me a month's notice.' The Canon pressed his index finger to the salmon-like extremity of his pointed jaw. 'A month's notice would be just about right. That way I'll be able to give you a reference. It will be a good reference although you don't deserve it. You needn't worry on that score. I'll make no reference to anything but

257

your teaching record. A fellow like you would have no bother getting a job in Dublin now or even England where they're crying out for teachers.'

Monty Whelan sat dumbfounded, unable to believe his ears as the Canon unravelled his plans for the future. There could be no denying that he had given the matter considerable thought.

'Before you go any further,' Monty suddenly interrupted the Canon's genial outflow, 'I may as well tell you that I have no notion of resigning. Get that into your head once and for all. I have done nothing wrong, nothing that I need be in the least ashamed of, so unless you have something further to add I'll be on my way.'

'You'll be on your way all right, Mister Whelan, on your way out that door and out of Dirrabeg school for good.'

'You have no such power,' Monty's voice registered its first trace of doubt.

'As you well know,' Canon Tett spoke more authoritatively than at any stage during the interview, 'I have the sole power of hiring and firing teachers in all of the parochial schools. I am the school manager and reserve the exclusive right above all others to hire and fire.'

'Yes. Yes,' Monty Whelan was forced to concede, 'the school manager has the right to hire and fire but without justifiable cause the school manager is just chasing his tail.'

'Well now, Mister Whelan, I'm sorry indeed that you should force me to declare the other option open to us. Unless you resign I will be left with no alternative but to fire you.'

'This is ridiculous!' Monty Whelan was becoming less sure of his ground. The Canon cleared his throat and rubbed his hands together before launching into another assault, this time from new ground.

'Would you be so good as to tell me, Mister Whelan,' he asked unctuously, 'what absentees you had from your class this fine Spring day?'

258

'Absentees!' Monty echoed the word in bewilderment. What was the old fool driving at now?

'Come on Mister Whelan, the name or names of the absentees from school today?' The Canon sat back further in his chair, his hands now extracted from his pockets and cradled behind his head as he awaited the information which he had solicited. Monty Whelan bent his head thoughtfully, his teeth tentatively touching the knuckles of his left hand as he sought to remember who might have been absent.

'There was only one absentee,' he recalled.

'And pray, what was her name?' The Canon was on his feet, hands now joined behind his back, a more magisterial approach to his interrogation.

'I believe it was one of the Drillies,' Monty Whelan revealed the information reluctantly wondering what new card the Canon had up his sleeve.

'It was indeed one of the Drillies,' the Canon confirmed, 'a daughter of Mickey and Rosie Drillie, a fine pair of honest, hardworking people God bless them. And did Mary Drillie's sisters not tell you why she was absent Mister Whelan?'

'I believe they said something about her having to go to town with her mother.'

'Exactly so,' Canon Tett corroborated, 'it was indeed something about her having to go to town and where do you think she went as soon as she landed into town? Would you care to take a shot at guessing her destination?'

'I have no idea, Canon.'

'She came here to me. The poor child hasn't been the same since she saw you and Mrs Fleece together on that awful day before Christmas. She told her mother of what she had seen as soon as she arrived home and the poor mother out of a false sense of loyalty to you, Mister Whelan, decided to say no more about it until her conscience got the better of her and she came here with her daughter. Young Mary Drillie saw you through the school window kissing and embracing Mrs Fleece. She

259

became frightened and ran off behind the school wall with another little girl, the wrenboy's daughter Moira Ring. They remained in hiding in fear and terror until yourself and Mrs Fleece left the school.'

Monty Whelan sat ashen-faced and speechless. What the Canon said was probably true. There had been scurrying sounds which could have been made by children. He had looked over the school wall but he had not looked down. It had been no more than a cursory glance. Now that he reflected on the matter there could indeed have been children hiding under his very nose. On a few occasions he had seen the younger girls peering inwards into the classroom after school. This time he had not noticed. He had been too preoccupied with his visitor.

'I haven't made contact as yet with the Ring girl but if you force me into doing so I will certainly interview her and hear what she has to say if she hasn't already been cautioned by her parents to deny all knowledge of the matter.'

'All they saw, if they saw anything or if they were there at all, was a simple embrace and an innocent kiss.'

'An innocent kiss!' The Canon fumed, 'an innocent kiss between a married woman and a single man. There can't be such a thing. What they saw was a passionate kiss and a lecherous embrace, the prelude to God knows what, the prelude to something so awful that the poor children ran off to hide themselves.'

The Canon pursed his lips, pressed his chin with his index finger and spoke in a matter-of-fact tone.

'There's no hurry with the resignation. Write it out sometime during the next few days and drop it in here to me or if you like put it in an envelope and post it to me. I'll notify the Department of Education and they'll be in touch with you regarding your gratuity and pension. If you ask me you're getting off lightly. I will, of course, have to notify the bishop but I don't think he will consider taking any further proceedings against you, not when I tell him you resigned without protest.'

260

Monty Whelan sat motionless scarcely able to believe that he was surrendering so abjectly. Although the Canon might exaggerate he had unwittingly scandalised two young girls. There could be no doubt about that. The honourable thing to do, under the circumstances, would be to resign. Monty also surmised that the Canon had not been bluffing when he threatened to fire him. The more he thought about it the less secure his position appeared. The story was certain to spread and spreading would be embellished and distorted so that remaining on at the school, even if he were permitted to do so, would be out of the question.

'I think that's about all, Mister Whelan.' The Canon was standing at the doorway of the study, his right hand indicating that Monty should precede him to the foot of the stairs where it so happened Nora Devane was most industriously dusting the banisters. She had heard most of the exchanges and she could always give her imagination free rein when it came to filling in the missing pieces.

'Today is Monday,' the Canon was saying, 'if you had it ready by Wednesday it would be a great help.'

'You shall have it tonight, Canon. For obvious reasons I can only give a week's notice.'

'That will suit fine.' The Canon tried hard to smother the chuckles which would reveal his overpowering sense of triumph. At the doorway he stood with his right hand extended. 'Well,' he declared expansively, 'we must now look to the future and try to forget the past. Let us shake hands in God's name.'

'No thank you, Canon,' Monty replied coldly, 'you shall have my resignation but I reserve my hand for those I trust and respect.'

Monty Whelan stood silently for a moment in the doorway and drew on his gloves. He sported what he hoped was a non-chalant look as he moved off. He desperately needed to sit down somewhere. His legs felt like jelly beneath him, his head

261

dizzy, his hands trembling as he emerged from the main entrance to the presbytery. As he walked slowly, carefully measuring every step, he managed to raise his right hand to acknowledge a salute from a passer-by.

In the presbytery hallway the Canon rubbed his hands together and firmly affixed his ancient hat on his head.

'If there's a call I won't be far away,' he informed his housekeeper. 'I'm just going across the square to Crolly's.'

Nora Devane put her duster to one side and folded her hands preparatory to lifting the receiver. She thought of several people all at once. The question was, however, who was the worthiest as well as being the most likely to be of worthwhile assistance to Nora in the future. There would be just time for one comprehensive call and no more. She thought of Ciss Fenley but instead settled for Estelle Munley. Estelle was the needier of the two and the information would boost her standing among those she was forever trying to emulate. Off-hand Nora Devane could think of nobody who would be more appreciative. As she was about to lift the receiver the phone rang.

Seventeen

MONTY WHELAN DECIDED to absent himself from the funeral of Father Alphonsus Donlea. The evening before he had attended the ceremony for the reception of the remains over which Bishop Collane had presided. He had tendered his resignation by letter to Canon Tett less than an hour after their fateful altercation in the presbytery. With all the parochial schools closed so that schoolgoers might attend the curate's funeral Monty felt, in one sense, that Father Donlea's demise had been a providential intervention.

There would be nobody to peer or pry while he reclaimed his personal possessions from Dirrabeg National School. He had been tempted to leave them behind but the likelihood would be that the new teacher would have them removed anyway to make way for her own aids.

The transfer from schoolroom to car of his Encyclopedia Britannica alone involved four journeys. The other books accounted for as many more. He decided to leave behind the local maps which should be of considerable interest to the incoming teacher.

Monty knew Angela Crolly to be a somewhat affected young lady who spoke with an accent he could never quite trace to any one source. He had always found it rather grandiose and haughty. He fervently hoped that she would not allow this ridiculous artificiality to spill over into the classroom. The

Dirrabeg scholars would see through her at once and would be less influenced by what she said than her manner of saying it. Schoolchildren were fond of taking off their teachers and it was vitally important, therefore, to preserve an attitude which would not encourage mockery or mimicry. Given the opportunity the children of Dirrabeg would behave like any others.

An overwhelming sense of loss assailed Monty when he stood with his back to the fireplace and gazed down at the rows of empty desks. He had, as yet, given no thought to the future nor had he confided his trauma to Daisy Fleece. He had been tempted to go to her after writing the letter of resignation but he felt afraid she might lay most of the blame on herself. Had she not presaged his present plight from the very beginning of their relationship!

Hands thrust deep in pockets he moved slowly towards the window. Traces of the recent hail and snow were to be seen on the hilltops. The crested plover flocks had broken up and were now moving out in mating pairs from the fields where they had sheltered across the winter. Later they would regroup before embarking on the long passage back to Scandinavia. Their plaintive, puling cries suited his downcast mood. He covered his face with his hands and shook his head at the folly that had brought him to his present pass. Soon, like the plover, he too would be obliged to migrate but, thankfully, no further than England where he would be certain to secure a position as a teacher. He had seen the advertisements in the English Sunday newspapers, the ones he was permitted to read by the Irish censors. He would somehow inveigle Daisy into going with him. If necessary they would bring her mother. He would sell the house in the square, not that he needed the money but he felt it would be best to pull up his roots altogether if they were to have any kind of life in England. It was, he knew only too well, somewhat late in life for the crossing of Rubicons. Still, there was little in Trallock that he would really miss: the Bus Bar, of course, and the Halpins, the Gaelic football and a

264

few select friends.

He would sorely miss Dirrabeg and its people. The children would be an irreparable loss. He would meet with Daisy on the morrow. He would go direct to the house this time. First, however, he would drown his sorrows. He had not drunk for several days. He had realised, after his last meeting with Daisy at the wrendance, that he would make a poor partner if he persisted in drinking as he had been doing, not that she had tried to extract a promise from him or anything like that but he felt he owed it to her to moderate his intake. When the knock sounded on the school door he was on the point of departure.

'Come in,' he called, not knowing who to expect. Bluenose shuffled in followed by Rubawrd Ring and Donal Hallapy. They stood for a moment hangdog at the classroom door.

'Is it true?' The question came from Donal Hallapy. Monty nodded.

'But you did no wrong.'

'Let us not talk about it, Donal. My resignation has been handed in. I am due to finish here at the end of the week but I have, in fact, finished as of now. My possessions are in the boot of the car. I won't be coming back.'

'You're not going without saying goodbye to the children,' Rubawrd Ring pleaded.

'I'm afraid so Rubawrd. I could not face them. You will say my goodbyes for me, all of you. Do that much for me and I will be eternally grateful.'

'But what will you do?' Donal Hallapy asked after they had promised him to see to his pupils. Briefly Monty outlined his plans. As they listened they shook their heads regretfully. After he had finished Donal Hallapy stepped forward, urged on by Bluenose and Rubawrd Ring.

'The people of Dirrabeg don't like what's going on. They're talking of keeping the children from school as a protest.'

'Do that,' Monty said fiercely, 'and the only ones to suffer will be the children.'

265

'The people feel you have been badly wronged,' Donal went on. 'They feel they should do something. Some even spoke of burning the school.'

'My friends,' Monty Whelan laughed. 'I appreciate what you are trying to do but if you want to help me the best thing to do is to convince your children that they must make life easy for their new teacher. If they do that I'll be sure that my time in Dirrabeg wasn't wasted.'

'It's a terrible thing,' Rubawrd Ring protested, 'that a man of your calibre must face for a foreign land while upstarts and rogues rule the roost here at home.'

'We're in a foreign land as it is,' Bluenose corrected him, 'at least those of us that resides in Dirrabeg. We talk a different tongue to the townies of Trallock and they laugh at us for it. They scoff at us and ape us when our backs are turned. We dress different because it suits our way of life and they look down on us for it. It's becoming so that a man with a peaked cap and turned-down wellingtons is now a suspicious character and I wouldn't mind but the fathers and mothers of most of them that mock us were country people themselves. The town does that to people, makes them ashamed of their own, makes copycats out of 'em. They think there's only one world and that's a townies' world. We live in a foreign country, boys. Make no mistake but we're strangers in our own land. Then the priests come out and tell us when to hold our wrendances and when to end them. Did you ever hear the bate of it! They attack us from the altar of God because we play the music that was played by them that went before us and dare we even dance the set dances the way our mothers and fathers danced 'em. The oul' stock of Dirrabeg dare not get drunk for fear the clergy might excommunicate 'em. You'd think the clan of the round collar wanted us out of the place. It's like as if they were ashamed of us. There's nothing for the men and women of Dirrabeg. They'd sooner work in hell than work in Trallock where there's nothing thought of 'em. What would our boys and girls do but for England I ask you. Where would they go but with their caps in their hands begging work from farmers or the girls to Trallock to go into service with jumped-up mistresses not fit to lace their shoes and what about the man of the house that has a path worn to the altar? A Dirrabeg girl would want her legs tied together at night if she hoped to wake up sound in the morning. Don't talk to me about a foreign land. This is it, where we are now, at the bottom of the hills, on the verge of the bog and don't let no one tell you otherwise.'

There was a lengthy silence after Bluenose had said his piece. Finally Monty Whelan spoke.

'You'd make a mighty politician, Bluenose.'

'I forget what a politician looks like,' Bluenose retorted. 'It's so long since I saw one.'

'You know, boys,' Monty Whelan spoke solemnly, 'it was the hand of God that directed you three in that door. There I was in a state of the most diabolical despondence when you came along out of the blue. I had firmly resolved from an early hour this morning that when I finished my chores here I would spend the rest of the day quaffing Fred Halpin's whiskey and stout in his splendid premises in the town square. Yet, I thought to myself, for all its delectability and for all its beneficial effects drinking can, perversely enough, be a very sobering diversion unless one is fortunate enough to have trustworthy friends and companions in his company. As I stood there by the window pondering on my misfortune and wondering where in the world I would find companions of the required calibre, fate intervened and ushered in three noblemen from the heartland of Dirrabeg. If I had been asked in advance to choose three companions for the drinking expedition which I have in mind I declare to God almighty that you would be the three. I'll say no more. Let us be off to the Bus Bar.'

'Our duds aren't right for the town,' Bluenose pointed at his own and his comrades' clothes.

'And since when,' Monty asked pointedly, 'did Bluenose

267

Herrity concern himself about what townspeople might think of his clothes?'

'We're not all that well fixed financially you know,' Rubawrd Ring reminded him.

'Do you suppose I don't know that? This session, my friends, is to be on me.'

'Well, now,' Donal Hallapy put in his piece, 'it needn't be all on you for we are not without some credit in Trallock. Remember that we have, each of us, yourself included Monty, five and a half pints of stout or its equivalent in whiskey coming to us in the Bus Bar from the night of the wrendance. It's there waiting to be drunk and I have in my pocket the sum of eight shillings so that we are not exactly paupers.'

'I have a pound note,' Bluenose boasted proudly, 'and there's plenty at home if that isn't enough.'

'That settles it then,' Monty rubbed his hands together in anticipation.

'What about the curate's funeral?' Rubawrd Ring asked.

'He's well buried by now,' Bluenose replied, 'man dear, it's three o'clock in the day.'

'What about notifying our womenfolk?' Rubawrd asked.

'We'll meet the scholars on their way home from the funeral,' Donal told him. 'They'll do the job for us. That way there won't be any need for explanations until we arrive home.'

'Would it not be as well,' Rubawrd Ring added, 'if they were also to inform the Costigans and Mossie Gilooley.'

'Very well,' Donal Hallapy agreed, 'and what about Patsy Oriel? He's a man could use a day out.'

'All right,' Rubawrd Ring conceded, 'but we don't want too many. It's not a hooley we're having, just a farewell drink. Let the others of the wrendance drink their share whenever it suits them. I'm sure they'll find causes just as we found one now. There's always something or at least that's my experience of the world and just when you think there's nothing that's the very time the something turns up.'

'Yes,' Bluenose agreed, 'but the bother is that it could be a bad thing as well as a good thing.'

'Well, it's a good thing this time round,' Rubawrd returned.

'Indeed it is,' Bluenose endorsed, 'a man is surely entitled to more than his diet and his sleep and his woman, especially in the height of winter when there's nothing much to do.'

In the car Bluenose found himself with the globe of the world in his lap.

'Whereabouts are we here?' he asked Rubawrd Ring. Rubawrd lifted the globe and spun it slowly before placing a black-nailed, thorn-pocked index finger on the south-west of Ireland.

'Here's where we are,' he said authoritatively.

'Where?' Bluenose asked, peering in vain at the area pin-pointed by Rubawrd.

'There!' Rubawrd placed Bluenose's index finger under his own. 'Right there.'

'I don't see anything,' Bluenose said sadly. 'I wonder if we're really there at all. Eh, Master?'

'Hard to say,' Monty Whelan replied.

'Maybe,' said Bluenose, 'we only think we're there. Then if we are there and can't see ourselves because we're so small what's all the bloody fuss about! It's enough to drive a man to drink.'

'You never needed anything to drive you to drink,' Rubawrd chided gently. 'All your life you were pointed in that direction. All you had to do was follow your nose.'

When Canon Tett heard the news of Father Donlea's death he made immediate contact with Cork. He might have recalled Father Butt who had resumed his itinerary of sick calls after lunch but he felt that his curate would be more profitably employed attending to the needs of the living rather than the dead. He summoned his parish clerk instead. Shamie Deale

269

was an acknowledged expert in funeral preparations. The Canon provided him with the necessary details. His next step was to inform the bishop. Doctor Collane was most sympathetic.

'It was to be expected,' he informed the Canon, 'but it was his most devout wish to get back in harness and I didn't have the heart to deny him.'

'You did the right thing, my Lord, as you always do,' the Canon concurred and went on to tell the bishop of the circumstances surrounding the curate's death. He repeated his belief that it was the visit to the Dirrabeg wrendance that had softened the way for the lobar pneumonia which was to take its deathly toll. Then, apologising profusely for bringing the matter up at such a time, the Canon told of Monty Whelan's resignation and the reasons which led up to it.

'You did right to tell me,' the bishop assured him, 'and from what you tell me it would appear that you distinguished yourself in getting that resignation. Imagine the scandal if the fellow refused and entered into litigation. The parish would never live it down.'

'It will be hard enough to live down what has happened already, my Lord, and what is likely to happen in the future.'

'Is there more?' the bishop asked in alarm.

'Alas yes, my Lord,' Canon Tett reluctantly informed him and proceeded to describe the recent defections. He also gave it as his considered opinion that the transgressors would continue to stay away from mass.

'Then you know what you must do,' the bishop's tone was angry now.

'I will do whatever is necessary, my Lord. Have you anything in mind?'

The bishop cleared his throat in order to emphasise the gravity of the situation.

'Since you have asked for my advice, my dear Canon, you shall have it with a heart and a half although I would not

270

presume for a moment that I am fit to offer a man of your vast experience advice in the first place.'

The Canon acknowledged the compliment by tut-tutting deprecatorily.

'It would seem to me,' the bishop spoke solemnly, 'that what you require here is a mission and not just an ordinary mission but a mission which will rock the parish of Trallock to its very foundations. I know just the boys for the job. Mind you, I would not recommend them in ordinary circumstances but since desperate ills require desperate remedies we have no other choice.'

'To whom are you referring, my Lord?' Canon Tett's curiosity needed to be satisfied quickly.

'The Orvertian Fathers are the missioners to whom I refer, my dear Canon, and you may take it from me that when they are finished with Trallock, or more particularly with the town-land of Dirrabeg, your parishioners will be as pure as the driven snow.'

'Cost!'

'Cost!' Bishop Collane echoed the word to show that he sought clarification.

'I want to know how much they are going to cost,' the Canon almost shouted the question into the mouthpiece.

'How long since you have had a mission in Trallock?' the bishop asked, a more business-like tone entering his voice.

'There has been an annual retreat,' the Canon recalled, 'since I came but we have never had a mission in the parish during my time here.'

'Then, my dear Canon, you cannot be expected to be aware of the fact that a mission will more than pay for its cost. Can I take it you will be contacting the Orvertians, whose mother house is in Belfast by the way, within the next few days?'

'Of course, of course,' Canon Tett retorted eagerly.

'You will make your own financial arrangements with the retreat master. He will nominate a figure and you will whittle

271

him down until an amicable arrangement is arrived at. You will also arrange to provide hotel accommodation for the three Orvertian priests who will spend a full fortnight in the parish. You will be obliged to pay their travelling expenses from Belfast and back when their mission is completed.'

'But that could run into several hundred pounds, my Lord.'

'I am well aware of that, my dear Canon, but what you will do is hold a special silver collection instead of the customary copper collection during all the masses on the three Sundays embracing the mission.'

The Canon almost dropped the phone from his grasp, so overpowering was his desire to clap his hands at this novel and legitimate way of meeting the mission's expenses. He could scarcely hear the bishop outlining the other aspects of the undertaking as he imagined the collection table glinting with massive arrays of silver coins ranging from sixpenny pieces to half crowns.

'There will be no threepenny pieces,' he spoke to himself.

'Did you say something, Canon?' the bishop's voice cut across his thoughts.

'No, my Lord. Please carry on.'

'I can think of nothing else,' the bishop's voice had grown tired all of a sudden. 'Make your arrangements with the Orvertians and you'll have no regrets. I'll see you tomorrow evening please God at the reception for the remains of our dear departed colleague.'

'There's just one other thing, my Lord.' Judging from his tone the bishop quite rightly presumed that the Canon was reluctant to bring the matter up.

'Go on, my dear Canon. Say what you must say.' Bishop Collane seemed unusually amenable.

'I'll need a curate, my Lord, and in view of what has happened I must ask you to provide me with an able-bodied man with a bit of experience. The parish has taken more than its share of knocks in recent times, my Lord. Poor Father Donlea is gone

272

for good, the Lord be good to him and then there was Father
Stanley, a gorsoon you might say as far as parochial duties were
concerned. So you see, my Lord, if we got a solid man we
wouldn't be getting him before our time.'
The bishop was silent for a while. The Canon had made his
point and had made it well.
'Let me think about it, Canon. I'll mull on the matter
tonight. Do you think you could hold out until the diocesan
appointments are made in a month's time.'
'No,' the Canon shot back emphatically, 'I could not hold
out. With all due respects, my Lord, this parish needs an active
man and it needs him now.'
Father Alphonsus Donlea's mortal remains arrived at the
entrance to Trallock parish church at seven o'clock. A blinding
hailstorm swept the square as the coffin was removed from the
hearse by selected members of Trallock Confraternity. It
seemed as if the elements had resolved to remain unsettled
until Father Donlea was safely in his grave. Despite the storm
the bishop stood, mitre in hand, at the church entrance. At
his right hand side stood Canon Tett and at his left the Dean
of the diocese, Archdeacon Mulkare. Arrayed at either side of
the senior trio were three score curates and parish priests drawn
from the contiguous parishes and including several of Father
Donlea's classmates from Maynooth where he had been
ordained.
It was a most solemn and impressive occasion.
Despite the weather the church was already half filled. The
confraternity members paused at the entrance to allow the
bishop sprinkle the coffin with holy water before his Lordship
turned and preceded his priests into the church. The coffin
was placed in front of the main altar on plush-covered wooden
supports. The parish clerk unobtrusively stepped forward and
placed the late priest's breviary, stole and biretta on the coffin.
The service was over quickly.
Those priests who had expected some form of reception in

273

the presbytery were to be disappointed. Some repaired briefly to the Trallock Arms for refreshments. The remainder, because they would be obliged to concelebrate the solemn requiem mass on the following day, returned to their presbyteries. While Canon Tett failed to see the need for entertaining the rank and file of the diocese he extended warm invitations to both Bishop Collane and Archdeacon Mulkare. The latter, it was rumoured, would succeed Collane in the event of his surviving him. Archdeacon Mulkare, who complained of a heavy cold, declined the invitation.

'If I am to be here tomorrow,' he confided to the Canon, 'I'll need to retire early.'

'I have the man for you, Canon,' Bishop Collane informed Canon Tett as soon as they found themselves in the presbytery.

'And pray who might he be, my Lord?'

'He is Father Michael Dully. He is forty years of age. He has been curate for the past five years in the parish of Ballyvillane in the south-west of the diocese but now there's no longer any need for him there since more than half the population of that parish has emigrated.'

'He'll be welcome, my Lord.'

'By God, it's cold in here,' the bishop registered his disappointment as his eyes took in the single bar heater which substituted for a fire.

'Let us go into the kitchen,' the Canon suggested, 'it's warmer there.'

The bishop allowed himself to be led into Nora Devane's spotless domain. Nora rushed forward eagerly and falling on her knees kissed Doctor Collane's ring. The bishop helped her to her feet.

'You've met my housekeeper already I believe,' Canon Tett forged a smile out of his normally grim features.

'Yes, indeed. Nora isn't it?' Nora curtsied in acknowledgement of the episcopal recognition. It would be something to tell her cronies over the weeks ahead.

'I have the tea and sandwiches ready, Canon. I was going to bring them to the room.'

'There's no need for that my good woman,' the Canon spoke dismissively. 'We'll be taking our tea here.'

'I'll be off then, Canon,' Nora Devane picked up her cue instantly and, directing a sanctified smile towards the bishop, took her leave.

'This Father Dully I'm sending you, Canon, is a good man. His parish priest could not be more glowing in his evaluation of him.'

The bishop accepted a ham sandwich and allowed the Canon to pour him a cup of tea.

'You know,' Bishop Collane continued, 'I would have thought with the decimation of the Dirrabeg population through emigration that two priests could handle this parish.'

'The population of Dirrabeg has undoubtedly fallen, my Lord, but if it has the town population has increased in proportion and the remainder of the parish seems to be holding its own.'

'And your senior curate Father Butt, Canon. How is he?'

'He's all right I suppose when you consider what's on the market these days. I left him off to entertain some classmates of Father Donlea God rest his soul.'

'And may God rest all the poor souls,' Bishop Collane responded by rote. He rose abruptly.

'Well, my dear Canon Tett, I had better be on my way. Tomorrow is another day. Oh, by the way!' The bishop proposed his final question with a stentorian laugh. 'I don't suppose you have any notion of retiring.'

'Retirement!' Canon Tett's laugh was explosive and natural. 'Retirement, my Lord, is the furthest notion from my head.'

On the morning of the funeral the Hallapy children left home at half past eleven. The funeral mass was scheduled to begin at twelve thirty. They were joined by other schoolchildren on the road to Trallock. Luckily the morning rains had vanished and the sky overhead was clear. Johnny Hallapy recalled for his sister and brother how the dead priest had accepted his cup of porter at the wrendance.

'That's what I'm going to be when I grow up,' Johnny Hallapy expressed the sentiment to himself, 'is a priest like Father Donlea.'

The children would not be attending the mass. By arrangement they would meet with Ciss Fenley in the town square and there join in double file with all the other schoolchilden of the parish to form an extended guard of honour which would stretch from the church entrance to Healy Street.

As soon as the cortege in its entirety had passed into Healy Street on its way to the graveyard and the priests' plot their participation in the ceremony would terminate. All the teachers of the parish would be on stand-by to ensure that there would be no horse-play or tomfoolery. There would be no dispersal until the principal of Trallock Boys' School, Tom Tierney, gave the order. The children would then be expected to return to their homes and to remain there until the funeral obsequies came to an end. The teachers would take it upon themselves to patrol the streets to ensure that the regulations were observed.

The parish church of Trallock was filled to overflowing for the occasion. More than seventy priests, soutaned and surpliced, together with the canons of the Diocesan Chapter, the dean and the bishop concelebrated the requiem mass. The chief concelebrants were Canon Tett flanked by deacon and subdeacon, namely Father Butt and the new curate Father Dully. First the Office of the Dead was chanted by all the priests and the bishop. The voices of the diocesan cantors paced the recital to its close. After the reading of the gospel a total silence settled on the congregation. All eyes were focussed on the bishop who sat in the episcopal chair, crozier in hand. Slowly he rose and solemnly handed the crozier to an acolyte before leaving the central point of worship and ascending the pulpit.

276

The congregation sat rapt when he raised his right hand in tribute to their participation. Many of those present had never heard him speak. Almost all had seen him from a distance or had seen his photographs in local and national newspapers but here he was now, large as life, gazing down upon them with princely countenance. What more glorious diversion could any sane parishioner possibly desire!

'My dear people,' Doctor Collane's voice reached to every corner of the church, 'in the gospel which has just been read for us by your parish priest Christ says, "I am the resurrection and the life. He who believes in Me, even if he die, shall live and whoever lives and believes in Me shall never die."' He went on to define the gospel message in the simplest terms and referred at length to the great faith and courage of the dead priest. As he spoke the vast majority of the congregation marvelled at the power of his voice and the clarity of his diction.

Directly underneath the pulpit sat Faithful Ferg. While his expression might suggest otherwise he paid little heed to Bishop Collane's homily. Inwardly he was seething. The only other topic of conversation in the town, apart from Father Donlea's death, was the resignation of his brother Monty. If, for a moment, he could just lay his hands about his brother's neck he would cheerfully strangle him. Apart from the disgrace and the gossip he found it unbearable to conceive that Daisy Fleece would submit herself to the ultimate degradation with Monty. He would make the scoundrel pay for bringing shame on the good name of the family. He would make him suffer in return for making his family suffer.

The bishop's voice carried clearly to the square outside. Apart from the two lines of schoolchildren, several hundred in number, there was a large number of parishioners who had failed to gain admittance to the crowded church. The children from Dirrabeg National School formed a small part of one line at the left hand side of the church gate near the hearse. For the most part they kept their heads down, not so much out of deference to

277

the bishop's oration but because of the taunts and grimaces of the town children. From the moment they arrived in the square they had been subjected to every form of ridicule. Their reaction to the accustomed baiting had been to bow their heads, sure from past experience that it would wear itself out in due course.

When the Smiley children arrived and opted to take their places with their country cousins the behaviour of the town children underwent a dramatic change. The Smileys might not have shoes on their feet or warm overcoats to their backs and they might be hungrier than most but they knew how to use their knuckles and were therefore greatly respected in and out of school.

Tom Smiley stood next to his first cousin Katie Hallapy.

'You're prettier than any of them,' he told her proudly, 'and your dress is nicer than any of theirs.'

It was the first compliment ever received by Katie Hallapy from somebody in her own age group. She responded by succumbing to the first mature blush of her life.

In the church the mass was nearing its conclusion. The bishop, crozier in hand, mitre firmly fixed on head, had once again risen from the episcopal chair to recite the Prayers of Final Commendation. Then came the sprinkling of the holy water, reminder of the baptismal rite. Then, swinging the incense-filled thurible, reminding all of the need of prayer for the dead priest, the bishop circled the coffin as the aromatic puffs of incense smoke drifted through the congregation. The parochial choir launched itself into an enthusiastic rendering of 'Nearer my God to Thee'. Many of the congregation joined in. As the coffin was borne away by the confraternity members to the waiting hearse the seventy priests, canons, archdeacons and bishop preceded it, singing the De Profundis. From the unison of the chaste, restrained voices, the sense of loss came through. Women wept openly as the coffin passed by. The church would always look after its own with discipline and dignity.

Eighteen

THE DIRRABEG CONTINGENT, driven by Monty Whelan, arrived at the Bus Bar as Bishop Collane was leaving the presbytery, accompanied to his car by Canon Tett, Father Butt and Father Dully.

Bluenose had never seen a bishop before. 'He looks like any other man,' he remarked to Donal Hallapy upon being told who he was, 'except maybe he's in better condition and there's more of a shine to him.'

A light snow had begun to fall.

'It was to be expected,' Rubawrd Ring pointed out as they stood watching the trio outside the presbytery. 'I saw the hares grazing in one of the low fields in the noon of the day, a sure sign of snow.'

As soon as the bishop's car moved away Canon Tett withdrew hurriedly, brushing the mote-like flakes from his shoulders. Father Butt raised his hand and waved it at the group outside the Bus Bar. Only Monty Whelan returned his salute. Father Butt advanced hesitantly towards them followed by Father Dully. It was clear that his intention was to introduce the new curate. The Dirrabeg party turned on their heels and sought refuge in the Bus Bar. Monty Whelan hesitated for a moment but followed suit when Father Butt decided to hail him. The curate stopped in his tracks, saddened and disappointed but understanding Monty's reluctance to meet with him. He would

279

call to his house in due course and clarify his position. He would make it clear that he totally disapproved of his enforced resignation.

'That was an excellent meal,' Father Dully commented as he still fondly savoured the taste of the roast turkey which Nora Devane had served for lunch.

'Yes, it surely was excellent,' Father Butt commented wrily. 'In fact it was the best meal I ever consumed in that presbytery.'

Where was the point in enlightening the junior curate regarding the everyday presbytery diet? He would find out in time that he had partaken of rare parochial fare and that he was unlikely to taste the likes of it again for the duration of Canon Tett's ministry.

'The stories I heard,' he was holding forth again, 'would make you believe that Trallock curates were in danger of being starved to death.'

'You can't believe all you hear, Father,' Father Butt was weary. He had been deeply shocked by the death of Father Donlea. He would be free for the oncoming weekend and would spend it with his sister. He desperately needed to confide in somebody. The one man whom he trusted and respected more than any other, short as had been the renewal of their acquaintance, was the man he had helped bury a short while previously. He had decided from the moment he heard of his appointment to keep Father Dully at a respectful distance until he had sufficient time to determine his exact mettle. Let him grow accustomed to the Canon and form his own opinion. Let him learn from experience of the devious stratagems and undertakings of Nora Devane. Friends had already intimated to him that Father Michael Dully was as shrewd an operator as was to be found in the diocese, a man who kept his cards very close to his chest and who had yet to make a false move in the discharge of his parochial obligations. He was not, however, a Canon's man.

By six o'clock six of the Dirrabeg Wren had foregathered in the Bus Bar. There was the earlier trio who came with Monty

Whelan and latterly the threesome consisting of the Costigan brothers and Mossie Gilooley.

Patsy Oriel had arrived on the stroke of six and sat himself on the edge of the gathering, content to be respectfully attentive rather than involved, silently partaking of his entitlement of porter. Not until Tom Tyler arrived in civilian clothes later in the night was Patsy to become aware of the justification for the unexpected levee. Like Tom he held Monty Whelan in the highest regard. Indeed, if he were asked to nominate the man he admired most in the parish he would plump, like Tom Tyler, for Monty Whelan. On hearing that the Canon and the Crollies were involved more than any others in the downfall of his idol he resolved there and then somehow to avenge the wrong. There was little he could do about Canon Tett but the Crollies, P.J. and Junior, had wives. Patsy Oriel knew that he could trust Tom Tyler especially in any undertaking relating to Monty Whelan.

'I would dearly love, my friend,' said he in an aside, 'to bring them Crolly dolls down a peg or two.'

'No better man,' Tom Tyler whispered back.

'But a poor man like me with no access to their likes would have little chance.'

'Don't say that,' Tom Tyler laid a hand on his knee. 'There's to be a wedding here in the middle of May and the Crollies will be at it. Neither of those women are averse to a drink. There will be soft music and with it there will be soft lights. If any man on this earth can saddle the pair in question you are that man, Oriel.'

'I need new clothes and how would I crash the wedding?'

'You can buy new clothes, especially tweed, in the hustings for half nothing and as for crashing the wedding there comes a time in all weddings when joining in is only a formality. They'll be all so drunk at that stage that they won't know whether you're entitled to be there or not. Your problem, if you succeed, will be to find a place to park 'em. You might

281

leave that in my hands. I'll get a key to a vacant room off one of the girls in the hotel.'

'And I'll strike a blow for our friend,' Patsy Oriel chimed in.

'Indeed you will,' Tom Tyler whispered with a chuckle, 'and as well as striking a blow for your friend you'll be striking a blow for yourself and for your country and for Irishmen yet to be born.'

Both men laughed, smothering their outcries with their hands.

'We'll say no more about the matter for the present,' Tom Tyler advised, 'we'll talk about it again when the time is ripe.'

By ten o'clock the music was in full swing. A few hours before Donal Hallapy had dispatched his nephew Tom Smiley on a borrowed bicycle to Dirrabeg for his bodhrán. On his way he would collect Trassie Ring and her concertina. She would sit on the bar of the bicycle and if Tom tired she would replace him on the pedals while he sat on the bar. The only other instrument required was a fiddle and since Mossie Gilooley never travelled anywhere without his own ancient instrument there was no worry on that score.

At eleven o'clock sharp Canon Peter Pius Tett retired to his bed. Twice during the day he had distinctly heard the sound of a distant drum. The odd thing was that nobody else had heard it. The drum he heard had been a bodhrán. He would recognise its distinctive and accursed throbbing anywhere and now here it was again just as he was about to pull the clothes over his head. But what was this! He listened attentively for a while. So now the drumbeats were accompanied by music! What next, he thought! Now there was knocking on the bedroom door.

'Who is it?' he called out irritably.

'It's me Canon, Nora Devane.'

'What do you want, woman?'

'It's the music, Canon. I can't sleep with it. It's enough to drive a person out of her wits.'

Nora had been surprised more than once over the days since the wrendance of Dirrabeg when the Canon had asked her if she could hear the sound of bodhráns. Earlier she had seen the Dirrabeg drunkards entering the Bus Bar. Without question the music she had heard was theirs. It had its own distinctive and bawdy flavour. She would soon put a stop to it.

Canon Tett was immensely relieved that his housekeeper had heard the bodhrán and the other instruments.

'It sounds as if it's coming from the direction of the Bus Bar,' Nora Devane called out.

The Canon eased himself out of bed and drew on his threadbare dressing gown and slippers.

'Go downstairs, woman,' he commanded, 'and wet us a sup of tea. I'll alert one of these bucks.' With clenched fist he pounded on Father Dully's door. The curate opened it at once. He had been sitting on a chair by the open window listening to the music.

'So you can hear it too!' Canon Tett exclaimed triumphantly.

'Yes indeed, Canon,' the junior curate responded enthusiastically.

'You'll go out now like a good man,' the Canon charged, 'and tell them to stop or I'll have the Guards on them.'

'Tell them to stop! Me!'

'Yes, you,' Canon Tett replied firmly, 'do you think I'm talking to myself.'

'But Canon,' Father Dully was laughing now, 'my brief doesn't extend to the silencing of public house musicians. I wasn't trained for that and I refuse to be party to anything of the kind. Now goodnight to you, Canon.'

Silently he closed the door. The Canon stood as if paralysed. For a moment it seemed that he must collapse. He raised his hand as though to smite upon the door again but changed his mind and followed Nora Devane downstairs, his face filled with a perplexity she had never before seen. In the kitchen he stood with his back to the range, his face still drained of blood after

283

the shock of Father Dully's reply. Nora Devane was pleased to note that his composure returned after he had tasted the first mouthful of tea.

'I suppose,' he said resentfully, 'there's no point in knocking up the other fellow either.'

'Oh, no point at all, Canon,' Nora Devane agreed. 'I don't know what curates is comin' to these days, Canon. They should be reported to the bishop.'

'Shush now, woman,' Canon Tett cautioned, 'you tend to exceed yourself. Go out and get me the sergeant of the Guards' Barracks on the phone.'

Delighted to be entrusted with such a momentous commission, Nora Devane hastened into the hallway and lifted the receiver.

Upstairs in his bedroom Father Dully still sat by the window, an amused look on his face. The bishop's secretary had been spot on. The whole diocese would benefit if Canon Tett was put out to pasture.

'But,' the secretary had ended his appraisal, 'it wouldn't surprise me if he buried the whole danged lot of us!'

Father Dully was impressed by the Dirrabeg music, especially the bodhrán. Although a tolerably good pianist the bodhrán was an instrument about which he knew very little. Played as it was now he visualised endless possibilities for its use. From what he could hear, even at a distance, it seemed a far more sensitive drum than he had ever realised. The snowflakes drifted slowly by the open window, the occasional tiny particle alighting for a glittering moment before expiring on his coat and trousers. Reluctantly he closed the window wishing he was one of the happy throng in the Bus Bar. Always on his holidays, dressed in lay garb, he enjoyed long sojourns in run-down public houses. He preferred them to lounge bars and hotels. The patrons were friendlier and more interesting although sometimes truculent and needlessly bellicose. He suspected too that they knew he was a priest from the very beginning. The toilets

284

in such premises left a lot to be desired and the glasses from which he drank were not always as spotless as he would like but at least it was a contrast to the sterility and gloom of the presbytery to which he would have to return all too soon. It was an unexpected bonus if such taverns housed a piano. Sooner or later, for reasons he could never determine, somebody always asked him to play and depending on his mood he would sometimes oblige.

There had been one unforgettable occasion when a beautiful girl, her sallow face framed in dark, short-cropped hair, her hazel eyes bright with the spirit of youth, had spent the night with her hand gently touching his left shoulder as he played tune after tune on the upright piano. Sometimes during the softer passages he found that her body brushed against his elbow. It had all been very disturbing at the time but he had remained at his post. The setting had been a popular bar at a seaside resort on the west coast. When time was called the girl sat near him on the stool and asked him if he would escort her to the seafront guesthouse where she was staying.

Later he found himself walking along the sandy shore from which the tide had just receded. Her hand, soft and limp, rested in his. They had walked to where a glinting rocky outcrop loomed over the glistening strand. Here they stood silently listening to the sea's quiet monotone, not speaking, each happy to savour the beauty of the star-filled summer sky and shining moon which cast its golden light all around. Shyly she raised her head and looked with melting eyes into his. Suddenly she was in his arms, the touch of her body and fragrance of her soft hair overpowering him. For all that he kissed her gently, cupping her radiant face in his hands, enraptured by her loveliness, overwhelmed with guilt but unable to release her.

'I think,' she said nervously, 'that we might be able to sneak into my bedroom without anybody seeing us.'

He had let go of her instantly. A look of surprise and hurt appeared on her face.

285

'We don't have to go,' she blurted out the words contritely. 'We'll just stay here and walk. Please don't think I'm cheap. The truth is I have never invited anybody to come to my bedroom before now.'

'You're not cheap.' He took her in his arms again, 'it's just that you took me by surprise. If you don't mind we'll stay here a while. Then I'll take you home.'

'You're a priest, aren't you?' She looked into his face as she spoke.

'Is it so obvious?' he asked.

'No,' she said, 'it's not in the least obvious. I just guessed. For what it's worth I don't mind.'

He had not seen her again. He had deposited her at the guesthouse door just as the dawn was breaking. A crowing cockerel disrupted the stillness of the brightening morning. As he walked to his hotel he felt as Judas must have felt. Now with hindsight, listening to the music of the Dirrabeg Wren, he realised his behaviour, all things allowed, had not been truly sinful; decidedly foolish, yes, and unquestionably wrong but not truly sinful. Remembering the starlit skies and the muted murmuring of the ebbing tide, he knelt by the bedside to say his prayers. Later, before sleep, he would wonder for the hundredth time what became of her. It was a memory he would always treasure.

In the Bus Bar the music continued unabated. Song followed upon song and there were rousing choruses. Fred Halpin made no attempt after closing time to call for quiet. Tom Tyler had assured him that the sergeant had gone to bed immediately after the funeral, complaining of a sore throat and a wheezing in the chest.

When the knock came it was completely unexpected.

'Silence!' Fred Halpin raised both hands and issued the command a second time. In the ensuing calm the knocking sounded more menacing. It boded little good. It was a persistent knocking. Fred Halpin had no doubt that the person responsible was a member of the Civic Guards.

'I can't account for it,' Tom Tyler sat puzzled in his chair. 'Somebody must have phoned in and complained about the music.'

'Never mind us,' Patsy Oriel spoke for all present, 'you're the one that has to be got away, Tom.'

'True!' Tom Tyler returned, 'but how?'

'Your only chance is the roof,' Fred Halpin told him. 'There's a skylight. You'll just about manage to squeeze through.'

When Minnie Halpin returned from her inspection of both exits she revealed the grim news. The sergeant stood waiting at the back while two Civic Guards stood at the front. Persistent, thunderous knocking now came from the back as well as the front. In the attic Patsy Oriel and Donal Hallapy hoisted Tom Tyler onto their shoulders. Strong as they were they staggered under his weight. Grunting and straining he drew himself upward and outward until his body disappeared.

When Donal and Patsy returned to the kitchen Sergeant Shee was in the act of taking names, his cap under his arm. Only one of the Guards was visible. The other would be waiting at the rear of the premises in case some intrepid captive should make a run for it.

When all the names were taken the sergeant, followed by his unwilling minion, made an exhaustive search of every room and compartment in the house from the downstairs toilet to the attic. He found nobody. When he shone his torch into the room where Fred Halpin's two young daughters lay sleeping Fred had to be restrained by Bluenose and Timmie Costigan.

'I'll kill the bastard,' Fred Halpin shouted as Donal Hallapy seized him from behind lest he attempt to carry out his threat. The sergeant made no apology when the girls sat up in their beds screaming for their mother. In the scuffle that followed the sergeant lost his cap. Bluenose seized it as the sergeant endeavoured to protect himself from Fred Halpin's threatened onslaught. It was passed from one hand to another until it

287

ended up on the roof of an outhouse where it could be later retrieved.

'If God spares me for another Saint Stephen's Day,' Bluenose promised his cohorts, 'it will be my headgear for the Wren.'

At the front door as soon as the premises had been cleared, the sergeant proceeded to harangue Fred Halpin about the loss of his cap and the attempted assault.

'Have a look,' Fred Halpin pointed in the direction of the Trallock Arms Hotel from which a number of people were emerging.

'I declare to God if it isn't the quality,' Fred called out to the Dirrabeg men who stood nearby. 'There's the superintendent of the Civic Guards and there's the Crollies, father, son and mother and there's Phil Summers the accountant and if it isn't Mickey Munley the bookie! One law for them and another for Fred Halpin? Isn't that the way of it, sergeant! Answer up now like a good man.'

'You'll get your answer in court and so will the man who stole my cap.'

Bluenose approached slowly until he stood inches from the sergeant.

'I haven't all that much time left, sergeant, so it don't make that much difference to me if I hang for you which is what I'll do if you don't remove your stinking corpse from here. Who do you think you're playing with? We're no criminals. All we ever wanted was the right to play our music and take a few drinks now and then but you'd deprive us of that. Crikey it's a comical country that hires its lawmen to raid pubs and destroy the native music, that hires emergency men to grind us further into the ground. Piss off now for yourself unless it's trouble you want. Your duty is done here.'

The Dirrabeg men accompanied by Monty Whelan moved across the square. Here Monty parted with them. He thrust a pound note into Donal Hallapy's hand.

'Go and get Martin Semple to take the lot of you home,' he

said.

Monty shook hands with every member of the party. No further word was spoken. He lifted a hand in silent farewell and returned unsteadily to his house. In the kitchen he was amazed to see his brother Ferg. He was still more amazed at the flood of abuse which his brother hurled at him.

'So you've disgraced us again, you fornicating whoresmaster,' Ferg screamed as he clenched his fists till the knuckles showed white.

'To be the town drunkard wasn't enough for you. You had to be the fornicator-in-chief as well. What a philanderer we have in you. You're the talk of the bloody countryside. I'll never again be able to hold my head high over you, you wanton wretch that has the family name disgraced.'

Ferg's first punch, which landed above Monty's right eye, stunned him. Before the second blow reached its target he was already semi-conscious. Blow followed blow until he fell in an insensible heap on the floor, his face a bruised mass from which the blood flowed freely. Ferg still stood over him ranting like a madman.

'Whoresmaster!' he screamed as he discharged a mouthful of spittle on the form beneath him. 'My name is mud,' he cried out, 'and it's all over you and that whore of a Fleece one.' He discharge a second mouthful of spittle before departing the kitchen.

In bed Minnie Halpin recited the first decade of the rosary while Tom answered. Try as she might she could not concentrate on the prayers. It had been a disturbing night for her. Patsy Oriel's arrival, calm and serene as a monk, had unsettled her.

'You have an awful neck to show up here,' she had scolded as soon as she got him alone.

Patsy had hung his head in pretended shame. At the time Minnie Halpin had been carrying a bottle of five star port from the store-room to the bar.

289

'I have a mind to give you this across the head,' she spat out the threat. Patsy Oriel still stood silently, seemingly crestfallen. Minnie found herself at a loss for words.

'Promise on your oath you'll never come near me again you merciless wretch.'

'I promise,' Patsy Oriel slowly lifted his head, a large tear showing under his right eye.

'Go on with you then,' Minnie Halpin had cautioned although her tone was less severe, 'and make sure you conduct yourself while you're under this roof.'

'God bless you missus! God bless you!' he called after her. He had been on his way to the toilet at the time. As he piddled he addressed the organ in his hand. 'You got off with a caution this time Mister,' he said, 'you're a lucky man you're not behind bars.'

As Minnie Halpin hurried through the second decade in an effort to keep her mind free of earthly matters she thought of Tom Tyler for the first time. Had those who assisted him onto the roof remembered to reclaim him from that most perilous of perches three stories from the ground? Surely they had and upon recovering him had spirited him out of the back way after the sergeant had quit the premises. Her thoughts reverted once more to Patsy Oriel. He had the kindest of faces although he wasn't exactly what a woman would call handsome. She recalled the tear on his face, the moisture forming on the bottomless blue eyes, the sense of serenity one felt while dancing with him. She would never be able to explain her totally uncharacteristic lapse. She had been a virgin when she married and had never so much as even contemplated unfaithfulness to Fred for a solitary second. She reproached herself for such irreverent digression by fiercely pinching the flesh on the back of her hand.

Towards the end of the third decade she thought, once more, of Tom Tyler. If they had not remembered to deliver him from his adversity he would by this time have been stranded on the roof for more than two hours. There was always, however, the possibility that he might have descended with the aid of one of the drainpipes. On second thoughts she decided this would have been suicidal. Tom Tyler weighed seventeen stone and the pipes were both loose and rusted. She decided that she would consult Fred as soon as the rosary was recited. If he were still on the roof he would be half frozen by now. She tried, in vain, to remember whether or not he had been wearing an overcoat. Fred would remember. She pressed on unwaveringly now to the conclusion of her supplications.

'Fred!' she would sound as casual as she could, knowing how explosive his reactions could be.

'What is it, love?' he asked.

'Tom Tyler, Fred!'

Fred Halpin offered no immediate response. He lay unmoving beside her. She knew he was thinking. Suddenly he leaped from the bed.

'He's still out there. That skylight cannot be opened from the outside.'

'Do you remember if he had an overcoat?' Minnie would maintain her attitude of calm no matter what.

'No!' Fred Halpin was adamant. 'He had no overcoat. The poor oul' bastard must be frozen by now.'

He hurried upstairs to the attic followed by Minnie. As soon as he switched on the light they noticed the broken glass on the floor. Looking upward they could see Tom Tyler's accusing eyes under his snow-flecked, bushy eyebrows looking down at them. His face was ghastly, his remaining teeth, carious and gapped, chattering uncontrollably.

'Right, Tom,' Fred Halpin tried to sound reassuring, 'feet first and we'll catch you as you come down.'

His attempted descent was preceeded by an avalanche of snow, most of which fell on the Halpins who stood directly beneath the broken skylight in nothing but their pyjamas. As he lowered himself painfully into the attic his grip on the glass-

291

free frame of the skylight weakened. His fingers, numbed from the rooftop exposure, found purchase beyond their stunted capabilities.

'I'm coming,' he cried out in alarm before he crashed on to the attic floor bringing the Halpins with him. All three lay sprawled and breathless. Tom Tyler seemed unable to speak, his eyes like those of a wounded animal whose hour of expiry was imminent.

Minnie Halpin had quickly risen but fell immediately to her knees screaming with pain, her scantily-protected posterior bleeding from several places at the same time, much of the broken glass still embedded therein.

Apart from a few minor cuts Fred Halpin seemed to be none the worse for his ordeal. He lifted Tom Tyler to his feet and bade his wife follow them downstairs to the kitchen.

'Don't fret, love,' he comforted, 'I'll have Joe O'Dell here in a jiffy and he'll look after you.'

Later in the kitchen Minnie Halpin leaned over a chair, clad in a white slip, her freshly-tended buttocks still smarting. The cuts had needed several stitches. Joe O'Dell sat on a chair near the range, a pint of stout clasped in his hand. Fred Halpin and Tom Tyler sat nearby, clutching glasses of whiskey to their chests as Tom regaled them regarding the odd disposition of houses, streets and laneways as seen from his recently-abandoned outpost overlooking the square of Trallock.

'I saw things and people that I would never see in a lifetime down below. There are many mysterious comings and goings in a small town that can only be seen from heaven or the roof of a three-storied house. I saw people coming and going in the small hours, exiting from unexpected places and others entering places more unexpected still. It was the will of God that I was forced to spend a term on the rooftops, moreover on a night when the ground was so white that every moving figure down below was clearly discernable. A lot was revealed to me tonight, more than was ever before revealed to a Civic Guard in this

292

town. It took me a while to get used to the distance but once I got the range and the angles right I had no bother putting two and two together. Then the cold got the better of me when the snow started up again. I could see nothing after that. There is one thing that puzzles me, however. Why would Faithful Ferg be coming out from under this very archway after midnight. I mean the hoor doesn't drink and he certainly wasn't in this bar.'

'He was never in this bar,' Fred Halpin cut in.

'He wouldn't give you the heat of his water!' Minnie added as she painfully adjusted the slip over her tingling hind quarters.

'What was he doing there then?' Tom Tyler asked. 'Would he have been remonstrating with Monty?'

'Remonstrating?' Joe O'Dell laughed and swallowed from his pint. 'More likely he kicked the piss out of him. That would be the scoundrel's style, especially with a drunken man at his mercy.'

Tom Tyler sat up in his chair. 'And Monty was drunk,' he said, his expression one of alarm. 'I think I'll slip out and make sure all's well with him.'

Nineteen

DONAL HALLAPY ARRIVED at his home in Dirrabeg at one thirty in the morning. He found his wife waiting by the kitchen fire, a doleful look on her face, her hands pressed to her lap. What calamity now? Donal thought apprehensively as he laid the brown paper bag on the floor.

'There's a calf dead,' she spelled out the dreadful tidings at once.

'Oh Christ, no!' Donal struck his palm with clenched fist. 'How?' he asked.

'White scour.' Nellie Hallapy adjusted the turf sods in the cheerless fire. 'It was Tom found him.'

'It was the bull calf then, was it?'

'Yes. It was the bull calf.'

'How are the other cows?'

'They seem to be all right but the grey is near her time. You'd want to tend to her.'

'I'll see to her right away.' He stood silently for a while absorbing the shock. It had been a fine bull calf.

'This is a terrible bloody blow. I was depending on that calf. This changes things.'

'What do you mean?'

'I was thinking lately,' he sat by her side near the fire, 'that if things went against us this spring I would go to England for a spell until I made enough money to straighten us out. Six months should do it.'

'No,' Nellie Hallapy was adamant. ' I won't let you and the children won't let you.'

'We need the money, Nellie. I'm sick of being a pauper. I haven't a suit. I haven't shoes. I haven't an overcoat that a man could wear in public and I haven't a penny in my pocket.'

'I heard you say it all before Donal and something always turned up. Don't think about it now. What's in the bag?'

'Sausages, rashers, black-pudding, and a loaf of shop bread. I got no chance in the pub to spend the eight shillings so I called to Faithful Ferg's.'

'I could eat a cow,' Nellie Hallapy said and then casually, 'but of course that could be because I'm pregnant again.' Donal's mouth opened and closed soundlessly as he sought words to register his surprise.

'The night of the wrendance was it?' he asked after a while.

Nellie nodded her head.

'It was worth it,' Donal tried to sound cheerful.

'Worth it for you but 'tis me that will have to carry the child. The deed is done now. There's no more to be said. Go and tend to the cow and I'll put down the pan.'

The first faint light was showing in the east when the grey cow started to stitch.

'Oh Christ, no!' Donal used the expression for the second time that morning. The cause of his alarm were the two tiny hooves which had just appeared at the cow's afterpart.

'A tailways birth!' He had handled such emergencies before but there was always the danger that the calf would be smothered before the creature was extricated from its predicament. Gently he tied wet ropes around each leg; drawing on either rope alternately, he laboured to lever the birth outward. Using all his strength he heaved and strained till beads of perspiration fell from his forehead. The cow spread her hind feet outwards, her whole body stitching convulsively, knowing instinctively that her every effort was needed for the safe

295

delivery of her young. The longer the effort required the greater the likelihood of a still-born calf.

'Come on!' Donal called out in desperation, his fingers slipping so that he was obliged to find second purchase. This seemed to him to be more favourable than the first. The calf slowly began to ease itself out, first the hock and then a pause for a renewed effort. There was still a long way to go and time was running out. Then after a combined and most strenuous exertion from all three participants the hindquarters appeared.

'Come on!' Donal called out despairingly, terrified that too much time had elapsed. Inch by inch he laboured until suddenly the forequarters, followed by the head, shot forth of their own accord.

Outside the sky had lightened showing up the snow-covered fields. Donal laid the calf gently in a bed of dry hay but it was to no avail. The creature was dead, smothered by its own and its mother's exertions. Donal stood dejectedly in the doorway of the byre. Two dead calves in the space of twenty-four hours. He had never been dealt a harder blow in all his years of farming. Half of his calf crop wiped out in a flash. Was this the atonement demanded by God for having rejected the holy sacrament of the mass! If it was it was an excessive punishment but it would only determine him all the more to keep clear of Canon Tett's church. Hands thrust deep into pockets he stumbled out into the small haggard at the rear of the byre. A blackbird chattered crazily in a nearby hedgerow, the bright morning light exciting it into a sustained outburst. Soon other birds were singing. Thrush, lark and linnet joined in the bewildering chorus. Donal never realised that so many small songbirds existed in his tiny domain.

'Sing,' he cried. 'Sing, you bastards, while you can. Sing before the hawk comes down on you and tears your heart out the way God tears out mine.'

He walked slowly around the tiny enclosure several times, his head downbent, his heart heavy.

What a change from yesterday! he thought. The morning of the day before had been brimming with hope and pleasant prospects. He began to count the cost of his losses in financial terms. The two calves yet to be born, if they survived and survive they must, would just about pay for two bonhams. That was the biggest hurdle cleared. His main assets were that he had his health and strength, a great wife and beautiful children but how would he support them now with his income drastically reduced? God is good! he thought or was it that God had been good and was unwilling to favour him with His divine benignity any longer?

He stood depressed under an ancient black alder estimating the strength of his relationship with his maker.

'If this is the will of God,' he spoke the words aloud, 'then I want no more of it. I might as well be dead!'

The thought sobered him and he remembered others who had taken the easy way out by the expedient of hanging a rope from the bough of a tree or committing themselves to a boghole. He had once helped cut down such a victim of life's misfortune, a brother of Rubawrd Ring's whose efforts at farming had failed. He shuddered remembering the screams of the dead man's wife. Time to go indoors and break his own awful news. He returned to the byre and lifted the dead body despite the mother's protestations. She followed him to the back door of the dwelling house where he laid the body alongside the other. He would now need to drastically revise all his plans for the future. There must be some means, fair or foul, whereby he might supplement his income. He would put his mind to it over the remainder of the day.

By the end of March all the cows in Dirrabeg had calved. There had been numerous losses because of the white scour which went on an unprecedented rampage that particular spring. Every bogland smallholder with the exception of the Costigan brothers had fallen prey to the scourge. Rubawrd Ring, like Donal Hallapy, had lost two calves; Bluenose, for all his experience, lost one. Mossie Gilooley had seen one of his expire shortly after he had delivered it. The heart had failed moments after birth. They were losses that the families of Dirrabeg could ill afford. The year ahead had never looked bleaker. There was nothing of promise on the horizon save rumours of a parochial mission. There was a time when the menfolk of Dirrabeg would have welcomed such an event but now, with their faces firmly turned against religion, they would be denied the pleasure of a diversion as good as any. They would also be deprived of the opportunity to shrive themselves in the vastly more experienced confessional of the visiting fathers.

Often during previous missions they had found opportunities to visit the Bus Bar which played host to huge crowds when the missioners had done with their ministrations each night.

Nellie Hallapy would attend the mission as would the entire female population of Dirrabeg. It would be unthinkable for any self-respecting Catholic woman to absent herself. When word spread that the males of Dirrabeg were deliberately staying away the missioners would inevitably arrive at their doors and demand to see them. It was normal practice during all missions. As the mission days wore on and religious fever mounted the congregation would be urged by the zealous evangelists of the Orvertian Order to supply them with names and addresses of recalcitrants so that they might be saved from themselves.

Often the names of innocent people were placed in the special deposit box in the sacristy. Sometimes the names of known pietists with impeccable characters, veritable pillars of the church, were to be found mingled with the identities of the most sinful and hardened of reprobates. The wool, however, wasn't so easily pulled over the eyes of the eager Orvertians. They would have been well used to such acts of mischief from past experience and would consult with the parish clerk, Shamie Deale, before venturing forth on wild goose chases. Generally the names of the suspect non-observers were approved by the parish clerk and by his reckoning would be

298

well worth a visit. The missioners were often rewarded by some spectacular successes which resulted in much rejoicing on earth, or that part of it which was Trallock, as well as in heaven.

Two weeks were to pass before Monty Whelan considered himself presentable enough to appear in public. Although badly bruised from Ferg's beating there was no serious damage to the face, apart from two blackened eyes, a split lip which required one stitch and some minor abrasions on the cheekbone. When discovered by Tom Tyler he was in an unconscious state. Tom had immediately alerted Joe O'Dell who was quickly on hand to render professional assistance. On the evening of his third day in bed, during a visit from Tom Tyler his friend made the suggestion that he should notify Daisy Fleece of his plight. Monty agreed fully and Tom Tyler volunteered to make contact. When Daisy arrived late that night covered by the black shawl she was shocked beyond words at his appearance. Later, after he had explained his disfigurement, they spoke about the future.

'I blame myself for all that has happened,' Daisy blurted out tearfully after hearing of the interview with Canon Tett and the subsequent letter of resignation. 'I've ruined your whole life; I know how you loved teaching at Dirrabeg and now you're finished forever there, all because of me. I warned you that something like this would happen. I wouldn't mind so much but we didn't do anything bad. It was just a kiss.'

'Are we ever going to do anything bad Daisy?'

The unexpected question caught her completely off guard. Suddenly she found herself blushing. She turned her head away before answering. Daisy Fleece was essentially a shy woman but she was honest. She believed that he deserved to be answered. When the answer came it surprised him.

'When we put the shores of this hypocritical country behind us you and I will make love all the time, Monty Whelan, and I promise you that from my heart.'

'And when will that be, Daisy Fleece?'

'I'll have to write to my daughters and to my sister. There won't be any trouble there. They know all about you and they approve. My mother is the problem. Getting her to leave the home where she has spent the most of her life will be no easy matter at her age. I'll come around it somehow. I think you and I can be happy over there. Life owes us that much.'

'Come here,' he called, 'and give us a kiss at least.'

After the kiss she lay on the bed beside him. They spoke of the future until long after midnight when Daisy announced that she would have to leave.

'Much as I admire you in that shawl,' Monty told her fondly, 'I think the time has now come to put it aside and wear that grey tweed costume that suits you so well and, of course, that flimsy green headscarf that sets off your face so beautifully.'

Daisy laughed. 'I never dreamed a man would notice such things.'

'Those are only the externals,' he laughed back. 'I have noticed other things about you, such as your smile and your still girlish figure but I'll spare you the other details until I abscond with you from this land of saints and scholars.'

Another ten days were to pass before Monty ventured out of doors. The smudgy blackness had disappeared from his eyes. There were still vague patches of discoloration on his cheekbones and the solitary stitch still remained in his lip. Joe O'Dell had promised to remove it in a day or two. Despite prompting from Tom Tyler and Fred Halpin he had decided to take no action against his brother.

When news of the assault reached Canon Tett he shook his head dolefully and announced that Faithful Ferg was well within his rights.

'What else,' he asked Nora Devane who brought him the news, 'could a decent, God-fearing man be expected to do under the circumstances? I must call to see the poor fellow and try to get him to put the whole dirty business from his mind. How must he feel, the most industrious of men, the most atten-

300

tive and caring of husbands, the most provident of fathers! It's a wonder he didn't kill him. He showed great forebearance. Another man might have gone further.'

When, a fortnight later, Monty Whelan and Daisy Fleece appeared in public together for the first time many of the residents of the town square were scandalised.

Emily Crolly stood with hands folded in the main door of the Crolly emporium as though daring the couple to pass her by.

'What neck!' The comment came from her husband P.J. who joined her in the doorway. Behind her curtains Ciss Fenley sat with a grim smile of vindication on her face. Now the whole sordid business was out in the open for all to see. It was as if they were advertising their evil liaison and their future intent which, by all accounts, was to pull out lock, stock and barrel for that land of iniquity across the Irish Sea. Where, Ciss Fenley thought righteously, would sinners go if it wasn't to a land of sinners where prostitutes stood at every street corner and where there was free license for every sort of illicit relationship? Trallock was well rid of the pair. There had been a few times in the past weeks when she had been tempted to beard Monty in his den and point out to him the error of his ways, to even offer him forgiveness for all his past transgressions and open her virginal arms to him in spite of everything. How right she was to have smothered such thoughts! Now at last she knew that he could never measure up to her superior moral precepts. She could go into any court of law in the land and solemnly swear that she was intact. Indeed she could swear that no man had even as much as fondled any part whatsoever of her body. How could he, knowing as he did her undefiled immaculacy, allow himself to be paraded through the streets of the town by somebody who was no worse than a harlot? It was clear that the man was beyond redemption.

The Canon was to echo exactly the same sentiments when acquainted of the latest display of immorality by Nora Devane.

'If I had been present at the time,' he ranted, 'I would have

301

taken my walking stick and ran them out of the square.'

As Nora filled him in on the provocative disposition of the female and the swaggering gait of her philandering paramour he pointed upwards to the cracked kitchen ceiling with an avenging finger.

'God is not blind,' he shouted, 'and God will not forget this day of infamy in a hurry.'

If Father Dully entertained any feelings on the matter he kept them strictly to himself. Upon becoming acquainted with the facts at the cheerless breakfast table by Nora Devane all he said was: 'That is the way of the world my good woman,' which Nora interpreted to mean disapproval.

Father Butt was unreservedly on the side of Monty Whelan. Foolish and provocative as it might have seemed to flaunt her openly in the square he could not bring himself to condemn either one of them for an instant. The tragedy was that there was no loophole in the ethical structure of the Catholic church which might provide some form of justification for their type of relationship. The church was unequivocally hostile on such matters. It mattered not that her husband had deserted her twenty years before and that he might as well be dead as far as their marriage was concerned. This had no bearing on the issue and if she chose to live with another man the liaison would be sinful in the eyes of the church. What the Catholic church desperately needed, or so Father Butt thought, was some elasticity in its entrenched conservatism, some small degree of tolerance for situations such as the one in which Daisy Fleece unwittingly found herself. She was a chaste and lovely woman, a most devout Catholic as he well knew and the awful aspect of the whole business was that the church which should be sustaining and facilitating one of its most loyal and devoted members was actually ousting that member and imposing on her the undeserved label of adultress. The only time he had voiced his disapproval of similar situations in the presence of Canon Tett the older cleric's reply had been typical.

302

'Dogs bark and the caravan passes by,' he had responded pompously.

The female staff of the Trallock Arms Hotel gathered at the dining room window to watch the deposed teacher and his fancy woman pass by. Some had never seen Daisy Fleece before. One who had not was a young waitress from Upper Dirrabeg.

'She's beautiful,' she said breathlessly.

'Yes,' said her supervisor Moll Canty with marked reproof, 'but is she beautiful in the eyes of Our Blessed Lady? That is the question you must ask yourself, child.'

'She doesn't look like a fancy woman.' The observation came from a chambermaid, arms filled with linen, who had come to join the others at the window.

'They never do,' Moll Canty returned. 'It's a known fact that the devil's children have the faces of angels.'

'She's so stylish,' said the young girl from Upper Dirrabeg, 'she carries herself like a real lady.'

'Oh, she's a right lady to be sure,' came the contradiction from Moll Canty, a close confidant of Nora Devane.

In the Bus Bar the newly-arrived couple were greeted with a round of applause.

'Now!' Tom Tyler threw his hands outwards, 'it's all over and done with. They'll talk about it for a few days and then we'll have the mission and there will be other things to talk about.'

'Ye made a handsome couple,' Minnie Halpin said proudly.

'If I was a young man again with no wifely arms to restrain me I would pursue you to the ends of the earth,' Joe O'Dell roared as he seized Daisy in his mighty hands and lifted her high in the air before implanting a fierce kiss on her lips.

'Did ye see oul' Crolly, the hypocrite,' Moss Keerby withdrew from the doorway where he had been standing, 'and what harm but the hoor would go up on a midge!'

'He'd screw a rat through a manhole cover,' Tom Tyler addressed all within earshot.

303

'And you may bet,' Joe O'Dell observed without a smile, 'that he will be the right-hand man of the missioners as soon as they come to town.'

'Bad as he is,' Tom Tyler put in his piece, 'he's not nearly as slimy as Junior. Now there's a wretch has given a hard time to many a young girl.'

'What kills me,' Joe O'Dell added, 'is the way they parade up and down to the altar or is it how I'm being unfair? Maybe it's we who are the hypocrites and we the ungodly.'

'They're entitled to go to the altar and entitled to receive the host. Nobody denies them that,' Tom Tyler was quick to interpose, 'so long as they don't expect you and me to observe the same high standards.'

Monty and Daisy Fleece sat together at the counter.

'I'm glad that's over,' she whispered.

'It took courage,' Monty admitted as he took her hand in his. 'I was proud of you out there. It had to be done. We just couldn't quit our native place with our tails between our legs. As well as that we would be depriving them of their rights if we didn't scandalise them properly.'

'Will you miss the place?' she asked.

'Yes,' he answered, 'but the thought of spending the rest of my life with you more than compensates.'

'We'll be happy,' she whispered.

'Of course we will,' he told her, 'we're young enough to be lovers and old enough to appreciate the fact. I can't wait to land in England.'

Monty Whelan's departure created a void that would never be filled in Dirrabeg.

'There is no one now left to explain what kind of people we are,' Rubawrd Ring complained. 'With Monty gone there is no one to justify our existence. No matter how cornered we were or how despised we were he could always make a case for us. The last barrier between us and our enemies has been removed. We are now at the mercy of every smart Alec and

304

every gombeen man in the parish. Our champion is gone and there's no one to take his place.'

'He was as noble a man as ever I knew,' Bluenose put in. 'I don't know what we'll do now that he's gone. While he was around there was always someone we could turn to. They can say what they like about him but he had the respect of the people. He had the standing. It is the way of the Irish,' Bluenose shook his head sadly; 'we give away our cream and retain the skimmed. Where is his equal to be found now, I ask you? If I was a young man I'd follow him into exile. Better be with him than at the mercy of contrary priests and arse-lickin' holy Josies.'

There followed a time of great hardship in Dirrabeg. Mossie Gilooley lost his remaining three calves. When, as a last resort, he sent for the veterinarian it was already too late.

'I've told you people repeatedly,' the vet admonished, 'that you must not corral your calves in rails that have been painted with red lead. Sooner or later the calves are going to lick it and then you're stuck with lead poisoning and there's nothing I can do about that.'

There was no alternative but to allow their oldest daughter, a frail girl of fifteen, into service in Trallock. At least she would be reasonably well fed and her wages, small as they were, would help feed her brothers and sisters. Gertie Gilooley shed bitter tears the day they deposited their daughter in the house where she would be committed to service for a full year. She had always promised herself that no daughter of hers would ever demean herself by bowing and scraping before an upstart mistress, but cruel circumstances had ordained otherwise.

As the cold winds and rains swept the boglands there were other tales of misfortune before spring came to an end. Aided by Tom and Johnny Hallapy, Bluenose drove his cows and remaining calves to the April fair in Trallock square. Neither

305

he nor Delia were any longer able to cope with the milking of the cows or the feeding of the sucklings. Bluenose found that he had little control over the trembling which more and more usurped the steadiness of his hands. The stock had to be sold. There was no other solution. At least they would both be able to draw old age pensions now that they could prove that they had no visible means of support.

Bluenose was surprised to see Rubawrd Ring standing with his animal at the entrance to the square. It was no time to sell a two year old bullock. October would be the ideal time, when the after-grass fat would be rippling on back and buttock. But Rubawrd had no choice. Two nights before, Noranne Ring had called her mother into the bedroom and informed her with bent head that she was pregnant by Conor Quille. There was no need for alarm: he was standing his ground and prepared to do his duty. They would be married in England and arrangements had already been made. A job was waiting for Conor and Noranne's oldest sister would provide lodgings until they could rise to a place of their own.

'I'll sell the bullock,' Rubawrd announced as soon as the news was relayed to him by his wife. 'He'll pay their fares and leave them with a pound or two over.'

'You remember the little priest was in Trallock before Christmas?'

'Father Smiley wasn't it?' Rubawrd recalled.

'It's him will be marrying them,' Kit Ring told him. 'He's with the lads over and he's young like themselves. He'll not scold them.'

'There is no scolding over there,' Rubawrd responded angrily. 'Folk over there wouldn't stand for it. God is easygoing over there, not like here where He's never done with tormenting people, especially people like us with no substance to speak of.'

Towards the end of April the weather grew mild. The Dirra-beg smallholders fared forth into the boglands and cleaned the turfbanks of the uppermost scraws to make way for the

306

sleánsmen who would thrust their gleaming, right-angled blades into the soft, unresisting peat deposits which had accumulated, seven sods deep, over the centuries. Each turf-cutting meitheal consisted of three men, a sleánsman, a breensher who piked the sods, cut and shaped by the sleán and a spreader whose title would signify that his function was to spread the turf to the outermost edges of the turf bank. Two days of uninterrupted cutting were sufficient to supply the annual needs of the Dirrabeg smallholders, most of whom would cut for several extra days and dispose of the harvested peat in the late autumn and early winter to customers in Trallock. A number of householders in town owned their own turfbanks but rather than expose themselves to the wind and rain which swept regularly over the brown boglands they hired teams of Dirrabeg turfcutters to excavate their fuel supplies for an agreed sum. These commissions provided a desperately-needed source of extra income for the three- and four-cow smallholders of Dirrabeg.

Twenty

THE TURF-CUTTING was in full swing when the first of the Orvertian Fathers arrived in Dirrabeg. Father Hugh Mane was described by the retreat master of the mother house in Belfast as the gentleman of the mission although on this occasion he was also to play the role of advance guard. Rotund, bald-headed and perpetually smiling, he represented the diplomatic arm of the Orvertians. He arrived in Trallock on the late evening of the Sunday preceeding the opening of the mission. This allowed him a week to acquaint himself with the lifestyle and cultural background of the parish as well as getting to know the mood and humour of the parishioners.

When his back-up arrived on the following Saturday he would be able to provide them with the quintessential elements of his findings. He fully realised, however, that from a purely fundamental point of view he would be going nowhere without a thorough briefing from Canon Peter Pius Tett, the parish priest.

He was met on his arrival at the presbytery by Father Dully. The Canon had already gone to bed. He had earlier explained to his curates that he would need all his energies for the coming fortnight. It had been agreed that both Father Butt and Father Dully would take their annual leave during the fortnight of the mission; this, the Canon explained, would give the missioners a freer hand and a sense of total responsibility. He neglected to mention that he would be remaining on in the presbytery and that he would not be relinquishing a shred of his authority for the fortnight. When Father Dully pointed out that he usually took his holidays sometime during the later months of July and Autumn, the Canon had responded with a sigh of pretended sympathy.

'This is a special time, Father,' he had explained. 'A time when we must all extend ourselves a little and make sacrifices for the sake of the parish as a whole.'

Father Butt did not complain although he would have preferred a break during September or October when the harvesting would be completed and his sister free to accompany him on outings to Cork and Dublin or, indeed, wherever her fancy might indicate. Still, late April was a quiet enough time on his brother-in-law's hill farm. All the cows would have calved and the lambing would be completed.

Father Dully escorted the newly-arrived Orvertian to the hotel where he was warmly received by the manager and staff who assured him that they would be at his disposal day and night. Father Mane declined the offer of a meal. Tentatively Father Dully enquired if he would care for a drink only to be told that he had never indulged in his life.

'I have seen the misery it has brought,' he told the junior curate, 'and while I might sometimes endorse drinking in moderation I very much fear that there are few who are capable of drinking judiciously.'

Father Dully had been disappointed. He had drunk with other mission fathers – Passionates, Redemptorists and Dominicans – and they had, with the occasional exception, turned out to be both intelligent and restrained in the matter of alcoholic intake. He had not fully decided where he would spend his holidays. More than likely on the following morning he would sit behind the wheel of his car and drive to the other end of the country, probably ending up in Donegal before night fell.

The sobering thought that a retreat or mission might be in progress at his first port of call had occurred to him. Nevertheless, he would spend a night or two in Donegal, more than likely in some cheap hotel. He would cheerfully have gone abroad but his finances precluded any such possibility. He would after Donegal inflict himself, through necessity, on members of his family. There were two married brothers in the civil service in Dublin and a sister married in County Wexford. His parents were long dead. The proceeds from the sale of the modest family home had been divided equally amongst brothers and sisters. There had been no windfall since then. There would be a welcome for him when he called but all three as he well knew were in somewhat straitened circumstances with large families and inadequate incomes. Four days and four nights with each should just about exhaust his welcome. He would be unable, much as he might desire it, to make any contribution to his board and lodgings unless an extra round in the pub could fairly be described as compensation in part.

All the members of the Dully family were partial to pub outings on a regular basis and this left them chronically short of ready cash on occasion. There was no hardship as such but in each of the households the shoddy quality of the trappings and general disrepair would suggest that income might be put to more practical use. Father Dully's personal account was already drastically overdrawn in the bank.

The parish from which Father Dully had been transferred had never warranted the luxury of two priests. He was now permanently attached to the parish of Trallock from which it was expected Father Butt would soon be elevated to his own parish. As senior curate in Trallock Father Dully was sure that he would be able to reduce his overdraft but inevitably there would be a short and somewhat austere period before things fell into place. Meanwhile he would not concern himself with presbytery infighting. He would do his job but no more than his job.

'My philosophy,' he once told a classmate when they accidentally met at the seaside resort of Ballybunion, 'is to be found at the end of a stanza in one of my favourite songs, "The Old Bog Road". You'll recall where it says: "I'll draw my pay and go my way and smoke my pipe alone."'

'Doesn't seem to be a very Christian philosophy,' his former classmate had argued.

'Oh, but it is,' Father Dully had responded without hesitation. 'Each of us has his place and his own individual outlook and you could say that the sum of all our philosophies is comprehensively Christian. It all boils down to free will but free will that is well within the framework of Catholic thinking. My philosophy gives me a free hand and more important an individualistic approach and yet I am harnessed to the greatest religious movement the world has ever known. I am shackled but I am free because of my philosophy.'

Father Hugh Mane's knock on the door of Mossie Gilooley's tiny farmhouse consisted of two gentle raps with the knuckle of the index finger. It was a knock which was not meant to be answered. Father Mane lifted the latch before anybody within could come forward to see who was there. In a thrice his smiling presence was dominating the kitchen.

He had been driven to his destination in the Canon's Ford Consul by Shamie Deale, the parish clerk. The car would be at his and the other missioners' disposal until the mission ended with the renewal of the baptismal vows and the renunciation of the devil. Shamie had drawn to a halt under a giant whitethorn, very nearly in full leaf, obscuring the car and its passengers from view of the Gilooley house. This way Father Mane would find himself at the front door before the occupants could be alerted. Earlier he had descended upon the homes of two other Dirrabeg defectors. Both had flown the scene having spied his approach from a distance, leaving the unfortunate womenfolk to face the music. They had been tearful and

311

apologetic, assuring Father Mane that they would redouble their prayers for the salvation of their husbands' souls.

'Tell him,' Father Mane had assured the first of the females, 'that he need have no fear of me. Tell him to come to my confessional and if he is truly contrite I shall dispense the absolution his soul so desperately needs.'

'I will. I will, Father. I'll bring him in myself. I'll drag him after me if I have to.'

The second visit had followed a similar pattern. Mossie Gilooley, however, was caught redhanded sitting by the kitchen hearth, his pipe in his mouth, his hands still tingling after a long day breenshing turf. Without a word he rose, nodded politely in Father Mane's direction before making for the door through which the Orvertian had unexpectedly entered.

'Stay, stay I beg you,' Father Mane had entreated. He placed his upraised hands on Mossie Gilooley's shoulders and beamed upon him with smiling face. Mossie Gilooley was taken aback. He had expected to be harangued in Tett-like fashion whereas this gentle intruder seemed friendly in the extreme.

'Please, I beg of you,' Father Mane's eyes grew suddenly moist, 'do not turn aside from your God. It is He who has sent me here.' The priestly hands fell away from Mossie Gilooley's shouders and seized the fiddler's hands. He held them gently for a while, his sincerity undeniable, his compassion overflowing. Gertie Gilooley threw herself at Father Mane's feet and clutched his trouserfolds begging forgiveness and sobbing distractedly. It was precisely the diversion her husband so desperately needed to break away from the spell of the saintly influence which had almost melted his iron resolve. He ran gratefully from the kitchen.

Behind him Father Mane lifted Gertie to her feet and assured her of forgiveness.

At the end of two days devoted exclusively to Dirrabeg the gentle Orvertian failed to make real contact with even one defector. He was genuinely disturbed and worried. The womenfolk had all been contrite and sincere in their desires to have their husbands once more within the framework of the faith. There was little more he could do until the others came.

They arrived on the Saturday prior to the mission. First came the thunderous and outspoken Father Artie Craw and secondly the more mellifluous Father Shamus O'Shule. Curly-haired and dour of mien, Father Craw seemed now to be the only hope of salvation for Dirrabeg. Penitents had often confided to Father Mane that they had quite literally felt the hairs standing on the crowns of their heads while they listened to Father Craw's descriptions of the lamentations of the lost souls who resided permanently in hell.

Father Shamus O'Shule on the other hand was capable of bringing tears to the eyes of reprobate and murderer alike with his glorious account of the after-life in the regions of heaven. Fathers Craw and O'Shule complemented each other ideally while Father Mane looked after the organisational work which included everything from tracking down recalcitrants to the formulation of mission policy for the fortnight and the drawing-up of a programme for each of the two weeks, first of which would be devoted exclusively to women and the second to men. Special sessions for children would be organised for pre-scribed afternoons.

On the Monday morning after his arrival Father Mane was ushered into the presence of Canon Tett. At the Canon's invitation they conferred in the kitchen. It so happened that Father Mane was as strongly addicted to tea as the Canon. After several cups and two hours of questions and answers Father Mane felt that there was no more he could learn about the parish of Trallock.

He had hung on every word, sometimes in awe, other times in incredulity, as the Canon cited instances of pishoguery in Upper Dirrabeg. First was the report of the laying-down of a circle of thirteen hen eggs in a neighbour's field by someone who was envious of the ability of the would-be victim's hens

313

to produce phenomenal numbers of eggs. The evil circle would stop the hens from laying or so the neighbour hoped. Then there was the casting of a cow's afterbirth into the pastures of a successful dairy farmer. It was believed that such an action would result in wholesale abortions. There were instances of perjury, which was a reserved sin in the diocese, isolated cases of buggery involving livestock, down to the more mundane practices of sexual familiarity of one form or another, culminating with Canon Tett's pet aversion which was talking at the rear of the church and the entrances thereto by blackguards who should know better.

The Canon left the question of the Dirrabeg defectors and the scandalous saga of Dirrabeg school until the very end.

'Until very recently,' Canon Tett shook his head, 'I had a model parish here. I can't imagine what went wrong. Maybe I was too soft.'

It occurred to Father Mane that the Canon might be too old. Soft was a word that he would never ascribe to him.

'When things are going smoothly, Canon, we tend to take situations for granted and that is what may have happened here.'

Father Mane tried not to sound smug. 'But not to worry, Canon. When the Orvertians are through with this parish the evil will have departed and the good will have returned. Meanwhile you must not concern yourself. Leave matters in our hands and you won't have any regrets by the end of the day.'

The female mission ended on the third Sunday night of April. There was hardly a dry eye in the packed church at the close of Father O'Shule's final homily and certainly there was not a soul which was not truly shriven. Everybody was agreed that it was the most successful mission ever. Yet there were men in the parish of Trallock, middle-aged bachelors mostly, who roundly cursed the missioners. Certain more accommodating although less attractive females had suddenly stopped being liberal with their favours and thus it would remain for several

314

weeks after the missioners had departed the parish. No amount of coaxing, wheedling or bribing would induce them to revert to the old ways. A minority of these females would never again indulge their former boyfriends. Doctor Joe O'Dell would insist that this lunatic deprivation as he called it was responsible for a dramatic increase in the numbers committed to mental institutions. One demented soul, a wifeless agricultural labourer in his late forties, stripped himself down to his bare pelt and ran shrieking for hours through the countryside before his agonising delirium was arrested by members of his family. Tom Tyler it was who acted as his escort in Martin Semple's taxi which had been requisitioned specially for the poor fellow's transportation to the nearest mental institution.

'What happened to you at all, Jack my poor man?' Tom had asked sympathetically after they had put the suburbs of Trallock behind them.

'What happens to any man when the wick is cut off?' had come the response. There was another who positioned himself near the convent at the time when the older girls were departing the secondary school at the end of classes. There followed an exhibition of his genitalia which did not end until the last of the hysterical schoolgirls had disappeared from view. He was fortunate that the Civic Guards managed to spirit him away to the barracks before the outraged parents of Trallock could administer some instant justice of the physical kind. He was jailed for twelve months. There were other manifestations of sexual unrest but by the time the men's mission drew to a close a state of sanctified calm began to assert itself. The men's mission began on the final Sunday night of April at seven in the evening. At six o'clock the first of the parishioners from the outlying townlands trudged their ways through the town's entrances, bound for the parish church, the capacity of which would shortly be put to its severest test. It was expected that every man and youth in the parish from the age of fourteen to eighty would present themselves in the body of the church for this rare and fearful confrontation with the Orvertian Fathers.

There were many who trembled as the towering frontage of the church loomed into view. Others would sweat blood while the mission was in progress. Others would hide their blushing faces in perspiring palms as they listened to the catalogue of sins with which they had become all too familiar during their sojourn in the valley of tears.

On the Thursday night which was devoted solely to sexual transgressions the church was packed to more than its natural capacity with the sacristy being brought into use when no more could be fitted into the body of the church. The night before had been devoted in the same manner to the horrors of hell and the variety of hair-raising sounds and useless pleas emanating therefrom. Several men and boys fainted during the sermon and had to be borne from the church into the square outside where the fresh air quickly revived them and saw them eagerly returning for the remainder of the sermon without assistance of any kind.

On the Saturday afternoon before the final Sunday the three Orvertian Fathers sat around the table in the presbytery kitchen. Also present was Shamie Deale, the parish clerk, and Canon Tett. Nora Devane had been summarily dispatched for the week's provisions by the Canon. It emerged before the meeting ended that well over ninety-nine per cent of the population of the parish had attended confession and received absolution during the fortnight gone by. One would have felt that this should provide grounds for genuine celebration. By the missioners' reckoning three thousand five hundred and three souls had been cleansed of impurities between the confessionals, the hospital, the convent and visits to private homes. The population of Trallock, according to Shamie Deale, amounted to four thousand, two hundred and ten souls. This figure included every man, woman and child. However, when the number of children who had not yet reached the use of reason was deducted there remained the exact figure of three thousand, five hundred and thirty souls. This left a shortfall of twenty-seven unshrived parishioners. The Orvertians shook their heads despondently. Any less redoubtable order of priests would have been well pleased with the enormous percentage. By Orvertian standards, however, the mission was far from complete.

'Of course,' Shamie Deale reminded them, 'you must remember that an entire family of eight Smileys vacated the town just before the women's mission began. Three of the boys, Tom, Teddy and Bill and two of the girls, Sophie and Kathleen have all made their first holy communion. In fact Tom is confirmed. If you include the mother that amounts to six and if you take six from twenty-seven we are left with only twenty-one.'

Some of the gloom departed the depressed faces of the Orvertians.

'If you take the twelve from Dirrabeg,' Shamie Deale went on, 'and they seem determined to damn themselves anyway, we are left with nine.'

Whatever vestiges of defeatism remained were quickly erased from the now eager faces of the Orvertians. An announcement from the Canon was to impose an aura of victory where dejection and disappointment had recently flourished.

'Where are you leaving the Protestants?' he enquired of his parish clerk. 'It isn't but they're all damned anyway,' he cackled banteringly.

'May God forgive me!' Shamie Deale rebuked himself instantly for his inadvertent omission. 'A body would hardly notice the creatures in recent times they've become so withdrawn.'

'They had their day.' This time there was no trace of waggishness in the Canon's tone.

'Let me see now,' Shamie held up his left hand and began to count with the index finger of his right. 'Jasper and Henrietta Bowman is two. Sandy and Penny Latcher and their daughter Ivy brings us to five.' Shamie Deale paused, relishing his task,

317

his index finger stationary on the thumbnail of his left hand.

'The Misses Jackson,' Canon Tett cut in, irked by his clerk's attempts to remain in the limelight.

'Of course,' Shamie Deale pretended to be grateful, 'the Misses Jackson, Emmy and Prissy. That's seven all told and there isn't another Protestant in the parish.'

'Excluding the Dirrabeg defectors that leaves us with just two people,' Father Mane sounded thoughtful.

A radiant smile lighted up the face of Father O'Shule, beloved of the females of Trallock. No hint of a smile showed under the curly head of Father Artie Craw. Shamie Deale was to tell his wife Madge that night as they sat in front of the kitchen fire that the curly-haired Orvertian reminded him of nothing but an already well-blooded terrier who had been sicked upon the last remaining rats in a once populous sewer.

'Two, only two,' Father Craw spoke the words triumphantly.

'Only one, Father,' Shamie Deale informed him. 'The other has fled the coop.'

'Stop that silly chatter and tell us what you mean.' Canon Tett was becoming more irritated by the moment at the dominant role the parish clerk was playing in the proceedings.

'Sorry, Canon.' His tone was again full of immediate contrition. 'They're saying, Canon, that Moss Keerby the council worker took off with the Smiley woman and her children.'

'Who says that?' the Canon demanded angrily.

'I'm afraid 'tis common knowledge, Canon. The Smileys boarded the morning bus here in Trallock and Keerby boarded it at a crossroads about two miles outside the town. He carried two suitcases and he was dressed, or so they say, in his Sunday best.'

'And why didn't you let me know before this?' the Canon shouted the question, somewhat to the surprise of the Orvertians who had grown to like Shamie, having found him to be respectful and courteous as well as informative.

'How could I tell you, Canon, when I didn't know myself

till this very day,' Shamie lied.

The Canon muttered angrily under his breath. How in God's name, he asked himself, did Nora Devane slip up on this one. It was right down her alley and yet she had not come to hear of it. Was it possible she was slipping? She would be attaining to pension age in a short while. He would consider her future then.

Shamie Deale had informed Father Butt the moment he had heard, which was less than two hours after the Smiley exodus. Father Butt showed no surprise. He could not find it in his heart to condemn Moss Keerby outright and anyway there was nothing to suggest that there was anything more than a purely platonic friendship between them. Something more might certainly develop in the less Catholic climate across the Irish Sea but there was nothing anybody could do about that save the principals themselves.

Kitty Smiley's decision had not been taken lightly. Less than a fortnight before her leavetaking she had received word from a friend domiciled in London that her husband's winnings had run out and that he was contemplating a return to his native place. Kitty had immediately confided in Moss Keerby who volunteered to provide the passage money for herself and the children to the English midlands where Kitty had numerous friends and relations and where work was plentiful. She had accepted instantly. The following day she contacted her brother Donal and informed him of her decision.

'What are you going to do about Moss?' Donal had asked.

'I don't know what to do,' Kitty told him.

'Take the poor bastard with you,' Donal advised. 'Surely you're not going to let him behind in Trallock to die of a broken heart.'

'What will people say?' Kitty returned anxiously.

'It's not what people say that matters,' Donal told her. 'It's what you say and what your children say.'

That night Kitty put it to her children. First there were tears

319

and sombre faces at the prospect of Willie Smiley's return. Although often hungry and always without money the Smiley children had never been happier than during their father's absence. It was a time without beatings, scoldings and other forms of punishment. Moss Keerby called to the house most nights and sat by the fire with one or other of the girls on his knee. Sometimes he brought small paper bags of bullseyes. Other times his pockets would be filled with apples. He was a good storyteller. The children looked forward to his visits more than any other event during the long nights of winter and spring. After the rest of the children had gone to bed on the night after Kitty Smiley's visit to Dirrabeg she sat with her son Tom in the kitchen. No word passed between them for a long period. Finally Kitty Smiley spoke.

'What do you think, Tom?' she asked. 'You're the wise old man of the family. You've never given me bad counsel.'

'You can't leave him behind,' Tom spoke without looking directly at her.

'Look at me, Tom,' Kitty spoke the words tenderly. Tom Smiley lifted his head.

'He's too good a man, mother.' He spoke the words without trace of emotion. 'We all want him to come with us because he's always been with us. We could always count on him no matter what. He was our real father.'

They were the words Kitty wanted to hear. On the bus she sat next to the window with Moss Keerby by her side. The Smiley children sat together on the back seat, their faces radiant. For most of them it was their first bus ride. Only Tom and Sophie had ever been on a bus before. For all seven it was an experience to be cherished. Passengers who boarded the vehicle at the many stops along the way expressed their delight and appreciation of the handsome, well-behaved children who sat at the rear of the vehicle, content as if they had just arrived in heaven and would be staying put for all eternity. Many of the older passengers shook hands with the younger members

320

of the party when they alighted at the railway station in Killarney.

If the bus ride had been heavenly the train journey was equally so except that on the train there were flush toilets and wash basins which could be filled with hot or cold water. The whole business was almost too much for the younger members of the Smiley family. At Northampton station in England they were met by Nellie Hallapy's brother Mick Brady, a successful sub-contractor in the building industry. He looked appraisingly at Tom Smiley and Moss Keerby. His brother-in-law Donal Hallapy had been right. Moss Keerby was a fine man and young Tom Smiley had the makings of a fine man. They were the kind of combination Mick Brady would desperately need in the coming years, youth allied to experience. The house where the Smiley family would be staying was one of several semi-derelict buildings which he had acquired over the years. He had purchased them cheaply immediately after the war for those of his workers who might need them and had carried out the necessary repairs in his spare time during week-ends. It had been settled that Moss Keerby and Tom Smiley would start with one of Mick's work crews on the following Monday, Moss at the unprecedented wage of five shillings an hour and Tom Smiley, a month away from his fifteenth birthday, at the astronomical wage of three shilling an hour. Both were left gasping for breath after Mick Brady had divulged his rates of pay.

'The work is hard,' he warned, 'and the hours sometimes long but you boys do well by me and there need be no ceiling to your earnings.'

That night Moss Keerby shared a room with Tom, much to Tom's surprise. During the train journey from Fishguard to Northampton Kitty Smiley and the new man in her life had laid their plans carefully. Their lovemaking would be confined to times when there was nobody in the house. The children must never know. Both were agreed it would not be in keeping with the upbringing they deserved. Should Willie Smiley in

321

the meanwhile pass on to his eternal reward they would marry after a decent interval.

In the presbytery kitchen the Orvertian Fathers fidgeted as they waited for Shamie Deale to divulge the name of the only unshrived soul in the parish, defectors apart. Shamie seemed reluctant to part with the information. He explained that he was not a hundred per cent certain, that there was always the outside possibility of an innocent man being victimised, even disgraced.

'The name!' Father Artie Craw bellowed, his dense dark curls quivering on top of his head.

'The name, you fool!' Canon Tett insisted, 'and hurry up about it.'

'Shyle is his name,' Shamie Deale released the surname reluctantly.

Ned Shyle was an inoffensive cobbler who lived and plied his trade in one of the end houses of Carter's Row. On Saturday afternoons his wife Nora would mount her bicycle and journey to her widowed father's home in Upper Dirrabeg, there to spend the remainder of the day cleaning the house and providing a fresh shirt and underwear for her ailing parent. Later she would cook a meal and stay for the night, returning to Trallock for early mass on Sunday morning. Shamie Deale would testify that the same Nora Shyle never missed mass on week mornings either. She was known among her neighbours as a devout woman, perhaps a trifle too devout. She scorned scent and make-up, religiously combed her flowing hair every Monday and Thursday night and boasted that she had never entered a hairdressers.

'Maybe if she did,' Minnie Halpin once confided to her own hairdresser, 'Ned mightn't be so manky.' What Minnie said was true enough. Ned Shyle let it be known that he would not be averse to half-soling and heeling a pair of ladies' slippers without expectation of financial recompense provided the lady in question called on a Saturday night when he would be free

322

to receive her in privacy. One such caller turned out to be an unattached female from the neighbouring parish of Ballyleen. After her initial visit she took to calling every Saturday night.

Armed with this most damnatory evidence, the trio of Orvertians led by Father Artie Craw made their way to Carter's Row as soon as their normal Saturday night obligations were fulfilled. Darkness had fallen as they entered Carter's Row from Healy Street. Pedestrians in Healy Street abandoned whatever pursuits in which they were at the time engaged and followed discreetly, slipping silently into the houses of friends adjacent to the cobbler's when it became apparent that this well-known den of iniquity was to be the Orvertians' destination.

Father Artie Craw it was who smote upon the front door. Upon arriving at the door he had lifted his hand but had not brought it to bear upon the door until his colleagues had stationed themselves at the rear of the house. Not a soul was to be seen in Carter's Row, from one end to the other, when the thunderous knock sounded. Barely parted curtains flickered on every window upstairs and downstairs. Shadowy, barely discernable figures watched silently from behind partly opened doors. Father Craw stood with his hands folded, a look of the most intense determination on his zealous features. He saw himself at that moment as a true Orvertian, the reincarnation of the order's martyred founder, Blessed Oliver Orvert. Now more than ever did the long years of self-sacrifice stand in his stead.

Like all Orvertians Father Craw had spent a year of spiritual contemplation before being accepted as a first year student in the mother house in Belfast. There followed eight gruelling, torturous, excruciating years before ordination. These were followed by a three year stint operating from one of the order's houses in East London. Finally there was a sapping, backbreaking ten year purgatory in the mission fields of Borneo, a veritable crucible where the annual mortality rate among the Orvertian propagandists was never less than fifteen per cent and often as high as thirty.

The ten years in Borneo had strengthened Artie Craw mentally and physically but had taken their physical toll of Fathers Mane and O'Shule who stood somewhat shamefacedly at the rear of Ned Shyle's beleaguered abode. They told themselves they were present only because Father Artie had insisted.

'Open up in God's name!' The stentorian voice of their more aggressive confrere must surely strike terror into the heart of the ensnared adulterers, or had they observed the approaching Orvertians and managed to make good their escape just before Father Craw's insensitive descent upon their illicit love nest?

Before Father Craw could smite upon the door for the fourth time in as many minutes it opened partly to reveal the hastily-dressed figure of Ned Shyle.

'What do you want?' he asked innocuously.

'What I want is your confession,' came the reply.

Slowly Ned Shyle withdrew a hammer from behind his back. It was a heavy hammer with a long wooden haft.

'You've finished me,' he said weakly, advancing a step. 'I can never raise my head in this town again. Go, before I split your skull. Go!'

Father Craw took stock of the half-clad individual who confronted him so menacingly. The hand which held the hammer trembled and the eyes which were fixed so steadfastly on his seemed crazed and murderous. Slow-moving streams of spittle trickled to the corners of his chin from his compressed lips, blue in colour. Father Craw withdrew a step, the curls tingling as they had never tingled before. He withdrew a second step. Ned Shyle allowed the hammer to fall from his hand and returned to the interior of his house without closing the door behind him.

At the rear of the house the pair of stationary Orvertians were startled when the woman emerged from the door at the rear. She was so preoccupied with drawing a flimsy slip over the exposed upper half of her body and lower portion covered

324

by knee-length bloomers that she did not notice the riveted priests who stood embarrassedly watching her. Both Father O'Shule and Father Mane had been surfeited with the sight of female breasts in all shapes and sizes during their sojourn in Borneo, but never before had they beheld a bare bosom of the proportions which enhanced the shapely front of the adulterous female who stood mutely in front of them. Slip safely in place, she wilted visibly before the dispassionate eyes of the priests and bent to retrieve the dress which had fallen from her grasp as she hurried through the rear door. For several seconds she stood stock still before drawing the dress over her head. She wore neither hose nor footwear. No doubt these lay somewhere along her line of flight. Covered by the dress she nodded modestly and respectfully at the Orvertians before mounting her nearby bicycle.

The close of the male mission was a resounding success and on the Sunday night the final response to the the final question from Father Craw was tumultuous and deafening, the sound spilling out into the silent square and exultantly traversing the deserted streets until it faded and died. The question had been: 'Do you renounce the Devil with all his works and pomps?' It had been posed by Father Craw and the unanimous and immediate response of the fifteen hundred bearers of fifteen hundred flickering, eighty-five per cent wax candles, consisted of the words: 'I do.'

Despite the entreaties of their womenfolk the Dirrabeg defectors held fast to their resolve and spent the final week out of doors in the bogs. They devoted most of the time to cutting the turf, a team of three to each turfbank. They revelled in the silent monotony of the cutting, breenshing and spreading and when dinner time came round they sat in the lee of convenient turf ricks or hedgerows and spoke about many things, chiefly football and bodhrán making, never referring to the mission which had taken the town of Trallock in its grasp and wrung from it the very last ounce of sinfulness. Several sightings

325

were reported of a curly-haired missioner and whenever there seemed to be the slightest danger of contact the turf-cutters vacated the banks and found impenetrable refuge in the depths of the bog. Mention was made of the Dirrabeg defectors, albeit obliquely, several times during the men's mission.

On the morning after the final Sunday night the Orvertian Fathers left by bus for the mother house in Belfast. A large crowd gathered in the square to wish them goodbye and as the bus pulled out the hundreds of men and women congregated in its wake gave full vent to the stirring hymn 'Faith of Our Fathers'. Joe O'Dell stood in the doorway of the Bus Bar, a glass of gin and tonic clutched in his hand. He felt relieved that the missioners had departed. The sense of sanctity which had pervaded the town during the preceeding fortnight had served only to depress him.

'I suppose really I should be grateful to them,' he told Fred Halpin. 'Several outstanding bills have been paid during the last two weeks and before the piety wears thin I daresay I'll be in receipt of as many more but I was never a man for religion Fred. It gets me down. I don't mind missioners as such. They do more good than harm and there are people who need them the way some of my patients need certain medicines to sustain them. I'm different. If I feel in the need of religion I'll go in search of it but I'll shy off when it comes in search of me.'

It was Joe O'Dell who brought the news of Walter Fleece's death.

'That's if you can call it news,' he confided to Fred Halpin over the second gin and tonic, 'because the wretch has been dead for five years.'

Joe O'Dell had received the information from Mother Columba although nobody would ever know his source. In a lengthy letter to the Reverend Mother Monty Whelan had divulged the news of the death. He had himself received the information from Father Bertie Stanley who had asked a friend in Northampton, a detective inspector, to make enquiries.

Walter Fleece had married less than three months after arriving in England. He had successfully changed both his identity and his faith. He married his landlady, a practising member of the Church of England, and became a prized exhibit of his adopted persuasion. Conversions from the Catholic faith to its ancient flagellator were rare indeed. As a result Walter Fleece became something of a celebrity, a person to be cherished by the local pillars of his newly adopted faith. It would have been unthinkable after a while to embark on a church outing or to hold fêtes and bazaars without the presence of Walter. He never refused an invitation and it was this celebratory dedication which eventually led to his being identified five years after his death during a coach tour. His wife had cradled his head in her arms during the final moments of his expiry while all around faithful friends listened intently for the inevitable appeal said to be fervently expressed by all Catholics about to draw their last breaths. The ultimate plea for a Catholic priest never came and thus was vindicated his wife's belief that he would not abandon the faith they had shared for so long. Monty Whelan and Daisy Fleece were married immediately by Father Bertie Stanley. A week later he officiated at the ceremony between Conor Quille and Noranne Ring.

Willie Smiley arrived in Trallock a week to the day after his family's departure. A ticket home and two pounds subsistence money had been provided by the Salvation Army. His return was the talk of the town for several days. According to Nora Devane he wore the same shoes and clothes, seemingly unchanged and filthy in the extreme. He was greeted with considerable amusement by the town's layabouts and was followed to the empty house by several cornerboys who had agreed among themselves that his reaction would be worth noting. There was none. When he arrived the door was open and it was obvious at once that the interior had been ravished. Even the range which had been so firmly embedded had vanished. Neither was there a chair on which he might sit or a bed on

327

which he might lie. Without a word he left the desolate scene.

First things first, he thought. There was still a pound left from the Salvation Army subvention. As he neared Journey's End his followers dropped off and resumed their vigils at the town's corners. Willie Smiley felt frustrated. During the final stage of his journey he had decided to beat the daylights out of his wife regardless of the consequences. He reckoned she had well and truly earned any punishment he might inflict upon her, especially since she made no attempt to locate him towards the end of his exile, particularly when his money was gone.

In the envelope of the letter which Monty Whelan had written to Mother Columba there was a cheque for twenty pounds payable to Katie Hallapy. The money was to go toward the purchase of a new bicycle. Columba resolved to pay a visit to the Hallapy household in Dirrabeg as soon as possible after she had replied to Monty's letter. She opened by answering the several questions he had posed in his letter. His replacement at the National School in Dirrabeg ruled with a firm hand but it was rumoured in educational circles that if the attendance at the school suffered further decline it would have to be closed and its pupils obliged to attend school in Trallock. As far as she knew Bluenose and his Dirrabeg neighbours were safe and sound in their paganistic ways despite the best efforts of the Orvertian Fathers. Canon Tett seemed hale and hearty but was now often seen with his fingers in his ears endeavouring to shut out the sound of imaginary drumbeats. The Orvertian mission had been a resounding success if one did not take the Dirrabeg defectors into account. Columba made no reference to the humiliation of Ned Shyle the cobbler, merely stating that he had left Trallock suddenly and unexpectedly. Monty had mentioned that he would be writing to Father Butt, Fred and Minnie Halpin, to Tom Tyler and to Joe O'Dell. Columba felt that any one of these would be far better qualified to outline what had transpired in Carter's Row on the Saturday night before the close of the mission. The odd thing was that since Ned Shyle's disappearance his wife had started to use scent and make-up and had submitted her hitherto-undefiled head to the professional care of a a hairdresser. Columba briefly described a visit by the Orvertians to the convent on one of the afternoons of the female mission. They had heard confessions and spoken privately with each member of the community. Columba had been impressed by the efficiency with which they carried out their duties but apart from Father Hugh Mane was not so over-come by their manners. She described the honey-tongued Father O'Shule as a thwarted romantic.

'Now settled and secure in appearance,' she wrote, 'he reminds me of a mature bull with his big benign eyes and resigned gait. As for Father Craw of the curling hair we must be grateful that he is not permanently attached to the parish of Trallock.'

Columba's visit to Dirrabeg was not as successful as she would have wished. Donal Hallapy had been spreading dung on his rushy pastures when she arrived in Martin Semple's taxi. The sound of the car horn reached him in the tiny cutaway field furthest from the house. He upended the asscart and thrusting the four-pronged pike into the heaped cargo eased it on to the green surface while the mare grazed from the freshly sprung grass at her feet. It was the twentieth fall of dung since he had begun work at eight o'clock that morning. The loads already deposited stood in four neat rows waiting to be pike-spread as soon as the entire area of the field was provided for. It was tiresome, feculent work but without the laying on of the dung there would be a scarcity of hay before summer came round again. When the car horn sounded a second time he flicked the reins and smacked the mare twice on the croup with the palm of his hand. She was tired enough but she responded gamely to his inducement.

They sat with Columba for more than an hour but for all her persuasion would no longer consent to send Katie to the

329

convent in September.

'There's too much talk about me and my friends,' Donal told her.

'If there isn't talk about one thing,' Columba replied philosophically, 'there will be talk about another. The important thing to remember is that no matter what's said or what's done Katie will have to come first.'

'And that is exactly where she will be coming for we don't want her being pointed out and talked about above all the others. We want her to live normal.' Donal knew his words made good sense.

'And what's to become of her?' Columba demanded angrily. 'Where is she going to be educated the way she deserves?'

'I have plans,' Donal Hallapy turned his back to the women-folk and looked out the open door into the gusty April afternoon. 'I have positive plans.' He spoke emphatically, so much so that his wife wondered what he meant. She deduced from his manner of speaking that he had already made up his mind and knowing him as she did she felt that argument would be fruitless once he had resolved in his mind to do something.

'And what is it you plan to do?' Columba asked, the anger now absent from her voice.

'England.' Donal uttered the single word with a finality that made the pronouncement sound irrevocable. 'She'll have every chance there. I have come to the conclusion that we would all be better off there.' He turned and looked at his wife, a smile of triumph on his face. 'I'll go out now and spread what dung I have laid out and when I come back later in the evening we'll sit down and make our plans.'

Nellie Hallapy nodded and joined her hand together. The gesture was deliberate, an indication that she would not be saying anything at that time.

'I'm sorry.' Mother Columba reached into the folds of her habit and withdrew the cheque. She spoke in measured tones as she examined the figures on the rectangular chit.

'As the child's parents you know best,' she conceded, 'although I would dearly love to have a girl like Katie in the convent.' She sighed deeply as she rose.

'You had better take this,' she addressed herself to Donal who took the cheque in his hand and saw that it was made out to his daughter. Columba was speaking again.

'Before he went away he told me that it was his intention to provide Katie with a gift of a bicycle when she would be enrolled in the convent.'

'Then you had better send it back to him,' Donal informed her, 'because there won't be any need for a bicycle now.'

'He said in the letter,' Columba moved towards the door, 'that if Katie would not be going to the convent you were to have the money. Goodbye and God bless you both. Ireland's loss is England's gain.'

Nellie Hallapy remained seated while her husband continued to look out silently at the drifting clouds which were arriving in increasing numbers from the southwest. After a while she spoke. Her tone was subdued.

'What's all this about England?'

'I have decided to make an honourable surrender.' Donal's tone was equally subdued.

'And what about the cows?'

'I'll sell the cows.'

'And the meadows?'

'I'll let the meadows. Cuss the farmer will be glad to have them. I had thought to sell everything but who knows? Maybe one of the lads will want to come back some day.'

'Maybe 'tis ourselves will want to come back.'

'No!' Donal sounded adamant. 'I've had my fill of poverty and slavery. I've given all I'm going to give to this place. We have lives to live, you and I. Tonight you will write to your brother Mick and tell him to expect us.'

'When?'

Donal pondered the question for a moment.

331

'Mid-May,' he replied. 'We should be good and ready by mid-May.'

Suddenly an expression of alarm appeared on Nellie's face. 'The turf!' she cried out. 'What will we do about it?'

'There's no need to do anything about it,' Donal answered calmly, 'because as sure as you're sitting where you are every last sod of it will be stolen by them that'll need it more than we will the moment it's ready for burning.'

'Take this,' he said and advancing, laid the cheque in her lap. He glanced at the pot-bellied clock which stood on the mantelpiece. 'It's now three o'clock in the day,' he informed her. 'That leaves you plenty of time.'

'Time for what?' she asked.

'Time to borrow Kit Ring's bicycle and head for Trallock.'

'What's on in Trallock?' she asked.

'Coats is what's on there,' he told her, 'and dresses is what's on and shoes is what's on there and if you are not outfitted in the very best of all three when I come back here this evening I'll blacken every inch of your beautiful behind.'

Donal Hallapy hitched up his trousers, blew his nose loudly and went out of doors to untackle the mare. Free at last she rolled on the dried dirt passage which led to the by-road. She flailed the air with her four hooves and snorted in appreciation at the prospect of her fill from the springing clovers which beckoned from every side. In the cutaway field Donal lofted his dung-laden pike and shook the top-heavy fork into the wind, whistling happily as the dung-caked wisps and hard flakes settled on the green grass. He had experienced the overpowering feeling of having been free to give generously for the first time in his life. He would sell the cows and calves at the May fair in Trallock. Nellie would dispose of the hens in her own time. The mare would have to be sold. He looked forward to the journey, to the high wages but most of all, although he would never admit it to anyone, to attending mass once more.

Twenty-one

RUBAWRD RING, CAPTAIN of the Dirrabeg Wren, sat by the kitchen fire, his tired feet immersed in a basin of warm water. Earlier in the day he had led the youngest of his cows to be serviced by the white-head bull of the farmer Thomas Cuss whose verdant acres fronted both sides of the roadway for the better part of a mile between the cross of Dirrabeg to within a mile and a half of the suburbs of Trallock. The four year old bull, ponderous and rippling, in prime condition, raised his great head from the confines of his pen and surveyed the latest arrival to his domain. Thomas Cuss it was who opened the gate of the pen. With surprising agility and an unlikely but sudden turn of speed the white-head hoisted the greater bulk of his poundage on top of his consenting visitor without as much as a by-your-leave. The operation was completed in seconds. The white-head slowly dismounted, his head aloft, his front hooves plopping heavily on the concrete yard. He stood unmoving for a moment, his eyes drowsy, an abject figure of dejection and befuddlement. Then as he fully realised his obligations he advanced a step and nudged his latest conquest appreciatively on the shoulder before ambling back to his pen.

'I'll settle with cash this time,' Rubawrd Ring thrust his hand into his trousers pocket.

'No need for that, Rubawrd,' Thomas Cuss protested. 'You

can give me a day later in the year.'

'I won't be here later in the year,' Rubawrd informed him.

'I don't follow you, Rubawrd.'

'I'll be moving out,' Rubawrd explained.

'England eh!'

'England is right, Thomas, lock, stock and barrel; man, woman and child. Let me know how much is going to you and I'll be on my way.'

'Forget it,' Thomas Cuss told him.

'I'm grateful to you,' Rubawrd spoke thankfully.

'What about the others?' Thomas Cuss asked.

'They should start bulling any day now,' Rubawrd informed him.

Thomas Cuss fingered the grey stubble on his fleshy chin.

'I can take them off your hands if you like.'

'I had thought to take them to the May fair in Trallock. With the new grass coming up the demand will be there.'

'The grass is growing. I'll grant you that,' Thomas Cuss said, 'and they're good cows. Is it the cabbage or what?'

'The cabbage and other things,' Rubawrd replied.

'I'll give you as good a price as any,' Thomas Cuss promised. 'Just tell me what's on them and if it's any way reasonable I won't fall out with you.'

Eventually they settled on a price. It was agreed that Rubawrd would leave the serviced cow where she was and return immediately with the others. His wife had cycled to town with Nellie Hallapy, Nellie, the lighter of the two, sitting astride the rickety carrier. Kit Ring had gone to Trallock at Nellie's insistence. Rubawrd showed no surprise when he heard of Donal Hallapy's decision. He had been on the point of making a similar one himself and he resolved there and then to dispose of his cows to Thomas Cuss. He would hold his only remaining calf until the May fair. It would pay for one more farewell fling at the Bus Bar before he departed his native land.

When Kit Ring arrived from Trallock Rubawrd was drying

his feet with a threadbare towel. As though he were relating an unimportant everyday matter he filled her in on the historic events of the afternoon.

'What about the turf?' she asked.

'I'll make it up into horse stoolins and I'll sell it off the bank.'

He handed her the envelope stuffed with notes which Thomas Cuss had given him.

'We'll want new clothes and shoes and then there's the matter of our fare,' he said.

'Don't you want some of it?' she asked on the verge of tears as she beheld the wad of five pound notes which the envelope contained.

'No,' he returned firmly. 'I'll drink the calf at the May fair in Trallock and that will do me nicely. I'll have the turf money for the journey.' He pushed the basin aside with one of his bare feet and took her in his lap.

'Now, now,' he said gently as he felt her warm tears against his face. 'There's no need for that and well you know it. We'll do well over there. Sure isn't there more of us over there than there is here.'

'I know,' she sobbed, 'that's why I'm crying.'

Word of the impending departure of two of the leading members of the Dirrabeg Wren reached Mossie Gilooley through his son Mattie. He set out at once for Donal Hallapy's to find out if the story was true.

'It's true,' Donal told him.

'That settles it so,' he said. 'I'll sell the cows the May fair. I'm not going to be left behind to be excommunicated.'

A week earlier the brothers Costigan had left by bus for Dublin where they proposed to spend a night of drunkenness and debauchery before embarking on the ship which would land them in Holyhead. Stock and farm had realised nine hundred pounds. They decided to retain the house.

'You never know,' Peter had confided to Nellie Hallapy, 'we might want to come back for a holiday some time and if we

335

don't there's others in the family that surely will.'

'Mass is what I look forward to,' Paddy Costigan laid the cup of tea which he had been drinking on the floor of the Hallapy's kitchen and joined his hands together, 'mass and confession. Maybe I'll go to Father Bertie. I'd say he'd be soft on sins of the flesh.'

'And what sins of the flesh have you to confess Paddy?' Donal Hallapy asked with a laugh.

'You'd be surprised, boy,' Paddy Costigan replied with a toss of his head as he winked at young Johnny Hallapy. 'By the time I face Father Bertie I might have a few blistering tales to tell. Right, Johnny!'

'Right, Paddy!' Johnny Hallapy winked in return.

Canon Peter Pius Tett privately celebrated his seventy-ninth birthday on the thirteenth day of May. He made no mention of the occasion to either his housekeeper or his curates.

'What they don't know won't trouble them,' he spoke the thought aloud as he congratulated himself on having very nearly attained to his eightieth year. Most of his Salamanca classmates were dead. Offhand he could not recall one who was still in the land of the living. He stretched his long arms upwards over his head and with his longer, bonier legs kicked off the bedclothes. He peered through the bedroom window at the scene beneath. The square was thronged with people and cattle. Hastily he dressed himself. Ever since his arrival in Trallock he had made it a point to traverse the square and streets on the occasions of the big quarterly fairs. No harm to remind his rustic parishioners where the true authority of the town resided, to let them see whose bailiwick it was so that they might comport themselves with propriety and likewise see to the behaviour of their stock. The May fair morning was one on which he was always well disposed towards the farming community. The farmers, after all, were the mainstay of the parish even if their contributions to the upkeep of the church and clergy did not always measure up to his expectations. As he moved through the square, carefully avoiding the buff-green monticles of freshly-fallen dung, he stopped now and then to enquire about prices or to exchange views about weather prospects.

Everywhere he was greeted respectfully. All the exchanges were civil until he came to a corner of the square where Rubawrd Ring and Bluenose sat on the shafts of the latter's pony cart. The week before Bluenose had sold the pony and now a crude cardboard 'For Sale' sign indicated that the cart was also on the market. Loosely tethered to one of the wheels was the last remaining member of Rubawrd Ring's farmstock, a seven weeks old bull calf, the progeny of Thomas Cuss's white-head bull and a black heifer of less decisive strain. Bluenose's decision to forsake his cutaway farm and join his eldest daughter in the town of Northampton was seen as inevitable. The elderly couple had visibly declined after the rigours of the recent winter and spring. The move was seen as a sensible one. With the care and attention which their sons and daughters were prepared to lavish on them when they arrived in Northampton a new lease of life was assured them but it was the fact that Rubawrd Ring, Donal Hallapy and Mossie Gilooley were also Northampton bound that really decided him. At the end of May his oldest daughter and her husband would come to prepare them for the journey and escort them to their destination.

'I never thought I'd see the day,' Donal Hallapy laughed, well aware of Bluenose's abhorrence for the land of John Bull.

'And I never thought I'd see the day,' Bluenose shot back as quick as a wink, 'that Donal Hallapy's wife would be carrying the pattern of an Englishman around in her belly.'

Canon Tett stopped abruptly the moment he spotted Bluenose.

'Look what we have here!' he announced to nobody in particular. 'Fitter for you to be on your knees, old man, than flaunting yourself in public,' he threw out angrily.

'And fitter for you,' Bluenose answered without lifting his head, 'be making your will in some attorney's office for you'll

337

never see the month of July.'

'And you'll never see heaven, you scoundrel,' Canon Tett fumed.

'I'll see it in spite of you,' Bluenose rose to his feet and faced up to his tormentor. The Canon raised his walking stick and threatened to use it.

'Try that caper,' Bluenose warned, 'and I'll put you on the flat of your back, Roman collar or no Roman collar.'

'Ah, you're beneath contempt you godless wretch. I don't know why I bother with the likes of you.'

'Well, I can tell you, my man, there's no fear I'll ever again be bothering with the likes of you,' Bluenose threw out the words in triumph.

'You'll cry on your deathbed for a priest like all your equals.' Canon Tett raised an admonishing finger and shook it in Bluenose's face.

'That may well be,' Bluenose concurred, 'but if I do it won't be for you. It'll be for Father Bertie Stanley I'll be calling because that's the next priest I'll be facing when I go to confession in the land of John Bull!'

'Good riddance,' Canon Tett called back as he moved off through the fair. He had not relished the exchanges with Bluenose.

'Like all godless ignoramuses,' he spoke the consolatory words to himself, 'he has a rough and ready wit sufficient for the moment but easily forgotten after the heat of the give and take has died away.'

As the Canon proceeded with his itinerary the last remaining animal had been crowded into the square. Latecomers with cattle for sale would be obliged to stand their stock in Healy Street. The stench of cattle dung and urine was everywhere. Intermingling with the human smells the general effect must seem suffocating to the casual visitor. The rustic participants, however, relished the noise, the bustle and the overpowering fetor which grew more pronounced as the morning sun ascended the cloudless sky. The braying of hungry donkeys and the hysterical yelping of poorly trained dogs added to the general commotion. Yet it was all the very stuff of life to the hundreds of country folk who thronged the square. This was their day and they would make the most of it from morning till night, making regular but brief visits to the public houses where they would eventually settle as soon as their bawling charges had been sold. They would eat, too, in the kitchens of taverns like the Bus Bar, where steaming plates of boiled and peeled potatoes with bacon and cabbage or home-made mutton pies in soup-filled bowls and dishes helped to assuage the worsening pangs of ravenous, rustic hunger. The Hallapys, Donal, Tom and Johnny, had been on their feet since sunrise which was the time they had set out from Dirrabeg with the four milch cows and the pair of heifer calves. The journey to town had been slow and uneventful but they were fortunate to find a prominent location for the cattle in front of the church. Donal Hallapy received his first offer of fifty-eight pounds for cows and calves together at ten o'clock in the morning, four hours after their arrival in the great square of Trallock. Buyers had been cautious at the outset, preferring to wait until streets and square had absorbed their fill of cattle. Hence their early reluctance to make bids which might be considered acceptable.

'Here!' said the beefy, brown-coated, brown-booted buyer, 'I'll tell you what I'll do with you and after that you'll see me no more. I'll give you an even sixty pounds for the bunch and in doing so I could be wishing starvation on my wife and children.'

Donal stood undecided, unable to make up his mind. The price seemed reasonable but there was always the chance that he might fare better later in the day. Still, he thought, bids have been few all round and this is my first and maybe 'tis how 'twill be my last.

'My final word,' said the buyer, 'sixty pounds. Take it or leave it! There's hundreds here will be glad to hear from me.'

Donal still hesitated but a nod from Rubawrd Ring who had drawn near accompanied by Bluenose decided him. The buyer produced a thick roll of ten pound notes from a well-concealed inner pocket and counted out six into Donal's outstretched hand. Donal in turn reached into his pocket and withdrew a pound note which he handed to the buyer as luck money. The new owner located a raddle stick and imprinted a rough circle on the rumps of each of his purchases.

'Now,' he said, 'you'll stand them here until three o'clock which is the hour my drovers are due in town.'

'Fair enough,' Donal assured him, 'they'll be here waiting for them.'

After a quick shake hands the buyer took his leave and moved off quickly into the heart of the fair.

'A good price,' Rubawrd Ring nodded solemnly, 'a very good price.'

'I don't know,' Donal said not unhappily, 'I might have done better to wait.'

'No,' Bluenose cut in emphatically, 'it's a wise man who settles for the morning price.'

Later in the day Nellie and Katie Hallapy would walk to town. It was arranged that they would meet Donal at the Bus Bar where he would hand over the money for the purchase of suits of clothes, new boots for the boys and shoes and a summer dress for Katie. He would also look to his own outfitting sometime in the afternoon. Later Martin Semple would return Nellie and the Hallapy children to Dirrabeg together with the day's purchases and on the following morning he would present himself for the final time at the Hallapy home from where he would transport the entire family to the square of Trallock and to the bus which would convey them on the first stage of their journey to England.

Nellie's earlier misgivings about the abandonment of the family home and farm had quickly vanished. The new coat and frocks which she had purchased out of Monty Whelan's money had added a new dimension to her life. Her lifelong reluctance about journeying to town or further afield was now replaced by an eagerness to travel. The new clothes had made her look younger, made her feel better and re-awakened in her an outgoing attitude which had lain dormant for years. Men had started to notice her again. Her chief priority in England would be to look after her teeth. She had no doubt about their ability to survive, even to one day owning their own house, with hot and cold water, a washing machine, a refrigerator and all the other hitherto unattainable modern conveniences of which she could only dream until now. They would rise to a car too some day. Of that she had no doubt. During that heartbreaking stint of Donal's in the English midlands he had sent home more than enough to meet the family's needs and there had been enough left over to provide a better than normal living standard for several months after he had come home at her insistence.

Johnny Hallapy was the first to detect the awesome figure of Canon Tett. The elderly cleric had stopped near the church before casting an approving eye over the noisy, bustling climate, prior to partaking of the hearty breakfast which Nora Devane would have waiting for him. When his piercing eyes had taken in the general scene a perplexed look appeared on his face, a look occasioned by the presence before his very eyes of the accursed bodhrán player from Dirrabeg. Johnny Hallapy immediately retreated behind his father, covering his eyes with both hands and praying as fervently as ever he had prayed in his life that this terrifying minister of misfortune would pass by without indicting his father. His water flowed freely down the inside of his trousers; there was nothing he could do to stop it. Canon Tett, upon beholding Donal Hallapy and assuring himself after a lengthy surveillance that he was indeed the bodhrán player from the January wrendance at Bluenose Herrity's, lifted his cane aloft before pointing it in Donal's direction. Neither Donal nor young Tom Hallapy were aware of the Canon's proximity. The eyes of father and son were fixed on a barrow

341

of shimmering herrings which had suddenly been trundled into the scene. A tiny stall had been earlier erected next to the church gate and already a brisk trade in fresh fish was in progress. The barrowful of baleful-eyed herrings was unceremoniously upended into an empty crate on the ground beside the fish stall. There were many other stalls in the vicinity, some displaying periwinkles and seagrass, others golden strings of onions, assorted fruits and vegetables while more sported buns, lemonade and chocolate bars. There were numerous second-hand clothes stalls and a cockle stall where a woman in a white blouse and red apron disposed of pint glassfuls of freshly boiled cockles which could be consumed there and then or taken home to be re-heated in simmering milk.

The Canon stood speechless, with his cane pointed, still unnoticed by the throng. He looked about him in bewilderment, but no word came. His looks would seem to wish that the people in the vicinity would listen to the throbbing drumbeats which assailed his tormented ears. He gestured in perplexity to any who would heed him, his mouth opening and closing, words forming on his lips but no sound issuing forth. Vainly he gestured with his free hand while the cane remained pointed at Donal Hallapy. Now came the barbaric music, skirling, haunting and earsplitting and yet nobody seemed aware of this monstrous and pagan intrusion outside the sacred precincts of the church. As he signalled to all and sundry to come and listen to the cacophany, to bear witness to the sacrilege, he started to vociferate loudly but incoherently. By now quite a number of onlookers had gathered, among them Bluenose, Mossie Gilooley and Rubawrd Ring.

'What's the old fool jabbering about?' Bluenose asked.

'Seems to have lost his wits, poor chap,' Mossie Gilooley replied.

Rubawrd Ring stood silently watching. At first he was tempted to burst into laughter, but then the pathetic absurdity of the old man's feeble gesticulations and unintelligible effusions

342

struck a chord of pity. He turned away, unable to endure the sight of the slobbering, snivelling hulk to which Canon Tett had now been reduced. Donal Hallapy turned just in time to see the cane fall to the ground and to witness the disintegration of the man who had earned more fear and respect than any other in the parish of Trallock. Donal stepped forward to render what assistance he could but the Canon was stumbling hurriedly now towards the presbytery, his hands covering his ears, oblivious to the curious stares and concerned looks of his parishioners. Nothing mattered to him but to find sanctuary from the intolerable beating of the bodhrán and the accompanying music. In the presbytery he surprised both his curates in the cheerless dining room. He looked from one to the other, his eyes affrighted, saliva dribbling down to his collar from the sides of his mouth.

'Can you not hear?' he asked. He raised a hand aloft and cautioned them to be silent.

'Listen!' he called distractedly. 'Listen well now and you shall hear it the same as me.'

The curates sat rooted to their chairs listening for all they were worth, hardly daring to exchange glances, so engrossed had they become in their efforts to discern the sounds which were playing such havoc with the Canon. After a long silence, during which no sound whatever penetrated the walls of the presbytery, the curates exchanged looks of concern. It was Father Butt who spoke first.

'What sort of sounds exactly might they be, Canon?'

'You must be deaf,' the Canon threw back angrily, 'what sounds would they be but the sounds of the diabolical wrenband. There it is again, as plain as the day. Bodhráns, melodeons, fiddles and what have you. Look out now! They're coming into the house. See them!'

'But that's only the postman, Canon.' Father Dully spoke reassuringly.

'It's wrenboys I tell you. I'm getting out of here.' So saying

343

he staggered to the foot of the stairs and would have fallen to the floor had not his curates come from behind to support him. Between them they bore him upstairs to his room. Nora Devane followed closely behind. Father Dully turned and informed her coldly that there would be no need of her services, that she should return forthwith to the kitchen. In the bedroom they removed the Canon's collar as well as his shortcoat and shoes. Then they drew aside the bedclothes and laid him on the bed. Immediately he drew the clothes over his head, his body trembling, piteous whining coming from his tightly closed mouth.

'Stay with him. I'll fetch Joe O'Dell.' Father Butt was visibly shocked but in full control of the situation.

'He's been hearing the sound of the bodhrán for some time as you probably know,' Father Butt recalled. 'I won't be long.'

As he left the room the Canon raised himself in the bed and pointed with a whimper at the door, indicating that the wrenboys might be expected from that quarter. As Father Butt closed the door behind him the Canon lay back once more and drew the clothes over his head, his long, lean frame still shaking underneath, the same whimpering sounds rising and falling in the silence of the dreary room.

Later in the week Joe O'Dell was to explain to Mother Columba during a visit to an ailing nun that the Canon had fallen victim to a form of senile dementia. When pressed by Columba to elaborate Joe O'Dell sighed deeply before explaining. At the time they happened to be walking in the convent garden, an enclosed area which throbbed with birdsong.

'What it means in simple terms,' Joe O'Dell confided, 'is that our Canon has a sense of guilt in his subconscious. This guilt is capable of manifesting itself through hallucinatory experience. In layman's language the Canon has bodhráns in the brain. Worse than that, behind every corner and under every bed there are bands of wrenboys waiting to pounce. Already he has been subjected to shock treatment but without any noticeable effect. If it had been a labouring man or indeed

344

any ordinary person, he would have been committed instantly to a mental home. At the bishop's insistence, and I fully concur by the way, he will remain indefinitely behind closed doors in the Bons Secour Home where he'll want for nothing and where he'll receive special care.'

After the Canon's departure, which had been supervised by Joe O'Dell, who had closed the ambulance doors on the patient and accompanying nurse, the curates of Trallock, senior and junior, went about their business as usual. At one o'clock Father Butt would be obliged to preside at the marriage of Mick Summers, only son of the accountant Phil Summers of Hillview Row and a Dublin girl he had met while on a skiing holiday in Austria. Afterwards the reception would take place at the Trallock Arms, the adjacent ballroom of which would serve as a dining, drinking and dancing area for the two hundred guests who had been invited to the celebration.

So, four full days would pass before Bishop Collane could see fit to present himself at the presbytery of Trallock. His visit was brief and to the point. If Father Butt was willing he would be appointed acting parish priest until such time as a permanent incumbent could be installed. Father Butt had been in the Bishop's thoughts for some time. In each of Father Bertie Stanley's monthly reports the young priest had expressed concern, sometimes at length, for his friend the senior curate.

Bishop Collane had found the reports alarming. The number of Irish emigrants had increased dramaticaly since the beginning of the year. If the trend continued, and there was no reason to believe that it would not, one sixth of the population of Ireland would have settled in Britain by nineteen sixty. By Father Bertie Stanley's reckoning twenty per cent of these would gradually drift away from the sacraments and unless the Irish episcopacy faced up to the problem by immediately sending out more priests there was a danger that the number would swell further. There was nothing the bishops could do to stem the flow of emigration. The Irish government seemed totally indifferent.

'And why wouldn't they be?' Father Bertie had written, 'when the Irish economy is being buoyed up by the monumental remittances being sent home by the emigrants. They are few indeed,' Father Bertie continued, 'who do not send a large percentage of their wage packets to their deprived dependents in Ireland. There are now more people here from the rural hinterlands of our own diocese than are left at home. We must thank God for England for if all these emigrants were to return a bloody revolution must surely take place. The diocese owes it to the emigrants that their spiritual needs should be looked after. The country has failed them utterly in the material sense. We need hostels over here, more advice centres, more lay workers and above all more priests. At the moment I don't have time for a summer holiday. I will bring with me in October a detailed report. In passing let me say that the generosity of the Irish over here is unbelievable.'

'We find ourselves in a most unusual position here, Father,' Bishop Collane pointed out to Father Butt as the latter led the way to the presbytery dining room. 'Firstly, there is no vacancy for a parish priest. It would be unthinkable for Canon Tett to find out that he had been usurped during his illness. According to the doctors there will be periods of lucidity for some time but there seems to be little hope of recovery. If he heard he had been deposed it could well kill him. For this reason I am obliged to maintain the status quo here. If you are willing to serve as acting parish priest then the post is yours.'

'I'm willing,' Father Butt shot back quickly lest the bishop change his mind.

'It will mean that nominally Canon Tett is still parish priest of Trallock but to all intents and purposes you are in complete charge and answerable only to me. I cannot promise you any-thing at the end of the day. It is possible but unlikely that Canon Tett will survive me. If he should expire before me or if he relapses irretrievably into his delirium the usual diocesan changes will follow and a new parish priest will be appointed. I make you no promises, Father, except to assure you of my trust in you and to further assure you that from now until the new appointment you will have a free hand here. I shall await developments with interest and, of course, send you a new curate as soon as possible although that may take some time.'

As Father Butt shaved in preparation for the wedding ceremony only one niggling thought prevented him from fully rejoicing. Something would have to be done about Nora Devane. She was on the threshold of pensionable age and would be in receipt of a full contributory pension. There was a widowed sister with her own home in the townland north of Dirrabeg although situated in the next parish. She would be welcome there. He would present her with a parting gift of three months' salary after he had given her notice. It was more than she deserved. His sister would find him a suitable housekeeper, a decent, discreet person more suited to the delicate, sensitive role of presbytery housekeeper. As he left for the church he thought of Monty Whelan. Too late now to rectify that particular wrong, not indeed that Monty would ever return.

Patsy Oriel, capless and sporting a pencil-thin moustache, sat on a high stool at the function room bar in the Trallock Arms. Outside, the cattle, saving a solitary white heifer, had disappeared as had their owners and purchasers although an intrepid handful from Dirrabeg had remained on in the Bus Bar. Patsy longed to join them but first there was the business of the Crollies, Emily and Angela, mother and daughter. The tweed suit, grey in colour, sat magnificently on his lithe, shapely shoulders. He had purchased it earlier in the day for fifteen shillings in the market hustings from a loquacious vendor who told him that it had, until recently, been the prized possession of a schools' inspector now, alas, consigned to clay after succumbing to an unexpected heart attack. The moustache had been Tom Tyler's idea.

'You need a 'tache,' he had told Patsy as they hatched their plans a month before. 'You've seen photos of Clark Gable I take it?'

Patsy had nodded.

'Something along those lines would put you in the front line of fashion and, number two, it will help disguise you. You're not exactly a stranger to these parts you know. If you keep your cool and look aloof you'll pass muster for long enough to do what's to be done. If anybody asks you who you are let it be known that you are a surgeon taking a few days off from the operating theatre. They'll be all pissed out of their minds anyway.'

The day before the wedding Tom Tyler had taken Moll Canty the hotel supervisor aside and explained to her that he wanted a room for one night only for his friend Doctor Peuly who was taking a short break from his labours. While directing the good doctor to his room Moll Canty asked if he had ever stayed in the hotel before and when he answered in the negative she asked if they had ever met on a previous occasion. Patsy had shaken his head, utilising one of his more winning smiles to disarm her against further suspicion. With the key of the room in his pocket he made his way downstairs to the foyer and thence to the wedding reception. From the very beginning he ogled his prey relentlessly. For their part they acknowledged his every overture after finding out from Moll Canty that he was unaccompanied, a distinguished surgeon, and was staying the night. Emily Crolly found herself unaccountably disturbed by the sad blue eyes of the visitor. Then she acted even more unaccountably for upon hearing the bandleader announce that the next dance was to be a ladies' choice she made her way to where Patsy Oriel was seated and invited him on to the floor. She had meant to question him about the hospital, indeed hospitals to which he was attached and why, for instance, he had chosen a backwater like Trallock for his much-needed relaxation. These questions and others which occurred to her as she felt his eyes appraising her would remain unanswered forever. In his arms she found a tranquility that she had never before experienced. Words would have surely deflated the ecstasy which began to lay inexorable claim to her after they had put the first round of the dance floor behind them. If, at that moment, somebody had intervened and asked Emily Crolly her name she would have been unable to answer. Never before in her life had she experienced anything remotely resembling such wildly exciting and deliciously tantalising emotions. Yet there was also a sense of solace and contentment and all because of the bottomless blue eyes, melting and reassuring.

'What you have, Oriel,' Tom Tyler had once told him, 'is what the old women in the arsehole of Mayo, where I come from, used to call in Gaelic the power to put a woman Fá Gheasaibh which means under your spell. It is an old pagan power given to few and it's given only to those of the pure Celtic strain.'

Patsy had often pondered Tom Tyler's words, wondering whether or not the big Mayo man had made the story up. Only the night before Tom Tyler had asked Patsy if the power had ever failed him.

'Not that I can recall,' Patsy had answered modestly, 'but of course I was never really ambitious until now.'

Moll Canty was first amazed and then dumbfounded at the look of abandonment on Emily Crolly's face as she allowed herself to be led past the reception area and upstairs by Surgeon Peuly. Some fifteen minutes later, looking none the worse for her experience, she meekly followed her seducer downstairs, the look of abandonment replaced by one of mystification. She was to sit mystified, looking into space, until later in the night when she became aware that her daughter was dancing with the man who had only just had his way with her. How could she have let it happen? At sixty-one she had never yielded to

349

any man other than her husband. Could it be that the surgeon had laced one of her drinks? She had not seen him but it would certainly have been possible for him to do so at the bar. She suddenly felt a cold and overwhelming fury, the ecstasy now completely forgotten, revenge the only thought in her head. She resolved to call Angela aside as soon as the couple passed her way again. There was no doubt in her mind but that her daughter was a virgin. She rose to her feet panic-stricken. Her first instinct was to summon her husband and son. She smothered the thought instantly.

Angela and her partner were nowhere to be seen. She hurried across the dance-floor, almost knocking over several couples in her blind haste. She need not have concerned herself about her daughter. Angela Crolly had shed her virginity during her first train journey to Dublin at the insistence of a handsome young man she had not seen before or since. After that there had been scores of others. Encountering Patsy Oriel on the stairway where he had stopped on his way down to re-affix one of his suspenders, Emily Crolly was tempted to strike out at his face with all her might. Her concern for her daughter came first, however. She was shocked to see her through the open door of the hotel room lying in a semi-clad state on the bed, still moaning and writhing after her experience with the tweed-suited surgeon.

'Get up!' Emily Crolly screamed. 'Get up, you wanton bitch!'

Slowly, painfully Angela Crolly's eyes focussed on the towering form of her mother. She quickly regained her senses when she found herself being dragged from the bed to the floor where Emily kicked and slapped her. The screams of mother and daughter did not go unnoticed by Moll Canty, still shocked from the sight of Surgeon Peuly dragging an only-too-willing Angela Crolly in his wake to the room where he had only a short while before been engaged in the most intimate manoeuvres with her mother. Moll Canty had seen many strange things in her time at the Trallock Arms but this surpassed all.

Alas, the exclusive rights on the story were not to be hers alone. The two incidents had also been witnessed by a vigilant chambermaid well known for her addiction to gossipry. The screams still emanated from the room on the second floor. Time to intervene, Moll Canty told herself. Angela Crolly was on her feet but still struggling with her mother when Moll entered.

'To hell with you,' Angela was screaming at her mother, 'he had you before me and I didn't reprimand you.'

Eventually tempers subsided more from exhaustion than from Moll Canty's intervention.

In the gents' toilet Patsy Oriel shaved off his recently cultivated moustache with the safety razor which he had brought with him for that express purpose. Next would be a final visit to the reception area where he would briefly present himself in a less formal garb to his most recent conquests. He was to be spared the journey for the pair sat together in the foyer, the mother bedraggled and wan, now truly showing her age, the daughter dejected and spiritless. Near them sat Moll Canty, for the third time solicitously enquiring if they would now care for the coffee or tea which they had already twice declined. The three sat motionless and dumbstruck when Patsy Oriel appeared in the foyer. Involuntarily Moll Canty's hand shot to her upper lip when it dawned on her that the moustache had been shaved off. The features of the man in front of her had suddenly become all too familiar. Slowly Patsy Oriel removed the collar and tie and thrust them into his trousers pocket. From his coat pocket he produced a crumpled cap which he placed at a rakish angle on his head. Next he inserted the all too familiar pipe. When it seemed to him that all the parts had fallen into place he touched the peak of his cap politely and took his leave.

'Patsy Oriel!' The exclamation came from Moll Canty. This would surely be the talk of the parish until Gabriel sounded his horn. Gradually the cap-covered, pipe-bearing features imposed themselves on Emily Crolly's memory. Of course! She had reprimanded him once when his donkey had left its calling card at the entrance to the garden at the rear of the Crolly premises in the square. He had hung his head sheepishly as he led the animal away. Emily Crolly slid silently from her chair without sigh or moan. In all of three score years and one she had never fainted before.

The men of Dirrabeg sat silently in the Bus Bar. Not one showed signs of intoxication although there wasn't a single one who had not drunk his fill. The realisation that they would never again sit together in such surroundings had earlier dawned on every one. The headiness in the immediate aftermath of their decision to pull up roots had long since given way to loneliness for each knew, in his heart of hearts, that there would be no return. A better quality of life awaited their families but this was the only compensation apart from the fact that they had all arranged to meet in the Black Boy in Northampton on the first Saturday night in June.

'It's hard, boy, this leaving,' Bluenose had whispered to Donal Hallapy as Fred Halpin called time before disappearing suddenly, unable to make his goodbyes.

'Of course it's hard,' Donal whispered back, 'but we'll be putting poverty behind us and we'll be with our own.'

'A man stops being a man when there's poverty,' Rubawrd Ring interposed sadly.

'And a family stops being a family,' Mossie Gilooley added, glad that his daughter would be sure to find better opportunities than domestic service once they settled in England.

'There's nothing harder than pulling out after the best part of a lifetime,' he declared with bent head, 'but what can a man do if he wants to live his life and look out for his family.'

What makes it hardest, Donal Hallapy thought, is the fact that we are no longer young and that we have nothing to show for our time. Young folk transplant easily and, after a short while, will flower fully in distant places; not so those who have matured in their native haunts. Donal knew from experience that he would sorely miss the dawns and the sunsets, the freedom of fields and boglands, the sound of the tiny rippling streams, the songbirds' chorus in the mornings and the incomparable sense deep in one's being of belonging to a place. He knew that wherever he went or however he might fare he would always be part of what he was leaving.

'Last night,' he turned to Bluenose 'I secured the bodhrán you made for me to make sure it travels well.'

Bluenose smiled and slapped his thigh. 'It will remind us,' he said proudly.

'Yes,' Donal voiced his agreement. 'It will remind us.'

Printed in the United States
5131

9 780941 423809